D0424854

"PlagueMaker is so well-written and plausible that readers may have to remind themselves they're reading fiction . . . Highly recommended."

—Aspiring Retail

"Top-drawer thriller about moral grudges--and fatal fleas . . . what makes this work so well is the appeal of the characters, particularily the witty old Chinese scientist."

—KIRKUS REVIEWS

"Fans of Jack Higgins and Tom Clancy will want to read this enthralling thriller."

—HARRIET KLAUSNER, reviewer

"A page-turning, exciting book, Downs has used research and skill like few other authors to provide a real life thriller . . . An excellent suspense read."

—EILEEN KEY, www.DancingWord.net

"[*ShooFly Pie*] is a sizzler of a story that won't let you go."

—www.majestychristian.com

"Simply put, Downs's third novel . . . is strong enough not only to overtake CBA's bestsellers but also to take on the big boys in the ABA."

—FaithfulReader.com

"[In *ShooFly Pie*] all the elements that make for good fiction—among them, memorable characters, a colorful setting, a riveting plot, and believable dialogue —come together seamlessly."

—MARCIA FORD, www.faithfulreader.com

"Fans of the hit TV show *CSI* will love this fast-paced mystery!"

—www.Christianbook.com

"Do not miss this excellent novel filled with fascinating, multi-dimensional, unusual characters. The intrigue and suspense will keep you on the edge of your seat and reading late into the night."

—www.theromancereadersconnection.com

PLAGUEMAKER

OTHER BOOKS BY TIM DOWNS

Shoo Fly Pie
Chop Shop

Visit Tim's Web site at
www.timdowns.net

PLAGUEMAKER

Tim Downs

WestBow
PRESS

A Division of Thomas Nelson Publishers
Since 1798

visit us at www.westbowpress.com

Published in Nashville, Tennessee, by WestBow Press, a division of Thomas Nelson, Inc.

WestBow Press books may be purchased in bulk for educational, business, fund-raising, or sales promotional use. For information, please e-mail SpecialMarkets@ThomasNelson.com.

Publisher's Note: This novel is a work of fiction. Names, characters, places, and inci-dents are either products of the author's imagination or used fictitiously. All charac-ters are fictional, and any similarity to people living or dead is purely coincidental.

Library of Congress Cataloging-in-Publication Data

Downs, Tim.
  Plaguemaker / Tim Downs.
    p. cm.
ISBN 1-5955-4022-9 (hard cover : alk. paper)
ISBN-10 1-5955-4235-3 (trade paper)
ISBN-13 978-1-5955-4235-9 (trade paper)
    1. Bioterrorism—Prevention—Fiction.   2. Government investigators—Fiction.   I. Title.
PS3604.)954P58   2005
813'.6—dc22   2005012627

Printed in the United States of America
06 07 08 09 RRD 5 4 3

For my beautiful Joy

"Many women do noble things,
but you surpass them all.".

CHAPTER ONE

SPECIAL AGENT NATHAN DONOVAN lifted his tray table and peered down at the small plastic case wedged between his feet, just as he had done a hundred times before. It was a beverage cooler, really, nothing more, the kind he might have smuggled into a Mets game or taken to the Jersey shore. The simple red lid was unceremoniously duct-taped to the chalky white body, giving it an altogether unassuming appearance—as though it might contain nothing more than a frigid six-pack or a picnic lunch for two.

Well-meaning scientists at the University Hospital in Kuala Lumpur had plastered the thing with every cautionary label imaginable. Long strips of neon-green tape flashed the word *BIOHAZARD* at regular intervals; fluorescent orange stickers warned of CORROSIVE MATERIALS and CHEMICAL HAZARD; even the Radiology Department chipped in, adding a series of triangular black-and-yellow labels declaring: DANGER! THIS EQUIPMENT PRODUCES IONIZING RADIATION WHEN ENERGIZED.

Donovan had carefully removed all of them, for the same reason that half of his fellow counterterrorism agents in New York City declined to wear their FBI windbreakers: It just doesn't pay to advertise. The Malaysian authorities thought the shrieking labels would hold the curious at bay—Donovan knew they would have just the opposite effect. He

1

might as well hang a sign around his neck that says, "Look what I've got!" Only a fool or a novice stamps SECRET on the front of a secret document. A professional will take a plain blue cover every time.

At the University Hospital, words had buzzed around Donovan's head like Malaysian fruit bats. Microbiologists and disease specialists tossed around terms that he could barely pronounce, let alone comprehend—words like *panenterovirus, cytomegalovirus,* and *respiratory syncytial virus.* All he understood—all that was explained to him—was that Malaysian pig farmers were dying by the hundreds and no one knew why. The disease began with raging fever, followed by delirium, then sudden and irreversible coma. Those were the lucky ones; the less fortunate were left conscious to face the wasting agonies of vomiting, diarrhea, and internal hemorrhaging. Each path was different, but the destination was ultimately the same: a violent and certain death.

No one knew what it was, how it was carried, or how it was transmitted. The disease resisted all known antibiotics, even the big guns like streptomycin. That's what set off all the bells and whistles at the Centers for Disease Control in Atlanta: That kind of antibiotic resistance rarely occurs in nature. It suggests intentional genetic manipulation, and that raises the possibility that some idiot, or group of idiots, might be trying to play dice with the universe again.

No one knew what to do. On Malaysian hog farms, gas-masked soldiers trained their assault rifles on squealing pigs, decimating entire herds, while across town other farmers smuggled their own pigs past roadblocks to markets in other states, allowing the disease to leapfrog from region to region and, inevitably, from country to country. That's why the CDC wanted a look. It was only a matter of time; in the global village of the twenty-first century, there is no such thing as a local outbreak.

A local pathologist had managed to isolate the virus from the blood and spinal fluid of two cadavers before becoming one herself. Before her own brutal demise, she succeeded in growing a fist-sized lump of the stuff in a culture of porcine kidney cells. Scientists at the University Hospital placed the mucosal mass in an airtight metal container, surrounded it with dry ice, and packed it carefully in a simple red-and-white cooler, addressing it to the CDC's Division of Vector-Borne Diseases in Fort Collins, Colorado.

But one courier company after another turned the shipment down. No one would take the risk. No one was willing to say, "We'll absolutely, positively have it there by 10:30 tomorrow morning—unless we happen to drop it, in which case half the western U.S. will begin vomiting blood." That's why the CDC called the Joint Terrorism Task Force, and that's why they called New York: because N.Y. agents are known as the best and the toughest in the Bureau. And that's why the job went to Nathan Donovan: because no one was better, and no one was tougher.

He glanced down at the box for the hundred-and-first time. *Maybe no one was dumber,* he thought.

At the hospital, they had handcuffed Donovan to the cooler like a diplomatic courier. For most of the flight from Kuala Lumpur to Los Angeles, he sat with the box in the center of his lap, clutching the handle with both hands like an old woman in Battery Park. But it occurred to him that a single inadvertent gesture, like reaching out to a flight attendant for a bag of peanuts, could jerk the cooler off his lap and onto the floor. *But it can't fall off the floor,* he decided, so he removed the handcuff and slid the cooler between his feet.

He felt the aching stiffness in his back and legs again. He arched backward, and his 220-pound frame flexed the back of his seat like a beach chair. Behind him he heard an expletive in some unknown tongue, like the bark of a small dog.

For eighteen hours he had unconsciously squeezed the cooler between his legs, as if it might somehow squirt out and slide down the aisle like a wet bar of soap. Only now, on the final leg of his journey, did he begin to relax—but only a little.

The 737 lifted off from a westbound runway and headed out over the Pacific one last time before turning northeast on its two-and-a-half-hour route to Denver. Donovan surveyed the sea of heads around him: Some slumped back in restless slumber; others nodded together in intimate conversation. Some seats appeared empty, until a tiny pair of hands gripped the top of the seat and then quickly vanished again. There were heads of all shapes and colors and sizes; there was long hair, short hair, and hair long gone; there were streamlined ears tucked tightly back against skulls, and large, curling ears that jutted out like diving planes on a submarine.

Donovan didn't care. He was looking for eyes—eyes that turned away when he looked at them, eyes that lingered a little too long. He turned his left leg slightly and raised it until it bumped the seat above; he felt a reassuring metallic tap from the Glock beneath his pant leg. He hated the ankle holster; it made the gun too hard to reach. But in the current social climate, allowing fellow passengers to catch a glimpse of gunmetal from beneath a blazer was a definite faux pas, and Donovan found himself wearing the ankle holster more and more. *Better than no gun at all,* he thought.

They were passing directly over Santa Monica now. Out his window, in the distance, he could just catch a glimpse of the cliffs at Malibu. They continued to climb over the sprawling San Fernando Valley, gaining altitude for the hop over the San Gabriel Mountains ahead.

Then it happened.

Donovan heard the blast before he felt the concussion—from somewhere in the forward baggage compartment, he thought. The floor in the first-class galley buckled wildly and then flattened again. The shock wave traveled back the full length of the plane, causing the entire fuselage to ripple visibly. Donovan was astonished that the airframe could contort that far without disintegrating—yet somehow, the plane was still intact. Overhead compartments sprang open like a line of mousetraps, vomiting out carry-on luggage, briefcases, shopping bags, and a blizzard of coats and sweaters. Above each row of seats a rectangular door dropped open, and a tangle of tubing and bright yellow plastic dangled down like a sea of jellyfish.

In his mind, Donovan could see the bomb: a small device, probably homemade, nothing more than a few feet of wire with a timer attached to an explosive charge. No, not a timer, an altimeter—set to go off at cruising altitude to maximize the loss of life and disperse the wreckage as widely as possible. It was a small blast in relative terms—definitely not C4, probably not even TNT. Probably just a canister of gunpowder embedded in a cocktail of nails and ball bearings for shrapnel. A simple bomb, really, a beginner's bomb—the kind you could build for twenty-five bucks with parts from a local Radio Shack.

They were lucky, he thought. The blast had blown downward, away from the passenger compartment—but it must have ripped the belly out of the ship, and there were things down there you didn't want to lose, things like hydraulics, and landing gear, and fuel lines . . .

For an instant the entire plane was silent and still, a freeze-frame before the panic to come. Bodies were rigid, faces frozen in disbelief. Arms angled everywhere, with white-knuckled fists clutching at seat backs, armrests, fellow passengers—*the way a man grabs on to a limb when it breaks away from a tree,* Donovan thought. And it would do them just as much good—because outside the plane, he heard the trailing whine of the engines as they began to lose power.

Then the nose tipped forward, and the plane started down.

Donovan watched stone-faced as the image before him erupted into motion. There were shrieks and sobs and mournful wails, some more animal than human. Long-unsaid prayers were dredged up from childhood memories; complete strangers embraced; mothers clutched at wild-eyed children, combing hair and straightening collars as if they were preparing for school photos and not death. Some wept quietly, some spoke aloud to no one in particular, and some sat in peaceful serenity. And over the intercom, through tearful sobs, a flight attendant offered insane instructions on how to "prepare for an emergency landing."

Donovan looked out the window and measured the angle of their descent against the horizon; they were coming down like a mortar shell. It wouldn't be a landing; it would be a detonation, with six thousand gallons of high-octane jet fuel erupting on impact—half of it vaporizing in a roiling fireball and half of it spewing like napalm over whatever godforsaken neighborhood or trailer park happened to be nearby. The debris would be spread over half a mile; a week from now a DMORT team would be sifting through the wreckage, searching for bits of bone and tooth, fragments of DNA to offer comfort to grieving families. *They'll be mailing us home in envelopes,* Donovan thought. *That's all that will be left.*

He listened for the feeble voice on the intercom again and slowly shook his head. You can put your seat back in an upright and locked position, you can put your head between your knees, but you're still going to *die*. That's all there is to it; that's how it is. The good people of United flight 296 to Denver were dead, every last one of them, and there was nothing they could do.

Then Donovan looked down at his feet.

There sat the little red-and-white cooler nestled between his feet, blissfully unaware of its impending destruction. But—*would* the crash destroy the cooler utterly and completely? Inside that cooler was a life-form, and like all living things, it would do everything in its power to survive. He visualized the crash again: the nose-first impact, the pulverizing momentum of eighty-five tons of imploding metal, the incinerating belch of fire—no living thing could survive that.

Or could it? The virus was a living thing, yes, but it was a living thing sealed in an airtight container, packed in dry ice, cradled in thick foam, shielded by plastic armor . . . Was the cooler fireproof, he wondered? Would it disintegrate on impact? Would it melt? Would the plastic crumble, the dry ice vaporize, and the canister rip apart like a tin can in a campfire? Or would the plastic casing only fracture? Would it bounce and roll and ricochet, but still survive the impact?

Or would the blast throw the cooler free of the plane? Donovan had worked crash sites before; he remembered picking his way through the utter annihilation, every fragment of the plane and its contents reduced to inches—and then suddenly finding a handbag or an attaché completely intact, as though it had been gently set aside before impact. Would the cooler be the handbag this time? Would it crack, and split apart, and dump its living contents onto the surrounding debris?

And when the DMORT team worked its way through the wreckage, would some hapless deputy coroner lift the empty canister and peer inside? Would he casually toss it aside, then wipe the sweat from his forehead or rub the smoke from his eyes? And when he went home that night, would he kiss his wife? Would he hug the kids? Would he pat the dog and shake hands with a neighbor?

Donovan looked around the plane. It was a ghost ship, filled with specters already beginning to fade away. They were already beginning to grow quiet, already acquiescing to their inevitable doom. They were already dead, every one of them. There were maybe two hundred on the plane—but on the ground, there were millions.

Donovan looked out the window. He had about a minute, no more.

He jerked the cooler up onto his lap and began to tear away the long gray strips of tape. When he opened the lid, a silent mist poured over the sides and down onto his legs. From the center of the ice he slid a tall silver canister and began to tug at its lid. It opened with a dull pop. He held his breath and peered down into the black interior.

Then he turned to his right and dumped the gelatinous blob in the center of the aisle.

He watched: The mass seemed to hesitate for a moment, then dissipate into the carpet. It seemed to spread and grow, putting out feelers like a vine, reaching out just like the rest of the passengers for someone, something, to hold on to. But it didn't matter—it was unprotected now, and it had no more chance of surviving than they did.

Than *he* did. The thought crossed Donovan's mind for the first time. He took a deep breath and leaned back in his seat. He had never been afraid of anything in his life, and he was not about to start now. He closed his eyes and put death out of his mind. Why not? He'd never feel it anyway.

Then, from outside the window, he heard the rising drone of the engines, followed by a heavy, sinking tug in his gut. Everywhere around him people gasped and stiffened, anticipating the impact—but the impact never came. Instead, the nose of the plane began to turn upward. As the engines continued to accelerate, the 737 leveled off, then once again began to climb.

From everywhere on the plane came astounded gasps and great, heaving sobs of relief. Passengers stared out the windows in astonishment; they stared at one another in unspeakable joy; they stared at the ceiling and uttered silent thanksgivings.

But not Nathan Donovan. He stared at a fist-sized stain in the center of the aisle.

Then he heard a voice say, "What did you do?"

He looked up. There was a young boy standing in the aisle, staring with him at the spotted carpet. The boy looked up into Donovan's eyes; the eyes were dark and wet and sunken deep into the pale little face. He was terribly thin, and the sagging neck of his blue hospital gown draped down over one bony shoulder. On both elbows, white strips of surgical tape secured pads of folded gauze.

Donovan couldn't bear to look at the boy. He shut his eyes hard. "I'm sorry," he said in a whisper.

"I don't feel so good, Daddy."

When Donovan looked again, the boy was backing slowly away down the aisle. His hair was gone now, and tiny veins coursed over his head like pale blue threads. The skin of his face was sallow, almost transparent, and his skull was clearly visible beneath.

"Wait," Donovan pleaded.

But the boy kept getting smaller, and thinner, and farther away.

"Wait!" Donovan shouted after him. "I can help! I can fix this!" He dropped to his knees in the center of the aisle and began to furiously scrape at the spot with his fingernails—but the spot only grew larger. It spread to the edges of the aisle now and sent ominous tendrils creeping up the sides of the seats.

The boy spoke one last time in a distant voice.

"Why won't you help me, Daddy? Why don't you love me anymore?"

NATHAN DONOVAN SAT BOLT upright in bed and stared into the darkness. He ran his fingers through the cold, damp mat on his chest and wiped his hand on the sheet. He turned and looked at the clock.

It was 4:00 a.m.—the usual time for the dreams.

CHAPTERTWO

DONOVAN SQUINTED AT THE spots on the man's forehead. They were on the right side, just above his temple, but well below the graying edge of his hairline. They were fleshy little things—what did you call them? Not warts—they were the color of warts, but they stuck up too high, and they had little dark tips like mushrooms. That was it, just like mushrooms—but they couldn't be called mushrooms. Polyps, maybe? Cysts?

Donovan found them annoying and fascinating at the same time. What makes a man grow his own little mushroom farm on his forehead? Surely he could cut them off—one swipe with a straight razor and a few days with a Band-Aid would take care of them. But no, he had to keep them—not in some nether region where fungus belongs, but on his *head*—and just an inch above his brow, making eye contact with the man virtually impossible. *Maybe it was a test,* he thought; maybe it was something that psychiatrists regularly do to see what kind of response they get from their patients. It could be—he'd never been to a psychiatrist before. Maybe after he left, the man would peel them off one by one and place them in a little box—

"Mr. Donovan, can we try to focus?"

"Sorry." Nathan shifted in his chair and resettled himself. But he didn't try to make eye contact—that was futile. He tried to focus instead on the open manila folder on the man's desk.

9

"You were a Marine," the psychiatrist said.

"Yes."

"You were in ordnance removal. Tell me about that."

Donovan shrugged. "People made bombs. I took them apart."

"Did you enjoy the work?"

"It fit me."

"How so?"

"I'm analytical," he said, carefully measuring his words. "I like problem solving."

"Do you like explosions?"

"If you like explosions, you join the artillery. In ordnance removal you only get one."

The man looked down at the folder and turned a page. Donovan leaned to the left slightly, trying to catch a glimpse of his opposite temple.

"I see you grew up in Ohio."

Donovan rolled his eyes. "Look, let me save you some time here. I grew up on a farm in Ohio. Some people spend their lives trying to escape small towns; some people spend their lives trying to get back. I wanted out. I enrolled at Ohio State to study engineering, but I switched to criminology because I was nineteen and I found the exams were easier to take when I was drunk. I joined the Marines because you can't do squat with a criminology degree, and besides, I liked their dress uniforms—still do. I went with ordnance removal because I spent my whole childhood blowing things up, and it sounded like a great career. I must have done okay, 'cause after a few years they sent me to the Academy as an instructor. That's where the Bureau found me; they do a lot of recruiting there. I was just the kind of guy they were looking for: I had a college degree, command experience, and I could make things go boom—or not go boom—whatever they needed."

The psychiatrist smiled slightly and closed the folder.

"Mr. Donovan, do you know why you're here?"

"Of course."

"Tell me."

"I'm here at the request of my supervisory special agent."

"That's it? Just a casual request to drop by and pay the psychiatrist a visit?"

"I'm here under my supervisor's orders."

The man paused. "Do you think you need to be here?"

Donovan felt a knot tighten in his stomach. He hated questions like this—they made him feel silly and childish. It reminded him of his basic training in ordnance removal, when the instructor asked, "Do you think you should cut the blue wire or the red wire?" How should he know? *Tell me what to do or let me blow myself up, but don't ask stupid questions.*

"You tell me," Donovan said evenly.

The psychiatrist opened the folder again and took out a multipage report. "You joined the FBI in 1996. You requested assignment in New York. Why New York?"

"They had the reputation—the best and the brightest. Besides, they told me I could have any assignment I wanted, as long as I picked New York. Nobody wants it—too expensive, lousy hours. You get up at 4:30 just to beat the traffic through the tunnels."

"But that didn't deter you."

"I'm a Marine. I'm used to the hours."

He returned to the report. "Sixteen weeks at Quantico," he said. "And then?"

"The usual freshman runaround. Six months on the 'Applicant Squad'—running background investigations, manning the call center, working surveillance."

"And then you moved to counterterrorism. Why counterterrorism?"

"Like I said: I like solving problems."

"You can solve problems sitting behind a desk."

You're right, Donovan thought. *You can solve little paperbound problems while you sit behind a desk growing mushrooms on your forehead.*

"I enjoy activity."

The man looked up. "Do you enjoy violence?"

Donovan didn't reply.

The psychiatrist turned a page of the report and slowly scanned the text. "In April of last year, you were involved in a hostage situation in Brooklyn. Tell me about that."

Donovan studied the ceiling while he organized his thoughts. "It was in Dyker Heights," he said, "a few blocks off Eighth Avenue. Italian couple, single-family dwelling. The wife heard a noise downstairs, sent her husband down to take a look. He walked into the living room, found a guy carrying out his TV—the guy shot the husband dead on the spot. The wife heard the gunshot, called NYPD. They arrived before the guy could get away, so he took the wife hostage. He told the cops he had a bomb, threatened to blow the whole place up. That's when NYPD called us—a bomb is considered a weapon of mass destruction, and that automatically involves the Joint Terrorism Task Force. We sent out a WMD squad; I was first on the scene."

The man nodded, verifying Donovan's account against the text. "And what happened when you got there?"

"I took up position on the front porch of the house, just to the left of the front door."

"Is that standard procedure in a situation like this?"

Donovan shifted uneasily. "It's a little difficult to define 'standard procedure' in a situation like this."

"Well, let's try. Who was in charge that night? Who had jurisdiction?"

"NYPD was the first responder, so it was their ball game—until we showed up, that is. In a WMD scenario, the FBI always has jurisdiction."

"So as the first FBI agent to arrive on the scene, you assumed command."

"No, not exactly. It's not that simple; we don't always just take over. If NYPD has things under control, we sometimes let them handle it."

"And in your opinion, did NYPD have things under control?"

Donovan paused. He began to construct his sentences more carefully now, like a man stacking high explosives.

"They had the basics covered. They established a perimeter, they set up a command center, and they had a hostage-negotiation team on the way. I felt, however, that they were failing to capitalize on certain tactical advantages."

"Such as?"

"Speed. The element of surprise."

"And in your experience with hostage situations, have you found *speed* to be a great advantage? You know, of course, that the first fifteen minutes of a hostage situation are the most dangerous. Time is almost always on the side of the hostage negotiator."

"*Almost* always. In this situation, time was working against us."

"How so?"

"The shooter had already killed once—he would be much quicker to kill the second time. What did he have to lose?"

"What about the bomb?"

"I didn't believe there was a bomb."

"Why not?"

"There was no purpose for a bomb. It didn't fit. A bomb requires forethought; a bomb requires planning. Nobody walks around with a bomb just in case they need one—I know something about this."

"And the NYPD officer in charge—did he agree with your assessment?"

Donovan paused. "He did not."

The psychiatrist turned back to the report again. "And so, against the wishes of the commanding officer, you broke perimeter and, gun in hand, simply walked up to the front door—'cowboylike' is the term the officer used."

"Too bad—I was going for Dirty Harry." Donovan bit his lip the instant the words left his mouth. This was no place for humor. The mushroom-man was not his bar buddy or his locker partner; he was a Midtown shrink hired by the Bureau to evaluate his mental and emotional stability. He cursed his own stupidity and lack of judgment and pulled the reins in tight again. The psychiatrist made a small note on a legal pad before continuing.

"According to the report—correct me if I'm wrong—there was a large picture window to the left of the door. You heard sounds from the shooter and the hostage in the living room, so you simply stepped in front of the window and took aim. The shooter fired first, shattering the glass, at which time you fired twice, striking him once in the head and once in the abdomen."

"Yes."

The psychiatrist paused. "Mr. Donovan, can you understand why this behavior might be described by some as 'cowboylike'?"

"I considered it an acceptable risk."

"An interesting term. Perhaps we can explore what you mean by 'acceptable risk' at a later time. Mr. Donovan, you seem to make a habit of taking risks no one else would find acceptable."

Donovan drew a breath and spoke slowly. "I heard the shooter and the hostage in the living room. I could hear the woman speaking—whimpering is more like it. The shooter's voice sounded agitated, confused, unstable. In light of that, I felt that the best approach was to distract him suddenly, try to throw him off guard. In his confused state of mind, I felt confident that he would release the hostage and confront me, giving me a firing opportunity."

The man nodded thoughtfully, considering the rationality of Donovan's account. "But according to witnesses, several seconds elapsed between the time you stepped in front of the window and the shot that broke the glass."

"I had to give the shooter time to spot me, release the hostage, and give me a clear line of fire."

"Did you have to give him time to shoot first?"

Donovan shrugged. "It only seemed fair."

The words seemed to remain in the air and float, like little globules of nitric acid injected into glycerin. To Donovan's surprise, the statement shocked even him.

"It only seemed fair," the psychiatrist repeated slowly. "Mr. Donovan, I'd like to give you a minute to reflect on those words."

Donovan thought it was just a figure of speech, but true to his word, the psychiatrist delayed a full minute before speaking again. It was a heavy, plodding, torturous minute.

"Have you ever actually been shot?" the psychiatrist asked at last.

"No."

"Do you have a desire to be?"

Stupid, idiotic question. "Of course not."

"Mr. Donovan," the psychiatrist said, squinting at him, "do you have any delusions of personal invulnerability?"

Donovan felt the knot in his gut spreading out over his body, filling his limbs with an aching restlessness. He felt adrenaline beginning to chew at the ends of his nerves until the tips of his fingers began to tremble like tuning forks. His throat twisted into a sodden, knotted rope, and the hair on his neck stood out like wire.

He continued to stare straight ahead, motionless, expressionless, smothering his growing anger like a leaden blanket wrapped around a pipe bomb. For weeks at a time he kept the demon locked safely in the basement, but from time to time he heard the familiar footsteps on the wooden stairs and he knew it had to come out. He had learned to conceal its presence, and it was an almost perfect disguise; but the demon was like a man buried alive, locked in a coffin, clawing at the lid and begging to be released. To hold it inside took everything Donovan had.

The psychiatrist rose from his chair, stepped slowly around to Donovan's side of the desk, and leaned back against the edge. He crossed his legs at the ankle; the move brought his right foot within inches of Donovan's own. Donovan felt a blue-white spark arc between them.

"You married in 1998," the psychiatrist said with an infuriating softness. "Tell me about that."

"The bride wore white; I wore black," Donovan said.

"Are you uncomfortable talking about your marriage?"

"Do you know anyone who's *comfortable* talking about a divorce?" Donovan imagined himself making a quick, sweeping motion with his right foot, taking the man's legs out from under him and sending him crashing to the floor.

"Tell me about your wife," the man continued.

"My *ex*-wife is a professor of political science and international relations at Columbia. She's an expert in the psychology of terrorism. She does piecework for the Bureau—that's how we met."

"Two professionals working in demanding careers," the man said thoughtfully. "That can put a lot of stress on a relationship."

Don't play head games with me, Donovan thought. *And for God's sake don't sympathize! You don't know me, and you don't know my life—just write me a hall pass and let me get back to class.*

"There was a lot of stress," Donovan said, parroting the man's own words.

"What would you say was the cause of your divorce?"

"Irreconcilable differences."

The psychiatrist shook his head. "That's just a legal term. What would you say was the *cause*?"

Donovan slowly looked up. He knew when their eyes met, his rage would become evident, but he didn't care anymore. He felt humiliated, he felt violated, and he wanted it to stop. "Does anybody really know?" he said in his lowest voice.

"I think you do."

Donovan glared at the man. There he stood, leaning against the desk, arms neatly crossed, waiting patiently—*pleasantly*—for Donovan's reply. He was just like the guy in Dyker Heights, an intruder in somebody else's home, knocking over furniture that didn't belong to him and dumping out drawers filled with secret and intimate things. What did he care? It wasn't *his* garbage. He could go home at the end of the day and leave somebody else to clean up the mess.

Donovan set his jaw and said nothing. The psychiatrist noted the stillness and changed his tack.

"Tell me about these dreams you have."

"What dreams?"

"It's in your file. A friend mentioned it."

Some friend, he thought. "Everybody has dreams."

"I'm talking about dreams of futility, dreams involving unsolvable problems, recurring dreams, dreams that won't let you sleep at night."

"Who doesn't have dreams like that?"

"Healthy people," he said.

"You know any?"

"Tell me—how do these dreams end?"

"I wake up."

He nodded. "Are you still having them?"

Donovan locked eyes with him. "No."

The psychiatrist held his gaze for a moment, then slowly turned away and took a seat behind the desk again.

"You're just the kind of guy the Bureau likes," he said, scribbling illegible notations on his legal pad. "You can dismantle a bomb without breaking a sweat. You can stand in front of a terrorist and let him take the first shot. I'll bet you didn't even flinch, did you?"

"You make it sound like some kind of neurosis."

"It is—but for the Bureau it's a very useful neurosis. They know you'll approach any situation with total abandon, with utter fearlessness. You'd walk through fire if they asked you to. That makes you a useful guy, Mr. Donovan; you get the job done—that is, as long as those qualities of yours are directed at the bad guys."

"I received a commendation for my actions in Dyker Heights—for courage under fire."

"Publicly, the Bureau calls it 'courage.' Privately, you've got them worried—*that's* why you're here, Mr. Donovan. They're wondering if this exceptional courage of yours isn't really something else. Over the last two years you have been unnecessarily placing yourself—and others—in harm's way. Don't worry, the Bureau will continue to present you with nice little awards and commendations right up until the moment you get yourself killed—and you will get yourself killed, Mr. Donovan; it's only a matter of time. The Bureau knows that—they're just hoping you'll be a good boy and die alone."

Donovan made no reply. He just sat in silence as the psychiatrist completed his notations. When he did, he tore off the top sheet from the legal pad, placed it in the folder, and smoothed it shut.

"The Bureau is paying me to do a psychological evaluation on you," he said. "Okay, here it is: I think you've got two problems, Mr. Donovan. You're angry, and you're afraid."

Donovan pinned him with a searing stare. "I've never been afraid of anything in my life."

"Interesting," the man replied. "I say you're angry and you're afraid—you say you're not afraid of anything. You ignored my comment about anger, Mr. Donovan—why is that? It's because you can't deny the anger; you feel that every day. You feel it right now, don't you? I can see it in your face: I get a little too close, and you light up like a highway flare. It's your fears that you don't recognize, and I think you have a whole closet full—and not just the ordinary bogeymen. Why don't you feel fear, Mr. Donovan? That's the question you need to ask yourself; that's the question only you can answer. But let me give you a clue: Fear and anger work together. Anger is like a roadblock; it's like a barricade. It tells you where you can go and where you can't. When you begin to feel fear, anger blocks the way—it says, 'No more.' When someone gets a little too intimate, anger steps in and says, 'That's close enough.'"

Donovan had no idea what to say in reply—but he knew he had to throw this dog a bone or he'd never let go of his leg. "Okay," he said with a sigh. "You're right. I do feel anger. I guess I—"

"Don't patronize me, Mr. Donovan. I've treated you with respect today; you can at least do the same for me. You and I both know you are light-years away from dealing with this problem. To do that, you have to go to a dark place—and you're not ready for that."

Donovan stood up. "Enough of this crap," he said. "You want to help me? Then let me get back to work. Look, you say this is something I have to work out for myself, right? Well, I can't do that by crawling off in some corner and contemplating my navel. If you really want to help me, help me get back to *work.*"

The psychiatrist seemed lost in thought for a moment—then he flipped open the folder again and made a quick inscription on the top page, adding his signature with a flourish.

"Do you prefer the Jets or the Giants, Mr. Donovan?"

"I'll take the Jets."

"I figured. Do you know what I think whenever I watch the Jets play? I think, *Thank God for the NFL! There go a dozen men who might otherwise be in prison.* That's you, Mr. Donovan. You're a very dangerous man—but I suppose you're less dangerous on the job than off."

The psychiatrist extended his hand. Donovan shook it quickly, then headed for the door.

"You said something," the psychiatrist called after him. "You said, 'Nobody walks around with a bomb just in case they need one.' Funny thing."

"What's funny?"

"You do."

CHAPTER THREE

THE BODY LAY HALF on the carpet, half on the white ceramic tile. It lay faceup, with its eyes half-closed in a dreamy, faraway stare, as though the victim had been utterly bored by the details of his own violent death. There was a single bullet hole near the center of the forehead—*a 9mm, maybe a .357,* Donovan thought. The flesh around the entry wound was smooth and even, and there was no powder tattoo, indicating that the shot was fired from at least a couple of feet away. The bullet had exited at the back and disappeared. Donovan looked across the sprawling loft to his right, where a couple of NYPD forensic techs searched the walls and ceiling for a telltale hole or crack. He shook his head; they could be looking for an hour in a place this size.

The exit wound itself was invisible, concealed by the skull, but the hole had allowed a crimson liquid to form a remarkably symmetrical puddle under the head. *Just like the halos on the angels in those old paintings,* he thought.

Donovan looked to his left; there were no old paintings here. The carpeted portion of the loft comprised an extensive private art gallery, dotted with objects of every conceivable size and shape and color, but nothing recognizable—nothing "objective," the art people would say. The loft was in TriBeCa, the old industrial section below Canal Street, where the exorbitant rents of SoHo a few blocks to the north once forced less-affluent artists and gallery owners to take up residence—that is, before TriBeCa became equally prohibitive. The loft still showed traces of its garment factory roots, with plumbing stacks and gas conduits snaking across the smoky walls like a map of the Manhattan subway. Throughout the room, freestanding panels of teak or pecan stood awash in brilliant light, each bearing a canvas screaming its own colorful obscenities. In front of each panel, acrylic display stands offered gifts of bronze and chrome and twisted glass. An electrical grid hung suspended from the black ceiling, where the blue-and-white rims of glowing halogen spotlights glowed like planets at sunset.

In the center of the far wall, under the brightest spotlights of all, stood a single display stand. It was square and large, about eighteen inches on a side. It rose no more than six inches from the carpet—and it was empty.

There was a sharp rap on the open door frame.

"Hey, Donovan."

"Hey, Poldie. You just getting here?"

"Nah, I was talking to the neighbors. Upstairs, downstairs, across the hall." The man started into the room.

"Hold it—put these on first," Donovan said, pointing to the blue surgical booties covering his own shoes. "There, by the door."

He was a heavy, thick-chested man. As he lowered himself, he extended his arms back toward the floor, then froze for an instant before dropping the final six inches like a sack of wet laundry. He landed with a huff and reached into a nearby box for a pair of the elastic coverings.

Leopold Satwyck—"Poldie" to everyone who knew him—was in his midfifties, a thirty-year veteran of the NYPD. He was not Polish; he was a Polack—there's a difference, Poldie said. He was a proud representative of one of the still-distinct ethnic communities that surround the East and Hudson Rivers. His features were thick and rough. His eyes were permanently underscored by purple-gray parentheses, and his nose was a bulbous lump of paste-colored orange peel with a lacework of intricate red and blue threads. His chin had long ago doubled and was in the process of multiplying again. If Poldie had a trademark, it was his hair; it was as thick as piano wire. No matter how hard he tried to plaster it down on the sides, it simply refused to be tamed. By the end of the day, rebellious gray strands stood out from his head in proud defiance—the Polish Rebellion, Poldie called it. In bad weather, Poldie looked like a cat in a wind tunnel.

They were an odd couple, Poldie in his starched white button-downs and Windsor-knotted ties, and Donovan in his navy crewnecks and Dolce & Gabbana shades. But then, that was the point of the JTTF—thirty different agencies joining together, old eyes paired with young, so that together they might spot things that a single pair of eyes could miss.

Donovan watched Poldie's face redden as he stretched to pull a bootie over the tip of his shoe.

"Hey, Poldie, you need some help there?"

Poldie looked up with a smoldering stare. Donovan loved it—it was Poldie's patented look, the one that said, "I'd shoot you, but I wouldn't want to waste the bullet." The look was a legend at headquarters; it was said to have the power to wither desk plants and cause computers to freeze. Subordinates and clerical workers steered well clear of Poldie just to avoid "the Look," but Donovan considered it an off night when he failed to merit at least one.

Poldie struggled to his feet again and started across the carpet, stopping to examine the various objets d'art along the way.

"You like this stuff?" he said, leaving no doubt as to his own opinion. "My dog leaves better art than this."

"Don't knock it. This is expensive stuff."

Poldie shook his head. "*Artists* are supposed to suffer, not viewers." He padded across the carpet to Donovan's side.

Donovan glanced at him. "Hey. Did you tell somebody about the dreams?"

"What dreams?"

"You know what dreams—my dreams. Who did you tell?"

"Nobody. Mayer, maybe. He asked me."

"He asked you. He says, 'Is Donovan having dreams?'"

"No, he asks me if you're okay. I say, 'Sure.' He asks, 'Is he sleeping enough?' I say, 'Who sleeps enough?' But he just stands there, looking at me—you know how he does. So I say, 'Maybe he has dreams sometimes. Maybe he wakes up a lot.'"

"*Maybe*," Donovan said. "Poldie, you got a mouth like the Holland Tunnel."

Poldie's one irredeemable quality was his tendency to talk—to anyone, at any time, about anything crossing his mind at the moment. Poldie was like a man with a Plexiglas skull; you could actually see the workings of his mind. He formed his thoughts right in front of you, darting down one mental alleyway after another, spitting out words and then searching for thoughts to fit them. Poldie liked to say, "Sometimes I talk so fast I say things I haven't even thought of yet." It was funny—most of the time.

Poldie looked at the body. "He's the best-looking thing in here. How much you asking?"

"A neighbor called it in," Donovan said. "He says there was a big party here night before last, some kind of gallery event—an opening or something. Says he dropped by the next day to pay a visit, but there was no answer. Tried a couple more times, then he got suspicious, so he called NYPD. This is how they found him."

He gestured to the left and right, outlining the basic layout of the unit. "The gallery is the carpeted area. Over there, the ceramic tile, that's a kitchen and foyer. Down that hallway, there's a bedroom and an office. No sign of forced entry. Might have been somebody he knew—maybe somebody from the party."

"Maybe somebody who likes art," Poldie offered. "So who called the JTTF? Homicides are NYPD's job. This one should belong to Manhattan South."

"That's who called us."

"How come?"

Donovan motioned to one of the forensic technicians still searching for the elusive bullet. "Lieutenant, would you please explain to my big-mouthed partner why Manhattan South thinks a regular homicide might be of interest to the JTTF?"

The technician carefully knelt down by the victim's head. "It's this," he said, outlining a spray of tiny red dots that radiated outward from the head. "We might not have seen them if it wasn't for the white tile."

Poldie shrugged. "Blood spatter."

"It's not blood spatter. Blood spatter occurs when a bullet or weapon causes blood to spray on surrounding surfaces. But this victim was standing when he was murdered—he fell backward and landed in this spot. But these little dots, what you called 'blood spatter,' surround the head as if he were shot lying down."

"So it happened when the head hit the ground."

"Look at the little dots," the technician said. "Look how even they are—almost as if they were airbrushed. Blood just doesn't splatter that way. It's too viscous—the dots would be larger, and all different sizes."

"Then what is it?"

"I can answer that," said a voice from the hallway.

They looked up to see a man rounding the corner from the back bedroom. He was tall and angular with broad shoulders and large hands. His clothes looked somehow unsettled, as if they had stopped by for a visit but were deciding whether or not to stay. He wore sagging khakis that puddled around a pair of broken-down Reeboks. He wore a gray Penn State Athletics shirt under an open-fronted button-down that didn't match in any conceivable way. His head was an inverted triangle, with a broad, contemplative brow. Under that thoughtful brow stood the largest pair of spectacles that Poldie had ever seen—and he said so.

"Holy—look at the specs! They look like Coke bottles."

The man stopped directly in front of Poldie and looked at him. Through the massive lenses his eyes were the size of brown chestnuts. When he blinked they momentarily vanished, then reappeared an instant later even larger than before.

"They're the size of boccie balls," Poldie said.

"Boccie balls," the man repeated. "Only in New York."

"Can I try them on?"

"Can I hold your gun?"

Donovan decided it was time to step in; there was an outside chance that Poldie might make the trade. "Poldie, I want you to meet a friend of mine—Dr. Nick Polchak. Nick, this is Detective Leopold Satwyck. Just call him Poldie—and whatever you do, don't tell him any secrets."

The two men shook hands, but Poldie never took his eyes off Nick's glasses. "Can you see through those things?"

"That would be the general idea, now, wouldn't it?"

"Poldie, Nick is a professor at N.C. State down in Raleigh. I asked him to fly up this afternoon when I got the call from Manhattan South. We've worked together before. Nick is a forensic entomologist."

"You're a bug guy!" Poldie said in amazement.

"I used to be a bug guy, but I grew up. Now I'm a bug man."

"How do you guys do it? I mean, all the flies and maggots and decomposing bodies?"

"We're shaking hands over a dead man," Nick said. "Do you detect a little irony?"

"Yeah, but we usually work with *new* dead guys."

Nick stared at him for a minute, then turned and looked at Donovan. "I'm assuming he's with you."

"Tell him about the blood spots," Donovan said. "Tell him what they are."

Nick squatted down by the legs of the corpse and gingerly slid up its right pant leg. "Look at this," he said.

Poldie grimaced. "Geez—he shaved his legs."

Nick looked up at him. "May I see your badge?"

"Poldie, look at the red spots," Donovan said, pointing. "See? They're on the other leg too."

"And also around the waist," Nick added. "That's the giveaway—fleas like to bite around the waist."

"The guy had *fleas*?"

"Let me show you something." Nick turned to his right and crawled on all fours to the center of the carpeted area; he motioned for Donovan and Poldie to follow. Donovan dropped to his knees beside him. Poldie

25

lowered himself a good deal more slowly, and his knees made a sound like crunching cornflakes. Nick took a sheet of white paper from his shirt pocket, unfolded it, and smoothed it out on the carpet's surface. To the side of the paper he made a few quick brushing motions, and tiny gray dots began to appear magically.

"There are thousands of them," Nick said.

Poldie lifted his hands from the carpet.

"Don't worry, Detective, they're all dead—every last one of them."

"How come they're all dead?"

"They were purposely exterminated. If we had a sample of carpet fiber analyzed, I'm betting we'd find traces of permethrin or hydroprene. Or they may have used an aerosol."

"But if he had the place exterminated, how come he's still got flea bites?" Nick looked at Donovan. "He's good at questions."

Donovan nodded. "It's his specialty. What did you find in the bedroom and office, Nick?"

"Nothing—not a single flea. And look at this." Nick crawled forward on the carpet, sliding the paper to a spot near the empty display stand. He brushed at the carpet again, and the gray spots began to reappear—but more than twice as many as before.

"There's a definite distribution pattern here," he said. "The flea population is densest here, by the wall. The number decreases as you move across the carpet toward the body. That means, of course, that the fleas were purposely released in the room."

"How do you know that?"

"This is not your ordinary flea infestation," Nick said. "Think about it: Over time, the fleas would spread out and become fairly evenly distributed. But here, they're concentrated all in one place—and I found none at all in the bedroom. Isn't that a little odd? The only way to explain this fan-shaped distribution is if the fleas were released from a single point—my guess would be from right over there," he said, pointing to the empty display stand. "That seems to be the locus. From that point, they worked their way across the carpet toward the foyer."

"Why would they do that?"

"Fleas are attracted by motion. They probably sensed activity in the busier part of the room and went after it. It wouldn't be an easy trip—this is thick carpet, and a flea's hind legs are shaped like little jigsaw blades. Most of them never made it; apparently some of the more aggressive ones did."

"The fleabites on the legs?"

"And the dots of blood around the head. It's fecal matter, Detective. Fleas feed on blood, but most of it passes through them undigested. It gets left behind in tiny red dots. Your forensic guys are sharp; beginners usually mistake it for blood spatter."

Donovan elbowed Poldie, earning him his second Look of the evening.

Nick stepped to the center of the room and looked around. "So here's the scenario," he said. "Someone purposely released thousands of fleas in this room."

"Why?"

"Your guess is as good as mine."

"A prank, maybe? A competing gallery owner? A disgruntled buyer, somebody who thought he got ripped off and wanted to get even?"

"I doubt it," Nick said. "We're talking about thousands and thousands of fleas here. You don't just have your dog roll around on the carpet to create an infestation like that. Rearing an insect population this large is a laboratory procedure. It takes time, and money, and expertise—trust me on this. Somebody went to a lot of trouble to do this. Besides, you've got a dead man here. It would be naive to consider the fleas and the murder as two separate events—especially when you consider that the fleas were exterminated *after* the murder took place."

Poldie held up both hands. "Whoa—you're way ahead of me here."

Nick looked at him. "Now, there's a surprise."

"How do you know that?"

Nick stepped to the empty display stand, turned, and started slowly across the carpet toward the body. "The fleas worked their way through the carpet, attracted by motion and exhaled carbon dioxide. When they got here, they found the victim already dead."

"Why dead?" Donovan asked. "How do you know he wasn't still alive?"

"The bites on the waist," Nick said. "Fleas like the waist area, but it's a matter of access. A flea can jump maybe eight inches, no higher. That gives it access to the ankles and legs of a standing figure—but to reach the waist, it needs to find someone lying down."

"In the bedroom," Poldie said. "You know, 'Don't let the bedbugs bite.'"

"There are no fleas in the bedroom, remember? They're all out here. This is where the fleas found him—he had been murdered just a few minutes before."

"Now, wait a minute," Poldie complained.

"It's the bites," Nick said. "A flea is something like a mosquito—when it bites, it injects a little saliva into the wound. That's what creates the red bump—it's a histamine reaction. But histamine reactions occur only when a person is living—and for a few minutes after death. Your boy here died instantly; the fleas arrived when he was lying down; ergo, immediately after death. And one more thing: Fleas feed only on *warm* blood. They were attracted to the blood around the head—but only while it was still warm. That wasn't long."

"But the fleas are all dead," Donovan said. "Are you saying someone came in and exterminated *after* the murder?"

"That would follow."

"But why?"

"The only possible conclusion is that someone didn't want us to find the fleas—which only strengthens my premise that the two acts are connected."

Donovan stepped to the display stand himself and retraced Nick's path across the carpet. "Somebody dumps the fleas," he said, "then somebody—maybe the same guy—shoots the victim in the head. The fleas cross the carpet, find the body, and help themselves. Then somebody comes back and exterminates the place. Who would do that?"

"Not him," Poldie said, nodding at the body.

"I'd say that's what you're investigating," Nick said. "Lucky for you, the detective has already narrowed the search."

Poldie looked at Nick with undisguised admiration. "You guys are amazing," he said. "You're worth whatever they pay you."

Nick turned to Donovan. "The detective mentioned money. We're friends now."

Donovan shook his head. "Nick and I have an agreement. He's here as a professional courtesy."

"*Courtesy*," Nick said. "That means two weeks from now the FBI will mail me a certificate and a Junior G-Man badge. Gee willikers."

There was another knock on the door. An NYPD officer leaned in the doorway and said, "There's a *Times* reporter downstairs. He wants to talk to someone."

"I'll go," Poldie said.

"Just the basics, Poldie," Donovan reminded him. "Until we know more. When you're done, follow up with the neighbors again. Ask about anybody unusual entering or leaving the building. Look for personal angles. Ask about anybody with a grudge against the deceased—you know the routine. And check with the super; see if the building has a surveillance system—there may be videos."

"Got it." Poldie started off toward the door.

"Hey, Poldie," Donovan called after him. "Keep the JTTF out of it, okay? Just tell the reporter it's an NYPD case."

"That reminds me," Poldie said. "Why *did* they call the JTTF on this one? What's the big deal about a bunch of fleas?"

"They're all the same species," Nick responded. "*Xenopsylla cheopis*, the Oriental rat flea."

"So?"

"They should be *Ctenocephalides felis*—cat fleas. That's the most common flea in the U.S. The Oriental rat flea is common to Europe and the tropics—not New York."

"Is that important?"

"Could be. They can carry bubonic plague."

CHAPTER FOUR

MACY APPROACHED THE FIRST uniform she saw and flashed her credentials.

The officer shook his head. "Uh-uh. Nobody allowed inside the perimeter. Take the detour around to the—"

"You people sent for me," she said. "Check with your boss."

The officer slipped the radio from his belt and held it diagonally across his mouth. "LaGambina," he said, holding the credentials at eye level. "I got a Dr. Macy Monroe here, professor of political science and international relations at Columbia University. Somebody send for a tutor?"

There was a crackle of static and a distorted voice—an urgent, emphatic voice.

"Yes sir. Right away." The officer turned back to Macy with a good deal more decorum. "My apologies, ma'am. Captain says I'm to escort you immediately to the command post. If you'll follow me, please."

"I can find it," she said, stepping across the yellow barrier tape. "A bunch of big guys in uniforms, right?"

Macy had been surrounded by books in the Graduate Reserve section of Low Library when her cell phone went off. She had an office, of course, but she preferred the solemn atmosphere of the old place with its spectacular view across the quad. Her office was just too quiet; she needed a little distraction to stay focused, and a few rustling pages and muffled coughs were just the thing to occupy her peripheral thoughts. She loved the long wooden tables and the intimate, eye-level lighting. She always surrounded herself with stacks of books, the older and thicker the better, a forbidding mountain of knowledge just waiting to be conquered.

She had meant to set her cell phone to vibrate, but she always seemed to forget, despite glaring reminders plastered throughout the library. When the piercing trill went off, shattering the tomblike atmosphere, she had to flash an apologetic grin at a dozen pairs of condemning eyes.

"Hold on," she whispered into the phone, then scurried down the stairs and into the bustling lobby to take the call.

Now, just thirty minutes later, she found herself in a residential/commercial section of Forest Hills, a proudly Jewish section of Queens. It was a beautiful street, lined with tightly packed buildings sporting colorful awnings and cascading flower boxes. It had a village atmosphere, as serene in its own way as any library. On the ground floor of each building was a clothier, or deli, or market; the two or three floors above were invariably residential, occupied by business owners and their extended families. The pristine sidewalks were ordinarily crowded with shoppers, strollers, and scurrying children—but not today. Inside the police perimeter the streets were as quiet as the southern Negev.

Rounding a corner, Macy saw a group of officers gathered around a Technical Assistance Response Unit. Most of them wore NYPD black, but a handful of navy FBI windbreakers mingled among them. *A WMD squad*, she thought, feeling a sudden twinge of anxiety that bordered on nausea. She quickly scanned the heads for a familiar face; he wasn't among them, and Macy relaxed again.

A senior NYPD officer spotted her first and waved her over. He looked over her shoulder as she approached.

"I told LaGambina to escort you," he growled.

"I told him not to. What can I do for you, Captain?"

The group closed in around her, and quick introductions were made. Someone shoved a steaming Styrofoam cup into her hand.

"Macy—like the department store?" someone asked.

"Only younger," she said. "Younger and cheaper" was the line she used with girlfriends, but not with black shirts and Bureau boys. She liked to get a laugh as much as the next person, but not at her own expense. Respect was hard to come by with these people; she wasn't about to give it away.

"Where's our boy?" she asked.

The commanding officer pointed across the street. There stood a Jewish grocery with a green-and-white awning overshadowing a red-trimmed door. Beside the door was a long display window, with the ends of crowded white shelves just barely visible through the glass.

"He's an Arab boy," the commanding officer said. "Fifteen, maybe sixteen years old tops. He charged in wearing a standard bomb vest. Witnesses tell us it was gray and bulky and had a series of pouches in it—all of them full. Looks like a manual detonator; he held it in his right hand."

"Hostages?"

"None. He rushed straight to the back of the store, shouted something in Arabic, then froze. For some reason he hesitated; that gave everyone in the store a chance to get out."

"So we've got a barricaded suspect. How long has he been in there?"

"We got the call about forty-five minutes ago. We were here and set up in fifteen. We've got a TARU and a hostage-negotiation team from the 112th Precinct. We've got a tactical unit setting up over in that alley—we like to keep those fellas out of sight until we need them. They're studying the building blueprints now."

"Let's hope we don't need them. Have you been able to make contact with the boy?"

"No. We captured the phone line going into the store, and we keep ringing him, but he won't answer the phone. He could be dead."

"Could be—we have to assume otherwise. Maybe the phone is in a bad place—maybe it puts him in a line of fire."

"We thought about throwing in a cell phone. We decided to wait until you got here."

"Good idea. People wearing bombs don't like to see small objects rolling across the floor toward them."

Macy turned to one of the men with bright yellow letters emblazoned across his back. "You must be the WMD guys," she said. "What can you tell us about this bomb?"

"Not much." The man shrugged. "We can't get a look at it—all we've got to go on is what witnesses have told us. Sounds pretty standard—probably eight kilos of C4 in a series of vest pockets."

"How bad is that?"

"It could bring the building down—maybe the ones on each side with it."

"Maybe we should let him," another agent said.

"Excuse me?"

"He's alone in there. If he wants to go out with a bang, I say let him. It's better than risking any of our people trying to walk him out. Sort of an unscheduled urban-renewal project. I'll bet these old buildings are insured for twice what they're worth anyway. What do we have to lose, a few knishes and some blini?"

They looked at the grocery store again—still no sign of movement in the shadows behind the glass. They could hear the ring of the telephone inside the TARU van. "Still no answer," a uniformed woman called out.

From around the corner came the muffled sound of struggling, shouting, pleading. An instant later a young, dark-haired woman broke into view, running toward them with an NYPD officer in close pursuit. He grabbed her by the left arm and spun her around, momentarily halting her advance, but she tore away and started forward again, running directly for the store. This time the officer tackled her from behind, breaking her down like a Giants linebacker. She hit the street headlong with her arms pinned to her sides, but she lifted her face toward the store and continued to scream uncontrollably. Macy took a step forward.

"I can't understand a word she's saying!" the officer shouted, pulling one of her arms behind her back and positioning the handcuffs.

"It's Yiddish!" Macy called back. "Let go of her hands!"

"Are you nuts? I've been trying to—"

"Do it!" Macy shouted.

The officer released the woman's left arm; she began to point frantically at the grocery store front. Macy's eyes followed her hand to one of the second-floor windows. At the sound of the woman's desperate screams, the draperies swung aside and two tiny faces pressed against the glass. One smiled, and a little hand waved from side to side.

"Let her go!" Macy shouted to the officer. "Get her out of here, but let her go!" She turned to the ashen-faced FBI agent. "He's got two hostages now—still want to let him blow the place up?"

She turned to the NYPD commander. "Get me your tactical commander—I need to know if there's a way to reach those kids without being seen."

Now she charged to the TARU van and looked inside. "Who's the chief negotiator? Who's in charge here?"

A detective from the 112th raised his hand.

"May I have a word with you, please?"

He stepped out of the van. Macy took him by the arm and turned him quickly aside.

"I need your help," she said. "I need a good secondary negotiator out here. I need somebody who's had training in this, somebody who knows the ropes."

"In other words, you're taking over."

She took a step closer and spoke in a low, even voice. "Look—I've got a doctorate in international relations. My field of study is the psychology of terrorism. I've got two areas of regional expertise—one is the Middle East. I'm fluent in Arabic. That's why they sent for me, okay? Nothing personal—it's not about you."

He tried to look as indifferent as possible. "It's your show. What do you want to do?"

"Get me a throw phone. I'm going in."

The tactical and NYPD commanders approached from behind. "You're going to *what*?"

"It's the only way," Macy said.

"Not a chance," the NYPD commander replied. "I asked you here to advise, not to get yourself blown up."

"I don't want that either. I've got vacation coming."

"I'm not giving this boy a hostage."

"He's got two already—he just doesn't know it yet." She turned to the tactical commander and shook his hand as she spoke. "Have you had a look at the building? Can you get to those kids?"

"The front door leads directly to a stairway," he said. "It's visible to the entire store. There's a fire escape in the back—but there's a big security window in the back of the store too. We don't know where this kid is holed up; there's a chance he could see us approaching from any angle."

"What about the roof?"

"We could come up through an adjacent building and cross over, then rope down through a third-floor window. But there's a problem with sound—this place is as quiet as a church. If a window breaks, if the floor creaks, this kid could hear us coming a mile away."

"Then you need a distraction inside."

"Wait," the commander said. "We could call the second-floor apartment—get the kids to open a window, maybe even sneak down the stairs and make a break for the front door."

"No," Macy said. "The last thing we want is a phone ringing on the second floor. There's a chance the boy hasn't even thought about who might be upstairs. Make sure your people secure *all* the lines going into the building—we don't want some worried relative trying to call in."

Now the hostage negotiator spoke up. "If somebody's going in, it should be me. That's my job; that's what I'm trained for."

Macy thought about the NYPD hostage negotiator training process: A few weeks of classroom training and you get a certificate allowing you to intervene in domestic squabbles and disturbances involving disgruntled employees and people who stopped taking their medication too soon. She should know; she wrote the training manual.

"No," she said. "It's got to be me."

"Why?"

"Look, I speak Arabic. He may not be answering the phone because he doesn't speak a word of English. If you walk in there and the first word you say is in a foreign tongue, that may be all he needs to remind him that you're the enemy."

"I don't have to say a word. I can just take in a phone and back out."

She shook her head. "There's another reason. You're a man."

The three men glanced at one another, but no one knew what to say in response.

"It's like this," Macy said. "An Arab culture is a patriarchal culture. That means men control most of the ostensible power. That boy is in there ready to blow himself up because he believes that's how you get yourself a river of honey, a river of wine, and seventy-two virgins. A *man* told him that; in Arab cultures, the relationships between men and boys are very complex and very powerful.

"But in patriarchal cultures, women also exert enormous influence— but they learn to do it in indirect ways. In fact, some cultures are patriarchal in form only. The women have the real power; they just allow their men the appearance of control."

Macy stopped. The men's eyes were beginning to glaze over. *This is the problem with critical-incident teams*, she thought. *There's an extreme prejudice toward action. Everybody wants to do something, but nobody wants to talk theory.*

"Here's the bottom line," she said. "If a man walks in that door, no matter what he says or does, he will be a visible reminder of duty, and courage, and *shame*—and that's when things go boom. An Arab boy will die for his father—but he will live for his mother. Get it?"

She took a handkerchief from her purse and scrubbed at her mouth and eyes. She pulled off her earrings and a bracelet and took a silver brooch from her left lapel. She instinctively reached for her ring finger, but it was already bare. She dropped all of it into her purse and pulled her hair back with a simple rubber band.

"How do I look?" she asked.

"Plain enough."

"Like a mom?"

"Not like *my* mom."

"Flatterer."

"If you're going in," the commander said, "then put this on." He held out a bulky black Kevlar vest.

Macy almost laughed. The gesture reminded her of her aunt Jean, who always brought a jar of her homemade preserves to a funeral. *It's human nature*, she thought. *When people feel powerless they always seem to offer the most ridiculous and useless things.*

"No thanks," she said.

"I'm afraid I have to insist. It's policy."

"Look, Captain. You and I both know that if the boy pushes the button, the only thing that vest will do is allow your cleanup squad to find a larger piece of my torso intact. No thanks—I can't go in there looking like one of your ninjas. I'm going in as a woman, and I need to look like a woman."

A TARU officer handed her a silver throw phone. "It's always on," he said. "Even when it's in the cradle it broadcasts. We'll hear everything you say."

Macy nodded. "Listen closely," she said. "When I'm talking to him, I'll be talking to you too. If I need anything, if I want you to do something, you'll know it." She turned toward the street.

"One thing," the tactical commander said. "I'm putting two shooters on the second floor across the street with a clear view of the store window. If things aren't working, if you can't talk him out, just lure him in front of the window. We'll do the rest."

Macy winced. If things didn't go well, she was to lure the boy out into the open where he could be neatly and efficiently murdered. *Some mother*, she thought.

At the door of the grocery, she paused. Her first words in Arabic needed to be flawless, without a hint of foreign accent or a trace of hesitation. She mouthed the words silently until the rhythm and cadence came back to her.

She reached for the door and then stopped. This was the hardest moment of all, like the first step into a dark cellar, when all the old fears come rushing out at once. For the police she put on an air of perfect confidence, but she had learned the hard way that dealing with terrorists is not a science; it's an art—a very imperfect art. Despite all her training and experience, she had no way of knowing what would happen when she opened that door. For all she knew, the boy might hate his mother; he might push the detonator at the first sight of her. A voice in the back of her mind asked her if she was prepared to die today. She shook off the thought and tried to refocus. There are some places your mind just can't go—not at a time like this.

She slowly opened the door. A bell jingled, and her heart jumped into her throat.

"Hello," she called out in Arabic. "May I come in, please?"

There was no response.

She slowly tiptoed down an aisle toward the back of the store, letting her words go before her. "May I come in? It's only me. I'd like to speak with you for a moment, if you'll allow me."

Still nothing.

"I'm a friend. I just came to talk. I've brought you something—may I show you?"

She rounded the end of an aisle. There was the boy, sprawled back against the glass of the deli counter, staring at her through eyes as black as Saudi oil. He held the detonator aloft in his right hand; his thumb stood poised above the button, and his hand trembled with uncertainty.

Don't look at the detonator, she reminded herself. *It's just a friendly visit.*

"Get out of here, woman!"

Macy bowed her head slightly in a display of womanly deference. She looked at him from the tops of her eyes. His skin was bronze, and his hair was thick and black. He was slender; his joints seemed larger than the adjoining limbs. A sparse tangle of facial hair sprouted from his chin, longer on the left than the right. *Just a boy*, she thought. *Not a foal, and not a stallion.* She wanted to shake her head. She wanted to say, "You sad little fool. What would you do with seventy-two virgins?"

"I brought you this," she said gently. "We thought the phone in here might be broken. This is for you, in case you want to talk to us."

"The time to talk is over," he said with angry defiance, but his voice was an octave too high to make it work.

"There is always time to talk," she said simply. She glanced around the room; beside the deli counter were a half dozen tables with wire-backed chairs. "May I sit?" she asked, pulling out one of the chairs.

"No!" he shouted back.

She showed him a look of injury and affront that bordered on anger. *Try a little guilt, kiddo. You don't talk to your mother that way.*

He lowered his eyes. "Sit," he grumbled.

She set the phone on the table nearest him and took a seat.

"Do you speak any English?" He shook his head. *Then he hasn't been here long*, she thought. *The Arabs in New York know they're a minority, and they pick up English fast.* "I apologize for my Arabic. Your language is so beautiful, and I speak it so poorly."

"It's not bad," he said reluctantly.

"My name is Macy. What may I call you?"

"Call me Shahid," he said—the Arabic word for "martyr."

She looked around the store. "You're all alone," she said for the throw phone. "May I ask where you're from?"

He glared at her. "You are with the police."

"I am not with the police—I am a schoolteacher."

"Then why are you here?"

"I speak Arabic. I've been to Jordan; did you know that? I've been to Lebanon and to Syria too." She left Israel out of it; no sense spoiling their little reunion. "I've been to Kuwait, and to Yemen, and to Saudi Arabia. I think I liked Saudi Arabia best—I love Medina." She watched for some sign of recognition, some hint of "Me too" in his eyes—but he showed her nothing.

"Are you hungry?"

The boy seemed taken aback. "I will not require food."

"Nonsense—you must eat to stay strong. I know a place not far from here—in Brooklyn Heights. Have you been there yet? You must go. There is a restaurant there; they serve a wonderful *shawarma*—you can have beef or lamb. I can send for some. May I?"

The boy said nothing. *At least he didn't say no*, Macy thought. She gently lifted the throw phone and looked at him as she spoke. "Did you get that?" she said in English. "*Shawarma*—they know what it is. Bedouin Tent on Atlantic Avenue. Take your time—and don't send it in unless I ask for it."

She hung up the phone and smiled.

"Do you have a sister at home? Someone like me?"

"You are much older than my sister."

"Your mother, then—is she about my age?"

"How old are you?"

"It's rude to ask," she scolded. "I'd like to meet your mother."

The boy sneered. "Perhaps she can clean your house."

Macy frowned. "You insult me *and* your mother. Still, I would like to meet her."

"Why?"

"Because I have met her son—and I would like to show her a picture of mine. Would you like to see?" She lifted her purse; the boy straightened and extended the detonator menacingly.

"It's just a purse," she said softly. She slowly turned and inverted it, spilling its contents across the table.

"You carry too many things," the boy grumbled.

"Women always do." She picked out her wallet and opened it to a section of small photographs in glossy plastic sleeves. The first was empty, but the faint contour of two heads was still visible on the plastic. She opened to the second photo, an image of a small boy no more than three. She slowly stood up from her chair, holding the wallet in front of her. *Either you come to me or I come to you*, she thought.

The boy measured the distance between them, then impatiently gestured for her to approach. She held the wallet at arm's length and approached until the wallet was within reach; he quickly reached out and snatched it from her hands. He gave the photograph a cursory glance and offered the wallet back, but Macy shook her head.

"Look at the next one," she said.

The boy flipped the plastic sleeve. The next photograph was an image of the same child—only this time he appeared tired, and frail, and bald-headed.

"What's wrong with him?" the boy asked.

"He had cancer. He's dead now."

The boy looked at her, unsure of what to say. For an instant, his countenance softened—then anger reclaimed him again. "What do I care about your son?" he said, tossing the wallet back to her. Macy let the wallet bounce off her chest and fall to the floor. She stood looking at it for a moment; when she lifted her eyes again, they were filled with anger of her own.

"What do you *care*?" she repeated. "How dare you. That was my son—and you throw him on the ground as if he were dirt. His life meant nothing to you—*nothing*. Well, it meant everything to me, because I was his *mother*. You know nothing about that, do you? Nothing about what it means to be a *mother*. You have no idea what it's like to watch your son waste away and die, to know that all your love and all your service were for nothing. You don't care about my son—but your mother would care. She would weep with me and hold me, because she is a mother too. She has a son, and she knows how it would break her heart to hear that he was dead—and not for something important, but for *nothing*.

"Men throw their lives away," she said with contempt, "and all women can do is watch and weep. No one thinks about the mothers—no one asks us how *we* feel."

She watched him as she spoke, waiting for his eyes to begin to soften, for his shoulders to round and droop. The anger was hers now; the power was hers. All that was left was his shame—but she knew that shame was still enough to kill them both.

The boy stared into space. "I have no choice," he said quietly.

"There is a saying in English," she said, holding up one finger. "He's in the back right corner. He has no weapon other than the bomb." The boy waited for the translation.

"It means, 'It's never too late to change your mind. There is always a choice.'"

"I cannot go back."

"Then you will have to kill me too." She held her breath. In her mind, she saw him shrug and press the detonator; she felt the heat and the impact and imagined her body catapulted backward across the store.

"You can go." The boy glared at her as he spoke. "I did not ask you to come."

"I will not go. You will throw away your life *and* mine—and then you will stand before the holy one and say to him, 'Let me into your Paradise. I am a *shahid*; I killed myself and *one woman*.'" Macy sneered. "How great will be your reward."

The boy just stared at the floor now. His anger and his power were gone; even his shame had been trumped by a greater shame. He was naked and alone, just a boy again, with no idea what to do next.

Macy took a step toward him. She lowered her eyes to the floor with his and spoke under her breath, as women do in the marketplace when they speak of intimate things. She prayed that he would not detect the trembling in her voice.

"There is a way," she said. "Outside there is a team of men. They are very large and very strong. They are highly trained, and they carry powerful weapons. They are known as a Special Weapons and Tactics team."

"Special Forces?" the boy said in awe.

"Yes, like Special Forces. They move very quickly and without a sound. If you were distracted—for even a moment—they would move in like shadows and overcome you. And who could blame you? Not even a great warrior could resist them."

Who could blame you? They were words of salvation, and they called to the boy like a crier from a minaret.

"I must ask one thing," Macy said even more softly. "The men outside, they have wives and children who wait for them at home. Before they come in, I must ask you to remove . . . this." She nodded, almost imperceptibly, toward the vest.

The boy stood silently, his mind racing.

Macy leaned forward until their heads were almost touching. "No one thinks of the mothers," she said.

The boy stepped back and began to fumble dumbly with the straps of the vest. "Yes," she said softly as he released each strap, soothing him like a groom with a nervous thoroughbred. She said, "Thank you," as he slid off the vest and set it on the floor beside him. Then she took him gently by the arm and walked him several feet away.

"Now *I* must ask one thing," the boy said. "I will not surrender to these men. They must *take* me."

"I understand," she said. "This is how it will happen: When I signal them, six men will enter this room. They will make a great deal of noise, and they will fire several shots into the wall. Do you understand? Not at you—at the wall. They will bend your arms behind your back, and they will bind your wrists with a plastic strap. Then they will help you to your feet and lead you out to a vehicle waiting outside." She paused. "Do you understand?"

He nodded fiercely.

"Then I will signal the men." She lifted the phone from its cradle and repeated the instructions in English. "Did you get all that?" she asked.

"We're on our way," said the voice on the other end.

She hung up the phone again and they stood in silence, waiting.

"Do you think I'm a coward?" the boy whispered.

Macy looked at him. "You did the hard thing. That's what courage is."

A moment later the door burst open, and six heavily armed men poured through and charged toward the back of the store. Macy could see their black ballistic helmets bobbing toward them like sea buoys. Three of the men pointed their Heckler & Koch submachine guns at the base of the wall and squeezed off a handful of single rounds. Macy stood perfectly still; better to let these men work around you.

She looked at the boy. "It will go easier for you if you lie down."

"They must *take* me," the boy repeated defiantly.

The men were happy to comply. One sweep of a boot took the boy's legs out from under him; a second man pinned him to the floor with a knee in the center of his back, while a third banded his wrists in a matter of seconds. They jerked him to his feet again; in their hands, the boy seemed to possess no weight at all.

"Easy, guys," Macy said. A lot of adrenaline was flowing in there—a lot of testosterone too—and it wouldn't take more than a kick or a jab from the boy to earn him a broken jaw or a rifle butt to the side of his head. *Maybe he'd like that*, Macy thought. *Something to show his friends—if he'll have any left.*

Three of the men searched under every table and counter in the store, while one gingerly disconnected the curling red wires from the bomb vest. The remaining two hustled the boy down the center aisle to the door; Macy followed close behind. Directly in front of the doorway, an NYPD van waited with its side door yawning wide. Macy stood in the doorway, watching as they turned the boy, tucked his head down, and shoved him into the center seat.

The boy stared at Macy with burning eyes. "I am Ali bin Ahmad bin Saleh Al-Fulani," he said.

Macy nodded as the door slid shut, and she watched as the van pulled away.

CHAPTERFIVE

EXPLAIN AGAIN ABOUT THE fleas," Mayer said slowly.

Nathan Donovan sat across from his supervisory special agent, the next man up the totem pole in the FBI's convoluted administrative hierarchy. Reuben Mayer was an old man, a veteran of countless reorganizations and regime changes at the Bureau, and nothing ruffled or surprised him anymore. He had seen it all, and there was simply nothing left to get all in a huff about. Mayer was like a man in slow motion, as if over the years he had learned to perform every thought, every word, and every motion with an absolute minimum of exertion.

He even looked slow. His shoulders were slightly rounded, the beginning of osteoporosis, and it caused him to slump slightly over his desk. The sacks under his eyes hung with such weight that his lower eyelids seemed to pull away from his eyeballs, leaving dark little pockets above. His face was long and drawn, and it widened at the bottom, where great sagging jowls bagged around his neck. It gave him the overall appearance of a melting candle, drooping under its own weight, as if at any moment his face might ooze over his collar and onto the desk.

To his reporting agents, Mayer's pace was maddeningly slow. They all searched for ways to speed along the weekly reporting process, but nothing seemed to help. At the Christmas party, they all chipped in and bought the old man a plaque for his office that read: "I have only two speeds: If you don't like this one, you'll hate the other." The gift was given anonymously; it had not been seen since. Reuben Mayer ran on his own timetable, and anyone trying to hurry him along simply earned a long, slow, forlorn glare—which only made the meeting longer.

Donovan sat impatiently while Mayer read his summary of the TriBeCa murder, his eyes sweeping back and forth over the text like weighty pendulums.

"There were thousands of fleas," Donovan said. "The Manhattan South forensic guys spotted them. They thought it was a red flag, so I brought in a bug man from North Carolina to take a look. He says no doubt about it, somebody dumped the fleas there on purpose."

"How does he know that?"

"By the number and distribution—but most of all, by the species."

"Species?"

"Yes sir. The way I understand it, fleas are named after the animal they feed on—so there are cat fleas, dog fleas, even people fleas. But these were Oriental rat fleas; they don't belong in New York, and—"

"So why do we care about fleas?" Mayer interrupted. His voice was a perfect monotone; it didn't even make the effort to rise for a question.

"Because Oriental rat fleas are known to be carriers of bubonic plague," he said. "That's why the forensic guys flagged it."

"Bubonic plague."

"Yes sir."

"Like in the Middle Ages, bubonic plague."

"I think so, sir, yes."

"Any of these fleas have plague?"

"No sir."

"And how do we know that?"

"My bug man. Apparently there's a way to tell just by looking at them under a microscope."

"He's sure about that?"

"Yes sir."

He looked down at the report again. A full five seconds passed before he added, "We should make sure about that." He closed the folder and extended it toward the out-box on the corner of his desk; he paused before letting it drop, as if his shoulder had suddenly locked or his sleeve had snagged on a hook.

"How do you want to proceed?" he asked.

"I think we should treat it like an ordinary homicide—because it probably is. Detective Satwyck is following up with neighbors, looking for people who attended the party, trying to find somebody with motive. I suggest we let NYPD find a perp; then we can ask him about the fleas."

Mayer nodded; no sense wasting a word. He dragged another folder in front of him now and lifted the cover as if it were a sheet of plywood. He began to read again, leaning on his elbows and rubbing his temples in long, slow circles.

"Tell me about the psychiatrist," he said without looking up.

Donovan hesitated. "I think it went well."

"Tell me about it."

"Well, he said . . . He thinks that I . . . You probably have it all right there in his evaluation, sir."

"You tell me."

Donovan could feel his teeth grinding. "He said I'm fit for duty."

Mayer's brown eyes turned up to Donovan like a Central Park swing. "He says you're angry."

Donovan shrugged. "Hardly worth the money."

"He says you might get yourself killed—or you might kill somebody." He paused. "Which is it?"

Donovan said nothing. Seconds went by.

The old man slowly closed the folder again. "He says you're fit for duty. That's good enough for me—for now."

Behind them, there was a knock on the glass panel of the door. Donovan turned and looked, grateful for the reprieve. A young administrative assistant stuck her head in the door.

"Sorry to interrupt. Mr. Donovan, you've got a call from overseas—I thought you might want to take it."

"Are we done here?" Donovan asked. He was halfway to the door before the old man completed his nod.

"I love you, marry me, bear my children," Donovan said to the woman as they walked down the hall toward his cubicle.

"I'll check with my husband," she said. There was no real reason for the interruption. Agents received calls from all over the world; it was standard practice for administrative assistants to take messages so that agents could respond at their leisure. But when Donovan was reporting to Mayer, his standing order was to be interrupted even for a wrong number.

"This is Donovan," he said, pulling on a wireless headset and flopping down in his desk chair.

"Well, hello," a voice said brightly on the other end. "This is London calling. Can you hear me clearly?"

"Yeah, they've got these things called 'satellites' now. They really do the job."

There was a chuckle on the other end. The voice was that of an old man, distinctly British.

"You'll forgive me," he said. "I never quite get used to the technology. I always imagine I'm speaking into a tin can with a long string stretched across the ocean."

Donovan smiled. He couldn't help imagining Batman's butler, Alfred, or Colonel Pickering from *My Fair Lady*—some quintessential British stereotype as seen through American eyes. The voice was the virtual opposite of Mayer's—it was lively and rich, and it had a musical quality that made you want to listen if only for the sound.

"I didn't get your name," Donovan said, reaching for a legal pad. He jotted down a single word: *Lee*. "So, Mr. Lee, why is the Queen calling the colonies today?"

"This is a private concern," the old man said. "Well, that's not precisely accurate; the matter I wish to discuss with you is of the utmost public importance. But I make no claim to represent the Crown or any governmental agency. I'm calling you purely as a private citizen."

"All right, then what can I do for you?"

"A most interesting newspaper article was brought to my attention just this morning. It appeared the day before last in your *New York Times*; it concerns an apparent homicide that occurred in a section of Manhattan known as *TriBeCa*. Am I saying that correctly?"

"Close enough. Why would a homicide in Manhattan concern you, Mr. Lee? Were you acquainted with the deceased?"

"I'm afraid I have no information that might help with your direct investigation, Mr. Donovan. No, the thing that caught my eye was the mention of . . . fleas."

"I'm sorry, did you say *fleas?*"

"Quite a number of them, I would imagine."

Donovan rolled his eyes; Poldie did the interview with the *Times* reporter. *Just the basics*, Donovan had told him. The big Polack—he managed to remember the fleas, but he couldn't remember to keep his big mouth shut.

"You'll have to excuse me, Mr. Lee; I haven't seen the story in the *Times* yet. What else does it say?"

"Is the newspaper account correct, Mr. Donovan?"

"I'm afraid I can't comment on that. The thing is, that information was never supposed to be released to the public."

"We may both be very glad it was."

Donovan paused. "How did you get my name, Mr. Lee?"

"The officer quoted in the *Times* article was a Detective Leopold Satwyck of the New York Police Department. I spoke with him this morning; he was most helpful."

"I'll bet he was."

"Tell me, Mr. Donovan, why is the FBI taking an interest in an ordinary homicide?"

"Again, no comment."

"Unless, of course, you suspect that it's not an ordinary homicide."

Donovan didn't reply.

"I suppose there are a number of reasons a case like this might fall under your agency's jurisdiction: It might involve organized crime, or drug trafficking, or interstate travel—"

"Look, Mr. Lee, let me save you some time here. I'm not at liberty to discuss an open investigation, okay?"

There was a pause. "If you're not at liberty to answer my questions, perhaps you'll allow me to simply make a few observations. You have no restriction against listening, do you? Trust me, Mr. Donovan, you may find my comments most helpful."

"I'm listening."

"As I see it, there are only four reasons an infestation of fleas at a crime scene might merit mentioning at all. First, if the fleas were discovered in an unusual environment—say, in an upscale neighborhood like your own TriBeCa. This suggests, of course, that the fleas were purposely introduced. Second, if the fleas were present in unusual number. Again, this raises the possibility that someone purposely interfered with the natural course of things."

"And why would someone want to do that?"

"Oh, you're allowed to ask me questions?"

Donovan said nothing.

"Are you still there, Mr. Donovan?"

"Still here."

"Very well, the third possibility is that the insects had an unusual distribution—say, a large population in one corner but nowhere else. This would suggest that the fleas had not been present long—and once again, that they were purposely introduced." He paused. "How am I doing?"

"No comment. This is fascinating, Mr. Lee, but we're talking about fleas here. A pile of fleas is hardly a threat to the city of New York."

"No. But an epidemic of bubonic plague just might be."

Donovan straightened. "Excuse me?"

"That's the fourth possibility, Mr. Donovan—that all of the fleas represented a single species, a species not common to New York. I assume you are aware that the Oriental rat flea is capable of transmitting plague?"

He paused. "We're aware."

"Then the species was indeed *Xenopsylla cheopis*?"

No reply.

"I see no other reason the Federal Bureau of Investigation would concern itself with these events," the old man said. "Especially the Office of Counterterrorism."

"Mr. Lee, are you some kind of insect expert? We already asked a forensic entomologist to consult on this case."

"That was very wise. And what did he have to say?"

"Are you an epidemiologist or an infectious disease specialist?"

"I am not."

"Then, Mr. Lee, I have to ask you: What is your interest in this case?"

There was a pause on the other end. "You might say I have a lifelong interest in this case."

Donovan waited, but there was nothing more. "Look," he said, "if you have information that bears directly on this case, the FBI would greatly appreciate any assistance you can give us."

"And I, for my part, am most eager to help. The question is how to best convey this information to you."

"Overnight it to us; I'll give you a billing number. Or you can fax it. If it's in electronic form, we can do it by encrypted e-mail."

"The issue is not a technical one," the old man said. "The information I have is of a rather . . . personal nature."

"If you consider it sensitive, I'll contact the U.S. Embassy and we can black-bag it."

"No, I mean *personal*—the kind of information best imparted face-to-face."

Donovan paused. "You want to meet?"

"I plan to be in New York the day after tomorrow. Would it be convenient to arrange a meeting then?"

"Give me a time and a place."

"Oh, let's do lunch," the old man said enthusiastically. "I never pass up a chance to dine in New York City."

"Lunch it is. Do you have a place in mind?" The old man spoke slowly while Donovan took down the address.

"Do you know it?"

"I know the general area."

"It's a date then. The day after next for lunch."

"One more thing, Mr. Lee. How will I know you?"

"Not to worry," he said. "Everyone on the block will know you."

CHAPTERSIX

N EW YORK HAS BEEN the most ethnically diverse city in the world since the 1600s, when barely a thousand residents already spoke fifteen different languages. Some think of the city as a tapestry, with hundreds of bright-colored threads woven tightly together in a seamless social fabric. In reality, New York is more like a mosaic, with hundreds of glittering tiles precariously held together by some invisible cement. On the Lower East Side of Manhattan lies the most enigmatic piece of this puzzle, a two-square-mile section of decaying tenements known as Chinatown.

The intersection of Mott and Canal Streets marks the financial center of Chinatown, where the jewelers and grocers of Canal Street join Mott Street's teahouse proprietors and restaurateurs. Nathan Donovan stood staring at a multistory concrete building with brightly lacquered balconies and a tiled roof that curled up at the corners like a pair of old slippers. *Pagoda*, he remembered, *that's the name for it.* He recalled the word with a sense of satisfaction, though he had few others in his vocabulary to describe the melee of otherworldly sights and sounds and smells that engulfed him. Canal Street stretched out before him, its sidewalks impossibly crowded with a sea of disembodied heads pulsing back and forth like corpuscles in an artery. Pedestrians dodged between narrow storefront merchants and sidewalk vendors hawking everything from firecrackers and baseball caps to fish balls and peanut cakes. Above them, a confetti of red and yellow banners displayed inscrutable Chinese pictographs; higher still, aging brick facades wearily supported black-iron balconies and rickety fire escapes.

One tiny shop, scarcely more than a flea-market stall, featured "genuine" Prada and Louis Vuitton. Above the open doorway a metal security shutter hovered, ready to crash down at the first hint of government interference. Donovan, a head taller than anyone on the sidewalk and dressed entirely in black, had caused more than one thriving business to close early for lunch that day.

Donovan hated to leave his Buick behind, and it was against company policy to do so; but parking in Chinatown was virtually impossible, and if his services were unexpectedly called for, he could travel on foot faster than he could retrieve his car from some subterranean parking garage. Instead, he took the subway to the Canal Street exit, where he worked his way past the fishmongers and apothecaries to the agreed-upon meeting place.

He glanced around, searching the passing throng for Western faces. He kicked himself for not insisting on a basic description; he just assumed that an elderly British gentleman would stand out in this crowd as clearly as he did. He looked to his right; just a few yards away, a man squatted by the curb, piling a heap of crumbling pork into a square of floured dough, then squeezed it in his fist until it resembled a wadded white napkin.

"It's called *wonton*," a voice said behind him. "Have you tried it? It's very good."

Donovan turned, but no one was there—at least, no one to account for the unmistakable British inflection. He searched the faces; there, at a small table at a crowded sidewalk café, sat an elderly Chinese man looking directly into his eyes.

The old man smiled.

"You can order off the menu if you like," he said. "They have exquisite seafood here, flown in fresh daily. But I suggest the *dim sum*—sort of like your American 'brunch.' That way, you can sample a whole variety of dishes."

Donovan just stared. He understood the words, but the accent was so incongruous with the face that it was like watching an old movie with the sound out of sync. The old man motioned him over and gestured to the chair opposite.

"You could have told me," Donovan said, pulling out the chair.

"What fun would that have been? You know, if I hadn't made eye contact, I'll bet I could have kept you guessing for quite some time."

"A whole afternoon of fun," Donovan said.

"Tell me, I'm curious: What were you expecting to see? Some dusty old Londoner, I imagine?"

"Something like that, yes."

"And instead you find?"

"Some dusty old mandarin."

The old man clapped his hands in delight. "I can't tell you how relieved I am to see that you have a sense of humor. It's something that I find Westerners lack—not the bawdy, barroom type of humor, but a sense of irony—of *subtlety*. You know, I have never met a truly wise man who lacked a sense of humor."

"I know some pretty smart people who are drop-dead dull."

"I'm referring to wisdom, not simple intelligence. The failure to distinguish between knowledge and wisdom is a common Western error. To you, it's all just 'smart' or 'dumb.' In the East we know better. Smart people are sometimes the biggest fools."

Donovan extended his hand across the table. The old man's grip was more vigorous than he'd expected. "I'm Nathan Donovan. You know who I work for; better not to say it out loud."

"Another sign of wisdom," the old man said. "And by now you have surmised that my name is spelled L-i, not L-e-e. Please, call me Li."

"And your first name?"

The old man's lips reverted effortlessly to his mother tongue. The name poured out like water; it was soft and flowing, with none of the abrasive consonant sounds common to the English language. It sounded something like "Shee Dong Lee," or maybe "Gee Dung Lean." It didn't matter—Donovan was lost after the first syllable.

"Li it is," he said.

A waitress arrived, and after a quick glance at Donovan, she exchanged prolonged pleasantries with Li. There was a rapid-fire volley of words—*like a series of bursts from an automatic weapon,* Donovan thought. Then there were smiles and quick nods, and then both of them turned to Donovan.

"If you insist on ordering à la carte," Li said, "then I recommend the honey-glazed garlic shrimp or the hot-and-pepper soft-shell crabs—but really, the *dim sum* here is not to be missed."

"Something simple," Donovan said. "Maybe some chow mein."

Li blinked. "Perhaps I should explain *dim sum* a bit more. The waitress will bring a cart to our table, filled with indescribable delicacies, and you may sample whatever your heart desires. Lighter, steamed dishes come first, followed by more substantial fare—my personal favorite is shrimp dumplings wrapped in seaweed and topped with a dollop of salmon caviar. After that comes dessert; you absolutely *must* try the custard tarts or the almond pudding."

"Chow mein," Donovan said to the waitress.

The waitress lowered her eyes. "*Low faan,*" she said under her breath.

Li nodded. "*Guey low.*" The two men watched until the waitress disappeared through a doorway.

"What did she say?"

"She called you a 'barbarian.'"

"And what did you say to her?"

"I quite agreed—and I added that you are a 'foreign devil.'"

"Thanks a lot," Donovan said.

"I hope you're not offended. I assure you, the word *barbarian* has lost its pejorative sense—most of it, anyway. In this case, some of it is deserved. I mean, ordering chow mein in Chinatown—really now. It isn't even Chinese, you know."

"And that makes me a barbarian?"

"The Chinese have used the term 'barbarian' for centuries to refer to all outsiders. It isn't just you; it's everyone. The fact is, the Chinese have always considered their culture to be superior to all others—an island of culture in a sea of mediocrity, you might say. It's hard to blame them; after all, the

Chinese were the first to introduce the abacus, the compass, the seismo-graph—even gunpowder. By the twelfth century our ships were already sailing the world; by the thirteenth we were using multistage rockets in naval warfare. We were the first to use paper, just a hundred years after Christ; Europe didn't catch on for another thousand years. We employed movable type four hundred years before Gutenberg did. And let's not for-get silk—we managed to keep that our little secret for three millennia."

"You must be very proud," Donovan said.

"We are—and deservedly so, don't you think? Until quite recently, China was always centuries ahead of the West. In fact, when England sent its first ambassador to China in 1793 to request trade between our nations, the emperor replied that China 'possessed all goods in prolific abundance' and had no desire to sample barbarian merchandise. I'll bet that put the burn on some British ears, don't you think?"

"I can't figure you," Donovan said. "Are you Chinese or British?"

"I like to think of myself as a citizen of the world—Chinese by birth and ancestry, British by training and tenure. I lived in China until shortly after the war, when I moved to England and matriculated at Oxford. I've been there ever since—though I have traveled extensively."

The waitress returned now with a two-level rolling tray packed with an assortment of colorful dishes. Li selected several with gusto; when he fin-ished, the waitress pulled a plate of rice and vegetables from the lower tray and set it unceremoniously before Donovan.

"The *low faan* needs a fork," he said.

"*Bot guey,*" she whispered, then departed again.

Donovan looked at Li.

"'White devil,'" the old man translated. "What did you expect?"

Li's face suddenly straightened. He looked over Donovan's shoulder at the street behind him. Donovan turned; from the crowded sidewalk, half a dozen young men approached and gathered slowly around their table. They were young—eighteen, maybe twenty years old. They were all Oriental, and similarly dressed—like Americans, like teenagers, but five to ten years behind the current style.

The tallest of the young men fixed his eyes on Donovan, slowly rolling a wad of gum from one side of his mouth to the other as he stared. He said something quickly in Chinese; it sounded somehow more guttural than Li's fluid tongue. Li responded calmly with just a word or two.

"What did he say?" Donovan asked.

"He says he would like to sit down."

"Tell him to pull up a chair."

Li translated Donovan's words, and the young man responded—but this time his voice sounded lower and more menacing.

"Well?"

Li hesitated. "He says he would like to sit in *your* chair."

Donovan stared back at the man without flinching. He slowly pulled back the left lapel of his blazer, reached into the inside pocket with two fingers, and pulled out his FBI credentials. He opened the leather folder, set it on the table, and slid it forward.

The young man picked up the credentials, slowly took the wad of gum from his mouth, and pressed it onto the center of the photograph on the lower left. Then he closed the folder, squeezed it tight, and tossed it back on the table.

Donovan felt his face flush. He slowly brought his left foot up to rest on his right knee. He put his right hand on his ankle, feeling for the leather ankle holster and the Glock within. He began to calculate the time necessary to draw the weapon, release the safety, chamber a round, and fire. He brought his left hand to rest beside his right and casually grasped the edge of his pant leg.

Suddenly Li jumped to his feet and began to bark at the men, scolding them in contemptuous tones and dressing them down in words that required no translation. He glared at each of them in turn until their eyes broke away and lowered to the ground; then one by one they slowly turned and swaggered back toward the street.

Li glared after them until they were a safe distance away; then he slowly took his seat again and looked at Donovan.

"They were Vietnamese," he said. "Did you notice the darker skin?

They're known as *sai low*—'little brothers' in the vernacular. The local tongs hire them as a sort of private police force."

"I thought they sounded different."

"They spoke Cantonese, not Mandarin. Cantonese is the language of southern China. Like many educated Chinese, I speak both."

"What did they want?"

"They wanted to know if you were bothering me. You must understand, your presence here is unwelcome—even an act of aggression."

"Why?"

"You are a *low faan*, you are rather large and imposing, and you are clearly a government official."

Donovan looked down at himself. "Is it that obvious?"

"When I arrived this morning, I stopped a *chong you bing* vendor and asked him, 'Have you seen an FBI agent today?' He said, 'At the corner of Mott and Canal. Be careful.' These people are used to being betrayed and abused by government officials, Mr. Donovan. To them you represent cruelty, fear, and corruption. They can spot a policeman a mile away. The 'little brothers' recognized you immediately."

"So they were just protecting you."

"Perhaps. Or perhaps they were trying to run you off so I would make easier prey. An old man in Chinatown is an easy target for the *sai low*. It's hard to tell with the Vietnamese; some are very ruthless. They have no problem with violence."

"Neither do I," Donovan said.

Li studied him. "I thought not. I had the impression that you were about to do something quite foolish—something that both of us might have regretted later."

Donovan said nothing.

Li frowned. "Mr. Donovan, you may hold your life lightly, but I want you to understand something: I am here because I have a mission to fulfill, and I do not wish to endanger that mission by associating with a man who cannot control his passions."

Donovan glared. He didn't like having his hand slapped; it made him want to slap back. But he held his tongue because the old man might have information he needed—and because somewhere inside, he knew the old man was right.

"What did you say to them?" Donovan grumbled.

"I rebuked them—something only an older man can do. I told them they were rude and lacked good breeding; that they were insulting my guest and dishonoring me. In the East, the elderly are still respected. When they are not, it is a source of shame. They thought to take advantage of me because of my age; I turned my age against them. I used my most powerful weapon, Mr. Donovan—I used *wisdom*. As a result, we are able to continue with our lunch—me with my assortment of Eastern delicacies, and you with your mockery of Chinese cuisine."

Li leaned closer now and lowered his voice. "And you, Mr. Donovan—how would *you* have dealt with the young men?"

"Given a choice? I would have beat the snot out of them."

"'Beat the snot out of them'—what a very American thing to say. You would have engaged in fisticuffs with six men?"

"I've done it before."

"Yes, I can imagine—you're quite a formidable-looking fellow. And what would have happened when the first of the young men reached for his weapon? Then you would have been forced to reach for yours. I assume you are armed; I assure you they are."

The old man reached across the table and picked up Donovan's credentials. He pulled the leather folder open, and long pink filaments stretched between the covers. He grasped the wad of gum with his fingers and began to pull it away.

"You don't have to do that," Donovan said.

The old man ignored him and continued working. He scraped the remaining traces away with his fingernails, then polished the photograph and the seal of the attorney general with his napkin.

"I said, 'You don't have to—'"

"It had to be done," Li said matter-of-factly. "I did what was necessary, and nothing more." He held out the folder to Donovan—but when he reached for it, Li held on until Donovan looked into his eyes. "That is the lesson you must learn," he said. "To do what is necessary—and nothing more."

Donovan dropped the credentials back into his pocket. "Look, Mr. Li—"

"Just Li, please."

"Li—I didn't come here for a lecture on anger management, okay? I get that from my psychiatrist."

Li raised one eyebrow. "Oh?"

"Which is none of your business. I came here because of a phone call—a phone call that interrupted a very important meeting, by the way. You said you had information for me—okay, here I am. I'd like to know why a man like you is interested in fleas."

"Oh, not just fleas," he said. "I employ a clipping service in London whose job it is to scan several of the world's major newspapers. They are instructed to alert me whenever certain words appear—like the word *flea*."

"You get a call every time somebody uses the word *flea*?"

"Only when it occurs in an unusual context—say, in the Metro section of the *New York Times*. That's a bit unusual, don't you think? Tell me something, Mr. Donovan: The fleas you discovered in TriBeCa—they were Oriental rat fleas, were they not?"

Donovan hesitated.

"Come now," Li said. "I've come all this way at my own expense—surely you can tell me that much."

"Okay—they were Oriental rat fleas."

Li nodded. "Just as I feared."

"Because of their ability to spread bubonic plague?"

"Yes. More than a hundred species of fleas are capable of transmitting the disease, but *Xenopsylla cheopis* is particularly adept at it."

"On the phone you mentioned an epidemic of plague in New York City. What did you mean by that?"

"How much do you know about bubonic plague, Mr. Donovan?"

He shrugged. "I know it's on the CDC's list of the five most dangerous pathogens. It's considered a major bioterrorism threat."

"A wise assessment."

"You think somebody tried to purposely spread plague with those fleas?"

"I believe it was some kind of failed experiment—a test of sorts."

"What makes you think so?"

"There are other words I search the world's newspapers for. Some of them are technical terms you would not be familiar with; a few of them are proper names. Are you familiar with the names 'Harbin' or 'Ping Fan'?"

Donovan shook his head.

"They are villages in Manchuria. What about the name 'Sato Matsushita'? Have you ever heard that name before?"

"Should I have?"

"I would be quite surprised if you had."

"Who is he?"

"I believe he is the one responsible for your flea infestation in TriBeCa."

"Why?"

"Because it is his life's mission to destroy the United States with an epidemic of bubonic plague."

Donovan slumped back in his chair and watched as the old man relished a bite of something that looked like a steaming dumpling with translucent skin.

"You don't seem too excited about it," Donovan said.

Li glanced up. "I can understand your alarm—but you must understand, what I'm telling you is hardly news to me."

Donovan took a moment to collect his thoughts. "Okay," he said, "let's assume for a minute that the fleas were put there on purpose. And let's assume they have something to do with bubonic plague—and those are both *big* assumptions. What makes you think this man had anything to do with it?"

Li carefully wiped his mouth and folded the napkin again before setting it beside his plate. "I understand that criminals sometimes have a modus operandi," he said. "A unique way of doing things that connects them to specific crimes—like the jewel thief who leaves a rose on the pillow beside his victim."

"You've been watching too many old movies on the BBC."

"But these identifying 'trademarks' do exist, do they not?"

"Sometimes."

"Very well, then. I believe what you have discovered in TriBeCa is the modus operandi of only one man—Sato Matsushita."

"Li, you keep saying you *believe*. Can you prove any of this?"

"No—but neither is it my imagination. What I am telling you is the result of six decades of careful research and investigation. I have been searching for Sato Matsushita for over sixty years," he said. "I need you to help me find him."

"You need *us* to help *you* find him? Li, the FBI is not a bunch of private investigators. If you wanted to find this man, why didn't you contact your own people? Why not talk to Scotland Yard or MI6?"

"Because Sato Matsushita has no interest in the British Isles. I contacted you because our interests overlap. My goal is to find Sato Matsushita, and your job is to protect the people of the United States."

"Why do *you* want to find this man?"

Li paused. "For personal reasons."

"I'm sorry, that's not good enough."

"It will have to do for now—until I know you better."

"Li, the FBI is not going to help *you* find somebody. If we determine that this Sato Matsushita represents a legitimate threat to the United States, then *we* will find him. The Bureau is not in the habit of allowing civilians to participate in official investigations."

"I think you have it backward," Li said. "*I* am allowing *you* to 'participate.' The search for Sato Matsushita will be just another case number for the Federal Bureau of Investigation—for me, it is my life's work. Besides, without my help you will never find him."

"Why not?"

"After World War II he effectively disappeared. I have been collecting information on him ever since. Much of my research cannot be duplicated; many of my interviews were conducted with sources long since dead."

"Do you have a photograph of this man?"

"None exist."

"Then how would you know him if you found him?"

"I have met him," Li said. "If I saw him again, I would know him."

"A man can change a lot in sixty years."

"I would know him, Mr. Donovan. I am probably the only man on earth capable of identifying him. That is why you must help *me* find him. If you do not allow me to 'participate,' you will not find him. And if you do not find him, millions of your people may die—beginning right here in New York."

"Look," Donovan said, "if you have information pertaining to this individual, then we'd like to see it. Give us your research—names, dates, historical records, whatever you have."

"You want my research without *me*," Li said. "I *am* the research, Mr. Donovan."

The two men sat in silence for a moment, eyeing each other. *Whatever the old man knows*, Donovan thought, *he isn't going to hand it to me in a gift-wrapped box.*

"You'd only slow us down," Donovan said.

"I assure you, I'm quite spry for my age. You'd be surprised."

"Look—if there's any chance at all that somebody wants to attack the United States, then you can understand that we need to check this out fast. Time is kind of important here."

The old man screwed up his face. "Time? Are you going to lecture a man on a sixty-year journey about the value of time? A man your age knows nothing about time, Mr. Donovan. That's the problem with you Westerners—you're so impatient. You want everything *right now*. That's what makes you Americans so superficial, like ducks that skim across a pond but barely touch its surface. Life is like a book, Mr. Donovan; it has great themes to be reflected upon and deep meanings to be rooted out. But you Americans think it's all about plot; you always want to skip ahead to the end to see how it all comes out, and so you miss all the richness; you miss all the subtleties. You have no sense of *story*; you have no—"

"*Okay*," Donovan said, throwing up both hands in surrender. "Then let's do it your way. I need to know about this Sato Matsushita, okay? So tell me about him."

The old man smiled. "That's *much* better."

CHAPTER SEVEN

Kyoto Imperial University, Japan, April 1942

NINETEEN-YEAR-OLD SATO MATSUSHITA stared at the thick manila folder that lay on the table before him. It was closed, with its label facing away. It was easy enough to read, though; it bore the name of Sato Matsushita.

He had never seen the folder before, though he knew what it had to contain—it was his school transcript, a summary of his entire life to date in a single stack of documents. It would contain a list of all of his coursework, from the elementary level to the present day, with the results of each major examination and each teacher's summary evaluation. "Brilliant," one had told him. "A born scientist," said another—but those were words spoken to his face. He wondered what private doubts and criticisms the folder might also contain, and he longed to look for himself—but such a breach of propriety would be inexcusable, and so he sat with his hands folded, waiting for someone with enough authority to open the folder and weigh his life in the balance.

The room was as silent as a temple. He looked out the second-floor window; it was spring in Kyoto, and he could see the tissue-paper tips of the cherry blossoms in full bloom. Golden sunlight poured through the window; he longed to move his chair in front of it just to feel the warmth. But the sunlight fell in the opposite direction, and in the shadow where he sat, there was still the chill of winter in the air.

The door opened abruptly, and a solitary figure briskly entered. Sato snapped to his feet, lowering his eyes in his most officious bow, awaiting permission to breathe again. The figure before him wore the uniform of a full colonel in the Kwantung Army.

"Sit," the officer said without courtesy.

Sato returned to his seat and raised his eyes for the first time. The man was tall, with a long face and nose. A sweeping mustache covered his upper lip, turning up slightly at the ends in a nod to Western fashion. When he removed his hat, Sato saw that he was bald. The face was altogether as sterile as a surgeon's table, except for the eyes—they were wide and black, and as piercing as a sword. The colonel said nothing for a moment; he silently studied the details of Sato's face, without ever meeting his eyes.

"Do you know who I am?"

"Sir, everyone at Kyoto knows who you are," Sato said. "You are Shiro Ishii, chairman of the Department of Immunology at Tokyo Army Medical School."

Ishii grunted. "But I am an alumnus of Kyoto Imperial University."

"Yes sir. I read your dissertation: 'Research on Gram-Positive Twin Bacteria.'"

The comment earned Sato a small nod. Sato knew he had to be careful; Ishii was known as a man with an insatiable ego, and such a man expected to be fondled—but not without art.

Ishii opened the folder and began to scan the pages within. "You are only nineteen, and yet you are in your fourth year."

"Yes sir."

"You have completed coursework in bacteriology? Serology? Pathology?"

"Yes sir. And I have done graduate research in both epidemiology and preventive medicine."

"Preventive medicine," Ishii said. "Are you aware of the water filtration system I developed while serving as chief of the Water Purification Bureau?"

"A brilliant invention, sir. It single-handedly stopped the spread of cholera among our troops in China." Sato was also aware that Ishii had profited handsomely from his invention. Word around the university was that the manufacturer had paid Ishii more than fifty thousand yen in "thank-you money" for exclusive manufacturing rights.

"And do you know the source of the cholera outbreak?"

Sato said nothing. Cholera and typhus had been the bane of armies since ancient times. The source was simply tainted drinking water or poor sanitation.

"The Chinese," Ishii said decisively.

"The Chinese, sir?"

"Do you not find it curious that in a single year *six thousand* of our finest troops contracted cholera?"

Hardly our "finest troops," Sato thought. The soldiers assigned to China were widely considered the dregs of the Imperial Army. Who knew what primitive sanitation practices prevailed among those peasants?

"That does seem odd, sir."

"Our intelligence sources tell us that the Chinese purposely polluted their wells, rivers, and streams with the cholera pathogen."

It seemed unlikely. Both cholera and typhus were fragile organisms; the Chinese would almost have to dump them in the river on one side while the Japanese troops drank from the other.

"It was a deliberate attempt at biological warfare, Mr. Matsushita. And since that time, I have been responsible for the development of a top secret counterbiological program known as Unit 731."

It was hardly a secret. Every graduate student at Kyoto had heard of Unit 731, and most of the undergraduates as well. But its daily activities and the focus of its research were largely unknown; for security purposes, the facility had been established in rural Manchuria, far from prying eyes. All that was known about Unit 731 was that it was assigned some of the best and the brightest of Japan's medical researchers—and that once assigned there, they virtually disappeared.

"But—biological warfare was outlawed by the Geneva Convention of 1925," Sato said. "China was a signatory to this convention."

"And why do you suppose biological warfare was forbidden?"

Sato hesitated. "Because it is immoral."

"No—because it is *powerful*. In 1928 I undertook a two-year inspection tour of Western nations: Italy, France, Germany, Russia, the United States—and many others. I assure you, our enemies are actively engaged in biological warfare research. They pursue this knowledge in secret, hiding behind a false and worthless agreement. The Geneva Convention was intended for *us*, Mr. Matsushita—nations of honor and integrity. Just as our enemies seek to deny us access to steel and petroleum and rubber, they wish to deny us access to *knowledge*. The Geneva Convention was intended to keep us in helpless ignorance while our enemies gained a strategic advantage."

Ishii rose from his chair and stepped to the window. In the sunlight his skin looked pale and uneven, revealing a man who had spent too many hours under laboratory light. He stood with his hands folded behind his back, rocking slightly from heel to toe. It was not a posture; it was a pose—like everything Ishii seemed to do.

"Since the turn of the century, Japan has led the world in military medicine," he said. "In America's war with Spain, fourteen men died of disease for every one killed by a bullet. Just ten years later, in our struggle against Russia, we reduced the death toll from disease and infection to just 1 percent. Now we must put this knowledge to use in defense of our nation." He turned and looked at Sato. "It is my privilege to present you today with your military commission. You will enter the Kwantung Army under my command at the rank of physician second-class—first lieutenant, if you will."

Sato was incredulous. "Sir, I have a semester of school left—and then there is graduate school."

"An unnecessary luxury," Ishii said with a wave of his hand. "You have precisely the qualifications I require. You will complete your medical education in the field, under my command."

"But, sir, I—I have a younger sister. I am her only family."

Ishii shrugged indifferently. "We are all orphans, are we not? Sons and daughters of the emperor, but orphans nonetheless. I take from your sister a humble student, but I will return to her a hero in the battle for the Greater East Asia Co-Prosperity Sphere. A worthy trade, I'm sure she will agree."

Then Ishii turned and exited as abruptly as he had arrived.

THAT EVENING, SATO'S SISTER watched him, wide-eyed, as he packed a bag with his few belongings.

"Where are you going?" she asked.

Sato paused. "A school assignment."

"What kind of school assignment? Where?"

"It is a research project. Not here, not in Kyoto—in the field."

"In the war?"

"No, not in the war—but for the war." He turned and looked at her, and he saw the look of terror and abandonment in her eyes. He felt sick to his stomach. He sat down on the cot and took her by both arms.

"You have heard about the American Doolittle? You know what happened in Tokyo just last week?" News of the first assault on Japanese soil was everywhere. It involved just a handful of bombers, causing very little damage and only a few civilian casualties—but the psychological impact was enormous. The Japanese thought of their homeland as an impregnable island fortress, but just five months into the war, their sacred walls had already been breached. Some said it was an accident; some said it was an omen—but throughout the islands the fear was tangible.

"I have heard," she said.

"Japan is an island nation," Sato said. "Our enemies' homelands are far larger and richer in resources. We must find creative new ways to defend ourselves. That is my assignment. Do you understand, little one?"

She nodded. "*Wakari masu.*"

Sato returned to his packing. A minute later, he felt a hand tugging on the hem of his white *hadajuban*.

"When can I come to you?" the little girl whimpered.

Sato wheeled around. "Why must you be so selfish? Are you the only one to sacrifice? Shall I tell the emperor, 'We must lose the war, Imperial Majesty—Emiko cannot be inconvenienced'?"

The little girl began to weep. Sato longed to embrace her, but it was better for her to be strong now. "Wipe your eyes," he said. "You are a very lucky girl, you know. I have a friend at the university; his family has agreed to take you in. Do you know where they live, Emiko? At the *seashore*. Think of it—you may even have your own boat."

The little girl wiped at her eyes with the backs of her hands. "When will you come back?" she asked.

"I will come back," he said. "This will be good for both of us—you will see. '*Ame futte ji katamaru*,'" he quoted. *Ground that is rained on becomes hard; adversity builds character.*

"Promise you will come back."

Sato smiled. "Don't I always come home from school?"

TWO DAYS LATER, SATO found himself on a military transport bound from Tokyo to Manchuria. Out the window, he watched the endless green-and-brown patchwork of fertile farmland rolling by below. A single black line cut like a stitched wound through the center of the quilt; it was the South Manchurian Railway, stretching eleven hundred kilometers from the coastal ports into Manchuria's hinterland.

The plane began to descend now. Sato looked up ahead and let out a gasp. Coming into view was an enormous industrial complex, as large as the sprawling steel mills of Osaka. No, it was even larger—he counted sixty or seventy buildings covering five or six kilometers of land. Some of the buildings were long and narrow, like boxcars on a track; others were enormous rectangles surrounding grassy courtyards. A central building, one of the largest, was encircled by a wide moat and a towering brick wall topped with rolling razor wire.

He roused a sleeping soldier beside him. "Ping Fan?" he shouted over the drone of the engines.

The soldier peered out the window. "That's the lumber mill. See the little square buildings? *Ro* buildings, we call them. They're for the *marutas*—you know, the logs."

"There's a lumber mill here?"

The soldier shook his head, pulled his cap down over his eyes, and settled back to finish his nap.

To Sato's surprise, the transport plane did not land at Ping Fan, but continued north another hundred kilometers or so before settling down on a macadam runway in an expanse of empty pastureland.

When Sato climbed unsteadily through the exit hatch, an enlisted man twice his age awaited him with a thick white garment folded under one arm.

"Mr. Matsushita," he said with a cursory bow. "Welcome to Anda Proving Ground. You will need this. The colonel instructs you to suit up immediately."

Sato held up the heavy garment. He had never worn a complete biological suit before; the midlevel pathogens he had handled at Kyoto required nothing more than latex gloves and a mask. He looked up at the soldier, who was half-concealing a grin.

"I will require your assistance," Sato grumbled.

"*Hai.*" The soldier snapped a quick salute, then quickly and expertly guided Sato through the convoluted series of zippers, seals, and linings. Before pulling on the heavy cylindrical hood, he glared at the soldier one last time.

"That is all I require," he said. "Return to your duties." It was his first order as an officer in the Imperial Army; he was certain the story would be recounted with particular glee in the enlisted men's quarters that night.

The narrow rectangular window of his hood provided only a limited range of vision. He turned from side to side; it was like looking through a magnifying glass, with only what was immediately before him coming into focus. Across the field, he saw a group of standing figures. He started toward them, watching the ground at his feet and thinking how much it was like peering out the window of the airplane.

He thought about Emiko; he had thought about little else the last two days. To have to send her by train, to have to send her *alone* . . . They had never been apart for more than a day since Emiko was a little child. That was the benefit of a student's life—the structure, the schedule, the predictability. He had hoped to finish his graduate education, then take a position there in Kyoto—perhaps at the university. It was a simple, unambitious plan, but it would have allowed them to be together. Now here he was, across the sea and a thousand kilometers beyond. Surely the officers at Unit 731 brought wives and families with them—why not a sister? But how could he make such a request—please, can my sister come along? They would think him a fool; they would call him a *boy*—and in his heart, he knew that's what he was. He was a boy who needed an idiot corporal to help him dress.

Lost in thought, Sato bumped headlong into a standing figure and stumbled backward.

"I'm sorry," he stammered, "I didn't see—"

He focused the narrow window on the figure before him. It was a Chinese peasant, a man, perhaps twenty-five or thirty years of age. He was tied against a tall board set vertically into the ground. His hands were bound behind him, and his knees were wrapped tightly together to prevent his body from slumping. He wore some kind of primitive headgear, and a simple sheet of rusting boilerplate hung from a rope around his neck to cover his chest. Other than that, he was completely naked—and he was dead.

"It protects the vital organs from shrapnel," Colonel Ishii said with a rap on the iron plate.

Sato looked up, startled.

"When the bomb explodes, pieces of the casing fly everywhere," Ishii said. "We can hardly test the efficacy of the pathogen if the subject dies in the initial blast."

Sato looked around him; he was standing in a ring of concentric circles. In the center was a small stand surrounded by a halo of soot and debris. In each of the surrounding circles stood at least one vertical board, to which a Manchurian villager was bound, radiating outward from the center like planets around a sun. The top of the first board was marked "30 meters," the second read "40," and so on back at ten-meter intervals. There were fifteen figures all together. Most were men of various ages, but a few were women. All were dead. From one silent figure, viscera hung from a gaping incision like sausages in a butcher's window.

"Most disappointing," Ishii said. "There is no sign of infection at any distance. The pathogen is apparently being destroyed in the initial explosion. This will be your challenge, Mr. Matsushita: to perfect a means of distributing the pathogen alive and in a virulent form. I have every confidence in you." Ishii whirled and headed off across the field.

Sato wrestled off his hood and dropped to his knees.

THE STORY WAS INTERRUPTED by the trill of Donovan's cell phone. He held up one finger to the old man while he took the call.

"Sorry," he said, folding the phone shut again with a dull click.

"I detest those things," Li said. "It interrupted the flow of a perfectly good story."

"My partner found something he thinks I should see. I need to break this off—but I want to get the rest of this story. Where are you staying?"

"Right here."

"In Chinatown?"

"Why not? The food is excellent." He glanced at Donovan's uneaten lunch. "Most of it, anyway."

"Let's meet again—but let's pick a different place next time, okay?"

"Where did you have in mind?"

"I don't know," Donovan said, glancing around. "How about America?"

74

CHAPTER EIGHT

WHERE YOU BEEN?" POLDIE asked. "I can't keep this guy on hold all day."

"Sorry," Donovan said. "Took me half an hour to work my way up Canal." He stepped inside, and Poldie shut the door behind him. "What's up?"

"I talked to the neighbors," Poldie said. "I found a guy who was at the party. I asked him if he had a guest list, if he knew anybody else who was there; you can guess how that went over. He didn't know anybody; he was a total stranger—but I pressed him on it, and he finally produced a couple of names—this guy was one of them."

"Where is he?"

"In the kitchen—making us some cappuccino," he said with a lift of his little finger. Poldie was the type who thought coffee tasted better from a Styrofoam cup, but he wasn't stupid. A cop knows never to refuse an offer of hospitality. He would have said, "Yes, please," if the man had offered him tea and crumpets.

The address was in the historic Cast-Iron District of SoHo. The sprawling living room was done entirely in neutral tones to highlight the undoubtedly original artwork that dotted the room. On one wall hung a triptych of glossy panels with slashes of blinding color across each. On a glass coffee table, a twisting pile of polished chrome spiraled up toward the ceiling. *Very posh,* Donovan thought, *very expensive*—the kind of place that made you want to stuff your hands in your pockets and stand in a corner of the room.

"How did it go with the English guy?" Poldie asked.

"Chinese guy."

"Huh?"

"It was L-i, not L-e-e. He's Chinese, but he lives in England. That's why he wanted to meet in Chinatown—he likes the food."

"I can't eat that stuff—eel brains and turtle heads and all. Turns my stomach."

"No, you like kielbasa—mystery meat stuffed in a pig intestine."

"Now you're talking."

"You know, the guy was eighty years old."

"No kidding—and he still eats that garbage?"

Donovan glanced down at Poldie's abundant girth. "He was skinny too. Maybe you should try a few eel brains."

"Let's not get personal. What did the old man want?"

Donovan hesitated. "It sounds crazy."

"Try me."

"He says the fleas were no accident. He claims there's a guy who wants to attack the U.S. with bubonic plague—some old Japanese scientist. Says he developed the process during World War II, but he never got to use it— so he's still trying. Li says he's been tracking this guy for sixty years."

Poldie rolled his eyes. "Too many turtle heads," he said.

"Maybe."

"C'mon, Donovan, that's the biggest tall tale I've ever heard."

"Have you heard the one about the two airliners that flew into the Twin Towers and knocked them down?"

"Let's not get paranoid here."

"Did you ever talk to a crazy person, Poldie? This guy wasn't like that."

"I've talked to a lot of liars. Maybe he's a good one; he's had eighty years to practice."

"Maybe."

"You believe this cock-and-bull story?"

"No—but he seems to believe it. I mean, why did he fly all the way over here—just to tell me a lie? I think it's worth running a background check on him."

"Good idea. Get the name of his retirement home. Find out if there's an old Japanese guy who's been stealing his slippers."

Just then an enameled doorway swung silently open, and a man appeared carrying a teakwood tray and two silver-rimmed cups. He was a slender man, immaculately dressed, with close-cropped gray hair and hollow blue eyes. He glanced from Poldie to Donovan and back again, as if estimating the two men's combined weight.

"I thought I heard the door," he said meekly.

Poldie stepped forward. "Let me take that for you. Thanks, that looks just great. Mr. Hollister, I'd like you to meet my partner—this is Special Agent Nathan Donovan."

The man blanched. "You're with the FBI?"

Donovan extended his hand. "Don't let it throw you," he said. "We're just like the NYPD, only with better-looking wives." The attempt at humor was in vain. The man had a look of ominous foreboding, as if his doctor had just summoned an associate to the examining room. "Seriously," Donovan said, "there's been an ongoing partnership between the Bureau and NYPD ever since 9/11. It's a regular thing."

Poldie looked at Donovan. "Mr. Hollister has something I thought you should see. He's been a big help here, no kidding." Poldie plopped down at one end of the sofa; he sank into the cushion like a rock in a sling. On the coffee table in front of him was a scattered pile of glossy photographs. Poldie patted the cushion beside him, and Mr. Hollister eased his way over and gently took a seat. Donovan considered taking the other end of the sofa, but he decided against it; being surrounded by the NYPD and the FBI might have been more than this guy could handle. He pulled up a chair across from them and sat down.

"These are photos Mr. Hollister took at the party," Poldie said.

"No kidding," Donovan replied. "What kind of a party was it, Mr. Hollister?"

"What kind?"

"You know—was there a specific purpose for it? Somebody's birthday? Some kind of celebration?"

"Just a social gathering, as far as I know."

"Maybe a gallery event of some kind?"

"I really wouldn't know."

"Was there a printed invitation?"

"We covered that," Poldie said. "It was just word of mouth."

Let him say it, Donovan thought. *I want to hear his voice.* He gave Poldie a quick look, then began to pick through the photos on the coffee table.

"Did you know the deceased, Mr. Hollister?"

"Well, yes, of course. He was the host, after all. We were casual acquaintances, that's all."

"Did you know anyone else at the party?"

"No."

"You're sure about that?"

"Quite sure, yes."

Donovan held up one of the photographs. "You're in this one."

The man blinked twice. "I'm sure I loaned the camera to a stranger. You know—just to get into a picture." If he had been hooked to a lie detector, the stylus would have gone off the paper and up the wall. Donovan gave him his most reassuring nod.

"This is what I wanted you to see," Poldie said. He collected half a dozen photos from the table and began to place them in front of Donovan one by one. Each was a crowded shot of partygoers huddled in the same section of the room. In each photo the faces changed, but the setting remained the same.

"So?" Donovan said.

"Now look at this one." In the final photograph, the group had divided—

some to the left, some to the right. In the center of the photo, visible for the first time, was the square display stand—and it was not empty.

On the display stand stood a tall earthenware vase of some kind. It was a good three feet tall, reddish brown in color, with faded black symbols and images around the neck. It was ancient looking; there were two ear-shaped handles, but one was broken in half, and the other looked chipped and eroded—*like iron in seawater,* Donovan thought. He looked up at Mr. Hollister with his best poker face.

"You seem to be an art collector yourself, Mr. Hollister."

"It's just a hobby."

"You have some nice pieces here. Tell me, how do you decide what to buy? I mean, a guy like me would get taken for sure."

"Well, a collector has to ask a lot of questions. You seek professional advice. You never make the decision to purchase alone."

"You must have learned quite a bit over the years about painting, and sculpture, and—what do they call those scratchy-looking prints?"

"Intaglio."

"Say—you sound like a professional yourself, Mr. Hollister."

"Not really. I guess you could say—that is—in some circles I'm considered something of an expert."

"I thought so." Donovan held up the photo of the earthen vase. "Can you identify this object, Mr. Hollister?"

"No."

Donovan glanced at Poldie, who nodded with his eyes.

"As 'something of an expert,' can you describe it for me?"

Hollister took the photo and studied it nervously. "It looks very old," he began.

"Yes, it does. How old would you say?"

"I have no way of knowing."

"It looks like it's made of clay, like a flowerpot. Would you agree?"

"It would appear so. It's hard to say from the photograph."

"But you saw it in person."

"Yes, well, I—it was an entire gallery of artwork, you know. It's hard to remember any single piece."

"Even for an expert like you?"

"Even for me."

"Mr. Hollister, do you suppose this particular piece was valuable?"

"I would think so, yes."

"More valuable than any of the other items in the gallery?"

"It's impossible to say."

"Funny thing," Donovan said. "The day after the murder, when we examined the gallery, this piece was missing. As far as we can tell, it was the only object missing. Any idea who might take it?"

"Of course not."

Donovan glanced around the room at the man's own extensive collection. "I'll bet these were all expensive," he said. "Are they insured?"

"Certainly."

"With a single company?"

"Yes."

"So if I contacted your insurance company, they could show me an inventory of your entire collection."

"I suppose so. Why?"

"We checked with the company that insured the TriBeCa gallery. They gave us an inventory. Every item on the list was accounted for—but this vase was not on the list. What do you make of that?"

"I have no idea."

"Make a guess. Give us an expert opinion."

He paused. "I can only surmise that it was a recent acquisition—something he had not yet had time to insure."

"That's a good thought. Any other ideas?"

"None at all."

"Poldie, any thoughts? Help us out here."

Poldie rubbed at his chin. "One possibility," he said. "Maybe it was stolen. You can't insure merchandise that's illegally obtained."

"Now, see here," Hollister protested. "I attended a simple social gathering and that's all. I know nothing about stolen merchandise or artwork that was illegally obtained."

Donovan smiled. "Of course you don't," he said in a tone that clearly implied, "Who are you kidding?" He paused for a beat and then said, "Well, Detective, I think we've taken enough of this gentleman's time. I don't think we'll be needing to bother Mr. Hollister again." Donovan began to rise from his chair; the look of relief on Hollister's face was evident.

"Oh—one small favor," Donovan said, picking up the photo of the earthen vase. "May I borrow this? I promise I'll return it."

CHAPTER NINE

Special Agent Elizabeth Mowery pressed a key on her laptop computer, and the photographic image on the screen changed. "Now, here's an exemplary piece," she said.

Donovan studied the image. It was a mask of a woman's face—at least, he thought it was a woman. More like a woman than a man, anyway. The face had no expression. A rich woman, he thought, one with enough money to have herself carved in stone—but not enough money to have it done right. Maybe her kid did it. Yeah, that's what it looked like, a kid's third-grade art project. The lips were just two little snakes of clay, pressed on and smoothed out flat. The eyes were just two almond-shaped holes— "I can't do eyes," the kid probably said. The eyebrows were a pair of arching curves that joined in the center, like a giant bird landing on her forehead. The hair is where the kid got bored—just a series of flat smudges parted down the center. The cone-shaped nose was broken off at the end—probably dropped it on the way home. *It was a joke,* Donovan thought, the kind of project any six-year-old could whip up with a can of Play-Doh and a half hour to kill.

Agent Mowery sighed. "Beautiful, isn't it?"

"Fabulous." Donovan nodded.

"This is from Uruk. It's Mesopotamian, more than five thousand years old."

Mommy, look what I made you. How nice, honey—what is it? It's you! Oh, thank you, I'll put this in a special place. Then the kid runs off to play in the Euphrates and the mom thinks, Geez, do I look this bad? I've got to get down to the spa. *She hides the thing in the back of a drawer somewhere, and five thousand years later it turns up as great art.*

They sat side by side in a darkened conference room at the FBI's New York headquarters at 26 Federal Plaza. Elizabeth Mowery was assigned to the Bureau's Art Theft Program, a part of the Major Theft/Transportation Crimes Unit. The laptop was connected by wireless network to the National Stolen Art File, a photographic database of stolen art and cultural artifacts from all over the world.

Mowery pressed another key. "Now, this is a fragment of a limestone stele, showing the king hunting lions."

"Swell," Donovan said. "Did you recognize the object in the photo I sent you?"

She clicked back to the index and searched for that particular image. "Here it is."

Donovan looked at the image: a tall earthen vase with ear-shaped handles—one broken, one still intact.

"That's the one," he said. "What can you tell me about it?"

"It's Babylonian, sixth century BC. A terra-cotta funerary jar from the time of Nebuchadnezzar."

Donovan stared at her blankly.

"Didn't you ever take a class in art history?" she asked.

Why would he want to do that? In college, Donovan's policy was to avoid any class that dealt with names, dates, or places—in fact, any class that required a state of complete consciousness. "Never could squeeze it into my schedule," he said.

"*Mesopotamia* means 'between the rivers,'" she began with irritating simplicity. "It describes the area between the Tigris and Euphrates

Rivers—modern-day Iraq. It's home to one of the oldest continuous cultures in the world—maybe *the* oldest. First the Sumerians lived there, then the Assyrians, then the Babylonians—that was their heyday, around the sixth century BC. Nebuchadnezzar was the most powerful king in the world at the time. He built the Hanging Gardens of Babylon, remember?"

"Sure," he lied. "What about the jar?"

"It's a funerary jar—where the ashes of a famous person or a beloved family member would be stored. It's made of terra-cotta—a reddish clay that's hard-fired in a kiln. Mesopotamia is famous for its clay; Babylon was built almost entirely out of glazed mud-brick. Have you ever seen the Ishtar Gate? It's incredible. I think I have a photograph of it here somewhere—"

"Boring an FBI agent is a federal crime," Donovan said. "Tell me about the jar."

"It was stolen from the Iraqi National Museum of Antiquities in April of 2003. Remember?"

Donovan did remember. When American troops first entered Baghdad and Iraqi forces retreated, the Iraqi people looted the museums, the hospitals, the government offices—even Saddam Hussein's palace. CNN broadcast images of smiling Iraqi citizens carting off beds, office furniture, ornate fixtures, even a porcelain bathtub. They took everything that was not tied down.

"The museum was stripped bare," Mowery said. "More than fifteen thousand artifacts were stolen and twenty thousand more damaged. It was a national tragedy—an entire cultural heritage just disappeared. And it could have been prevented, if we hadn't been so busy protecting our interests in Iraqi oil."

Donovan had a different perspective. An invading force was like the tip of a spear—pointed at the end. The first troops into Baghdad were concerned with nothing more than dodging enemy sniper fire; the second units in were responsible for securing the city's critical assets, and museums just weren't very high on the list. It wasn't just museums that were looted; it was libraries, shops, and businesses too. In virtually every part of the city, Iraqis robbed Iraqis blind. There was simply no way to protect all of Baghdad from itself. As an ex-Marine, Donovan knew that "strategic objectives" were all a military force could ever hope to achieve. The National Museum was Iraq's past, but the oil fields and refineries were its future. For Donovan's money, they got it right—but this wasn't the time to argue politics.

"How much of the stuff has been recovered?"

"Most of it," she said. "When the looting began, it was like a fever— people just grabbed anything that looked valuable. They didn't give much thought to what they were going to do with it later on. I mean, where does an average citizen sell a three-thousand-year-old relief carving? It's not like you can scalp it in a back alley somewhere—and there are international laws prohibiting the sale of stolen archaeological and ethnological arti- facts. I think the Iraqi people realized that they had only robbed them- selves, and the stolen pieces began to mysteriously reappear again."

"But not this one."

"No. This one and a handful of others are still out there."

"How valuable is it?"

"To the Iraqis, it's priceless. It has no real value, of course—no precious metals or inlaid gems. Its value is completely symbolic. Remember, Babylon represents Iraq's glory days—the time when they ruled the known world. It's a little like us losing the Liberty Bell."

"Any idea where it went?"

"Sure," she said. "Want to see it?"

Donovan wasn't sure he heard correctly—but before he could ask for a clarification, Mowery rose and headed for the door, beckoning for Donovan to follow. He pursued her down a series of short hallways, past intricate mazes of cubicles defined by fabric-covered panels with metal trim. Donovan didn't mind his own cubicle once he was seated at his desk; it was only when he stood and looked across the office that he felt like a drone in an endless beehive.

Mowery opened a door and entered. Donovan looked at the doorway before stepping in behind her. *How does she rate a door?* He looked around the tiny office, packed with bookshelves and paper. *At least she has no window*, Donovan thought, and he felt a little better about his own cell in the hive.

Mowery sat down at her desk, picked up a handful of messages, and began to shuffle through them. Donovan stood across from her, waiting. She looked up at him as though she were seeing him for the first time.

"Oh," she said casually, pointing to the corner. "There you go."

Donovan turned. There, in a crowded corner, sat the funerary jar with a stack of magazines and a small green plant resting on top.

"Where did you find it?" he asked.

"In a private showroom in the back of a gallery on the Upper East Side. Very posh, very respectable, very illegal. We had been watching the place for quite a while. We picked it up about two months ago."

"Two months? But the photo I gave you was taken just a week ago."

She pointed to a spot behind Donovan. He turned again; there, in the opposite corner of the office, sat another funerary jar identical to the first.

"They're fakes," she said. "We've uncovered three so far—the one in your photo makes four."

Donovan said nothing.

"Look," she said. "Not everyone looting the Iraqi museum was an amateur. There were people there who knew what they were doing. The amateurs, they grabbed the shiny things—the jewelry, the ivories, the bronzes. The professionals went for things like this—things of real value, things worth the risk of selling on the black market—things that can be *copied*."

"Copied?"

"Why sell one when you can sell half a dozen? Think about it—it's the perfect scam. You steal a priceless artifact, a remnant of King Nebuchadnezzar himself, and you let it be known that it might be available for sale—at the right price."

"What's the 'right price'?"

"Half a million, maybe more. But there's no negotiation, because it's a once-in-a-lifetime opportunity and a one-of-a-kind object—or so the buyer thinks. Before the sale, you hire a local artisan to make a few copies.

After all, what does it take—a pile of Iraqi clay and a pottery wheel? Then you sell the copies, but you keep the original.

"New York is the perfect mark for a scam like this: The city is filled with unscrupulous private gallery owners who would jump at the chance to add a piece of Babylonian history to their personal collection—illegally or not. So the gallery owner makes the purchase, and he finds some clever way to sneak it past Customs. And if he somehow later discovers that his prize acquisition is a fake, what's he going to do? He can't exactly go to the authorities, now, can he? What would he say? 'In violation of Title 18 of the U.S. Penal Code, I have knowingly purchased a stolen artifact from the Iraqi National Museum—and I want my money back.' Like I said— it's the perfect scam."

"So that's it? It's just about money?"

"Three million bucks for half a dozen clay pots? Pottery Barn should do so good."

"Where do these fakes originate? Do we know?"

"We're working on that. Probably not Iraq—too much risk of discovery there. Our best guess is Syria; a lot of things crossed the border there at the start of hostilities."

"Syria?"

"Could be. We're pretty sure the fakes are made somewhere near the original area. A Middle East return address is important in a sale like this. A genuine Babylonian relic can't exactly arrive from Tijuana, now, can it?"

Donovan thought for a minute. "The vase in my photo—what did you call it? The 'funerary jar.' It was there one day and gone the next. When we showed up to investigate the murder of the gallery owner, the jar had been taken. Any thoughts?"

"Stolen art makes good stealing," she said. "It's uninsured, and the theft can't be reported. Maybe your gallery owner did one private showing too many."

Donovan nodded. "These funerary jars—are they always empty?"

Mowery paused. "I've never been asked that before."

"Ignorance is my specialty."

"They're almost always empty," she said. "The jar itself is fired in a kiln to harden it, but the top is just a clay plug left to air-dry. It's much more fragile, so it tends to break apart over time. Somewhere along the way, the contents always seem to get dumped out. People want the jar, not a bunch of ashes."

"Would a gallery owner know that?"

"Hard to say. A lot of them have more money than experience."

Donovan started for the door, then turned back. "Oh, one more thing: Could you use these jars to transport fleas?"

"Fleas?"

"You know—little jumping things."

"I guess so. But why in the world would you want to?"

CHAPTER TEN

THE WOMAN BEHIND THE information counter was young. Her hair was short and artificially black, with bangs cut straight just above her eyes. Her lipstick was purplish-red, so dark that it made her skin look like plaster. From the left side of her nose, a tiny silver post protruded. A book was open in front of her on the counter: Chaucer's *Canterbury Tales. Probably a college student,* Donovan thought, *maybe from Columbia.* He cleared his throat, and the young woman looked up.

"I'm looking for some place called the Cuxa Cloister," he said. "Can you help me out?"

"Through that doorway and to the left," she said. "You can't miss it."

Give me a break, he thought. *This is New York—you can miss anything here. You can miss a turn and spend the next fifteen minutes honking at taxicabs. You can miss a whole neighborhood if you blink at the wrong moment. You can miss your subway stop and end up on the wrong side of town—or even worse, in Jersey.* Donovan could easily miss the Cuxa Cloister, because he had no idea what a "cloister" was—but he wasn't about to look stupid in front of some twenty-year-old nymphet.

"Isn't this whole museum called the Cloisters?" he asked.

"That's right."

"So—I'm looking for a cloister inside a cloister."

"Basically, yes."

"How many cloisters do you have here?"

"Five altogether. The Cuxa is the largest."

"The largest in what way?"

"Size."

Donovan frowned. "I'm looking for an old man," he said.

"We get a lot of them here."

That figures, he thought. "They do love their cloisters, don't they?"

"They do."

"This is a Chinese man. He's in his eighties, but he looks younger. He's about five foot three, speaks with a British accent. Have you seen him?"

"Yes."

"Where is he?"

"In the Cuxa Cloister. Through the doorway and to the left."

Donovan glared at her and started for the doorway.

"Hey," the young woman called after him.

He turned.

"A cloister is a courtyard surrounded by covered hallways on all four sides. Each hallway has an open colonnade facing the courtyard."

She winked.

"Thanks," Donovan grumbled.

She was right—he couldn't miss it. Through the doorway and to the left, Donovan found himself in a long passageway. To his left, the wall was solid stone. The roof above him sloped down from left to right, where it was supported by a series of rounded stone columns joined by semicircular arches. The archways looked out on a kind of central garden; two narrow sidewalks crossed in the center, dividing the garden into grassy quadrants dotted with coarse, untrimmed shrubberies. At the far corner, he saw an old man sitting quietly atop a low wall. Donovan waved; there was no response. *Who knows*, he thought, *the old guy could be almost blind*.

"Li," he called out as he rounded the corner. There was no answer. *Maybe he's deaf too*. "Li!" he shouted. Still no response.

Donovan was standing right beside the old man now. Li sat with his head bowed and his eyes closed with an almost deathlike stillness. Donovan reached out and shook him gently. The old man slowly opened his eyes and looked up.

"Do you have any idea what a cloister is?" Li asked.

"Of course. It's a courtyard surrounded by covered hallways on all four sides."

"A cloister is a place of solitude, a place of quiet reflection—which you just managed to shatter. This cloister was brought here stone by stone from a monastery in France. Eight hundred years ago, Benedictine monks used to sit on this very wall in a discipline of silence."

"Sorry. I thought you dozed off."

"I was meditating."

"On what?"

"On life. On death. On the universe and my small but meaningful part in it. Don't you ever meditate?"

"Never had much time for it."

"You mean you've never had much use for it."

"Life is busy, Li."

"Life is too busy to have time to think about life—ironic, isn't it? You know, Blaise Pascal once said that the distinguishing characteristic of humankind is *distraction*. We don't like what we see when we slow down long enough to look at our lives, and so we keep ourselves distracted—we fill our lives with all sorts of trivial stuff and nonsense. That way, we never have to confront our emptiness or longing; we simply don't have time for it. How very convenient."

Li studied him for a moment. "What about you, my busy young friend? Suppose you closed your eyes for a moment and shut out all the busyness and noise and distraction—suppose you looked into your *soul*. What would you find?"

"I think I'd fall asleep."

"Excellent. It requires peace to fall asleep. Is that what you'd find there, Nathan—peace?"

"Look, Li—"

"I know"—the old man sighed—"you don't have time for this."

"Next time, I pick the meeting place."

"What do you mean? This is the perfect meeting place."

"A museum?"

"Not just any museum. This is the Cloisters—the largest collection of medieval art and architecture in the Western Hemisphere. I thought it would be the perfect setting for today's discussion."

"Okay, fine. Now can we get to the subject?"

"I'm sorry. What is the subject?"

"Bubonic plague in New York City."

"Oh, no, that's not the subject at all. That's just a subplot of a much grander story I was unfolding—before I was rudely interrupted, that is."

"Then let's get back to your story. You were telling me about Sato Matsushita, remember? A scientific whiz kid at nineteen, drafted into the army in 1942, assigned to a biological warfare unit in Manchuria. He shows up, discovers that they're doing human testing."

Li frowned. "You've stripped all the flesh off my beautiful story. You've left nothing but bones."

"That's my job. What happened next?"

"Over the next three years, Sato was exposed to the full range of Unit 731's activities. There were 150 buildings eventually constructed at Ping Fan. Buildings Seven and Eight were used to house the *marutas*—the logs for their sawmill, you see. In Building Seven males were imprisoned; in Building Eight, females and infants. Rural Manchuria provided an inexhaustible supply of human beings for experimentation; about two hundred unfortunate Chinese or Koreans were kept there at any given time. They were all 'criminals,' of course—convicted of espionage, or anti-Japanese sentiment, or some other trumped-up charge. They were sent to Ping Fan on 'special consignment,' and they were never heard from again. Buildings Seven and Eight were connected by tunnel to the experimental laboratories and the crematorium. That's where they all ended up, of course—every last one of them."

Donovan shook his head. "How many people are we talking about?"

"Well, now, that's a very interesting question. During the years that Matsushita was present, about three thousand souls. That's just at Unit 731; at other laboratories around China, perhaps six thousand more. But those were just the laboratory casualties; the real horror resulted from the field experiments."

"Field experiments?"

"A laboratory can only produce theories; theories have to be tested in the real world. Beginning in 1939, Unit 731 began to conduct field experiments in selected Chinese provinces. Wells were infected with cholera. Sweet cakes laced with paratyphoid bacteria were left near fences and trees for children to find. And in the most effective experiment of all, plague-infected fleas were released from airplanes to rain down on unsuspecting villages. The epidemics that resulted spread like wildfire to neighboring areas. You know, there are areas of China where plague outbreaks still occur to this very day.

"So—how many people are we talking about? To make an accurate assessment, we must include both the laboratory deaths and the field trials; we must also include the deaths that resulted from ongoing epidemics. In total, the best estimate is a quarter of a million people."

Neither of them said anything for a minute.

"And Matsushita participated in all this?"

"Unwillingly at first. I think it troubled him greatly, the whole concept of biological warfare. He was in many ways a moral person, you see—at least at the beginning. But evil has a hardening effect; the conscience can be seared until the scar tissue that remains has no nerve endings at all. At first, it was all unthinkable; then it became a necessary evil; after that, it was just his job. I believe more evil has been committed under that rubric than any other: 'I was just doing my job.'"

"Li—how do you know all this?"

"Much of it is a matter of public record. By the end of the war, both the Allies and the Soviets were well aware of the activities of Unit 731. If you remember your history, the Soviet Union waited to declare war on Japan until the very last days of World War II. Their intention was not to assist in the fighting but to seize some of the spoils of war for themselves. The situation in Manchuria was much like that in Berlin: The Allies and the Soviets paired off around the plunder, seeking every opportunity to strengthen their position in the postwar world. That included, of course, a grab for the best Japanese scientists."

"Including Unit 731 scientists?"

"Why not? Your own space program was made possible by Nazi rocket scientists. One day they were raining V-2 rockets down on London; the next day they were respectable engineers working for NASA."

"But after the war there were trials for Nazi war criminals."

"Yes—but Europe was very different from China. The chief victims of the Holocaust were the Jews, a cohesive and homogeneous people. They pursued their assailants; they championed the cause of justice. America has a large Jewish population who felt personally aggrieved by the Nazi atrocities; the Russian people suffered greatly at the hands of the Nazis as well. There were several parties who were unwilling to allow Nazi war criminals to escape unpunished.

"But in China, neither the U.S. nor the Soviet Union were the victims. *We* were the victims—the Chinese. But postwar China was not a unified society—it was just a collection of isolated farms and villages. We had no champion; we had no one to pursue justice for us."

"So the Unit 731 scientists went unpunished?"

"The Allies had more important things to worry about. After all, the end of World War II was the beginning of the Cold War. And what was more important, raking up the muck of a war that both sides wanted to forget, or looking to the future? Besides, China was about to turn Communist—that didn't win us any sympathy from the West. And Japan, America's old enemy, was now a critical ally in the war against Communism. The Americans decided that it was not in their best interest to reopen old wounds. Instead, they struck a deal with the devil: In return for their biological warfare research, the Unit 731 scientists were granted immunity from prosecution."

"You're joking."

"The commander of Unit 731, Shiro Ishii, died of throat cancer in

1959. Some of the scientists became captains of industry; others went on to hold esteemed positions in government or academia. All died peacefully in their beds."

"And Sato Matsushita?"

Li smiled. "What do you say we stretch our legs? I want to show you something."

CHAPTER ELEVEN

"**H**ERE WE ARE," LI said. "These are known as the Nine Heroes Tapestries." In a rectangular room just off the cloister's west wall, four ancient tapestries hung from floor to ceiling. They were black and red and gold mostly, with occasional patches of bright blue interspersed throughout. Each one featured a series of royal-looking figures—*sort of like the characters on playing cards,* Donovan thought, all seated in some kind of ornate cathedral setting. The tapestries were in pieces, each one patched together from variously sized fragments to create a single panel.

Li studied them admiringly. "So tell me, what do you think of them?"

"Big," Donovan said.

"A profound observation. Anything else?"

"Old."

"They are indeed. They were made in the late 1300s for the brother of the king of France. They portray nine great heroes from the past: three pagan, three Hebrew, and three Christian. There are Hector, Alexander, and Julius Caesar; Joshua, David, and Judas Maccabaeus; Charlemagne, King Arthur, and Godfrey of Bouillon. I'm proud to say that one of them was a fellow servant of the Crown. None of them, I might add, were American."

"King Arthur was just a legend."

"Bite your tongue." Li stepped back and gestured to the set of tapestries with open arms. "Tell me, seriously—what do you think?"

Donovan looked again. Black backgrounds and bad drawing—to him they looked like the black velvet paintings of tigers and bullfighters he used to see for sale at gas stations in Queens—"$9.99 with fill-up."

"Stunning," he said.

Li grinned from ear to ear. "You see? I knew you were not the barbarian you pretend to be."

"Look, Li, I've had enough art history for one week."

"Oh, this is not about art. I brought you here for a different reason. You see, tapestries like this served a practical function in the Middle Ages. They were used to cover windows—to keep out the Black Death."

"The plague?"

"Or the Pestilence, as it was known then. In the late 1340s, plague took the lives of twenty-five million people in Europe. That was one-third of the population—a quarter of a billion people in today's terms. The Black Death was unique in all of human history. It's no exaggeration to say that it changed the path of Western civilization.

"Let's walk," he said. They exited the same way they came in and began to amble slowly down the cloister's empty halls.

"The Black Death actually began in China. Did you know that? The Tartars brought it with them from the steppes of central Asia. In 1345 they laid siege to the city of Kaffa on the Black Sea. The siege lasted two years; during that time, the plague broke out among the Tartar troops. According to eyewitnesses, thousands died every day—like arrows raining down from heaven, they said.

"The symptoms were easy to recognize: First there was a sudden fever, then chills and weakness, followed by enormous and painful swelling in the armpits or groin—those are the 'buboes' from which the disease takes its name. Next came exhaustion, lethargy, and delirium; after four days of this agony, the poor wretch would perish from respiratory failure. This manner of death produced an overall purplish color—thus the 'Black Death.'

"The Tartars had a problem on their hands—how to deal with thousands upon thousands of diseased and decomposing corpses. Then someone came up with a bright idea: They decided to catapult the bodies over the walls of Kaffa and into the city. Soon there were mountains of dead within the walls, witnesses said. In no time at all the plague broke out among the Venetian traders who inhabited the city.

"Now the Tartars had blockaded the land in front of the city, but not the sea behind it. So when the Venetians saw the plague erupting, they fled to their ships and put out to sea—and they took the plague with them. By 1348 the plague had reached Italy—first Sicily, then Genoa, and then it spread from harbor to harbor all over the Mediterranean. The seaports were the key; there are ghastly stories of plague ships sailing into port with no one on board alive. Eerie, don't you think?

"From the seaports, the plague spread like a flame across the continent. England was hit as hard as any; the population of England didn't return to its preplague level for more than four hundred years. All told, more than twenty-five million died: the rich and the poor, the nobleman and the peasant, the priest and the pagan. The plague, you see, is not a respecter of persons."

"And the Tartars started it all with their catapults," Donovan said.

"In a way, yes. They made an intentional effort to spread the disease to the enemy. It was one of the first deliberate attempts at biological warfare."

"It sure worked."

"Actually, it did not—they just thought it did. You see, the mechanism of bubonic plague was not clearly understood for another five centuries. Plague is *enzootic*. That means its natural home is in certain types of animals—voles, gerbils, even the prairie dogs of your American Southwest. That's why plague can never be eradicated; it will always survive in some rodent population, hidden away in vast underground burrows.

"Now, from time to time the plague decides to move up the zoological ladder—no one really knows why. From a gerbil host, it may jump to a wild grass rat; from the grass rat, it moves on to the urban brown rat; from the brown rat, it attacks humankind. But the intermediary in this whole process—the truly responsible party—is the *flea*. That's what the Tartars didn't understand."

"So the Venetians weren't really infected by the bodies," Donovan said. "They were infected by fleas *on* the bodies."

"Most likely, yes. As strange as it may sound, bubonic plague itself is not all that contagious. But certain kinds of fleas are especially adept at transmitting the disease. Fleas feed on blood, you see, and fleas are a common parasite found on rodents. When a flea bites a plague-infected rodent, it draws in the bacteria with the blood. The bacteria begin to multiply wildly in the flea's foregut, blocking off its stomach entirely. Now the flea, infected with plague bacteria, begins to starve. Its hunger becomes insatiable; try as it may, it cannot take in more blood—so it frantically jumps from host to host, taking the disease along with it. Every time it bites, it injects a little saliva—and twenty thousand bacteria along with it.

"When those catapulted bodies landed, the fleas fled in search of another host, and the Venetians were close at hand. That's how the disease was spread in Kaffa; that's how the bubonic form of plague is always spread."

"And that's why you picked up on the fleas in the TriBeCa story."

"Yes—because fleas can be purposely employed to spread plague. Your entomologist identified the fleas in TriBeCa as *Xenopsylla cheopis*—the Oriental rat flea. That is the species that was responsible for the carnage in medieval Europe. Sato Matsushita knows that; Unit 731 did extensive study on Oriental rat fleas—how to rear them, how to artificially infect them with plague, how to successfully introduce them into a human population. The Oriental rat flea is precisely what one would employ to create an epidemic of bubonic plague—if one were so inclined."

"And you think Sato Matsushita is so inclined."

"I'm certain of it."

Donovan stopped and waited until the old man turned to look at him. "Why, Li? Why would an eighty-year-old Japanese man want to launch an attack of bubonic plague against the United States?"

"Because he didn't have the opportunity sixty years ago."

"So? There's unfinished business in every war: bombs that don't get dropped, shots that don't get fired—"

"And shots are always fired *after* the surrender is signed. There is always unresolved anger; there is always the desire for revenge."

"Sixty years later?"

"In this case, yes."

"Come on—nobody carries a grudge that long."

"Sato Matsushita was assigned to Unit 731's plague program. The program was fraught with problems; chief among them was finding a way to distribute plague-infected fleas alive and unharmed. They tried different types of bombs, but the fleas were always destroyed by the blast."

"They should have tried a shaped charge—it would have directed the blast away from the payload."

Li paused. "You seem to know something about bombs."

"I was in the Marine Corps—in ordnance removal."

"You made bombs?"

"I made them; I took them apart."

"That must have taken a great deal of courage."

"We called it 'controlled insanity.' Some days required more control, others more insanity."

Li thought for a moment. "Which do you possess more of now?"

"Li—the story."

"Oh, yes. Well, as an expert in this area, you'll appreciate Sato's solution to the problem. He developed an entirely different type of bomb. It was a hollow ceramic shell, designed to be dropped from an airplane by parachute. The nose cone fell away and dropped to the ground; when it struck the ground, it sent back a radio signal, setting off a charge just powerful enough to shatter the ceramic shell and release the thirty thousand fleas within. With this technique, over 80 percent of the fleas survived."

"A ceramic bomb. Very clever."

"Yes—and so successful that it was decided to employ the bomb against the city of San Diego."

"You're kidding."

"The plan was code-named Operation Cherry Blossoms at Night, and it was slated for September 22, 1945. They had only one problem left to solve: how to get an airplane close enough to America's West Coast to deliver the bomb."

"How about a carrier?"

"There were none left—by 1945 the Imperial Navy had been decimated. There was only one possibility: a top secret submarine developed by the Japanese navy. It had a large cylindrical compartment on top—a kind of hangar if you will, capable of stowing a folding-wing aircraft inside. The submarine could sail undetected within striking distance of the coast, then surface and launch its airplane. It was just the ticket."

"But."

"But the Japanese navy would not risk exposing one of its few remaining vessels in a frivolous attack on a civilian population center. They knew an American invasion was imminent, and they wanted to save the submarines to launch kamikaze attacks against U.S. carriers."

"So Operation Cherry Blossoms at Night never happened."

"No. The war came to an end in August, just six weeks before the scheduled attack."

"And you think Sato Matsushita still wants to carry it out?"

"Some form of it, yes."

"Are you sure this guy is still alive?"

"No."

"But you think he is—even though he would be over eighty years old."

"*I* am over eighty years old."

Donovan paused. "It all sounds crazy to me. But the way I see it, there's no way to know whether there's anything behind this theory of yours unless we find this guy and talk to him."

"An excellent idea—and as I told you before, I have been trying to 'find this guy' for more than sixty years now. I will require your resources to help me do so."

"No offense, Li, but why should we help you when we can do it ourselves? You said yourself that all this is a matter of public record."

"That's quite true. Everything I've told you today can be gleaned from any university library—but you won't be able to learn anything more."

"Why not?"

"As the end of the war approached, the Unit 731 scientists saw the handwriting on the wall. Each one knew he had to strike some kind of bargain in order to save his own skin. Shiro Ishii, for example, went to the Allies—but how many sources of information did the Allies require? Sato Matsushita understood this, so he went to the Soviets. After the war, Matsushita disappeared behind the Iron Curtain. That is where his trail ends."

"But somehow you were able to track him."

"Yes."

"Then so can we."

"If your people attempt to locate him without my help, they will reach a dead end. Try if you wish; it's a waste of valuable time. You'll find that Sato Matsushita simply vanished from the face of the earth."

Donovan shook his head. "You underestimate the FBI."

The old man raised one eyebrow. "You underestimate me."

Li turned and continued down the corridor. Donovan watched him for a moment before following. He was an old man, but he stood perfectly erect; no slight hanging of the head, no rounding of the shoulders, no sign at all of brittleness or osteoporosis. He looked ten years younger than most Americans his age—maybe twenty. *Maybe that's what you get from eating eel brains and turtle heads,* Donovan thought. There was an energy about the old man, a self-assurance, a sort of lightness in his step—almost a swagger. Donovan wondered if he would have the same quality when he was eighty; he wondered if he had the quality now.

And his mind—no doubt about it, the old man was as sharp as a razor. But this story of his, it was so—*unbelievable.* That was the problem: The story was incredible, but the man himself almost compelled belief. Could it be true? Could there be something to this bizarre story of his? And did this eighty-year-old man have knowledge that the Bureau could never attain on its own? Donovan looked at him again—*sixty years is a long time to collect newspaper clippings . . .*

Maybe the old guy's right, Donovan thought. *Maybe I do underestimate him.*

The old man had reached the corner now; Donovan started after him. "Li," he called, "I want to show you something." He reached into his blazer pocket and removed a glossy four-by-six photo. "Can you identify this object?"

Li studied the photo. "It looks like an urn of some sort."

"That's right—it's called a funerary jar."

"It's very old—Mesopotamian, if I'm not mistaken. The relief work around the neck—the images of the lion, the bull, and the ram—they're all symbols of Near Eastern royalty. It might be Assyrian—perhaps Persian."

"You really know your art history."

"Well, it's more artifact than art. At my age, one takes an interest in older things—since I'm rapidly becoming an artifact myself. What is the significance of this object?"

"It's a copy of an item stolen from the Iraqi National Museum of Antiquities. It turned up in that gallery in TriBeCa; then it disappeared again. The fleas in the gallery—they spread out from a definite point, from the exact spot where this was on display. Li—there's a good chance the fleas were transported in this funerary jar."

Li examined the photo more closely.

"It's made of clay," Donovan said.

"Yes." Li nodded. "One might call it *ceramic*."

CHAPTER TWELVE

Damascus, Syria, present day

SATO MATSUSHITA STROLLED QUIETLY down the long, high corridor of *Souk al Hamidiyeh*, the ancient marketplace that stretched five hundred meters from west to east across the old city of Damascus. For five thousand years Damascus has been a crossroads of civilization, and the old bazaar still reflected it. Arabs, Kurds, Armenians, and Turks mingled together with Western tourists. Styles of dress ranged from Europeans in haute couture to bearded Bedouins in flowing robes and traditional checkered headgear. Half a dozen languages could be heard, but Arabic rose above them all; it was an Arab market after all, and in the *souk* the Arab tongue is still the language of commerce.

The corridor's walls were a beehive of tiny shops, booths, and stalls, offering wares of every imaginable kind: richly colored carpets woven from goat or camel hair, woven baskets and raffia, embroidered silk brocades, copper pots engraved with intricate arabesques, and wooden boxes delicately inlaid with exotic woods. Shoppers and browsers crowded around the stalls, while eager tradesmen wandered the aisles, holding their wares aloft and recounting their virtues. European tourists haggled clumsily with seasoned vendors, shaming them into settling for only twice what each item was worth. Hard-won treasures traded hands with a flourish, while euros and dollars and pounds flowed invisibly under tables and behind backs.

The bazaar was centuries old. It had been built and rebuilt many times; this incarnation dated from the thirteenth century, built atop the ruins of an old Roman fortress. That's what Sato liked about the *souk*; that's what he liked about the city itself. Damascus is one of the oldest continuously inhabited cities on earth, and one of the most frequently conquered. First the Egyptians, then the Israelites, then Assyrians, Greeks, Romans, Turks, Ottomans, and French—and each one built their palaces and markets atop the civilization that came before it, like a deck of shuffled cards. That's what the old man liked; all of Damascus was built on the ruins of something else. It seemed somehow appropriate, and it served as a reminder of what could be.

Sato passed directly down the center of the aisle, looking neither to the right nor to the left. He wasn't there to shop. He took this path almost every afternoon, using the jostling crowds and the cacophony of voices to help him transition from the solitude and silence of his research at the Scientific Studies and Research Center. For Sato it was a kind of cleansing ritual, a sort of bathhouse for the soul. The noisy, crowded bazaar was the soaping-up; the rinsing-off came at the eastern end, where the bustling market gave way to the magnificent Umayyad Mosque.

The sprawling, marble-covered courtyard was the atmospheric opposite of the *souk*. It was peaceful and serene, surrounded by stone colonnades and intricate mosaics. In the center of the courtyard was the ablutions fountain, marking the midpoint between Istanbul and Mecca, the meeting point between East and West. Like most of the buildings of Damascus, the mosque was only the most recent occupant of its location. Its courtyard had been a place of reflection for three thousand years: first by the Aramaeans, then the Romans, then the Christians, and finally the Muslims just a scant millennium ago. Sato walked slowly and silently across the courtyard, breathing the ancient air and remembering the past. That's what Damascus allowed him to do—*remember*. Moscow did not; Baghdad did not. Modern cities were so forward-looking, always in a hurry to forget the past; but Damascus *was* the past, a place where everyone lived among the ruins.

He exited the courtyard now, cleansed and refreshed, and circled behind the mosque to one of the city's better coffeehouses, the Alsham Alkadima. The café was crowded but relatively quiet. Small groups of men huddled around tables, sipping tea and coffee and drawing on old pipes, playing backgammon and dominoes and nodding their heads gravely about politics and business and war.

Sato took a table where he could be seen from the door. A waiter approached and made a slight bow.

"*Ahweh*," Sato said. "For two."

"How do you take it?"

"*Murrah*," Sato said. "I prefer my coffee bitter. *Mazbuta* for my friend."

"Cardamom? Orange blossom water?"

Sato shook his head, and the waiter left.

A few moments later, an Arab approached Sato's table. He looked half Sato's age, though his skin was rough and weathered and his precise age was difficult to determine. He was dressed simply, in a khaki jacket with a coarse wool sweater underneath. A thick mustache jutted forward from his upper lip, streaked with threads of gray. He had coarse black hair peppered at the temples. On his left cheek was a horizontal scar; it started as a tiny slit just below his eye and widened as it went back like a gash on a melon. It slashed back around the side of his face, cutting a barren swath through the middle of his sideburn. The scar stopped just before his left ear, which was missing except for a curling twist of flesh.

His name was Raheem Khalid. He was Syrian by birth and had been a soldier since boyhood. Khalid had crossed many borders since his youth to add his weight wherever the Arab balance of power was threatened in the Middle East. He fought against the Israelis in southern Lebanon; he joined guerrilla raids against the West Bank and the Golan Heights; he fought against the Kurds in northern Iraq. In 1991 he joined with the Iraqis in their battle against the American-led coalition. He lost a brother and his left ear to an American M16, and in the process gained a lifelong foe.

Khalid nodded a greeting. "Dedushka," he said simply—the Russian word for "grandfather."

Sato looked up. "I've ordered us a Turkish coffee."

Khalid grunted and took a seat. "*Turkish* coffee—the name is insulting. Syrian traders brought coffee to Istanbul four hundred years ago—now they send it back to us with their name on it. They are worse than the Americans."

"No one is worse than the Americans."

The man lowered his eyes. "No."

The waiter returned now with a steaming *Rakweh*. He placed a demitasse cup before each of them, but no spoon. He poured slowly into each cup to evenly distribute the thick sediment. The two men waited in silence until he left.

"This place is too crowded," Khalid said. "Too many ears."

"Too many is enough," Sato said. "If you listen carefully, Khalid, you will hear all sorts of intrigue in here. Our voices will not stand out."

"I don't like it."

"That's what coffee is for, is it not—striking deals and hatching plots? That's why the Turks liked your coffee; that's why the custom caught on. Now—tell me about New York. I have already been briefed; I know that your test has failed."

"It appears that you were right," Khalid said.

"Tell me."

"We found buyers for four of the jars," he said. "All made it past U.S. Customs successfully—all were delivered to their respective buyers. We made an enormous profit—almost two million dollars U.S."

Sato frowned. "This is not about money."

"It takes money to accomplish so great a task, Dedushka."

"It also takes a successful delivery system. Tell me about the test."

"We sent the first three jars empty—just to test the waters, just to make sure they would make it across the border. We sent the fourth jar with the—" He glanced around for listening ears. "We sent the fourth jar full."

"And?"

"It, too, arrived safely."

"Then the test was a success—yes?"

Khalid hung his head. "We sent an operative to retrieve it. He was to steal back the jar so we could verify that the contents had survived the trip. When our operative got there, he found that the jar had been somehow damaged, and the contents had been allowed to escape."

"So he silenced the buyer with a gunshot to the head and left thousands of fleas behind," Sato said, glaring at Khalid. "Yes, I know—I read all about it in the *New York Times*."

"He exterminated the fleas before he left," Khalid grumbled. "The Americans should never have found them."

"The Americans *did* find them."

"No one will make the connection to you," Khalid said.

"Do I have your assurance of that? Just as I had your assurance that this ridiculous plan of yours would work?"

"It was not my plan. It isn't my money, so I don't make the decisions."

"No, your superiors do—but they are not *my* superiors, Khalid. They have made an inexcusable error in judgment; they have risked exposure of my entire strategy. So I ask you, in what sense are they superior? No. From now on, we will do it my way—just as I have said from the beginning."

"It's their money," Khalid said. "They want to do it their way."

"Perhaps we'll find them more humble and teachable after this embarrassing failure," Sato replied. "Tell them I will make no further concessions; tell them I will allow no more outside interference."

"They won't like it."

"Remind them what I offer in trade: a true weapon of mass destruction with an efficient and utterly untraceable delivery system. It will claim a minimum of a million lives—perhaps twice that many. The economic and social impact on America will be irreparable. I offer your superiors what they have always sought—what they attempt to gain for themselves with their silly little bombs and devices. I have spent sixty years perfecting this system, Khalid—should I now let them alter my plan with their foolish and ignorant suggestions? No more; never again. Tell them I offer them my weapon, my way—or no weapon at all."

"I will tell them," Khalid said.

"Tell them also why this foolish plan of theirs failed. A flea is a fragile animal. It must feed on blood—warm blood—and it requires oxygen and specific environmental conditions to survive. To pack thousands into a tiny container and then expect them to survive in uncertain conditions for an extended period of time is sheer folly. It did not work sixty years ago, and it will not work today. I must accompany the fleas, Khalid. I must feed them and nurture them until the moment before they are employed."

"They did not want to risk you," Khalid said. "They thought it safer to attempt to send the fleas alone."

Sato let out a snort. "Do they not strap bombs on their zealots and send them into Jerusalem cafés? If they want a hundred dead, do they not sacrifice one? I offer them ten thousand times a hundred—are they not willing to risk one to get it? You and I know the real reason for their fear, Khalid. They are more than willing to risk me; it is their own cowardly necks they are unwilling to risk. If I am captured, I could expose them all. Tell them that is the chance they must take. Tell them that without great risk, there is no great glory."

"I will tell them as you say."

"Good. They will listen to you."

"You overestimate me, Dedushka. I am just a soldier."

"You are more than that, Khalid. We have been associates now for more than a decade—since I first came to Iraq from the Soviet Union, when you were just a young lieutenant in the Republican Guard. We almost persuaded them then, didn't we? We almost had our chance. But it was not to be—not then, not there. When the Iraqi army was destroyed, when the situation there became unstable, it was you who invited me here. You arranged my sponsorship, my housing, my laboratory at the Scientific Studies and Research Center. It was you who saw me safely across the border into Syria, along with the seeds of my research. If I have neglected to say so, I want you to know that I am grateful. I consider you almost a friend."

Sato finished his coffee and turned the cup upside down on the saucer. "Now we must send for a fortune-teller. That is the Turkish custom: When the cup cools, the fortune-teller will read the grounds that remain in the cup. She will tell us our futures."

"I don't need a Turk to tell me my future—I will make my own future."

"Yes," Sato said. "We will make the future." He leaned forward now and spoke in a somber tone. "Listen to me, Khalid—I want to remind you of something. This strategy, this system of mine—you know that it is more than a weapon; it is my life's mission. I have spent sixty years in pursuit of this single goal. Please understand that I accept the assistance of your superiors only because they serve my mission. Your superiors, your country, even you, Khalid—everything is secondary to my mission."

"And I serve you because your mission and my mission are the same."

Sato nodded. "A common purpose. Is that not the source of all true friendship?"

CHAPTER THIRTEEN

Brookhaven, New York

Danny Cardello paced the floor of his office, staring out the big glass window at the chaos on the factory floor. His young fireworks company, Pyrotech, had doubled in size in only three years—then doubled again in just the last three months. His headaches had doubled, too, and the Italian sausage he'd wolfed down for lunch was burning a hole in his gut like a Roman candle. He looked again. There were bodies everywhere, people he didn't even know, scurrying across the factory floor like so many ants. *Some family business*, he thought. *Growth is good, but this is like cancer.*

Danny's company was just a young upstart in the competitive, family-dominated fireworks display industry, but less than a year ago, *Pyrotech* became an industry buzzword when Danny managed to accomplish a startling coup de grâce. In a spectacular demonstration of overpromising and underbidding, he had managed to wrest away New York City's Fourth of July Fireworks Spectacular from the legendary Souza family, which had held the concession for more than twenty consecutive years. Danny found it surprisingly easy; all he needed to do was grossly exaggerate the capabilities of his company and promise magnificent, never-before-seen effects—never-before-seen because they didn't yet exist.

And there was one more little hitch: To pull off the New York display as promised, Pyrotech would have to take a loss. The event would be a major financial hit, almost enough to sink the company—but it could be worth it for the promotional value alone. Live from New York, broadcast all over America on NBC, the Fourth of July Fireworks Spectacular— brought to you by Pyrotech, the little company that could. Danny knew that all the premier fireworks displays in the U.S. were dominated by a handful of "fireworks families"—the Souzas in California, the Gruccis in New York, the Zambellis in Pittsburgh. You don't make money in the fire-works business by selling bottle rockets to kids. You go for the big events—New York, Boston, Philadelphia, San Francisco. Danny had man-aged to snatch the goose while the giant was sleeping; now all he had to do was hold on until one event led to another, and then came the golden egg. Then he could charge what he was worth.

But first he needed to deliver the goods in New York. It wasn't enough just to land the contract—that was just a business deal. He had to beat Souza soundly—he had to put on a show no one had ever seen before. If he didn't—he could just see the headlines: "Pyrotech Bombs in the Big Apple"; "Pyrotech Fizzles—City Regrets Change, Begs Souza to Return"; "Pyrotech Announces Plan to Sell Variety Packs in Wal-Mart Parking Lots." He felt the ball of fire burning in his gut again. He opened a desk drawer and took out a bottle of Mylanta.

He mentally reviewed the terms of the agreement: forty thousand shells—did he promise *forty*? That was five more than Souza ever did. He promised four separate firing locations—Souza offered only three: on the East River, just south of the Brooklyn Bridge, and across from Liberty Island. Danny threw in the Hudson River too. Now people would be able to watch the fireworks from all five of New York's boroughs—even the Bronx. Twelve hundred shells going off every minute, all perfectly synchronized with the music—it would take thirteen miles of wire to pull it off, eight sepa-rate barges, and seventy thousand feet of steel and plastic mortar pipe.

But the logistics he could handle; the logistics were just business too. His biggest headache was the finale. To land the contract, he had to prom-ise the biggest, baddest slam-bang finale in the history of fireworks, one that would make old people coo like pigeons and babies pop out their pacifiers. *What is it with finales?* he wondered. You could detonate a nuclear warhead and people would still ask, "When's the finale?" *But that's the way it works*, Danny thought. In fireworks, you live or die by your finale—and Danny's Fourth of July Fireworks Spectacular was currently on life support, because Danny had no finale.

He had spent the last eight months traveling the world in search of something new, something never before seen. He hit all the major pyrotechnics markets—Italy, Portugal, China, Japan—but all he found was more of the same. There were chrysanthemums, peonies, starbursts, and showers; yellow ribbons for the troops and smiley faces for the kids. Just the same old, same old—maybe a little louder or brighter, but certainly nothing that would impress the been-there-done-that citizens of New York. Danny looked out the window again. Maybe he could just invite everyone to Brookhaven, then torch the whole warehouse at once—maybe that would do it.

"Danny, you have a call on line one."

"No calls," Danny said.

"It's from overseas."

"Where overseas?"

A pause. "Syria."

Syria? Who did he know in Syria? "Take a number."

Another pause. "He's very persistent. He says you'll want to talk to him."

"Who is it?"

"How should I know?"

"What does he want?"

"You want to have this whole conversation through me, or you want to take the phone call?"

"You're fired," Danny said.

"Then you can make your own dinner tonight. He's on line one."

Danny lifted the receiver. "Yeah, Danny Cardello."

"Mr. Cardello, thank you for taking my call."

It was some old guy; he sounded Japanese. "Look, you caught me at a bad time here," Danny said.

"I understand. With the New York City display just weeks away, I imagine things are very busy there—*very* busy."

"I didn't catch your name, Mr.—"

"Mr. Ogatsu. Is my family name familiar to you?"

Was he kidding? The Ogatsus were the oldest fireworks family on the planet. The Souzas had been in the business for only a century, the Gruccis a little longer; the Ogatsus of Japan got their business license in the seventeenth century. Their modern-day company, Marutamaya, was known all over the world.

"My wi—my secretary said this call was from Syria."

"Yes, that's right."

"Marutamaya is based in Tokyo."

"And also Ibaraki and Yamanashi. We have thirty-two factories all together. Have you visited us?"

"Sure, just a few months ago. Have we met?"

"No, sorry to say. The Ogatsu family has dispersed over the years. I now reside in Damascus. Though many of our family now live abroad, some of us still maintain an interest in the family business. My particular interest is in research and development."

"Good for you." Danny didn't have time to trade fireworks stories with some old coot who made his own sparklers at the retirement home.

"It's unfortunate," the man said. "Because I no longer live in Japan, buyers don't bother to visit me. They assume that one man alone could offer nothing that an entire factory could not. But I believe the creative process is always individual in nature. Great discoveries are made by gifted individuals, not by committees. Don't you agree?"

"Uh-huh." Danny was shuffling through paperwork, waiting for an opportune moment to end the call.

"Tell me, please: Is your program for the New York display complete yet?"

"What? Oh, sure, months ago."

"That's too bad. I had something quite unusual to show you—something that might have made a significant contribution to your presentation."

Danny stopped what he was doing. "What are we talking about here?"

"Are you at a computer?"

"Sure. Just a minute." He swept a pile of papers onto the floor.

"I'm going to give you an Internet address. You'll find a link to a com-pressed video file there. The video was taken in the Syrian Desert not far from here. Do you have a moment to view it? It will only take a minute of your time. I'll hold on while you look."

Danny entered the URL and waited. The screen that appeared was practically empty. *I hope his pyrotechnics are better than his Web design*, he thought. There was a single link in the center of the page; Danny clicked it, and a smaller window appeared. He enlarged it to fill the screen.

The screen was completely black. Danny was about to say, "It's not working," when a flash of light at the bottom of the screen revealed a single steel mortar against a desert backdrop. The flash was followed by a thun-dering boom, then darkness again—but a few seconds later the screen erupted in light.

In the center was a slow-rising column of glittering silver and gold, so bright and so full that it looked solid to the touch. As the column reached its peak, it suddenly exploded, sending tendrils of brilliant green sprawling across the sky, dripping like watercolors as they went. From the tendrils, curling leaves of yellow began to appear, beginning at the center and spreading out toward the tips. There were hundreds of them, and they were crisp and clearly defined, not just the usual quick streaks of light that disappeared almost before they could be seen.

An instant later, leaves of the deepest blue began to appear, and Danny's jaw dropped open. He understood the chemistry of fireworks: Strontium gives you red; barium, green; sodium, yellow—but nothing gives you blue. A true blue was the holy grail of pyrotechnic chemists all over the world—and yet here it was, the deepest blue he had ever seen. The blue leaves gave the image depth, making it appear almost three-dimensional.

Now the tips of the tendrils exploded into dazzling clusters of pink and red, and the figure was complete. It was a cherry tree—the image was clear and sharp and unmistakable. It was nothing like other patterned shapes, the primitive hearts and stars and circles common to fireworks displays all over the world. There was no guesswork here—no one would ever say, "Was that a bow tie? I thought it was a dog bone."

And it *lasted*—that was the most remarkable effect of all. The chemical pellets that fill an aerial shell are consumed in less than a second; the first sequence of an effect disappears long before the last ever takes place. But *this*—it was as though the image were painted on the sky. The column, the tendrils, the leaves, the blossoms—they were all still there, just sitting and glittering like jewels in the desert sky.

An instant later, the entire image disappeared all at once.

Danny just blinked at the screen. The kid in him wanted to shout and cheer; the fireworks expert wanted to sing praises; but it was the businessman who spoke into the phone. "Very interesting," he said.

"Have you ever seen anything like it?"

"There was one in Lisbon," he started to say, but he caught himself. What was he doing? This man knew things about fireworks that Danny had only dreamed of. All he had to do was offend the man, all Mr. Ogatsu had to do was hang up his telephone, and Danny would lose this masterpiece forever. "Never," he said. "Mr. Ogatsu, I have been to fireworks demonstrations all over the world in the last few months, and I guarantee you there is nothing like this anywhere."

"I'm so glad you like it."

"I have to ask you something. Has this video been altered in any way?"

There was a pause on the other end. "You insult me."

"No—wait. I'm not suggesting that you did anything, Mr. Ogatsu; it's just that—well, put yourself in my place. This is so different, I just have to know for sure."

"I assure you, the video was not edited or retouched in any way. The effect you saw was exactly as it appears."

"How did you get the blue? I've never seen a color like that before."

"You understand, of course, that I cannot reveal family secrets. I will tell you that I have personally made discoveries I do not even share with the rest of the Ogatsu family."

Danny could barely contain himself.

"I was hoping you could make use of this effect in your New York display—but as you said, your program was completed months ago."

"No! I mean, it was—except for the finale. And the finale is everything, you know. I've been looking for something really different, something that would really cap off the show. Mr. Ogatsu, this is exactly what I've been looking for."

"You can still include it, then?"

"Absolutely."

"I'm so glad. I'm very proud of it. I was hoping it could be introduced at some larger event, and not just at closing time at some minor amusement park."

"Well, the Fourth of July in New York is the biggest event of all. I'd be proud to include your effect in my show." He took a breath and held it. "Let's talk about price."

"I was thinking about a thousand dollars per shell. That seems reasonable."

Danny wanted to do handsprings. A thousand per shell for his finale? It wasn't possible—he couldn't get off that easy. "That's more than fair," he said. "In fact, I think you're undercharging. Let's make it fifteen hundred a piece."

"Very well, if you insist. How many shells will you require?"

"Eight—one for each of the barges."

"Yes—I think that will cover things quite nicely."

"And I'd like to talk to you about an exclusive arrangement."

"Exclusive?"

"Yes—I'm willing to pay a premium if you'll agree not to sell this shell to anyone else until after the New York show."

"I'm aware of no other major displays before your own."

"Still, just to make sure. You understand—this is something completely different, and I don't want anyone else to steal our thunder."

"I agree—this is something that should be reserved for New York. Very well, it will be an exclusive arrangement."

"Done," Danny said with finality, hoping to block any possible escape.

The old man paused. "There are a couple of conditions I would like to mention," he said. "They must be considered a part of our agreement, and they are not open to negotiation."

Danny's heart sank a little. "Such as?"

"First, I must accompany the shells. I will not ship them; I will bring them to you in person. You can arrange the technical details—the placement of the mortars, the wiring, and so on—I will send you whatever specifications you require. The shells themselves will not arrive until one day before the event."

"That's acceptable."

"Please understand, the workings of this shell are a closely guarded secret. I do not wish to insult you, but you and I both know that if I allow my shell to travel unaccompanied, it will be a very brief time before my effect finds its way into another family's recipe book."

"I understand your concern," Danny said. "What else?"

"Second, I must accompany my shells to your barges, and I must personally oversee their loading and launch."

"Ignition is all done by computer."

"Of course. I simply wish to make sure that each of the eight shells is successfully launched. I must be certain that none remain behind; a failed shell can still reveal its secrets."

"That makes sense. Agreed."

"Finally, no one is to touch the shells but me. No one is to examine them. No one is to assist me in any way unless I specifically request his help. I hope I do not appear overly cautious, Mr. Cardello; as you know, in this business a secret has a very short life span. I simply wish to preserve my secret as long as possible."

"I'd feel the same way. Is that everything?"

"Those are my terms."

"Great! I'll get a contract together before the day is over and have it on your desk the day after tomorrow."

"There is no hurry. I consider our verbal agreement binding."

"One more question, Mr. Ogatsu. I was amazed at the way your effect extinguished all at the same time—almost like a sign switching off."

"Thank you. That was not an easy task."

"I want to use your shells as my grand finale—fire them off from all eight barges at the same time. My question is: Can they *all* be synchronized? Can they all be timed so that everything goes black at once?"

"I promise," the old man said. "Everything will go black at once."

SATO WAITED A MOMENT before dialing again.

"Khalid," he said. "Have you spoken yet with your superiors? Ah, good. When you do, please inform them that I have already reinstated my original plan. I have made the necessary contact in New York, and everything has been arranged. Yes, I know, Khalid—please forgive my apparent haste. Our friends will understand that if we allow this opportunity to pass, we must wait another full year—and they do not wish that delay any more than I do.

"Please inform your superiors that I will require the form of transport specified in my original plan—I'm certain they have the resources to arrange this on short notice. I will wish to set up a temporary lab in the lower cargo hold. It will require adequate ventilation and an air-filtration system—I will send them all of the specifications they need.

"And, Khalid—remind them to follow my instructions to the letter. We do not want a ghost ship arriving in New York Harbor."

CHAPTERFOURTEEN

THE CLOCK ON THE wall was the old-fashioned mechanical kind, the kind with a ticking second hand. It would have been bearable in a noisy cubicle, or hanging in some busy hallway. But in an office like this—four walls, door closed, quiet as a crypt—it was maddening. Donovan sat across from Reuben Mayer, waiting in concealed agony while the old man studied his weekly report. Mayer sat hunched over the folder, utterly motionless except for an almost imperceptible swinging of his head from side to side. From the corner of his eye, Donovan watched the clock's second hand advance. It made a hollow clicking sound that echoed off the walls, and the pitch seemed to change slightly from tick to tick—that particularly annoyed him. The second hand seemed to hesitate before jumping on to the next black hash mark—it seemed like two or three seconds at least. *What kind of a clock is that? What's wrong with a nice electric clock with a sweeping second hand—or better yet, an LCD with no hands at all?* Donovan wondered if it really wasn't a clock at all. Maybe it was some kind of voodoo metronome, casting a spell over Reuben Mayer, making sure that he could never move faster than a lava flow—

"You think he's nuts?"

"I'm sorry?"

"The old man—this Li character—do you think he's nuts?"

"No sir, I don't. Eccentric maybe, but not crazy."

Mayer glanced up. "'Eccentric' can get you put in a home. Is he senile?"

"I don't think so. He's highly educated—he's got a PhD in biochemistry."

"I'm talking about his rational processes. Any gaps in memory? Signs of confusion? Loss of concentration?"

"He's as lucid as you are, sir."

One slow blink from Mayer. "Maybe it's just an old man's fantasy," he said. "A story he tells to get some attention. A tall tale, a fish story, the one that got away."

"He flew all the way from London to tell this story."

"Why not? He meets with the FBI; he consults with the CIA. Something to tell his friends back home."

"It's possible—but I don't think so."

"Why?"

"I ran a background check on him after our first meeting. His full name is *Zhong Ren Li*—I'm not sure how to pronounce it. He immigrated to Great Britain after the war and enrolled at Oxford. When he finished his degree, he moved to Linz, Austria, and went to work for a man named Simon Wiesenthal. Wiesenthal was a survivor of the Mauthausen concentration camp. When the war ended, Wiesenthal started collecting evidence against Nazi war criminals. He opened the Jewish Documentation Center in Linz, staffed by thirty volunteers—apparently Li was one of them. Remember Adolf Eichmann?"

Mayer slowly cocked his head to one side. Donovan winced; he had just asked a Jew if he remembered Adolf Eichmann.

"I believe so, yes," Mayer replied coolly.

"Well, Eichmann was hiding in Buenos Aires under the name of Ricardo Klement when Wiesenthal's group tracked him down. It turns out Li played a big part in that capture."

"A Nazi hunter," Mayer said. "I'm impressed."

"That's my point, sir. Li's not the sort of man who needs to make up stories—he's got plenty of his own. And his record shows that he has the knowledge and experience to track a man over time and across continents. Whether Li's story turns out to be true or not, Li himself is a credible source."

Mayer studied the report again. "Tell me about this plague-maker fellow. What's his name—Santo?"

"Sato, sir. It's Japanese."

"I saw it here somewhere." Mayer slowly spread the pages of the report.

"It's Sato, sir."

"Here it is. *Sato*."

Donovan gripped the arms of his chair.

"It says here that at the end of the war, this Sato went over to the Russians—then all trace of him disappeared."

"According to Li, yes."

"According to Li. Have you checked that out?"

"Yes, sir. There was definitely a Unit 731 in Manchuria, just as Li said, and it was as bad as anything the Nazis handed out—human testing, medical experiments, the whole nine yards. It's a matter of historical record."

"And what was Sato's role in all this?"

"That's hard to say. In the documents seized after the war, there's only one mention of Sato Matsushita—in a roster of scientists employed at Unit 731. But there are no records of his research or activities while he was there."

"So as far as we know, Sato Matsushita is just a name," Mayer said. "Everything else your boy has told us could be legend. He could be making it all up."

"It's possible. I don't think so."

"Why?"

"Because Li has spent the last sixty years searching for this man."

"According to Li."

Donovan didn't reply.

"And after Sato went over to the Soviets, what happened then?"

"Like Li said—he disappeared from the face of the earth."

"But Li has further information."

"He says he does, yes."

"Information that only he possesses."

"Yes."

Mayer paused. "That makes him a very important fellow, doesn't it?"

Donovan felt his face flush. He knew what Mayer was saying—that Li might very well be nothing but a lonely old man seeking attention, a one-time Nazi hunter reliving the glories of days gone by. It could all be a fantasy—a story—a *lie*. The only reason Donovan had to believe Li was the power of the old man's personality—but Mayer had never met Li, and with nothing to consider but the pathetic handful of facts in Donovan's report, Mayer had no reason to believe at all. Donovan suddenly felt stupid; no, it was worse than that—he felt *naïve*. But for a reason he couldn't fully understand, he did believe Li—and the fact that Mayer did not made him angry.

"So you think the old man is nuts?"

"I think this whole thing is nuts," Mayer said. "I think this Li is a bored old man jerking your chain. I think this Sato character might be just a figment of his imagination—some old bogeyman left over from the war. I think his trail disappeared because *he* disappeared a long time ago."

"You want me to tell the old man to pack up and go home?"

"Yes—but the ADIC doesn't."

"The assistant director in charge?" Donovan sat up a little straighter; the ADIC was the Bureau chief over all of New York City.

"I passed your report upstairs," Mayer said. "The ADIC thinks we should follow it up."

"Why?"

"Because it's a post–9/11 world, Mr. Donovan. You know all the flak we took after the Trade Center—the FBI should have seen it coming; there were clues, but we didn't follow them up. In the current political climate, we can't afford to leave any stone unturned. Your orders are to stick with the old man—at least until we can *prove* he's nuts. Let's find out if this Li really has anything we want. Tell him that we welcome his cooperation, and collect whatever information he has."

Donovan paused.

"Problem, Mr. Donovan?"

"The situation is a little—tricky."

"Tricky?"

"Yes, sir. Li says it's his life mission to find Sato Matsushita. *He* wants to find him. He's not offering to assist us; he wants the FBI to assist him."

"Now, that *is* nuts."

"That's what I told him—but he's determined."

"So apply some leverage. Tell him he's impeding a federal investigation."

"He's a British citizen, sir. And he approached us, remember?"

"What are we supposed to do, give him a badge and swear him in?"

"No—I just think we have to play it his way for a while. What do we have to lose?"

"Time," Mayer said. "The ADIC wants to expedite this. If the old man really is nuts, we've got all the time in the world. But if there really is anything behind this story of his, then time could be critical."

"What do you want me to do?"

"Get an expert opinion."

"On what?"

"The old man's mental condition. His psychological makeup and motivation. The feasibility of this plague scenario of his."

"You want to use somebody inside the Bureau or take it outside?"

"Outside."

"Any recommendations?"

"I've got a name for you." Mayer slid a second folder across his desk and opened it. "Dr. Macy Monroe," he read from the top page, "Professor of Political Science and International Relations at Columbia University."

Donovan felt the floor drop away beneath him like the Parachute Jump at Coney Island. If he had a penny in his open palm, he was sure it would have floated into the air.

"You gotta be kidding."

"'Ongoing consultant to the CIA, the State Department, and the

Office of Technology Assessment,'" he read. "'Specializes in the psychology of terrorism and international terrorist threat assessment.'"

"Wait a minute—the Bureau can't require me to work with a family member."

Mayer looked up. "What family member?"

"Come on, Reuben—you know Macy's my ex-wife."

"That makes her an ex–family member. More like a friend."

Since when is an ex-wife like a friend? Donovan thought. He felt sick to his stomach.

Mayer continued to read. "'Past lecturer in Foreign Policy Studies at the Brookings Institution. Member of the Livermore Study Group. Adviser to NYU's Center for Catastrophe Preparedness and Response.' Quite a pedigree," he said.

"I'm not questioning her qualifications. I'm saying I can't work with her."

"Why not?"

Donovan fumbled for an explanation. "What I mean is, she can't work with me."

"So if we ask her, she'll turn us down."

"Yes. No—I don't know what she'd say."

"Let's find out," Mayer said.

"Since when is it Bureau policy to go around hiring ex-spouses?"

"It's Bureau policy to hire the best people we can find," he said. "Always has been." He turned back to the folder again. "'Regional expertise in both the Middle East and Japan.' Now, there's a coincidence." He glanced up. "This says she speaks both Arabic and Japanese."

"Plus some French," Donovan grumbled.

"Four languages," he said. "Did you ever win an argument?"

"Reuben, I'm begging you—don't make me do this."

"It's done," Reuben said. "Her name came down from the ADIC himself. The most qualified person in this city—maybe in the country—just happens to be your ex. Sorry," he said. "I'd get over it if I were you."

125

Donovan glared at him. "Did you ever try to 'get over' an ex-wife?"

"Do you call her, or do I?"

"I do."

"Good. Questions?"

"Just one," Donovan said. "Who do I shoot?"

"Anybody but your ex-wife," Mayer said. "She's on the payroll now."

CHAPTERFIFTEEN

THE CHALK ON THE blackboard made a quick clicking sound, like a mouse with a piece of hard candy. Macy's right hand moved in large, brisk strokes, spelling out the words *ASYMMETRICAL WARFARE* in capital letters.

"Who can tell me what this means?" she asked, turning to the class.

"Fighting on your own turf," one student offered.

"Give me an example."

"David meets Goliath," said another.

"Good—let's talk about that one. Who remembers the story?"

A dozen hands went up.

"Okay. This was a Middle Eastern territory dispute, with Israel in one corner as usual. Who was in the opposite corner?"

"Palestine?"

"No—but you're not far off. Anybody else?"

"The Philistines."

"There you go. Here's a piece of historical trivia for you: The name Palestine is derived from the word *Philistine*. Now the Philistines occupied the coastal region of Israel, what we now call the Gaza Strip. The armies of Israel and Philistia were about equal in number and strength, so nobody wanted to make the first move. It was a standoff, and it lasted for a month and a half.

"Then one of the Philistines suggested a way to break the tie: Each army would pick a champion and the champions would slug it out, winner take all. So—who went to bat for the Philistines?"

"Goliath," someone said in his best Darth Vader voice.

"And for the Israelites?"

"David!" Scattered applause from the classroom.

"Right. Now, David was just a boy—maybe fifteen or sixteen years old. The king at the time was a man named Saul. Saul called David into the locker room to help him suit up for the big game. Saul gave David his helmet, his armor, his sword—but they were so big on David that he couldn't even walk. He looked like that character from the Looney Tunes—you know, the little guy with the big Roman helmet. What was his name?"

A hand shot up in the first row. "Marvin the Martian," a young man said, grinning. "His sidekick was Commander K-9 the space dog, and his favorite weapon was the Illudium PU-36 Explosive Space Modulator."

Macy looked at him. "What year did World War I begin?"

The student's face went blank.

"I thought so," she said. "Anyway, David couldn't fight in Saul's armor. Somebody tell us what was going on here—describe the situation for us."

"Goliath wanted David to fight on *his* terms," a woman said.

"What terms were those? What were Goliath's assets?"

"Size. Strength."

"Exactly. He was over nine feet tall, and he was covered with armor from head to foot. Like our Third Armored Division—he was big, armed to the teeth, and practically invulnerable. Those were his assets; what were his liabilities?"

"He was dumb."

"Maybe," Macy said. "Or maybe he was just used to people doing things his way. You can get careless that way, can't you? What else—what were his weaknesses?"

"He was slow."

"Ah," Macy said. "He was *slow*—and in warfare, speed is a critical advantage. Now—what were David's assets?"

A muffled voice from the back of the room: "Rocks."

Through the laughter, Macy made a slight bow. "A double entrendre at eight o'clock in the morning," she said. "I don't know what you ordered at Starbucks this morning, but keep it coming. Okay, David had courage— another critical advantage. But he had something else too. What was it?"

Silence.

Macy stepped back to the blackboard and tapped her chalk by the large white letters. "He had *this*," she said. "David had the ability to think outside the box. Goliath wanted him to fight a traditional battle; Saul wanted him to fight a traditional battle. But David knew that would be suicide. He could never defeat Goliath on Goliath's own terms. He had to fight *his* way; he had to capitalize on the assets he had. David had speed, and quickness, and expertise with a nontraditional weapon: the sling. Goliath's armor was designed to withstand the point of a spear and the edge of a sword—but not a rock to the forehead."

Just then the door at the back of the classroom opened. The hinges were silent, but the glass panel made a brittle, rattling sound. Nathan Donovan slipped into the back of the classroom as inconspicuously as any tall, dark-suited federal agent could. He took a seat and nodded for Macy to continue.

Macy rarely broke stride in the middle of a lecture. She slowly gained momentum when she taught, like a locomotive building up steam, and she was just as hard to stop. She sometimes continued her lecture right through the bell, while sheepish students with next-hour classes collected their books and crept quietly away until only a single listener remained— some sympathetic soul who couldn't bear to be the last to go and leave Macy talking only to herself. Once the train was up to speed, Macy was oblivious to all interruptions: raised hands, late arrivals, coughing fits, even fire alarms. But when Donovan entered the room, she stopped and looked; it was enough to turn half of the heads in the classroom.

Macy attempted a recovery by returning to her lecture with renewed enthusiasm, which only made the few who were still oblivious turn and study Donovan as well. When Macy realized there was no use fighting it, she stopped.

"By now you've all noticed that we have a visitor," she said. "The 'Man in Black' in the back of the room is Special Agent Nathan Donovan of the FBI. Relax, he's not here because of anything you did—not yet, anyway."

Donovan cupped his right hand and did his best Miss America wave.

Macy pointed to the blackboard. "Mr. Donovan graduated from the Big Ten, so this may be asking a lot of him, but—can you tell us how the Bureau would define this term, Mr. Donovan?"

"Terrorism," Donovan said.

"I'll bet that's the term Goliath used when David pulled out his sling."

Donovan shook his head. "I'll bet the term was 'Uh-oh.'"

The class laughed; Macy kept a straight face. "The term 'terrorism' isn't particularly helpful," she said. "It describes the effect an attack has on its victim, but not the motivation for the attack. And if we never understand the cause, we won't be able to prevent it from happening again."

"You understand the cause of terrorism?" Donovan asked.

Macy glared back. "I understand the reason for asymmetrical warfare. So do the Palestinians; so does al-Qaeda; so does every outgunned and outnumbered guerrilla force in the world." Her countenance softened now. "And so does this class," she said. "So what does the story of David and Goliath have to do with the military situation in the modern world? Anybody?"

"It's David versus Goliath everywhere we look," someone said.

"And who represents Goliath in your scenario?"

"We do—the U.S."

"We're the bad guys?" Donovan said from the back of the room.

Macy took the comment in stride. "No, we're the *big* guys. And who represents David?"

"Everyone smaller," a young man said. "Everyone who lacks our technology; everyone who can't match our level of military spending. Just about everybody."

Macy nodded. "This is the important point here, people: *David can't fight in Saul's armor.* In today's world, America is unparalleled in military technology, training, and supply. No one is even close. So we roll in with our Third Armored Division and we call out to the enemy, 'Bring out your guns! Line up your tanks! Come on out and fight like a man!' By which we mean, 'Come on out and fight *our* way.' And when anyone is actually stupid enough to try it—like Saddam Hussein in the first Gulf War—it ends up looking more like a video game than an actual battle. And we love it—why shouldn't we? It demonstrates our absolute superiority, and it holds our losses to a bare minimum.

"But the enemy isn't stupid—that's what Goliath forgot, and that's what got him killed. If the enemy doesn't have guns and tanks, he'll come at you with a sling and a stone."

"What if you take away his sling?" Donovan asked.

"Anybody can make a sling," Macy said, "and rocks are everywhere. You can't take away all the world's slings—that's a waste of time. If a man wants to kill you, he'll find a way to try."

"Then what do you do?"

Macy looked at him. "You find the man first."

The bell rang, releasing the palpable tension; there was an almost audible sigh of relief from the class. When the doors crashed open, it was like pricking a balloon; students poured out like escaping air. Only one student remained, carefully repacking her books and papers into a backpack. She stopped abruptly and glanced around, mortified to find herself alone. She quickly scooped the rest of her belongings under one arm and hurried out.

Donovan rose and came forward.

"Thanks for your contribution to the class today," Macy said, returning her own books to a leather attaché.

"I love 'Bible Hour,'" Donovan said. "Did I miss the snack?"

"What do you want, Nathan?"

He paused. "Can we sit down?"

"Is it necessary?"

"It would help," he said. "Please?"

They both took seats on the folding wooden amphitheater chairs.

"I never did like these seats," he said.

"You never liked classrooms."

"That's true. I guess I never was much of a student. At least you get to stand up and teach."

"You have to pass a couple of classes before they let you teach," she said. "It's sort of a requirement."

Donovan tried to slow things down. "How are you doing?" he asked.

"In what capacity?"

He rolled his eyes. "Come on, Macy, it's a simple question. I ask, 'How are you doing?' and you say, 'I'm doing fine.'"

"Is that what you want to hear?"

"I want to hear how you're doing."

"I'm doing fine. Anything else?"

The door suddenly opened, and a student stepped inside. He glanced at Macy and Donovan and instantly read the expressions on their faces; he looked like a mosquito caught in a bug zapper. He backed out quickly and shut the door behind him.

"This is not a personal visit," Donovan said.

"That's good. I haven't seen you in, what—almost a year? And then, without any advance notice, you drop in on my classroom. I'd hate to think this is your idea of a personal visit."

"I thought about calling," he said.

"But you didn't."

"I thought it would be too hard."

"Lots of things are hard, Nathan. Life is hard sometimes—"

"Let's not go there, okay?"

There was a moment of awkward silence.

"So if this is not a personal visit, why are you here?"

"I need your help," he said.

She paused. "You need me to *help* you."

It was a simple sentence, but it was like an iceberg; a tiny, innocent tip concealing a thousand tons of coldness below.

"I've got a lot on my plate right now," she said.

"This is not a personal request," he said. "The Bureau wants your opinion on a case we're working on—a case *I'm* working on."

"They want *me* to work with *you*?"

"Well . . . yes."

"Don't they know about us?"

"Of course they know. They don't care. You're the most qualified person for the job, that's all."

Macy squinted. "They want *me* to work with *you*?"

Donovan groaned. "I told them it wouldn't work."

"You told them you couldn't work with me?"

"No, I told them *you* couldn't work with *me*."

"Where do you get off telling them that?"

"What?"

"If you can't work with me, that's one thing—but don't try to make this out to be my problem."

"Macy, how are we supposed to work together? We couldn't even stay married."

"That's a little different, don't you think? Did they say I have to love you?"

"Of course not."

"Did they say I have to respect you?"

Donovan glared at her. "All they told me is that I can't shoot you."

"Well, do you think you can manage that?"

"Right now I'm not so sure."

"What kind of case is it?"

"It involves bubonic plague, and Oriental rat fleas, and a guy with a very long memory."

"I like it so far."

"Look—last week an old Chinese man came to see me. He told me a story you wouldn't believe—I'm not sure *I* believe it. It's either the biggest news of the century or the biggest whopper of all time, and we can't tell which. We have to know if the old man is crazy or not. That's why we need your help."

Macy stood up, closed her briefcase, and started for the door. "Tell them to count me in," she said. "'Crazy' is one of my specialties."

Donovan watched until the door shut behind her. "You're telling me," he said.

CHAPTER SIXTEEN

Tartus, Syria

KHALID STEPPED ON THE gas pedal, and the old Peugeot accelerated along the empty highway. The road to the port city of Tartus was almost new, a part of the recent network of highways and railroads connecting the inland cement factories and fertilizer plants with Syria's two major ports: the venerable old port of Latakia and its younger and more industrial brother, Tartus.

The drive was straight and level and required no thought at all. It allowed Khalid's mind to wander. His thoughts went back to Iraq, to the time almost fifteen years ago when he first met Dedushka in Baghdad at a briefing of battlefield commanders. It was December 1990, and the Americans were amassing their forces along the Saudi border in preparation for war. Everyone knew it was the final briefing before the American offensive would begin, and everyone waited on the edge of their seats for the high command to reveal the strategy for the Iraqi defense.

Khalid was dumbfounded when a tiny Oriental man was escorted to the podium—but when he was introduced as a Soviet biological weapons specialist, they all understood. Then the air became electric, supercharged with anticipation. Every officer in the Republican Guard knew about Iraq's biological arsenal; some of them had seen these weapons firsthand when they were tested on the Kurds just a few years before. All of them wondered if Iraq would have the courage to use them against the Americans. The talk was everywhere; the possibility hung over them like a gleaming scimitar.

The threat was directly implied when Saddam Hussein spoke of the "mother of all battles." No one believed Iraq's imported armor would last for long against the Americans' inexhaustible resources. The "mother of all battles" was an apocalyptic term, and Iraq's pitiful collection of jets, tanks, and aging Scud missiles would never bring about an apocalypse. The only thing powerful enough, the only thing *terrifying* enough to usher in the end of days would be an invisible onslaught of bacteria, viruses, and toxins. That, and only that, would be enough to defeat the Americans.

Khalid was elated when the old man began to speak. He outlined a plan for the battlefield deployment of biological weapons if the Americans attempted to approach Baghdad. The plan was simple and foolproof, but it would require great courage and sacrifice. As the Americans attacked, the Iraqis would fall back, allowing the enemy to advance. But, the old man said, a line of courageous volunteers must remain in their positions to seed the desert sands with a combination of anthrax spores and plague-infected fleas. Then they would bury their equipment before their positions were overrun, giving the Americans no indication of what had been done. As the Americans advanced, they would be infected; when they withdrew, they would take the deadly pestilence with them. Within weeks, disease would decimate the enemy's forces, perhaps even leaping across the ocean and devastating the American homeland as well.

For the volunteers, there could be no gas masks or protective clothing—nothing that might reveal the presence of biological agents. That would mean, of course, the death of every volunteer either by bullet or by disease. But that was the price to be paid, he said; that was the price to be a martyr. The old man spoke with such quiet confidence that it seemed like a price even a child should be willing to pay—a price he himself would gladly pay for the chance to punish the Americans.

And we were willing, Khalid remembered, *every last one of us. We stood and cheered. We were ready to volunteer to the man, gladly offering our lives to halt the American advance—but then our own commanders spoke, and we were horrified.*

135

The decision to use biological weapons, they said, would be made by each individual field commander. The authority belonged to us; the decision would be ours. We were mortified—it was clear to us what they were doing. The decision would be ours—and the responsibility too. Our commanders were cowards; they were unwilling to take responsibility for such a decision. They hoped we would have the courage they themselves lacked. We knew that if it went well, they would surely take credit for the success; but if it went badly, they would deny any knowledge of our actions. We would be martyrs, yes—martyrs who died to protect our commanders' careers.

There was an astonished silence in the room. I looked at the old man, and I saw that on his face was a look of horror equaled only by my own. And all at once I understood. I understood that we were somehow brothers—not brothers of blood, but brothers of will. We were the only two men in the room with the strength of will to strike back at the Americans, regardless of the cost.

That night, Khalid sought out the old man. Their conversation was quick and direct, almost in shorthand, as though the conversation had already taken place and they were only repeating the lines. They seemed to read each other's minds; they somehow knew each other's thoughts. They were not servants of Iraq, neither one of them; they were servants of a higher cause, and that cause would not be served by this weak-kneed and futile defense against the American forces.

When Dedushka spoke, it was almost a spiritual experience for Khalid. He spoke of his native country and what he called *bushido*—the warrior spirit his people once lived by. Raw courage, self-sacrifice, unstinting obedience, and utter contempt for death—this was the way of the warrior. He spoke with disgust of the dwindling will of modern nations. He said that the warrior spirit now must reside with individuals, those with the will to do what must be done. When Khalid mentioned his Syrian birth, the discussion seemed to accelerate. There are people in Syria, Khalid told him, people with connections and power. There are men who possess this warrior spirit—men who still live by *bushido*.

On a cold, clear night less than a month later, as American bombs rained down on Baghdad, Khalid and Dedushka calmly drove across western Iraq toward the Syrian border. In the backseat was a large steamer trunk.

Khalid's connections in Syria received Dedushka as a gift from Allah. The weapon he described to them was beyond anything they had imagined possible. He was provided with a house in Damascus, a generous stipend, and a laboratory at the Scientific Studies and Research Center. He was given whatever he requested without hesitation: equipment, supplies, even an isolated testing site in the Syrian Desert. To the Syrian government, Dedushka was simply a visiting research scientist; to a handful of wealthy Arab businessmen, he was their future and their hope.

And Khalid had served the old man ever since, acting as a mediator between Dedushka and his anonymous sponsors. For years they had accepted the old man's judgment as if it were the Koran itself; but lately, things had begun to change. They were becoming impatient, demanding, even critical. Perhaps too much time had passed, and their original excitement for the old man's plan was wearing thin. Or perhaps someone else now had their ear, turning their eyes and hearts in a different direction.

Khalid wondered: Why was he summoned to Tartus on such short notice? What was the purpose of this meeting? Khalid had communicated the old man's demands—his request for transport by ship and the specifications for the temporary lab. Was any of this objectionable? These people were said to own twenty ships—was this too much to ask? Perhaps it was the timing; perhaps they resented the old man's initiating his plan without their prior approval. But if it was only a question of timing, surely they would relent. After all, what choice did they have? The plan was already under way.

Khalid was in the heart of Tartus now, driving along the waterfront and watching the dry-bulk carriers and Ro-Ro vessels that lined the wharfs like cups on a shelf. Black-and-yellow forklifts darted back and forth across the docks, lifting pallets of fertilizer and phosphate, disappearing into yawning cargo holds and then suddenly reappearing. He turned away from the waterfront and drove three blocks, then parked his car at the address he had been given.

He entered the restaurant and glanced around at the lavish surroundings: soaring sandstone arches and draping date palms towering over an oasis of white linen, silver, and imported china. He was almost instantly aware of the shabbiness of his own clothing. He straightened himself and stepped into the main dining room.

He found the man seated along the far wall, dining alone at a table for four. His elegance and manner caused him to stand out even in these exclusive surroundings. He was tall and very thin, dressed in an immaculate Western business suit of olive green. His tie was golden silk, and on the third finger of his right hand he wore an enormous gold ring to match. His skin was a milky chocolate color and perfectly smooth. He was completely bald on top, but the raven hair on the sides of his head flowed back into well-oiled curls. He ate quickly and efficiently, and when he chewed, the sinews of his jaw flexed under his skin like a stallion's flank.

He glanced up at Khalid with eyes as black as ravens. He continued to eat and jabbed at the chair opposite with his silver fork. Khalid sat down across from the man and turned his missing ear slightly away.

"It is a pleasure to see you again, Khalid."

"And you."

"Will you join me? The *mezzeh* here is excellent. Try the aubergine or the stuffed vine leaves."

Khalid shook his head. "Why did you call me here?"

"You've just arrived. At least have a little wine to wash away the dust."

"You received Dedushka's instructions? Everything was clear?"

"Quite clear."

"Have arrangements been made for the ship? And the lab—have all specifications been followed?"

"Everything has been done according to specifications—*our* specifications. Let us not forget who serves whom, Khalid."

"Dedushka says he will allow no more outside interference."

There was a pause. "We understood the message, Khalid. To be frank, we found the old man's tone a bit demanding."

"He was very disappointed by your test."

"Yes, I'm sure he was. It was regrettable, but nonetheless necessary."

"He doesn't see it that way."

The man smiled as he continued his meal. "And how does your friend see it?"

"He says it was a mistake to ever vary from his plan."

"His plan was a foolish fantasy, filled with unnecessary risks."

"He says you must be willing to take risks. He says that without great risk, there is no great glory."

The man glanced up for the first time. "Are we averse to risk, Khalid? Does our goal seem timid to you? We are willing to risk everything in this great venture—but there is a difference between a calculated risk and a foolish risk. That is what your friend must learn."

"He has perfected this weapon for sixty years."

"And are we children? Does he have the only gray hair among us? For how many years have we been working and planning in pursuit of this goal? He is but one man, and we are many. Greater minds than his are at work on this."

"He says the earthen jars were a foolish mistake. He says this failure shows that the fleas cannot be delivered in that manner."

"Is that his interpretation? We think differently. We believe this failure reveals a fundamental flaw in his entire strategy. These insects are obviously too fragile to employ for this purpose."

"The fleas will work—but the old man must accompany them. He must wait until the very last moment to load the fleas into the shells."

"He must *accompany* them," the man repeated. "We accepted your friend's fundamental premise, and we attempted a test to determine if his premise was sound. The test failed. Now—what have we lost? The cost of four excellent forgeries, that is all. There was no trail left behind, no connection to our people. Now, suppose your friend had accompanied the fleas—suppose *he* had been captured. That is what I call a risk, Khalid—a most foolish risk."

The man spotted a waiter, snapped his fingers, and pointed to his empty wine glass. He waited silently while the glass was filled, then dismissed the server with a nod. He looked across the table again.

"You must be careful, Khalid. I know that you respect this man—perhaps admire him. But you must not allow your personal feelings to cloud your judgment. Why do you suppose your friend insists on accompanying these insects? Do you think his presence is truly necessary? I will tell you what I think—I think he is a bitter old man seeking revenge, and he wants to taste his revenge with his own eyes. That is understandable—but very dangerous."

"This is not some petty revenge," Khalid said. "Dedushka has pursued this goal for sixty years—this is his *mission*."

"Does your friend think himself the only one with a mission? Are we here to serve an old man's wishes, or is he here to serve our cause? But perhaps this is too much to expect. Your friend is not really a friend at all, is he? He is not even one of us."

"The enemy of our enemy is a friend," Khalid said.

"No—the enemy of our enemy is a *tool*. An effective tool perhaps, even a faithful tool, but a tool must never be confused with a friend."

"Dedushka offers us an invincible weapon and the perfect delivery system."

"Dedushka offers us *one option*—one among many."

Khalid blinked. "You have other options?"

"Of course." Khalid watched as the man poked his fork into a deep-fried ball of falafel. "Your friend must learn to distinguish *means* from *ends*," he said. "The end he seeks is the destruction of the Americans. Very well, let him join with us in our efforts to accomplish that goal. If the means we employ are his own, all the better for him; but if the means are ours, he should still be satisfied that the end he desires has been accomplished. We serve the *cause*, Khalid. Servants of the cause must be willing to put the cause before all personal considerations."

The man drained his glass again, then looked directly at Khalid. "I must ask you something, my friend—I must ask where *your* true allegiance lies. Tell me, Khalid: Do you serve this man, or do you serve the cause?"

"I serve the cause," Khalid said weakly.

"Good—because I must tell you, there has been a change of plans."

"A change? What sort of change?"

"We have reviewed the old man's strategy carefully. We think there are elements that remain useful. There are other elements, however, that we wish to abandon. We believe they would be unreliable, and we find them unsatisfying. We intend to implement our own strategy—one that maintains the sprit of the original plan while incorporating our improvements."

Khalid felt sick to his stomach. "But—Dedushka's plan is already under way."

"That is problematic," the man said. "Your friend acted irresponsibly and without authority. We have no choice now but to accept his timing—but the plan that proceeds will be ours, not his."

Khalid stared at the tablecloth. "How will I tell him this? I don't know what he will say—what he will do."

"That, too, is problematic. We are aware of Dedushka's passion—his commitment to not only ends but means. That is why you will tell him nothing."

"What?"

"You will inform your friend that all of his demands have been met. His ship will sail from Tartus on the agreed-upon date. His lab will be located in the lower cargo hold, outfitted according to his exact specifications. That is all you will tell him; that is all he needs to know."

"Nothing more?"

"Nothing more."

"You are asking me to deceive him."

"I am instructing you to say nothing. That is quite different."

"And me," Khalid said. "What part do I have in this new plan of yours?"

"A very great part," the man said. "You will be in command when the ship sets sail. You will carry out the new plan. You will continue to serve, Khalid—you will continue to serve the *cause*."

CHAPTERSEVENTEEN

THE AISLES OF THE Chinatown apothecary were impossibly crowded. Behind a long glass counter, a wooden cupboard held hundreds of small square drawers, each with a curling brass tongue and a tiny nameplate bearing a mysterious Chinese symbol. The drawers contained all the secrets of the Chinese pharmacopoeia. There were roots, and leaves, and bundles of dried grasses tied with straw; there was garlic and figroot, bupleurum and jujube dates, magnolia buds and dried chrysanthemums; there were warty, bulbous herbs and flat, thin slices of earthy-looking fungi.

Li studied the displays of deer legs and bear gallbladders like a child in a candy shop. Across the store, Donovan and Macy stood watching him.

"So what do you think?" Donovan asked.

"I loved the Triple Eight Palace," Macy said. "These people know how to eat."

"I'm talking about Li. What's your first impression?"

"He's a remarkable old man," Macy said. "You'd never believe he's over eighty. I've got graduate students who aren't as focused and alert."

"Maybe he takes this stuff," Donovan said, picking up one of the few products with an English label. "'*Qing Chun Bao*,'" he struggled to pronounce. "'The Green Vitality Treasure. Promotes blood circulation, benefits heart and kidneys, counters fatigue. Useful for poor memory, senility, fatigue, poor resistance to disease, and strengthening the heart.'"

"If he uses it, I'm buying some," Macy said.

"What about his story? What do you think?"

"It's incredible."

"'Incredible' as in *amazing*, or 'incredible' as in *no way?*"

"Have your people been able to verify any of it?"

"The historical background all checks out. There was a Unit 731 in Manchuria during the war, and they committed all the atrocities Li described—and then some. It was as big an operation as he said—it rivaled the Manhattan Project in size and scope. They recruited some of the best medical researchers in Japan. And he's right about another thing: They got away with it. The Russians hanged a few of them, but most of them went on to successful careers in the private sector."

"What about this Sato Matsushita?"

"There's only one mention of him, in a roster of past Unit 731 scientists; that's the entire extent of what we could find. Once the Japanese knew they'd lost the war, they apparently destroyed every record they had on Unit 731."

"Can't say I blame them."

"Most of what's known has been pieced together from eyewitness testimonies, testimonies that Li says he's been collecting for sixty years—testimonies from people who are dead now, stories we have no way to corroborate."

"You think he's making them up?"

"You're supposed to answer that one."

"It's possible," Macy said. "It may be that Li is using Matsushita as a personification of evil, the way some people do when they ascribe to Hitler every atrocity committed by Nazi Germany."

"You're saying Matsushita could be mostly fiction?"

"Maybe. If you've spent your life pursuing Nazis and there's only one left, that one Nazi could begin to take on mythical proportions."

"So how do we separate myth from reality?"

"We keep talking to Li," she said.

Donovan looked at her. "Hey, I really appreciate this."

Macy turned away. "I'm not doing it for you."

They crossed an aisle stocked with iodine-colored jars of astragalus and ligusticum powders, and another lined with clear plastic bins of dried, crumbling leaves. Li stood by the long glass counter, shaking his head in delight.

"Here's something you won't find in your local London chemist's shop," Li said. "Deer antler velvet. It increases stamina, strengthens the immune system, and even enhances athletic performance."

"Thinking of trying out for the Olympics?"

"You never know," he said. "Did you take note of the final medal count in Athens? China is rapidly gaining on the United States, you know—I could be just the one to push them over the top."

"Do you really use any of this stuff?" Donovan asked.

"Of course. For a cold I take *yin chiao*, just as my people have for more than a century. For headache: chrysanthemum flower tea. For occasional constipation—"

"Hold it—that's more than I need to know."

"We were wondering about the secret of your vitality," Macy said.

"Ah. Is that what you two were whispering about over in the corner?" He looked at each of them and smiled. "The secret is: clean Christian living."

"I figured you for a Buddhist," Donovan said.

"Buddhism, Taoism, and Confucianism are the three largest religious traditions in China," Li said. "Most people practice a combination of all three: a little ancestor worship, a little family piety, and a dash of the divine thrown in for good measure. Sort of a vague, eclectic hodgepodge—like most of the religion in your own country. I was educated through the London Missionary Society school in Nanking. It was my dream to one day become a missionary doctor. The war changed all that; the war ended the dreams of a lot of people."

Just then, a small, smiling woman stepped from behind the counter and approached. Her eyes were large and black and surrounded by a paper fan of wrinkles that seemed to flutter when she smiled. Her hair was pulled back in a simple bun, and her skin was as smooth and translucent as vellum. Her manner was quiet and dignified, almost noble; her peaceful face radiated compassion and sadness at the same time. She said a few words to Li; he nodded and turned to Donovan.

"She wants to know if you would like to be examined."

Donovan did a double take. "Me?"

"She referred to 'the big one.' I believe that would be you."

"Is she a doctor?" Macy asked.

"She is a practitioner of traditional Chinese medicine—an herbalist, perhaps an acupuncturist as well."

"Why me?" Donovan said.

"Practitioners of traditional Chinese medicine are quite intuitive. Perhaps she senses something wrong about you."

"What a gift," Macy said.

"Is this a joke? What am I supposed to do, step into the back room and drop my drawers for some quack?"

Li winced and looked at Macy. "Does he *try* to be offensive?"

"No, it comes naturally for him. That's *his* gift."

Li turned to Donovan again. "In the first place, she is not asking you to 'drop your drawers.' You're thinking in terms of Western medicine, which is much more invasive; you won't have to undress, and she promises not to cut you open with any surgical instruments. In the second place, this is not quackery. There is a growing regard for traditional Chinese medicine among Western doctors. Some of your largest American pharmaceutical companies are studying herbal remedies, searching for the active ingredients in some of our ancient cures."

"Go on, Nathan," Macy said. "Let's find out what's wrong with you."

"Shut up, Macy."

"Her examination room is in the back," Li said, "just through that curtain. It would only take a few short minutes."

"Tell her thanks anyway."

"Come on, don't be such a baby."

Li's eyes drifted away in boredom. "I was told that you federal agents are fearless—walking through fire, facing a hail of bullets, that sort of thing. Apparently the stories are a bit of an exaggeration."

"All *right*," Donovan grumbled. "If it's the only way to get you two off my back."

Li nodded politely and spoke a few words; the woman smiled and led the way through the curtain with the three of them following behind.

Li leaned close to Macy. "He's rather easy to goad, isn't he?"

She nodded. "It's a guy thing."

The back of the shop was partitioned into two separate examining rooms by simple white sheets. The woman motioned for Donovan to sit down; she took a chair across from him and began to look him over as if he were a prospective plow horse. She turned his head from side to side, felt his throat, and peered into his mouth. She motioned for him to exhale, then shook her head with a look of disgust.

"She's right about that," Macy whispered.

"This is humiliating," Donovan said.

The woman spoke a single word.

Li translated: "Quiet."

The woman took Donovan's left hand in hers and turned it palm-side up. She placed both thumbs on his wrist, closed her eyes, and began to gently rub.

"What's she doing?" Donovan asked.

"She's taking your pulse," Li said. "Your pulse will tell her about the condition of your internal organs."

Donovan rolled his eyes.

A few minutes later, she abruptly dropped Donovan's hand and nodded confidently. She turned to Li and began her summary report.

"She says that in the Chinese theory of medicine, diseases are divided into hot and cold types. Apparently, you are afflicted with the hot type. Your breath is foul and your eyes are bloodshot; these are indications of overheated blood, the result of overwork and stress. Also, a poor diet."

Donovan glared. "You threw that in."

"Think of me as a physician's assistant."

The woman rose from her chair now and, still speaking rapid-fire, exited through the curtain and into the store.

"Her prescription is a tea made of American ginseng," Li said. "This will cool your blood. Not Asian ginseng—that would have exactly the opposite effect. She will prepare a prescription for you now. This concludes your examination."

Donovan rose. "Do I get a little sucker with a shovel on the end?"

Li frowned at Macy. "What is he going on about?"

"Never mind. The heat affects his mind too."

In the shop, the woman placed a piece of paper on an old bronze balance and weighed out the proper amount, handing the concoction to Donovan in a small paper sack. He held it away like a doggy cleanup bag. "What do I do with this?"

"You make tea with it and you drink it, of course."

"Does it really do anything?"

"Traditional Chinese remedies are time-tested," Li said. "Five thousand years ago, the great emperor Shen Nung was the first to research and catalog herbal medicines. According to legend, he personally consumed 365 different medicinal plants over the course of his life to test their effects."

"What happened to him?"

"He turned green and died from a toxic overdose."

"Of which one?"

"No one knows. Fortunately, he discovered tea before he died. Are we finished here? Let's take a walk."

It was dark now, but the sidewalks were still as crowded as the apothecary shelves. Most of the street peddlers had closed up after a ten- or twelve-hour day, but the shops and markets remained open, casting their orange and yellow lights halfway across the street. The throng had thinned just enough to allow them to walk three abreast, but the going was slow. Li flowed through the mob effortlessly, like a bee through a busy hive, and Macy followed at his side. Donovan found progress a good deal slower; his broad shoulders were like a moving barricade, and irritated passersby seemed to constantly rebound off him like pinballs off a bumper.

"I'm pleased that you could join us for dinner," Li said to Macy. "Your choice of the shark fin soup was excellent; it relieves me to know that not all of your people are barbarians."

"I told Nathan, 'The Chinese know how to eat.'"

"It's a very important part of our culture. You know, Confucius divorced his wife because she couldn't cook." Li paused to allow a change of topic. "So tell me, what did you think of my story?"

"I think you're a master storyteller," she said.

Li smiled. "A polite evasion."

"Not at all. I was simply commenting on your delivery."

"And my content? As an expert in the psychology of terrorism, I assume you're here to help the authorities determine the possible veracity of my story."

"Something like that, yes."

"I assure you, the story is true in every detail."

"No one's questioning your honesty, Li. No one doubts what Matsushita did in the past. The question is what he's likely to do in the future—if he's still around. When did you last see Matsushita alive?"

"In 1942."

"And you haven't seen him since?"

"No—though not for want of trying."

"Then how can you be sure he's alive?"

Li paused. "I'm afraid you won't like my answer."

"Try me."

"I know Sato Matsushita is alive the same way that practitioner knows Nathan has overheated blood."

"Li—that was just a guess."

"I assure you, it was more than that. I can't expect a Western scientist to appreciate this, but there is such a thing as *intuition*."

"You're wrong," she said. "As a psychologist, I believe in intuition. But you're dealing with the FBI here, Li. They've got limited time and resources—and you're asking them to commit those resources just because of your *hunch*."

"I've never liked that word," Li said with a frown. "All right—then let me suggest a more rational reason: Suppose a man is thought to be dead—but at the scene of a crime, his fingerprints are discovered. What would the authorities conclude?"

"That the man is still alive."

"Precisely—and this is what the FBI must understand: The Oriental rat fleas in TriBeCa were the fingerprints of Sato Matsushita—they could belong to no other. That reason alone should be enough to convince them that the man is still alive."

"And you're convinced that even after *six decades*, Matsushita still intends to use his plague weapon against the United States."

"If you knew the man the way I do, you would have no doubt either."

They stepped aside to let a street sweeper pass, collecting the fish heads, orange peels, and vegetable matter that choked the gutters from the day's commerce. Steam rose off the pavement as he passed, bringing with it a smell both sweet and foul.

Li glanced over at Macy. "You know, your presence here tonight gives me hope."

"Why is that?"

"The fact that they sent you tells me the FBI is at least concerned."

"They're definitely concerned—this kind of scenario is something we've been talking about for a long time. A lot of people today are worried about nuclear weapons; in my field, some of us are more concerned about biological attacks. Nuclear weapons aren't easy to make—not even the simple ones. It takes a lot of technical expertise, and the materials are extremely hard to come by. But any chemistry major with ten thousand dollars' worth of equipment and a lab the size of a bedroom can make herself a serious biological arsenal. That's what keeps me awake at night."

"Your fears are well founded," Li said. "A bomb or a chemical weapon destroys only what it comes in immediate contact with; a biological weapon spreads from one person to the next, vastly multiplying its effect."

"Several countries have developed biological weapons," Macy said, "but there are good reasons no one uses them. They're messy—no one can tell when the wind will shift and blow the pathogen back on you. They're uncontainable—if you start a real pandemic, how will you keep it from infecting your own people? And most of all, they're *taboo*—that's the biggest deterrent of all. There's an almost universal abhorrence of biological weapons, and nobody wants to be the first to use one."

"Yes—an *almost* universal abhorrence."

"But not in the case of Sato Matsushita."

"No."

Macy stopped and turned to him. "Help me understand that, Li—help me understand Matsushita the way you do. What's his motive? What's his driving force? What would make him willing to do the unthinkable?"

"It's really rather simple," Li said. "A man finds it easier to do the unthinkable once the unthinkable has been done to him."

CHAPTER**EIGHTEEN**

Japan, August 1945

IT WAS MORE THAN a mile by foot from the cottage to the University Hospital, but Sato didn't mind the daily walk. It gave him a chance to look at his new home. The seaside metropolis was now the eighth-largest city in all of Japan, home to a third of a million people, but it didn't look it. It was a peaceful, sprawling city, spread over six islands in the Ota River delta. Sato had arrived from Ping Fan by airplane less than a week before. From above, the islands of the city looked like the fingers of a crooked hand. The river bottom soil was rich black loam, where wheat and rice grew almost unattended. In the low, sheltering mountains that surrounded the city, fat yellow silkworms leisurely spun the fabric of the gods.

The mountains seemed to separate the city not only from the rest of Japan but from the rest of the world—from the fire, from the suffering, from the deprivation—from the war itself and the daily bombings that devastated so many of Japan's metropolitan areas. The city was like a Shangri-la, hidden away from all the plagues of civilization and all the ravages of war. Everyone had his or her own pet theory of why the city had been spared: Some said the city had no military significance, though in fact it was headquarters to the Second General Army and was an important port. Others believed it was because their citizens had so many relatives in the United States. Still others claimed that it was because of the city's great beauty; the Americans, they said, wished to preserve the city to use as a residential area after the war.

Sato didn't care. He was just grateful for this tiny oasis in the midst of so much horror—horror that he himself had been a part of until just a week ago. He thought of his three years of research at Unit 731. It never failed to bring a wave of—what was it? Shame? Guilt? But why should he feel this way? What had he done but his duty? He was recruited to serve his emperor, just as hundreds of thousands of his countrymen had been. And that's what he had done—serve his emperor. Unit 731 itself was established by royal decree; Ishii was a friend of the emperor himself. What more could any Japanese soldier do than serve the purposes of His Imperial Majesty?

It was not his place to question his superiors; it was not his place to challenge the overall strategy of the war. There were reasons for the things that took place, high and hidden reasons. It was war, and in war regrettable but necessary things took place. It was not as though he himself had done them—not his true self, anyway. In war, the soldier assumed the costume of war along with the duties of war. When war ended, the soldier discarded both and returned to his true nature again.

Besides, it wasn't as though they were human beings—they were Chinese. They were allies of the Americans, enemies of Japan. When Doolittle's bombers first dared to touch the skirts of Tokyo, it was the Chinese who received them with open arms. It was Chinese air bases that now launched American B-29s on their nightly raids, raining fire bombs and incendiaries on the wood-and-paper houses of Japan's cities.

It was war, and China was the enemy. And if China itself was the enemy, were not the individual Chinese? In war there were so many complexities, enough to drive a man mad; better for the simple soldier to focus on the duty at hand.

But Sato was sick to death of duty. He was secretly relieved when the Imperial Navy refused to release its I-400 submarines; he was relieved when he realized that Operation Cherry Blossoms at Night would not take place. For three years he had perfected his plague bomb, and it was a triumph of both biology and engineering—but to use it against a major city—against the Americans . . . No one knew what the full extent of the devastation would be. More important, no one knew what the Americans would do in response. An invasion of the Japanese homeland now seemed inevitable; farmers and peasants were now training at the seashore with pointed sticks as weapons, determined to resist to the last man—to the last child. How much worse would it be if the Americans came with a burning desire to wreak vengeance on Japan's own civilian population?

And when the Russians invaded Manchuria, Sato was relieved most of all. Then he knew that his duty was at an end; then he knew that Unit 731 would be destroyed, along with every trace of its research. He was relieved when Ishii granted his request for reassignment to the University Hospital here, where he could at last be reunited with his beloved Emiko. They now lived together in the heart of the city, in little more than a lean-to on a corner of his friend's property, but it was worth it. Here the war seemed already over. Here the healing had already begun, and Emiko would be a part of it. Her tender heart and gentle spirit were like a soothing balm for his soul.

He yawned. He had slept little the night before. There had been three air-raid sirens since midnight, but no one paid much attention. They were just a reminder that a war was still raging in some faraway land—but the mournful wail was still enough to interrupt sleep. Just an hour ago, a single American plane had been spotted high overhead, but it passed by without incident. Probably a weather plane, he thought. Perhaps taking reconnaissance photos.

He wondered about the time. He looked up at the university's clock tower, then remembered that the clock had ceased to work two weeks ago. He rounded a corner and started down a sidewalk, with a tall brick building on his left. A man passed on his right and stepped out into the street. Sato turned and called after him.

"Excuse me. Do you know the time?"

The man turned with a look of derision and pointed at the clock tower.

Sato shook his head. "It doesn't work. Hasn't for weeks now."

"That's Hiroshima for you," he said, pulling out his own pocket watch. "I've got 8:15."

Sato glanced at the tower. By the strangest coincidence, the clock on the tower was stopped at exactly 8:15.

At that precise moment, a blinding white light filled the street where the man was standing, followed by a blast of enormous heat. Sato's exposed skin stung and blistered; even behind the shelter of the brick wall, it was like opening the door of a furnace. The man in the street wore a white shirt and dark pants. The pants were instantly incinerated, but the shirt somehow remained. His thick black hair vanished, and his skin turned a crackled brown, like the mud when a pond evaporates. He opened his mouth, but no sound came out. For the first few seconds, everything was utterly silent—then a low, rumbling wall of noise hit, and with it a shock wave so powerful that everything in its path seemed to crumble away. The man himself was like a column of cigarette ash, standing one moment and then disappearing in a blast of wind.

The sky was an eerie yellow, and the air was filled with flying debris: stones, timbers, chunks of pavement, enormous sections of tiled roof and concrete wall, objects so huge that it seemed incomprehensible that they could be airborne for even an instant. Roofs were ripped off houses as if they were paper; telephone poles exploded like bombs.

Debris began to rain down on Sato now, pieces of brick and glass and wood from the wall beside him. He didn't know whether to run from the wall or hide behind it. There was no time to think anyway, and nothing to think about. Nothing like this had ever happened in Hiroshima before; nothing like this had ever happened in all the world.

He collapsed to his knees and covered his head with his arms. The rumbling grew in intensity until the sensation was shattering, until Sato was sure the universe itself would shake apart—but a moment later it subsided like an enormous passing train. When he looked up, the street was empty, and everything was preternaturally still. Then, from the opposite direction, the wind came back. Like a movie projector rewinding, the scene before him reversed itself; the city's debris came whirling back in winds of cyclonic force, bringing with it entire trees and pieces of houses from outlying areas.

It also brought fire. Flames leaped from building to building in blow-torch blasts, consuming every wooden thing in their path. The wind continued for what seemed like an eternity, and the sky above was a swirling maelstrom of smoke and dust in a haze of purple and red and brown. High above, a narrow column of smoke rose into the sky, swelling into a pinkish cloud at the top.

Sato staggered to his feet, wondering what to do first. He thought of his patients at the University Hospital—those who survived the blast would need his help now more than ever. There would be wounded and dying everywhere in the city, more than he could ever—

Emiko.

Sato imagined his sister in the tiny lean-to. There was no brick wall nearby for her, nothing to shelter her from the searing heat. He ran to the street and looked in the direction of the blast. He started back toward the city, into the heart of the devastation, his mind too frantic to even pray.

Blackened figures passed him everywhere, flooding out of the city. Some had no noses or ears; some had faces so swollen that they had no features at all, like mannequins in a clothing store. Some looked as though they had been dipped in blood; many were charred beyond recognition, and their flesh hung from their limbs in long curling strips. They held their arms in front of them and walked silently, without expression, without tears, like the dead returning to life—or the living on their way to the grave.

Sato knew what the blast was now; he knew what had happened—it was an atomic bomb. Japan's own scientists had spoken of the possibility for years now and had pursued it without success. Now America had perfected the weapon—and they had used it, without mercy and without hesitation. Sato knew that most of the people he saw would be dead by nightfall—and no scientist in the world knew for certain what the next few weeks would bring.

Surreally, it began to rain. The rising blast had taken with it half of the water from the Ota River, and great drops of water, black with dust and ash, fell like blobs of ink and pelted the half-naked and smoldering bodies, leaving long, gritty streaks on the skin that remained. The drops sizzled and hissed when they hit. Sato wondered if they were poisonous or contaminated. He wiped at his arms, and the flesh turned a grimy gray.

Sato stopped a man stumbling past. The outline of his nose was stenciled on his right cheek. "I'm looking for Emiko Matsushita," he said desperately. "Have you seen her?" The man looked at Sato as though he spoke a different language. He turned silently away and continued on his journey to nowhere.

At the Ota, Sato saw hundreds of burned and wounded people lining its banks, one by one leaping from the ledge and plunging through the wine-red scum that covered the remaining water. Few came up again; those who did slowly rose to the surface facedown. Each saw the fate of the one who jumped before him, but no one seemed to care. Anything was better than the burning.

The hypocenter of the blast was easy for Sato to trace. Near the university there were buildings still partially intact, with standing walls and portions of roofs still in place. Closer to the center, there was nothing but fragments of walls and blackened beams jutting up like the masts of a burned-out ship. Near the heart of the city, there was nothing left at all. The ground was perfectly level and covered in a thick layer of powder, as though a gigantic pestle had ground the city to dust. The periphery of the city was all in flames; at the center, there was no fire. There were no buildings, no statues, no trees, no bodies—no sign that life had ever existed there at all. It looked like the pit of an abandoned hell. From every crack in the ground, smoke and steam rose into the sky, turning the sun into a crimson ball.

He took his first bearings from whatever landmarks he could still recognize—the bend in the river, the Aioi Bridge—then he worked outward in circles, searching for the first recognizable outline of a street or structure. He found a main intersection and headed north, toward the mountains. He recognized a bank by its still-intact vault; he remembered its location and proceeded east. He continued in this way, working outward from the center, slowly picking his way through the smoldering rubble.

It took hours to find the cottage—or the place where it once stood. By nightfall he had located the property, which was nothing but a pile of smoldering refuse. In the corner of the lot lay a section of corrugated tin, now scorched and gunmetal blue. He scrambled across the pile of stone and timbers and pulled at the metal sheet; it crumbled in his hands like a rusted can. Underneath was a single figure, charred as black as coal. It was lying on its back with its knees drawn up in a sitting position. The two hands were raised to the face, covering both eyes.

Sato stared. It must be the wrong house, the wrong property. He could be mistaken; it was so hard to tell. Everything was in ruins; everything looked the same. He could be on the opposite side of town for all he knew. He was new to the city; how could he be certain? That was it—it was all a mistake. He would turn, and go, and search in another place.

It is not her. In the whole universe, it was the only thing Sato still knew. *It cannot be her.*

He reached down and took the figure by the wrists. He tugged; the limbs were rigid and hard. Then there was a cracking sound, and the cupped hands pulled away from the face. Underneath were two pale yellow circles surrounding half-open eyes. He looked into the eyes, and he knew.

He collapsed on the rubble and looked up into the sky. It was a strangely beautiful evening, without a cloud in the sky. He thought about weeping, but it was a faraway thought, like a man recalling a distant memory. Perhaps he should scream—but he had no anger, no rage, no feeling at all. He looked deeper into his soul; nothing was there. It was empty, abandoned. It was just a pile of smoldering timbers, a ruin of broken stones and twisted steel.

He looked down at Emiko. He wondered what sort of impotent god had allowed her a last split second to cover her eyes. What a useless gesture, what a laughable gift. But the gods themselves were laughable, weren't they, raining down fire from heaven while they sat idly by? Or were they idle? Perhaps they were just senile old men, straining to remember the names of long-forgotten mortals, eating the children's food but unable to give anything in return.

What kind of weapon could do this? He wondered about its size, its structure, its workings. Most of all, he wondered about the people who would use such a weapon. Did they know what it would do? Surely not. Surely it was the only one of its kind—or perhaps there had been no time to test the weapon in advance. Surely tomorrow, when the Americans examined photographs of the destruction, they would cover their own eyes in horror and shame.

Surely they knew that Hiroshima was a peaceful city, not an industrial center like Kobe or Osaka. Surely they knew that the population was largely civilian. It was a favored city, a protected city . . . Suddenly, Sato understood the nature of Hiroshima's "favored" status. The city was spared just as the fattest hen is spared for the feast. The city had been set aside for this specific fate. Emiko too—yes, Emiko too. She was scheduled long ago to die on this specific day, at precisely 8:15 in the morning—not by the will of the gods but by the will of the Americans.

He thought about the men who had dropped this weapon. Were they soldiers, conscripted into the army against their will, or were they eager volunteers? Were they scientists, just like him? Had they spent the last three years of their lives perfecting this device? And if the weapon had not been used, would they have been secretly relieved? Or did the weapon, once created, have a life of its own? Did the weapon demand to be used, simply because it existed?

In war there are so many complexities, he thought, *enough to drive a man mad.*

Quite mad.

He closed his eyes, collapsed on the rubble, and fell asleep.

CHAPTER NINETEEN

MACY FOUND HERSELF STANDING motionless on the busy sidewalk like a rock in the center of a stream. She wondered how long she had been standing there, lost in the details of Li's description.

"Li, how do you know all this?"

"That's what I keep asking," Donovan said.

"I mean, a lot has been written about the experiences of people in Hiroshima and Nagasaki—but how do you know all the personal details? How do you know about Matsushita's own experience?"

"From Matsushita himself," Li said. "After the war, Matsushita surrendered to the Soviets. In 1949 the Soviets held a war crimes trial in the city of Khabarovsk in eastern Siberia. Twelve former members of Unit 731 were prosecuted for crimes against the Russian people—Matsushita was one of the defendants. His presence was only for the sake of appearance, of course—the Russians understood that Matsushita was far too valuable an asset to hang over some petty offenses against the Chinese.

"The evidence presented at the Khabarovsk trial was based upon eighteen volumes of interrogations and depositions collected from the defendants over the previous four years. I was able to obtain those eighteen volumes; to my knowledge, they are the only copies in existence. In them,

Matsushita tells everything—about his plague research, about Hiroshima, about the loss of his beloved sister."

"What was the outcome of the trial?" Donovan asked.

"The defendants were given light sentences—two years of hard labor for most. Half of them returned to Japan within a decade. No one was executed."

"And Matsushita?"

"He went to work for the Soviet Union, as a pioneer in their budding biological warfare program. A trophy catch, wouldn't you say?"

Li looked at Macy. "So what is your opinion, Dr. Monroe—am I insane or not?"

"No one ever said you were—"

"Nonsense," he said, waving off her denial. "A crusty old man appears out of nowhere, with tales of ghosts from the distant past who have returned to wreak their vengeance . . . If the possibility of my insanity didn't occur to you, I would be disappointed."

"You're not insane," Macy said. "I wish you were."

Li smiled. "Why, Dr. Monroe, are you coming to faith?"

"The history of terrorism is divided into three phases," she said. "In the sixties and seventies, terrorist organizations like the IRA focused their attacks against a single enemy, against a single nation. In the seventies and eighties, terrorists began to operate internationally, but still under the sponsorship of a country—like Libya or Iran. But in the nineties, everything changed. Terrorist organizations began to operate independently, without any responsibility to anyone. Modern terrorists don't take hostages; they don't negotiate; they don't make demands. They just kill. It's not about what they hope to achieve; it's about what's going on inside of them."

"Then Sato Matsushita is a man ahead of his time."

She nodded. "Usually we're lucky. When a man goes off the deep end, he usually loses it completely—but every now and then, there's someone who loses all sense of empathy and compassion but still keeps his rational abilities. Those are the dangerous ones; those are the ones we have to watch out for."

Li turned to Donovan. "Your lovely companion is beginning to believe," he said. "What about you?"

"She believes the motive," Donovan said. "In a criminal investigation there are three things we look for: means, motive, and opportunity."

"So we have a motive," Li said. "And opportunities for a terrorist attack are everywhere, as I'm sure you know. That leaves only the question of means."

"A biological attack is no small undertaking," Donovan said. "A lot of people have tried it and failed. Even if Matsushita wanted to, are you sure he has the means to pull it off?"

"I'm quite certain."

"Well, I'm not."

"I know someone who might convince you."

"Who?"

"His name is Pasha Mirovik. I'm told he lives not far from here—I have no idea where. Your people will have to help with this; I believe it's something of a state secret."

"Okay—I'll check it out in the morning."

"Let's call it an evening," Macy said. "I'm teaching a summer session, and I have to give an exam in the morning."

Li smiled. "It would be a privilege to be a student of yours."

"I've enjoyed being one of yours. Thanks for the story."

"I'm full of stories. Next time I'll tell you another."

Macy shook his hand and started down the sidewalk.

"Wait up," Donovan said, catching up to her in two long strides. "I'll walk you to your car."

"I don't have my car. I took the subway."

"Then I'll walk you to the station."

"Are you looking out for me now, Nathan? Please don't." She wheeled and disappeared into the flood of oncoming pedestrians.

Donovan watched until the tip of her head was no longer visible, then turned back to Li. The old man had been watching them, observing. Donovan felt a flush of anger.

"Seen enough?" he asked.

"Oh, not nearly enough. How long were the two of you married?"

"Who said we were married?"

Li rolled his eyes. "Please."

Donovan paused. "Five years. How did you know?"

"There is a certain *tension* between you, the kind no two strangers can ever achieve. How does the old saying go? 'Heaven hath no rage like love to hatred turned.'"

"Confucius?"

"No, William Congreve—a fellow countryman. Perhaps you're more familiar with the second half of the quotation: 'And hell hath no fury like the wrath of a woman scorned.'"

"I know that part," Donovan said. The two men turned and started slowly down the sidewalk again.

"Care to talk about it?" Li asked.

"No."

"That seems unfair. I've told you some of my very best stories, and yet you refuse to tell me one of yours."

"You asked me to listen to your stories," Donovan said.

"A minor point. You know, I like Dr. Monroe very much. Will she meet with us again?"

"For now."

"*Macy*—what a curious name. Like the large department store?"

Donovan smiled. "I'll have to remember that one."

"The hostility between you seems a bit one-sided."

"What?"

"Dr. Monroe—Macy—she seems to harbor more anger than you do. Not that you're short of anger, mind you; I'd say you're positively seething with it. But she seems like less of an angry person—her anger seems to be directed only at you. Would you say this is true?"

"I wouldn't say."

They passed an alley, and there was a flurry of movement in the shadows. "Let me show you something," Li said. "I think you'll find this interesting."

They walked several yards into the alley, to the point where the street-lights could no longer penetrate and visual details disappeared into silhouettes. The alley seemed old and narrow, with a cobblestone pavement that dipped in the center, allowing a rivulet of runoff from the street to trickle down the middle. The walls were lined with wooden crates and old appliances, the castoffs of a dozen former shops and businesses. Along the left wall, near a wooden doorway, was a row of black plastic garbage bags.

Li lifted one of the bags, and two plump rats scurried out into the center of the alley. They were big—a full eighteen inches from nose to tail. They were brown in color, with sooty white underbellies. They were shaped like elongated pears, with bulbous ends that tapered to a point at the snout. In the half-light of the alley, their eyes were black and glistening.

"*Rattus norvegicus*," Li announced, "commonly known as the Norwegian brown rat. There are fifty-one species of *Rattus*, but this is the only one you're likely to find in New York City—it has chased away all of the others. Watch this."

He stamped at the rats with his right foot. Instead of fleeing, they rose up on their hind legs and made a hissing sound. "Aggressive, aren't they? Rats are very territorial; they're letting us know who the boss is here."

"They could use a cat," Donovan said.

"It wouldn't last long. These rats would make a meal of an ordinary cat."

"They eat cats?"

"They've been known to eat dogs too—even pigs. A rat will eat virtually anything—they're omnivorous. They eat naturally occurring foods, of course—by some estimates, a third of the world's food supply is consumed by rats. They eat grains and fruits and vegetables, but they especially love garbage—our garbage. Some experts believe that rats develop 'local food dialects.' That means they develop a taste for the ethnic foods of the neighborhood in which they live. These are Chinatown rats—a particularly fortunate group."

Li replaced the garbage bag, and the rats darted behind it again. He wiped his hands on his trousers and turned to Donovan.

"Rats depend upon human beings for their survival," he said. "That means they're never far away. They live in our basements, our attics, our sewers— perhaps under the floorboards of your own house. They can fit most anywhere.

An adult rat can weigh up to two pounds, but it can fit through a hole less than an inch wide. Their skeletons are able to collapse, you see."

"I grew up on a farm," Donovan said. "As a boy I once helped my dad tear up the old threshing floor in the barn. When we lifted the boards, there were hundreds of them underneath."

"They breed prolifically. Some say there is a rat for every person in New York City."

They started back toward the street now. The streetlights, though dim, seemed blinding in contrast with the darkness of the alley. At the corner they turned left and continued down the sidewalk. It was getting late now, and only a few stragglers remained.

"Thanks for the nature lesson," Donovan said.

"Oh, it was much more than that. I wanted to make three important observations: Rats live near humans, rats can go anywhere, and in a city this size, there could be millions. The Norwegian brown rat, you see, was responsible for transporting the fleas that decimated medieval Europe. If Sato Matsushita were to disperse plague-infected fleas in New York, these rats would carry the disease to every corner of the city."

Li stopped in front of an old brick building. "This is it," he said.

"What?"

"This is where I live."

Donovan looked up. The building looked ancient, decrepit, like most of the buildings in Chinatown. "This isn't a hotel."

"New York hotels are a bit pricey, especially for an extended visit. I'm staying in a *gong si fong*."

"A what?"

"A kind of boardinghouse. Very cozy, very inexpensive. Would you like to come up?"

There was an open doorway that led to a tiny foyer, illumined only by the streetlights from outside. On the left wall was a long-abandoned door-bell system for the apartments above; nothing remained but a tarnished brass skeleton with holes where black buttons once protruded. The wooden stairway was steep and hollow sounding and awkwardly narrow.

Donovan's shoulders almost brushed both walls as he climbed from stair to stair. At the top was a brief landing, and then the corridor turned left. It was dark except for a single lightbulb at the opposite end; the glow from the bare bulb gave the hallway a haunting, tunnel-like effect.

Beneath the lightbulb was a door. Li used a key to unlock a small padlock, and they both stepped inside.

They were standing in the living room of a one-bedroom apartment. The living room was divided into four smaller sections by sheets of unpainted plywood.

"I love what you've done with the place," Donovan said.

"It isn't all mine. Let me show you my room."

Li slid aside a plywood panel and gestured for Donovan to enter. Donovan had to duck and turn sideways to fit through the opening. The space inside was smaller than some closets, no more than six by six. Most of the space was taken up by a bunk bed; there was no other furniture in the room.

"I'm fortunate to have a window," Li said.

Donovan looked. The outside of the glass had probably never been cleaned—it was like looking through waxed paper. Under the window was the only shelf in the room. It held a Bible and a coffee mug with a red toothbrush inside. Beside it was a dimpled black case, the kind that might carry a small musical instrument. Li silently took the case and slid it under the bed beside a canvas duffle.

"Which bunk is yours?" Donovan asked.

"I selected the bottom—then my roommate arrived and assigned me the top. I had a prior claim, but he was younger and larger. I thought it best not to press the point."

Donovan sat down on the bottom bunk. He could lean forward and touch the opposite wall. From the plywood panels, a series of twenty-penny nails projected, providing the only closet space in the room.

"How many people live here?"

"Eight—though I believe it holds ten."

Ten bodies packed into this dump? Donovan had seen these places before. Some greedy landlord bought a substandard apartment, then divvied it up into four or five bathroom stalls and rented each one for half the going rate. The landlord made a killing, and the renters didn't complain. They couldn't—half of them were illegal aliens.

"Li, this place is illegal."

"But affordable."

"I can't let you stay here. How would it look for a guest of the federal government to be staying in illegal housing?"

"What does the federal government suggest?"

"We'll put you up in a hotel. There are a couple not far from 26 Fed that the Bureau uses for visitors."

"What about the food?"

"You can eat in the hotel restaurant. Just sign it to your room."

"Yes, but what about the *food*?"

"Stop whining," Donovan said. "It's a step up from England."

"But it's a step down from Chinatown. Besides, I already know my way around here."

"I don't. I get lost every time I come down here."

"Well, I certainly don't want to put the whole burden on you. There must be some solution that would be equitable for both of us. Let's think for a moment." Li stood there, staring at Donovan.

Donovan considered the time he had already wasted picking his way through the crowded streets of Chinatown. He thought about his three-hour field trip to the Cloisters, seventy blocks past Columbia. He thought about Li's annoying habit of selecting meeting sites for their educational value instead of proximity, and he wondered what his next choice might be—Boston? Then he thought about the realities of depositing the old man at a hotel: picking him up, dropping him off, making sure he ate enough lousy American food . . . *Forget it*, Donovan thought. *The only way to reduce the hassle is to keep him close at hand.*

"Why don't you stay with me for a few days?" Donovan offered.

Li brightened. "What a splendid idea! It would be so convenient, and it would give us much more time to *talk*."

Li was packed in an instant; everything fit into the canvas duffel. As

Donovan stepped into the doorway, a young Chinese man bumped into him. He was a head taller than Li, almost as tall as Donovan—but he had only half of Donovan's mass.

"Ah, my roommate," Li said. "Just in time to see me off."

Donovan and the young man squared off in the narrow doorway. Donovan locked eyes with him. "Do you speak English?"

The man nodded.

Donovan dropped the canvas duffel and stepped to the window. He shoved it open, then turned back to the lower bunk. He rolled up the mattress and bedding and stuffed it out the window; it disappeared silently into the alley below. He returned to the doorway and glared into the young man's astonished face.

"Now *you've* got the top bunk," he said.

CHAPTER TWENTY

DONOVAN PUSHED OPEN THE door and flipped on the light. Li stood in the doorway, peering inside. The central room was average in size and perfectly square. It was almost empty, except for a brownish-gold three-cushion sofa that slumped toward the center; one of the cushions was patched with crisscrossed pieces of gray duct tape. The sofa faced a small TV stand with spindly wooden legs that tapered to brass tips. On top of the stand was a nineteen-inch television with two chrome rabbit ears jutting out at the twelve and two o'clock positions; on the end of one was a crumpled piece of aluminum foil. From the center of the ceiling, a hanging lamp dangled from a length of tarnished chain. It was octagonal, like an Oriental lantern, but with panels of pebbled yellow glass framed in scrolling black metal. It was easily the ugliest fixture Li had ever seen.

"You consider this an improvement on the *gong si fong*?"

"There's no place like home," Donovan said. "Come on in."

Li took a step back and glanced from side to side. "There are prison bars on your windows," he said. "Is there something you're not telling me?"

"They're just for security."

Li glanced around the room. "If you don't mind my asking—what do you have to secure here?"

"Are you coming in or not?"

Li placed one toe on the matted carpet as if he were testing the thickness of ice.

"You can have your own room," Donovan said.

"Lucky me."

"Don't they have security windows in London?"

"Yes—in the bad sections."

"Well, the South Bronx is a tough neighborhood."

"I noticed that. There seem to be a number of dilapidated buildings."

"Just like Chinatown."

"Chinatown is simply old—a third of the buildings were built before 1900. Here the buildings just seem neglected."

"This part of the Bronx was practically abandoned thirty years ago. The whole borough was going under. Owners set fire to the buildings for the insurance money—there were twelve thousand fires a year here in the seventies. The city figured it would cost half as much to just gut the buildings and rebuild the insides as it would to knock them down and start over. The insides look pretty good; just the outsides look bad."

"Just the outsides," Li mumbled. "And this type of housing is legal?"

"Sure."

"Whereas the *gong si fong* was not?"

"Li—there were eight people living in a one-bedroom apartment."

"So the deciding factor is population density? If that's the case, New York City should be illegal."

"Will you stop complaining?"

"I'm not complaining. I'm just . . . readjusting."

"You should feel right at home here. In Chinatown you had what— Chinese, Koreans, Vietnamese?"

"Also Indonesians, Burmese, Malaysians, and Fujians."

"Well, here you've got Irish, Italians, Hispanics, and Russians. Take your pick."

"Who were the young men loitering on the street corners?"

"That depends on who owned the corner."

"And who owns *this* corner?"

"Me."

"Does everyone else know that?"

"I have to remind them from time to time. C'mon, I'll show you your room."

Through an opening in the far wall was a short hallway. On the immediate left was a closed door; straight ahead, a small bathroom; on the right, an open doorway. Donovan reached in and switched on the light. There was a flash of blue and white, and then the room went dark again.

"I'll get you a bulb," Donovan said.

"Please—take the one from that yellow lantern."

In the far corner was a single bed with a bare mattress; in the opposite corner was a particle-board dresser topped by a wooden frame but no mirror. They were the only two objects in the room. Between them, a closet with sliding doors stood open. One door was off its track, sloping down and resting one corner on the carpet. Inside the closet, a tangle of empty wire hangers was just visible.

Li sat down quietly on the edge of the mattress.

"I'll fix up the bed," Donovan said.

"The way you fixed my roommate's?"

Donovan smiled. "If I had a choice, I would have thrown your roommate out the window."

"You had a choice," Li said. "Why didn't you?"

"There's a little matter of the law."

"Ah, yes, the law. Is the law all that constrains you?"

"I don't like bullies," Donovan said. "I never have."

"Neither do I." Li looked up at him in the darkness. "I have fought against bullies all my life. A sad reality of life is that a time comes when a man must choose his battles. He must learn to fight in a different way— like a swordsman who loses his strong arm in battle. Do you understand what I'm saying?"

"I should have thrown him out the window with my left hand?"

"I'm saying that all men grow old. Young men fight with their bodies because their bodies are strong; old men fight with their minds because that's where true strength lies—in wisdom. The wise man puts away anger and violence before they betray him. He who lives by the sword dies by the sword."

"I'm not old yet," Donovan said.

"You're not wise yet either."

Donovan turned toward the door. "I'll get you some sheets."

"Nathan," Li said, "I want you to know that I appreciated that gesture very much. It was very decent of you—even noble. It's a difficult thing to grow old and to know that you can no longer defend yourself. Fifty years ago, I would have boxed his ears myself."

"Would that have been wise?"

"Touché." The old man smiled. "Can you sit for a moment?"

"Li—"

"Please." He patted the mattress beside him. Donovan let out a heavy sigh, then leaned against the dresser and folded his arms.

"May I ask you a question?" Li said.

"I figured you would."

"Do you always wear black?"

"What?"

"Black or navy blue—it's all I ever see you wear."

"It takes ten pounds off me. Macy taught me that."

"The Chinese prefer red—red symbolizes happiness, or wealth, or good fortune. Yellow is the color of nobility; green represents growth. To the Chinese, black is an unhappy color. Black is the color of servitude."

"Then I'm definitely switching to pastels."

"Nathan. Are you unhappy?"

Donovan groaned. "Li, you've spent your whole life worrying about Japanese war criminals and bubonic plague epidemics—are *you* happy?"

"You know, the Greek word for 'happiness' is *eudaimonia*. It means 'good spirit' or 'good soul.' To the ancients, happiness meant much more than some superficial feeling. It meant that everything was right with your soul."

"Is everything right with *your* soul?"

Li paused. "Not yet. But it will be."

"It's dark in here," Donovan said. "Let's go out to the family room."

"The 'family room'—that's rather euphemistic, isn't it? The *gong si fong* was more family-oriented than this place."

"What did you expect? It's a bachelor pad."

"But you were not always a bachelor."

"Let's not go there, okay?"

Li looked around the room again. "I'm a little surprised by your living conditions."

"It's *affordable*."

"I had little choice in living arrangements; I would think you do. I assumed that federal agents were paid better than this. Do any of your associates live in this area?"

Donovan shook his head. "The commute's a little long."

"Yes, the commute. Tell me, do most FBI operatives enjoy approximately the same standard of living?"

"Look," Donovan said. "Most married agents live over in Jersey, in some nice little FBI neighborhood like Woodbridge, or maybe down in Monmouth County. Single agents live wherever they can find affordable housing."

"Like this?"

"How would I know? I haven't visited them all."

"And when you were married—where did you and Macy live?"

"We had a house—near the rest of them."

"I've heard divorce can be quite expensive."

"I'm not paying alimony, if that's what you're wondering. Macy makes more than I do."

"Child support?"

Donovan didn't reply.

Li looked at the dresser behind Donovan. Now that his eyes had adjusted to the darkness, he could see small shards of mirror still protruding from the wooden frame.

"I'd like to tell you a story," Li said.

"C'mon, Li, it's late. I'm off duty."

"You're off duty from gaining wisdom?"

"Is it a short one?"

"Is the path to enlightenment a short one?"

"Tonight it is. Give me the abbreviated version, okay?"

"If you insist—but it really hampers my style. Once there was a man—"

"Is this a Chinese story?"

"Of course. All great stories originated in China. The Greeks lifted a few, but the stories were originally Chinese. Now, where was I? Oh, yes. Once there was a man who possessed a magic ring, a ring that could make him invisible. But the ring was so precious to him, he feared losing it so very much that he took the ring and hid with it in the center of a mountain."

"Li—this is Lord of the Rings."

"You've heard it before? That rather spoils it."

"Everybody in America has heard it before."

"I never should have told it to Tolkien. Anyway, when the man emerged from the mountain and looked at his reflection in a stream, he realized that he had become a salamander."

"I don't remember that part."

"The story was later embellished to fill the pages of a book. Now, tell me, what is the lesson of the story—*my* version?"

"Men shouldn't wear jewelry."

"You're not trying."

"I give up."

"Don't you see? We are influenced by the things that surround us. Darkness begets darkness."

"I see darkness," Donovan said, "and I want to go to bed. I'll get you those sheets. You need anything else?"

"Just a few seconds to unpack. In the morning, what will our agenda be?"

"I need to track down that name you gave me."

"I suggest you check with your government's witness protection program. They might be able to help."

"Will you be okay here by yourself?"

"Just slip some food under the bars from time to time. Pleasant dreams, Nathan."

"You tell me a scary story and then you say, 'Pleasant dreams'? Some grandpa you are."

"Think about the story."

"I have—the elf woman was hot."

"Think about *my* story."

Donovan flipped off the light switch, but nothing happened. *Darkness begets darkness*, he thought.

CHAPTER TWENTY-ONE

Don't lift until I tell you," Donovan's father said.

"Right." His father worked the pry bar along the edges of the long wooden planks. They creaked and groaned as they began to separate from the barn floor for the first time in years. A crack began to widen; Donovan squeezed his fingers in and felt for a solid grip. His father pried up one end just enough to force a two-by-four into the hole, then wedged a cinder block underneath it to use as a fulcrum.

"Okay," his father said simply, and they both began to lift.

The plank suddenly gave way, landing with a crash on the floor beside it. The gap left by the plank revealed a fist-deep space beneath it, and it seemed to be alive. It was swarming with a wriggling mass of brown and gray and white fur.

"Barn rats," his father said. "Lots of 'em."

Suddenly, the rats began to flow up and out from under the planks, like water bubbling up from a sewer. They kept coming, and coming, until there were thousands of them covering the remains of the threshing floor. There were too many, far too many, and it frightened Donovan. He stamped his foot at them and shouted, but the moment he did, he knew that was a mistake.

They turned and looked at him, and then they all began to rise up on their hind legs and hiss. It was a small sound at first, like a handful of garden snakes might make, but rat after rat joined in until the sound was like the growl of a jungle cat.

Then they all fell silent at once, and Donovan turned to run—but his father stood calmly, with his gloved hands resting on one end of the standing two-by-four. The rats swarmed up and over the man in an instant, covering every inch of his body.

Donovan raced to his father and grabbed two rats by their backs. They were thick and muscular, and they twisted in his hands like two sinewy eels. One turned and sank its curving yellow teeth into the base of his thumb. He felt no pain, but he threw the rats away from him and reached for two more, ripping them away from his father's face.

But it wasn't his father at all. Now it was a young boy, standing and crying softly.

"Make them stop," the boy sobbed.

Donovan felt a wave of panic. He began to pull the rats away faster and faster, but the instant he tore one away, another wriggled in to take its place.

"Help me," the boy pleaded, but he was invisible now, covered entirely in a roiling mass of squealing, scurrying fur.

And the pile began to grow smaller, and the voice grew fainter.

In desperation, Donovan grabbed for the two-by-four and swung at the center of the pile. The impact felt thick and rubbery. Rats flew everywhere, shrieking and hissing through the air. He swung again and again until the pile disappeared completely, but there was nothing inside.

"Daddy!"

DONOVAN JERKED UPRIGHT IN bed. He was breathing hard and fast, and his jaws were aching. *It's a wonder I have any molars left*, he thought. He didn't bother to look at the clock—he knew what time it would be.

No use trying to go back to sleep—there never was. By the time the adrenaline wore off, it was always time for work anyway. He got out of bed and stood directly in front of the window unit air conditioner. The old machine throbbed and groaned, and the plastic panel on the front made a buzzing sound. He jammed it with the butt of his hand, and it stopped—but several seconds later it returned again like an annoying mosquito.

He pulled on yesterday's crewneck and a pair of slacks and stepped into the hallway. Li's door was open just a crack. He tiptoed across the family room, turned the dead bolt on the front door, and closed it quietly behind him.

The night air had a slight coolness to it, and there was a gentle breeze that rose and fell like waves on a seashore. It was late June, still more spring than summer, when the New York air becomes thick and stagnant and the heat is impossible to escape.

At the street he stopped and looked both ways. *Which way tonight?* It didn't matter. He had no place to go anyway—he just had to *move*. Anything was better than lying in a bed in the dark with no chance of escape into the oblivion of sleep—and even when sleep came, it always brought the dreams. In the last year, Donovan had learned that there are different kinds of darkness. There's the darkness that fills the alleys of the South Bronx at night, the kind you can walk into and out of, and there's the darkness that comes from inside—the kind you can't fight or escape, the kind you can only lie there and feel, paralyzed and screaming, while it takes its own sweet time.

Just then the yellow streetlights to his right clicked off, recycling for a few moments, and he took it as a minor omen; he turned right and headed into the darkness. The streets were almost empty at four o'clock; they always were. *You learn a lot when you don't waste time sleeping,* Donovan thought, *things that other people never know.* You learn that every city has a cycle of life and death that repeats itself day after day. In the morning the city is an infant, full of hope and limitless possibilities. By afternoon it's already full grown, burdened with the endless responsibilities of life. The evening is the city's golden years, those pitifully few remaining hours that only a handful are allowed to enjoy. Then at midnight the clock silently strikes, and old age falls like a heavy curtain. The next two hours are a kind of death kick, when the feeble and dying frantically try to strengthen their grip on life. Two o'clock is a kind of funeral, when coffin doors are shut tight and lights are put out, and for the next three hours the city lies smoldering in its grave, awaiting its daily resurrection. Donovan looked at his watch. *Just my luck*, he thought, *to be alive when everyone else is dead and dead when everyone else is alive.*

He wandered for half an hour before starting for home again, keeping to the coolness of the shadows. He turned down alleyways, the narrower the better, and cut across vacant lots littered with the detritus of other people's lives. He emerged from one alley and heard voices; on a street corner he saw three men huddled together, some of the living dead who inhabit every city at night. As Donovan approached, the men looked up. He stopped directly in front of them. One mumbled a reluctant greeting, but Donovan said nothing in reply. He just glared at each of them, one by one, until they silently shuffled aside to let him pass. He pushed by them, bumping the shoulder of one, listening hard for any half-whispered curse or remark—anything to give him an excuse to turn back. He even hunched down a little as he passed, trying to look smaller than he was, but none of them were fooled. Maybe they had heard about him, the man in black who walked the streets at night. Maybe they were friends of the men who hadn't been as cautious—the one with the broken jaw, or the one whose forearm had snapped in two like an old broom handle.

Back at the house, Donovan quietly let himself in and bolted the door again. He walked to the kitchen and pulled the coffeemaker out on the counter. He opened the top and peered in at the filter; there were still some grounds left over from the day before. He sniffed. *Strong enough to squeeze out a little more caffeine*, he thought. *I'll just run it through twice.*

Then he heard a noise, and he froze. He was used to being alone in the house, and the only sounds he heard at night were inhuman: the pulsing of his air conditioner, a sudden crack from the walls as the old framing cooled and contracted—sometimes even the quick scurrying of feet in the rafters over his head. This sound was different—it was a high-pitched cry or groan, the kind a wounded animal might make.

Donovan thought about his Glock. He wasn't stupid enough to take it with him when he went out at night; it would be where it always was, on the nightstand to the right of his bed. He started down the hallway, then stopped. The sound was coming from Li's room. He put an ear to the crack and listened: The old man was crying—but it was unlike any human cry Donovan had ever heard. It was pure grief, raw and unadulterated. There was no anger or pettiness or self-pity in the voice. There was no shame or restraint either—the grief was simply there, and it flowed out of the old man like sap from a wounded tree.

The grief came in rolling waves. First there was a low groan, punctuated by woeful laments in broken Chinese; then his words began to quicken, and his voice rose until it crescendoed in a mournful wail and receded again in gentle sobbing. Donovan suddenly wondered if he himself had ever really cried in his entire life—when his mother passed, when he found his father hanging from the rafters in the barn, even when little Jeremy died. No, not even for Jeremy—not like this. Compared to Li's grief, he wondered if anyone else had ever cried at all.

Donovan thought about knocking—but it seemed somehow unholy to interrupt this moment with a sudden rap on a doorframe. Instead, he silently pushed the door open a few inches and peered inside. Li knelt on the floor in front of his bed; on the mattress was a faded black-and-white photograph of a young Chinese couple standing in front of a stone well. They were dressed ceremoniously, in long silken robes with dark-colored belts. They held hands, and they were grinning from ear to ear.

Each time Li's lament began to rise, he would take the faded photo from the bed and clutch it to his chest, rocking back and forth and weeping at the ceiling. When the weeping subsided, he would carefully return the photograph and study it again, waiting for the next wave to come rolling into shore.

Donovan felt suddenly ashamed. As an FBI agent, he was used to interrupting people at awkward moments. He had arrested men at dinner with their families, in bed with their wives—he once even dragged a man off a toilet in a public restroom. This was different. Those were embarrassments, those were inconveniences—this was something worse. He reached for the doorknob to pull the door shut again, but he moved too quickly and the doorknob made a slight rattling sound. Li turned and looked at him.

The two men stared into each other's eyes but said nothing. Donovan's mind raced, searching for some acceptable excuse, or even better, some glib remark that might reduce his offense from a blasphemy to a minor faux pas. But he could think of nothing to say; after a few seconds he simply lowered his eyes and quietly shut the door.

He stood in the hallway for a moment, then crossed back to his own bedroom and sat down on the edge of the bed, staring across the hall at Li's closed door.

What do you know? he thought. *I'm not the only one who can't sleep.*

CHAPTER TWENTY-TWO

Sato Matsushita knelt before a small Shinto shrine in his Damascus apartment. In the center of the shelf was a box made of Japanese cypress in the shape of a temple, with a door that opened on tiny brass hinges. In front of the box were three white bowls containing rice, water, and salt, and on either side were fresh cuttings from a Syrian olive tree.

Sato neatly scripted a wish on a small prayer paper, then opened the little door and placed the paper inside along with all the others—all bearing the same identical words. He bowed his head and closed his eyes for a moment; then he rose and stepped the few paces to his bed, the only other object in the room. He took one corner of the blanket and pulled it down diagonally across the bed, folding it as crisply as a piece of paper. He sat down on the edge of the bed and pulled his feet from his slippers, leaving them perfectly aligned on the floor beside him. He turned ninety degrees and tucked his feet under the blanket, pulling it neatly up over his body as he reclined with his head in the precise center of the pillow. He stared at the ceiling for a few moments, blinking; then he closed his eyes and willed a dream to return to him, a dream that he had carefully crafted one element at a time every night for sixty years.

By SEVEN O'CLOCK, TENS of thousands already line the shores of the East River, setting up lawn chairs and spreading out blankets in anticipation of the event still two hours away. The FDR Drive is closed from Fourteenth to Forty-second Streets, providing thirty blocks of unimpeded view. In the center of the river, just below the tip of Roosevelt Island, three black barges sit silently in the water, each one honeycombed with hundreds of steel and fiberglass pipes. Across the river in Queens, hundreds of thousands more crowd rooftops, balconies, and parking lots. Soon every driveway and backyard patio within eyeshot will be filled, every spot that allows an unobstructed view of the western sky.

Just below the Brooklyn Bridge, two more barges lie deep in the water, midway between the boroughs of Brooklyn and Manhattan. The streets around the South Street Seaport and the Brooklyn Heights Promenade are already packed tight. In the final light of day, the towering skyscrapers of Manhattan cast their shadows clear across the river; in the deepening darkness, tiny figures scurry about like insects. Up the Hudson, two more barges are positioned across from the Village, and the piers along West Street and on the opposite Jersey shore are all crowded with people.

Farthest to the south, a single barge lies anchored in the Upper Bay, equidistant between the tip of Manhattan and the shore of Liberty Island. The view from this barge is spectacular, breathtaking, unparalleled in all the world. This is the master barge—this is where I will stand. From here I can see the entire skyline of Manhattan, its soaring spires glittering with dots of light against the darkening sky. From here I can see four of the city's five boroughs, containing 80 percent of the city's eight million inhabitants. From here I can see five of the eight rectangular barges, closing around the city like the teeth of a giant beast.

It is eight o'clock now. The sky is clear, and the air is perfectly still. The ground is still warm, but a cool blanket of air settles over it, creating an inversion that will keep the tiny fleas from being blown away by gusts of wind. Tonight the sun will set at exactly 8:30 p.m. At 9:03 civil twilight will end, when the sun dips precisely six degrees below the horizon and objects can no longer be clearly distinguished by the naked eye. The phase of the moon is a waning crescent with only 3 percent of its disk illumined, just a tiny silver sliver in the summer sky. At 9:04, when the first cannon shells are sounded, the sky will be almost completely black.

Young men recline on grassy medians and tune their radios to the musical simulcast. Mothers pass food around on paper plates and keep a watchful eye on wandering children. Fathers hold toddlers in their laps, pointing into the skies and building anticipation. Some take advantage of the darkness to embrace, while others scout for better locations, staking out new territories and waving for friends to join them. And still more people come, pouring out of the city and pushing toward the rivers, packing against the banks like drifting grains of sand.

Now it is nine o'clock, and I take a seat on the edge of the barge and allow my legs to hang down over the water. On the western horizon a line of light grows thinner and brighter, like the last light from a dying candle. As darkness settles, the night grows somehow quieter, as if the entire city is holding its breath before letting out its first astonished gasp. In a few moments the Americans will celebrate their day of independence, and I will celebrate with them—I will celebrate the independence of my soul.

And then it begins.

From all eight barges simultaneously comes a thundering cannonade that echoes off the sides of the buildings. Seconds later, the sky lights up in cascading showers of silver and gold. I can hear traces of the patriotic refrains that synchronize the barrage, and I can imagine the oohs and aahs and the scattered applause arising from the appreciative crowds. The detonations grow faster now, more than a hundred every minute from my barge alone, and I can feel the vibration of each explosion as it sends its shell rocketing into the sky.

I look out over the city. There are floral shells that cover the sky with multicolored blossoms. There are golden brocade crowns that drape down over the water like the branches of weeping willows. There are skyrockets that make spiraling silver columns as they rise, and there are spangled star mines that rise invisibly into the night before erupting in startling reds and greens. The sky explodes in time with the music, fortissimo and pianissimo, and everywhere faces light up in wide-eyed wonder.

It is a spectacular display, truly a work of art. It is a fitting closing ceremony for the world's most powerful city.

At last the finale approaches, and the sky is like a black fabric ripping apart so that the sun shines through from behind. Rockets, streamers, starbursts everywhere; the music rises to a fevered pitch, and then suddenly stops—one last detonation can be heard, lower and louder than any before it. The city holds its breath. Seconds later, eight brilliant cherry trees stand glistening in the nighttime sky—and then simultaneously vanish. In the silence that follows, I can hear the roaring cheers from the surrounding shores.

Now the sky is dark again, but it is not empty. The air is filled with clouds of smoke, and bits of ash and paper rain down everywhere. Some pick bits of wadding from their hair or clothing. Some brush away still-burning sparks or embers. Some absentmindedly scratch at the tiny, biting specks that dot their necks and arms. And in the gutters and alleys near the rivers, rats snap angrily at their haunches and then scurry into drainpipes and sewers.

Even before the applause dies away, people start back toward the city. Eyes turn away from the nighttime sky; blankets are gathered, belongings collected, children taken by the hand to begin the long walk home. Back to houses and apartments; back to childhood homes and hotel rooms held only for a night; back to Upper West Side lofts and tenement slums; back to New York City—and back to cities all over the eastern United States.

The first symptoms appear just two days later, first among the elderly and the immune-suppressed. The symptoms are minor—just a cough, or a chill, or a slight fever. They scold themselves for going out in the nighttime air, and they make a mental note to dress warmer next time. They take their favorite over-the-counter remedies and retreat to their beds.

But the next day they feel no better, and soon they are visited by friends, by loved ones, by little grandchildren bringing consolation and comfort. They sit together in the same little rooms, breathing the same air. There are coughs and sneezes; there are handshakes and kisses and hugs.

A cat plays with a dead rat in an empty lot. A child pets the cat. A mother embraces the child. The woman makes love with her husband. The husband shakes hands with a client. The client boards a jet for home. A woman greets the man at the airport. And so the Pestilence travels, with its own mass-transit system and port authority, taking in every sight in the city and visiting every corner of the nation.

The next to take ill are the children; because they breathe faster than adults, their lungs are more susceptible to inhalational agents. Soon even the healthy and strong begin to experience fever, headache, weakness, and shortness of breath. There are rumors of an influenza outbreak. Pharmacy shelves are stripped bare; physicians' waiting rooms and urgent-care centers are crowded to overflowing. Doctors make their first inaccurate diagnoses: pneumonia, bronchitis, flu. Broadband antibiotics are prescribed, hoping for a panacea. The first specimens of bloody sputum are sent to laboratories to grow cultures, a process that will take forty-eight precious hours to complete.

Within six days the Pestilence erupts all over the city—but in different forms, with different effects. In some victims the plague is bubonic. Agonizing purplish masses appear in groins and armpits and necks, pus-filled tumors the size of oranges. Fevers rise to brain-boiling temperatures, and everywhere they collapse in exhaustion and delirium.

In others, the plague goes directly to the bloodstream. The blood in their vessels begins to thicken and clot. Pustules open; purpuric lesions appear; the tips of their fingers and toes turn scarlet-black.

And in others, the plague is in the lungs. Pulses race; they pant like winded animals, stopping only to cough up bright red blood, ejecting particles of pestilence everywhere. There is no one to care for them; they lie untended on soiled sheets, their skin cold and dry from endless diarrhea.

A dozen genetically altered strains release invisible toxins into the blood. Each strain multiplies like a colony of tiny immigrants, claiming a portion of the city for its own. In Brooklyn, *myelin* toxin predominates. People lie paralyzed in hallways and on bedroom floors, staring helplessly up at the ceiling, choking to death on their own vomit.

Botulinum claims Staten Island. The toxin binds to nerve endings, blocking the signals that command muscles to contract, always beginning in the head and spreading downward. Eyelids droop, and speech slurs. They cough up blood but cannot swallow. Then the toxin reaches the lungs, and frantic victims struggle for final breaths of air.

Anatoxin A makes its home in the Bronx, where bodies drop to the ground in midstride. *Microcystin* prefers the suburban feel of Queens, causing liver enlargement, stupor, and shock. And Manhattan, the great melting pot, opens its doors to everyone. All over the city, toxins reveal their deadly surprises like exploding fireworks. There are starbursts of purple and red and black everywhere. Some sag slowly to the ground like brocade crowns; others drop like cannon shots. Some leave trails behind them like blazing skyrockets; others seem to appear out of nowhere, then vanish before your eyes. And the sounds are everywhere—the shrill cries, the booming shouts, the rocketing screams.

State and local health officials rush to the scene with neatly bound contingency plans tucked under their arms. But in their darkest dreams they never imagined something like this. They try every palliative in their pharmacopoeia: streptomycin, tetracycline, gentamicin, doxycycline. But nothing seems to work—nothing even helps.

There is no way to isolate the disease. Quarantine is impossible—the disease seems to have emerged everywhere at once. They desperately attempt to quarantine the city itself. They close airports and bus terminals; they barricade highways and shut down trains and subways. But it's far too late for that. Airplanes have already departed; trains have left the stations; ships have put to sea. Soon children of the plague will appear everywhere, like tiny blossoms sent out by a colossal floral shell.

And I will walk the streets of New York, just as I walked the streets of Hiroshima sixty years ago. But this time there will be no fiery sky, no choking clouds of dust. All the buildings will still be standing, all the parks still green and lush—but all the guilty will be dead or dying. And I will walk among them hand in hand with Emiko, and we will see the final blackness together—the blackened faces, the blackened limbs, the blackened bodies. We will see the blackness everywhere. Then at last there will be justice; then at last Emiko will have peace.

Truly a fitting end for the most powerful city in the world.

Truly a work of art.

CHAPTER TWENTY-THREE

LI STOOD IN FRONT of the open refrigerator and peered inside. It had the same desolate look as the rest of Donovan's house—just a handful of random items scattered across the shelves without any apparent logic. There were olives with plump red pimientos staring out from a half-empty jar of greenish brine. There was an oven-ready cheese pizza shrink-wrapped against a circle of cardboard, with furry patches of green and blue encroaching from the edges. There were plastic bottles of ketchup and mustard—though Li could not imagine what they would be used for. And there was a solitary silver can in the corner, sporting a plastic necklace with five empty holes where its companions once stood. The refrigerator was dark; Li put his hand inside to make sure it was cold.

"Help yourself," Li said aloud. "How very generous of him."

There was a knock at the front door. Li removed the chain, twisted the dead bolt, and opened it. He found himself staring up into the face of a thick-featured man with heavy, drooping eyelids and untamable gray hair.

"Hey," Poldie said. "You're that Chinese guy."

"A shrewd deduction," Li said. "And I recognize that voice—you must be Detective Satwyck; I spoke with you on the phone the other day."

Poldie stepped past Li and into the house. "Where's Donovan? We ride together on Thursdays."

"You've just missed him. I'm afraid that's my fault; I sent him on an unexpected errand, you see. Can you stay for a moment? Please, sit down. I'd try to avoid the duct tape if I were you—it will leave an adhesive residue on that lovely suit."

Poldie shrugged, turned, and hovered over the sofa before dropping onto it like an ox backing into a stall. The sofa made a squealing sound.

"Can I get you anything? Some beer and olives, perhaps?"

Poldie gave the offer serious consideration, then ran a hand across his sprawling midsection. "Better wait for lunch," he said. "So—what's this errand?"

"Nathan is attempting to locate Pasha Mirovik."

"Who?"

"Pasha Mirovik—a Soviet scientist who defected to your country a decade ago. He may be able to provide information on the whereabouts of Sato Matsushita."

"Oh, right." Poldie groaned. "The big conspiracy."

Li smiled. "Tell me, how is your investigation into the TriBeCa murder proceeding?"

"Uh-uh," Poldie said. "I already got my hand slapped once for talking to you."

"That's very unfair; they really should be thanking you."

"Huh?"

"Think about it: If you hadn't made the on-the-spot decision to mention those fleas to the *Times* reporter, I would not be here today. If by some chance I do make some small contribution to this investigation, *you* will be the one ultimately responsible."

Poldie blinked.

"I find it remarkable," Li said. "How does a police officer develop that kind of instinct? You could have mentioned anything to the reporter, I suppose, but you chose to mention the fleas. How do you know which bit of information to release to the press? You must have planned your strategy well in advance."

"It's a gut thing," Poldie said. "You got to think on your feet."

Li shook his head in admiration. "Tell me—how long have you been at this?"

"Thirty years now."

"Well, that accounts for your uncanny intuition. And how long has Nathan been your junior partner?"

"Donovan? Since just after 9/11."

"Then he's just a novice compared to you. You must be a very patient man."

"Huh?"

"I mean, for a seasoned veteran to be constantly surrounded by so much inexperience. Young men can be so reckless, so impulsive at times—don't you think?"

"Well, we all had a little more gunpowder back then."

"*Gunpowder*—yes, an excellent metaphor. It seems to me that Nathan has an abundance of 'gunpowder.'"

Poldie shrugged. "It helps in a business like this."

"Are you married, Detective Satwyck?"

"Me? Sure." Poldie reached into his back pocket and pulled out his wallet. He removed a small glossy photo and handed it to Li.

Li studied the photo. She was a broad-faced woman with hair almost as wild as her husband's—only hers had been corralled into tight gray curls that gave the top of her head the overall appearance of steel wool. She had an unusually narrow forehead, as though her hair were a hat pulled down low. Her eyes were very wide and had a penetrating quality—like two rifles holding the viewer in a cross fire. To her credit, she was smiling, though Li found her smile strangely unexpressive—something like the grin on a camel. She had an altogether Wagnerian quality, and Li could easily imagine her suited out in a Viking helmet and full battle gear.

"A lovely woman," Li said. "Tell me, Detective, isn't this business of yours rather hard on a marriage at times?"

"How do you mean?"

"The anger, for instance—the *gunpowder* as you called it—what happens when you bring it home with you at night?"

"Well, Truda doesn't take any guff."

"No, I can imagine."

"We got a saying in the NYPD: When you sign up you get a gun, a badge, and a sleeper sofa."

"Is that also true of the FBI?"

"Sure—only they get pajamas."

Li nodded, though he had no idea what that meant. "I understand that Nathan was married at one time."

"Yeah, Nathan and Macy. They were the FBI poster kids for a while—Ken marries Barbie."

"They changed their names?"

"What?"

Li paused—following this man was like chasing a chicken.

"You referred to them as 'poster kids.' I assume this means they had an exemplary relationship at first."

Poldie frowned. "You always talk like that?"

"Please forgive me; it's my fourth language. I understand that Nathan and Macy later divorced."

"Well, that was because of Jeremy."

"Jeremy?"

"Their boy."

"Nathan never mentioned a son."

"He never will."

"Why not?"

"'Cause Jeremy died when he was four."

"How very sad. How did it happen?"

"The boy started having headaches. They took him in for an MRI, found out he had a brain tumor—one of those 'astral' things."

"Astrocytoma."

"What?"

"I'm sorry; please continue."

"Well, they tried radiation, chemo, even experimental drugs, but nothing stopped it. The poor kid just wasted away to nothing."

"And you were Nathan's partner during this time?"

"Yeah."

"Tell me—how did Nathan seem to handle all this?"

Poldie shrugged. "He didn't."

"He didn't?"

"He was there at first—for all the tests and procedures, I mean—and let me tell you, they did some god-awful things to that kid. But after a while, I think Donovan just couldn't take it anymore. He just sort of backed off."

"Backed off? You mean he emotionally withdrew?"

"I mean he didn't show up anymore. He let Macy handle it."

"Until the end?"

"Until the end."

Li shook his head. "And did Nathan talk to you about all this?"

"He didn't talk to anybody—he just sucked it up. I mean, it's not like we had a lot of time to hold hands and talk; this was just after 9/11, you know, and we sort of had our hands full."

"And what about Macy? Did you ever speak with her?"

"She called; she asked me to try to talk to him. And I did try, but I didn't get anywhere. Then after Jeremy died I called her—but nobody was talking to anybody then. It was all downhill from there; nobody could stop it. They split up after that."

Li paused. "Why do you think Nathan withdrew from his son?"

"How should I know?"

"I'm not asking for an explanation, Detective; I'm asking for your *instinct.*"

Poldie thought for a moment. "Did you ever have to watch somebody die—somebody you care about? And you can't do anything about it; you just have to sit there and watch?"

"I have experienced that particular horror, yes."

"Well, then you know—what it takes out of you, I mean."

"Yes," Li said. "I know."

Poldie shook his head. "I don't know what I'd do if it was me."

"No one ever does." Li looked around the room again. "So that's why there are no photographs—no memories of any kind."

"That's why."

Poldie glanced at his watch now, then began to pry himself out of the sagging cushions.

"Must you go so soon?" Li asked. "This has been so informative."

"Some of us have jobs," Poldie said. He stretched, opened the door, and stepped out onto the tiny front porch.

Li rose and followed after him. "By the way, has Nathan been involved in any other relationships since the divorce?"

"I don't think so."

"And Dr. Monroe?"

"Haven't heard of any, but it wouldn't surprise me. Have you seen her? New York men aren't blind, you know."

They reached the car now. Poldie climbed in and lowered the window.

"I enjoyed our little visit," Li said. "Thank you for taking a moment from your busy schedule."

"No problemo. And keep working on that English—it takes time."

CHAPTER TWENTY-FOUR

MACY WAS IN HER favorite outfit: a loose-fitting, long-sleeved pullover, a pair of baggy gray sweatpants, and thick cotton socks. It was her lounging outfit, her comfort suit. Macy loved the fall and winter because they allowed her to bundle up like this, and it didn't seem fair that she should have to give up the joys of warmth and coziness just because the earth decided to rotate on its axis. In the summer, she just fired up her air-conditioning and bundled up anyway. For three months every summer her electric bill was astronomical, but she didn't care. There were very few pleasures in her life right now, and a pleasure that could be purchased was a pleasure worth paying for.

She had just settled down on the sofa when the doorbell rang. When she opened the door, she found Li standing there grinning with his arms folded behind his back.

"Well, hello!" he said cheerfully.

"Li."

"The very same."

"Well, what are you—why are you—"

Li held up his hand. "Perhaps I can anticipate your first few questions. What am I doing here? I came to pay you a visit. Is this visit personal or professional in nature? That depends largely on your frame of mind. How did I get here? In one of those infamous New York taxicabs. Does Nathan know I'm here? There are many things Nathan doesn't know, as I'm sure you will agree."

Macy just stood there, dumbfounded.

"This is such a lovely front porch," Li said. "One could almost remain here."

"Oh—I'm sorry. Won't you come in?"

Li stepped in and brought out a small paper sack from behind his back. "These are scones," he said, "true English scones, not the crude American facsimiles, which taste like sawdust with a binding of glue. I don't mind telling you, it was no mean feat to find them. It seems provisions were a bit short at Nathan's house."

"They sound wonderful."

"You'll find there are two of them."

"Then all we need is tea."

"What a lovely suggestion." He walked to the sofa, took a seat, and looked back at Macy with a warm smile. Macy still stood in the doorway holding the paper sack.

"You're wondering why I didn't call first," Li said. "In point of fact, I did. I remembered that last night you said you were giving an examination today, so I called your office at Columbia University. I was informed that it was a morning class and that you planned to return to your home afterward to grade the papers. I can't say I blame you—this is really a lovely setting."

"How did you get my home address?"

"I told the departmental secretary that I was your aged uncle from Great Britain, who just arrived from Heathrow to find himself stranded and forgotten at LaGuardia. It was my first time in the States, you see, and everything was so big and confusing. If only she would give me your home address, I could take a taxi and meet you there. The story had just enough pathos to do the trick."

"You lied?"

"I did *research*—a subtle but important distinction."

Macy smiled, shook her head, and headed for the kitchen.

Li looked around the living room. It was a sensual room, filled with deep colors and rich textures. Most of the furniture was upholstered, thick and soft and inviting. The walls were lined with glass-front bookcases, filled to overflowing. The coffee table and end tables were covered with glossy-jacketed books and knickknacks, and green plants draped over every available corner. The walls were covered with framed photographs and personal mementos, including several of a young boy. It was a warm room, a welcoming room, the kind that put its arm around your shoulder and helped you off with your coat.

"It's remarkable," Li called into the kitchen.

"What's that?"

"This room—it's the virtual opposite of its counterpart in Nathan's house."

"That's no surprise."

"This is truly a *living* room. His is more of a dying room, if you get my meaning."

"I do."

"I understand that you and Nathan were married for five years."

Macy poked her head around the corner. "He told you that?"

"Oh, yes. We discussed the situation at length."

"Really. What did he have to say?"

"He told me all about the lovely home the two of you shared—in Woodbridge, I believe. He went on and on about it. I could bore you with all the details, I suppose, but I'd really rather hear from you."

Macy brought out the scones on a tray with a china tea set. "Are you lying now, or just doing research?"

"I'm lying. The truth is, I couldn't get a thing out of him. I was hoping I could do better with you."

"So the scones are just a bribe?"

"I prefer to think of them as an *inducement.* Storytellers have always gathered around fireplaces and tables, you know. There's something about breaking bread together that brings out the storyteller in all of us. Personally, I think it's a response to boredom. You can sit and watch one another masticate for only so long before someone breaks the monotony with a story."

"You want me to tell you a story?"

"You see? And we haven't even taken a bite yet."

Macy smiled. "What story are you interested in?"

"You mean I have a choice? How very generous of you. Personally, I would like to hear the story of Macy Monroe and Nathan Donovan."

"That's a big story," Macy said.

"I have all day. Feel free to begin anywhere."

"It doesn't have a happy ending."

"The best stories never do. Americans have a bad habit of sanitizing their stories, but the original versions are always so much more rewarding. Remember the tale of Goldilocks? In the original version, the bears became enraged and impaled her on a church steeple. And in the story of Pinocchio—what was the name of that pesky insect?"

"Jiminy Cricket."

"Yes, that's right. In the original version, Pinocchio threw a boot at him and squashed him against a wall."

Macy let out a laugh. "That doesn't make a very good Disney movie."

"My point exactly. Americans want all their stories to be 'Disney movies,' so they clean up the endings and lose all sense of the darkness and complexity of life. Your story doesn't have to have a happy ending. I like to think it doesn't have an ending at all—not yet anyway."

"Trust me, Li, it has an ending."

"Then I would be satisfied just to hear the beginning."

"I grew up here in the city," she began. "I did my undergraduate work at George Washington University down in D.C.—they were starting a terrorism studies program just about the time I came through. I did my graduate work at the University of St. Andrews in Scotland."

"I had no idea," Li said. "We were practically neighbors."

"You did your studies at Oxford, didn't you?"

"Yes—but a half century or so before your arrival. I enrolled at Oxford in 1947. I took a first in biochemistry."

"Then on to medical school?"

"No."

"I thought your dream was to become a missionary doctor."

"It was—but as I said, the war changed all that. The end of one dream became the start of another. A different dream required different skills and training."

"So what did you do after Oxford?"

Li frowned. "It's an old trick, you know. Every student knows it."

"What is?"

"Sending the teacher off on a rabbit trail by getting him to talk about himself. I'm not as vain as all that, and I'm not so easily put off. You were beginning to tell *your* story; I believe we left you at the University of St. Andrews."

"Right. Well, I did an MLitt in Middle Eastern and central Asian security studies, and I did my PhD through their Centre for the Study of Terrorism and Political Violence."

"You're giving me your résumé," Li said with a roll of his eyes. "I was hoping for a *story*."

"My résumé is a part of my story."

"Yes, but only a part—and not the better part. Suppose I told the story of Goldilocks this way: 'There was once a girl; little is known about her background. About the age of ten, she began to take walks in the woods. She displayed a tendency toward criminal behavior, including breaking and entering—'"

"Okay, I get the point. I'm used to dealing with the bottom line, Li. Maybe you should just ask me some questions."

"An excellent idea." He thought for a moment. "Tell me, how did you and Nathan meet?"

"He was a new agent assigned to New York City; I was an associate professor at Columbia. I did a seminar for the FBI on terrorist threat assessment. Nathan was in the class."

"I see. And what attracted you to him in the beginning?"

Macy took a moment to fold her legs under her. The question felt a little awkward from a man old enough to be her grandfather. "He's tall, and he's very good looking," she said. "That was enough at first."

"He has very good hair."

"Yes, he has good hair."

"I find him rather complex."

"That's one way to put it."

Li paused. "Tell me about your courtship."

She shrugged. "We dated for a few months. We were married a few months later."

"You must have been very certain."

"I suppose I was—at first."

"And how did he propose marriage?"

Macy squirmed. "That's a little painful to remember."

"Do you remember the cause of your divorce?"

"Of course I do."

"Is that painful to remember?"

"Sure it is."

"But it's *easier* to remember, isn't it? It's odd, isn't it, how much easier it is to recall hurt than joy?"

"Li, are you asking questions or giving me therapy?"

"Both, I hope. Questions are the most effective form of therapy I know."

Macy suddenly realized that she was gripping the arm of the chair. She forced herself to relax a little.

"I noticed the lovely photographs on your walls," Li said. "Did Nathan take them?"

"No. Why?"

"He isn't in any of them."

"No, he's not."

Li looked around the room. "You know, Nathan's walls are completely bare, while yours are crowded with personal memories. It's as if he's trying very hard to forget something, while you're trying very hard to remember."

Macy said nothing.

"I see several photos of a small boy."

Macy stood up abruptly. "I think the tea is ready," she said and turned toward the kitchen. It was such an awkward evasion, such an obvious admission, and she despised herself for it. In the kitchen she took a few moments to compose herself before returning with the steaming teapot.

"I apologize if I've offended you," Li said gently.

"That part of the story is painful for me," she replied. "Would you be offended if I chose not to tell it?"

"Offended, no. Disappointed, yes." She poured the tea, and they sat in silence for a few minutes.

"Are you enjoying your scone?" he asked.

"It's excellent. I hate to eat without a story, though."

"Am I really that boring?"

"No, I love to watch you chew. It's just that you're such a great storyteller. I thought maybe you might have one to tell me."

Li smiled at her. "You're not really surprised to see me this morning, are you?"

"I was surprised to find you at my door—but I expected to hear from you, yes."

"You've spoken with Nathan, then."

"He called me early this morning. He told me about last night—about you, and the bedroom, and the photograph of the couple in front of the well."

"This photograph?" Li reached into his coat pocket and gently removed the ancient photo. "Please be careful," he said, handing it to her. "It's the most precious thing I own."

Macy held it in her cupped hands and studied it. The brittle paper was veined with tiny cracks, and the emulsion had worn off around the edges. The image was clear, but coarse and grainy; in some spots individual particles of silver could be seen.

Macy looked up at him. "Li, this is you."

"Give or take sixty years."

"You haven't changed a bit."

"Who's lying now?"

"The young woman beside you is very beautiful."

Li didn't reply.

She handed back the photograph and waited as he carefully returned it to his jacket pocket. "I would very much like to hear the story of that photograph," she said, "but I understand if you would prefer not to tell it."

"I would prefer not to," Li said. "At least, not for the purpose of some psychological evaluation."

"I'd like to hear it as a friend."

Li studied her face. "If you wish to take in a dog, you must have a leash and a bowl and a brush—you must have the things necessary to *receive* a dog. You're asking me to tell you a story that is closer to my heart than anything in this world—so I must ask you, Macy Monroe: Are you so used to dealing with the bottom line that you'll listen only for names and dates and places? Have you been hurt so badly that you are unwilling or unable to feel someone else's pain? Do you have the things necessary to *receive* my story?"

"I think so," Macy said.

Li leaned forward on the sofa. "Most important of all—can you still weep?"

Macy paused. "I sure hope so."

Li nodded. "Then pour me some tea," he said.

CHAPTER TWENTY-FIVE

Congshan, China, August 1942

LI KNOCKED HARDER THIS time. "Give me my bride!" he shouted. "Must I break down the door?" The young men in the wedding party crowded around the cottage, poking and jostling and carrying on. One of them set off a string of firecrackers reserved for the wedding procession, intended to drive away evil spirits.

"She doesn't hear you," one of them teased.

"She doesn't *want* you," another added, and the group erupted in laughter again.

"Quiet, quiet," Li said, putting his ear to the crack. Inside, the bridesmaids barred the door against this would-be intruder.

"First you must pass a test," said a voice through the door. "Only courage and wisdom can get you what you seek."

"If I did not have wisdom, I would never have chosen Jin—and if I did not have courage, I would not be standing here in front of all these fools." Howls and laughter from the audience.

"You must answer a question," said the voice. "What does this expression mean: 'Waiting by a tree stump for a rabbit'?"

There were groans and hisses from the wedding party, but Li hushed them and stood a little straighter. "There once was a farmer resting by a tree stump," he said in a loud voice, "when a rabbit, racing by at great speed, ran into the tree stump and died. The farmer took the rabbit to market and sold it for a good price, whereupon the farmer said to himself, 'I will never have to farm again—I will wait by the tree stump for rabbits to come to me.'"

"And what does this mean?" the voice asked.

"It means if I have to wait outside the bride's door much longer, I will never get married." The wedding party began to cheer and applaud, but Li raised one hand and silenced them. "It also means that if the bridesmaids don't open the door, they will never receive their wedding gifts."

That did the trick. The door slowly swung open, revealing a wall of grinning women with outstretched hands. Li handed each of them a small red packet containing a single coin. As each received her gift, she stepped aside, until Li stood face-to-face with his bride-to-be. She was dressed in a red silk robe elaborately embroidered in gold and white and blue. Her feet were covered with a pair of scarlet slippers. On her head she wore an ornate phoenix crown, the symbol of the bride, and a veil of beaded strings hung down over her face. Li's own gown was black, with a bright red sash and a big puff of knotted silk on his chest. He wore red shoes as well, and his head was covered in a cap of cypress leaves to declare his adulthood and his new family responsibility.

"You are more difficult to obtain than treasure," Li said to his bride.

"Some man might consider me a treasure."

"I am that man," he said. "What have you been doing in here?"

"The married women have been teaching me how to be a good wife."

"Have you learned well?"

She smiled. "You will soon know."

Now an older woman pushed her way through the crowd, clucking and shooing at the bridesmaids like a hen. She stepped to the doorway and looked back at Jin. "Your good-luck woman is ready," she said. Jin turned and bowed to her parents, then climbed up onto the older woman's back.

"Wait!" another woman said, opening a red parasol over their heads. "Now you are ready."

Just a few yards from the cottage, a decorated donkey awaited the bride. Hanging from the back of the donkey was a silver sieve to strain out evil, and a metallic mirror to deflect malevolent influences. The good-luck woman carried her passenger as though she were weightless—which she was, compared to the burdens the woman bore to and from the fields each day. She turned and neatly deposited the bride on the donkey's back. Then the wedding procession started on its journey, led by a handful of dancers and musicians with far more enthusiasm than skill. At the head of the procession was a young boy carrying the bridal box, symbolizing the couple's hopes for fecundity. The bridesmaids scattered grain and beans on the ground before them, adding their own amen.

The journey ended about a hundred yards later, at an even smaller cottage on the opposite side of the village. A red mat was placed on the ground at the donkey's side to prevent the bride's feet from touching the ground. The couple stepped hand in hand into their new home together, and the entire assembly crowded in behind them.

Li and Jin knelt briefly before a family altar, then turned and bowed to each other—and with that simple gesture, they were husband and wife.

Now they turned to their friends and neighbors. "My wife and I want to thank you all for your generosity and good wishes," Li said. "And now, if you will excuse us, we are very tired."

At this, the whole room erupted in laughter and closed in around the couple. The men seized the groom and the women the bride, half dragging and half carrying them into the bedroom and depositing them on the bed, which was scattered with candies, lotus seeds, peanuts, and fruits. Everyone drew back from the bed now, waiting in silence until Li patted the sheets and nodded—then all the children of the village scrambled onto the bed with them, devouring the sweets and adding their own blessings for fruitfulness.

The next morning, Li and Jin sat at their wooden table and shared their first breakfast together.

"You seem tired," Jin said.

"I am."

"Perhaps you didn't sleep enough."

"Very little, I'm afraid."

"I suppose it takes a while to get used to a new bed."

Li grinned.

"According to custom, this is the day we must return to visit my parents."

Li's expression changed. "According to custom, we have up to three days to pay our respects."

"Today is as good as any."

"Today is not as good as any."

"Our cottage is empty; we have none of our belongings yet. What else do we have to do?"

Li put his hand on hers. "We could get used to a new bed."

Two days later, Jin watched as Li assembled a bedroll and a small pack of food and clothing for his back. "Married only three days, and already you're abandoning me," she said with a pout. "Haven't I been a good wife?"

"You are the best wife I have ever had."

"I wish you wouldn't go. Nanking is not safe."

"No. But everything I need for my studies is there: my books, my microscope, my papers—"

"Things that can be replaced."

"Besides, I must talk to the people at the Missions School. They are the ones arranging for us to go to England. These things take time, and the war is slowing everything down."

"I remember the stories you told about the Japanese soldiers—about what they did to the people of Nanking."

Li said nothing but continued his packing.

"You said thousands and thousands of our people were slaughtered— mutilated, burned, beheaded."

"Those were rumors."

"You believe the rumors."

Li did believe. In December 1937, the imperial capital fell to the Japanese. For the next two months, the occupying forces engaged in an orgy of atrocity against soldier and civilian alike, unrestrained by their commanding officers. If it hadn't been for the Missions School, Li himself might not have survived. At the first indication the city would fall, a handful of Americans and Europeans formed the Nanking Safety Zone in an attempt to protect some portion of the city's inhabitants from slaughter. The Japanese high command reluctantly honored the Safety Zone, which encompassed Nanking University, a women's college, and various government buildings. Because it also contained the American embassy, the entire area was granted a tenuous diplomatic immunity. The Safety Zone became a city within a city, ostensibly to provide protection for foreign-born visitors, educators, and missionaries. In reality, the Safety Zone became a place of refuge for endangered Chinese, the first stop in an underground railroad that spirited away countless noncombatants to safety in rural areas. When the Japanese first attacked Nanking, half the city fled; of those who remained behind, half eventually sought sanctuary in the Safety Zone; of those who dared to resist the Japanese, almost all perished.

Li himself remained in the city for more than a year, continuing his studies until the danger became too great. Then the directors of the Missions School sent him to Congshan, his "visit" sponsored by Jin's family—a visit that had lasted four years now. Jin was only a girl when Li first arrived, and at first he found it relatively easy to focus on his studies in her presence. Perhaps it was her youthfulness, or perhaps it was his own blindness—but with time his eyesight greatly improved. With each passing year he found himself more and more distracted, until he seemed to do little more than stare at Jin as she went about her chores. Li came to Congshan with a single-minded purpose: to serve God by becoming a doctor. It wasn't long before his plans expanded to include a physician's assistant.

Li stopped and looked at his wife. "The war is going badly," he said. "I cannot complete my education here in China. If I remain here, I will end up serving the Japanese. The Missions School has arranged for me to finish my studies in England—but this opportunity is fleeting, and we must seize it while we can."

"We will come back English," Jin said with a frown.

"We will come back *educated*," Li replied, "and we will be much better prepared to serve God and our people. There will be a very great need for doctors after the war."

"You don't have to go in person," Jin said. "Write the school a letter, as you've done all along."

For four years Li had communicated with the Missions School only by letter, making carefully guarded references to any future plans for fear that the letters might fall into the hands of the Japanese. The letters were a risk both for Li and for the school. If the Japanese discovered that Li intended to travel to England, he would be executed as a traitor; if it was revealed that the Missions School encouraged such a journey, it could provide the excuse the Japanese were looking for to shut down the Safety Zone once and for all.

"I can no longer communicate by letter," Li said. "There are too many specifics to discuss, and I can't risk putting them on paper. It would put us at risk, and also many thousands of people in Nanking."

"How will you reach the Missions School?" Jin asked. "How will you avoid the soldiers?"

"The school will help. If they can smuggle me out, they can smuggle me in again. I should think 'in' would be much easier."

"I'm frightened, Li."

Li took his wife by the shoulders. "I will be back in three weeks. Please pack our things. I expect that we will leave for England soon after."

They walked together down a dirt road to a hilltop where a stark white pagoda marked the entrance to their village. They embraced, and Jin began to weep.

"Why are you crying?"

"Because I know that you'll never return."

"I will return," Li said, "and then you'll feel silly because you wasted all these tears."

"Tears are never wasted."

Li turned away before he started weeping too. He walked quickly down the path, resisting the temptation to stop and look back. Until he crossed the next hilltop, he could feel a pair of eyes on the back of his head.

CHAPTER TWENTY-SIX

THREE WEEKS LATER TO the day, Li returned. He walked in double time for most of the last day; when he reached the final hilltop, he broke into a run. He had fantasized that Jin might be waiting for him at the pagoda, but of course that was impossible. She had no way of knowing the day or the hour he would return. He began to envision how they would meet: He would creep quietly into the cottage and surprise her, or he would be sitting nonchalantly at the table when she returned from the fields.

In the center of the road he passed a dead rat. A bad omen, some would say, but by now Li had learned too much science to hold much regard for the traditional Chinese prophecies and portents. But twenty yards ahead he found another one.

He stopped and looked. Neither rat was crushed or flattened, as it would be if the wheels of a passing cart had caught it scurrying across the path. The rats had apparently died of some internal cause. And out in the open—a most unusual behavior for the reclusive rodents. Then Li looked farther down the road, and he saw a dead cow.

He threw off his pack and started running.

On the outskirts of the village he found a man lying facedown, drinking from a puddle of scum-covered water. "What are you doing?" Li shouted to him. "Don't drink from that—the water is bad!"

The man looked up at him in a stupor, then flopped over onto his back with his head still in the puddle, staring blindly into the sky. Li could see that he was delirious, consumed with fever, and under each armpit there was a purplish tumor the size of an orange.

Li left him and hurried across the village to his own home. Along the way he saw dead rats scattered everywhere, more than he thought the village could have ever contained. He passed the body of a woman he could recognize only by her clothing; her body was stiff and bloated, and her skin was almost black in color. He passed a friend sitting placidly in the middle of the dirt road, talking to the air like a village idiot. He heard screams and mournful wails from behind shuttered windows and bolted doors.

At his house, he threw open the door and rushed inside. "Jin! Jin! Where are you?" He checked the bedroom, he looked in the backyard, but there was no sign of his wife anywhere.

He ran to the closest cottage and pounded on the door.

"Go away!" said a voice from somewhere deep inside.

"It's Li! I'm looking for my wife! Have you seen Jin?"

"Do you have it?"

"What?"

"The pestilence—do you have it?" The voice was a little closer now.

"I've been away for three weeks. I just returned today. Please, tell me what's happened! Help me find my wife!"

The door opened just a crack, and a wary eye studied him from head to foot—then the door opened just enough for a timid-looking man to wedge himself into the gap.

"Don't come inside," he said.

"What happened here?"

"Don't you know? Two weeks ago a Japanese plane flew over the village. It came out of the west—from over there," he said, pointing. "It circled over the rice paddies. There was smoke pouring out of its end. We thought it was on fire; we thought it was going to crash. Everyone came out to watch. But the plane flew away, and the smoke began to settle. It wasn't smoke at all."

"What was it?"

"It was bits of cloth, and beans, and wheat—so much wheat that people swept it up to use for chicken feed. A week ago, all the rats began to die—then the chickens, then the cattle. A few days ago people began to get sick too. It's all over the village—it jumps from house to house like a fire. It brings fever and thirst and terrible swellings. It takes one family but leaves another; it kills a mother but spares her child. What kind of a curse is this?"

"Where is Jin?" Li demanded. "Where is my wife?"

"Jin was kind; Jin was good. She helped everyone; she cared for them. Then two days ago she took ill herself—but Jin is lucky."

"Why? Why is she lucky?"

"Because the Japanese have come to help us."

"The Japanese? Where?"

"They posted a sign at the temple—they will treat anyone who comes for help. Jin didn't want to go at first, but her suffering was too great. She went just an hour ago. She thought—"

But Li was already running toward the temple. He couldn't feel his feet pounding the ground; he wasn't even sure he was breathing. His terror was beyond feeling. His thoughts kept drifting to unthinkable possibilities, and he refused to let his mind come to rest on any of them.

Fifty yards to the right of the temple, he saw a small band of Japanese soldiers climbing aboard a personnel carrier; a few of them were dressed in white biological suits. Li started toward them but thought better of it. What might he say or do in his anger, and what would they do to him in return? *Jin first*, he said to himself. *Jin is the only thing that matters*. He turned to enter the temple but stopped in the doorway.

At the end of the short aisle, in front of the altar, a woman's naked body sat bound to a wooden chair. Her head was covered by a hood, and it hung back and to the right. Her torso had been opened with a Y-shaped incision, from both shoulders to the breastbone and then down the abdomen to the pelvis. The wound lay open and gaping, and most of her internal organs lay steaming on the ground around her.

Li squeezed his eyes tight, like a man trying not to swallow poison. He felt an overwhelming rush of nausea. He dropped to his knees and vomited, but not enough—not nearly enough to get all the poison out. It was too late—he had seen the unseeable and thought the unthinkable, and he could never get the poison out of his system again.

Jin! My beloved Jin!

Li turned and looked at the soldiers. The last few were climbing aboard the truck now, joking and lighting cigarettes. Only one remained in his biological suit, flipping through papers on a clipboard. Li struggled to his feet and staggered toward them.

Jin was the only thing that mattered, but Jin was dead—now nothing mattered. Li had no idea what he would do when he reached the soldiers. He had no plan; he had no thoughts. He was pure rage; that's all that was left, and rage has a mind of its own. Rage would know what to do when it got there. Maybe rage would kill them all; maybe rage would get him killed. No matter; it was all the same now.

Li approached unnoticed. The man in the biological suit was facing away from him. Li stopped directly behind him, trembling uncontrollably. Then he reached up and ripped off his cylindrical hood.

The man turned in astonishment and stared at Li, and Li looked into his face. An hour passed, or maybe only minutes—perhaps just a single second. It made no difference. In that span of time, however it would be measured chronologically, Li recorded every form, every nuance of feature, every blemish and pore, every line and crease. The face burned into his mind like the brand from a searing iron, and it could never be erased. It was part of him now, a part of the pain and the horror, and it would stay with him for the rest of his life.

Suddenly, a soldier shoved the man aside. He glared at Li with a look of anger and contempt and raised his rifle waist-high. Li looked back with no expression at all. Then the soldier barked something, lunged forward, and plunged his bayonet into Li's abdomen. Li felt something tugging at his shirt from behind.

Li's expression never changed. He looked down at the bayonet as if it were protruding from someone else. An instant later he saw the blade withdraw again, stained with someone's blood.

Now he knew that he would die, and he felt a sense of gratitude. He stood perfectly still, with his arms at his sides, waiting for the darkness to come. He felt no pain; he felt peaceful, and distant, and removed—like a marionette being removed from a stage.

He imagined Jin in heaven, standing by a white pagoda, with her arms open wide.

Then everything went black.

MACY DROPPED HER HEAD in her hands and began to weep—so did Li. He matched her tear for tear, rocking back and forth just as he had done the night before.

They wept together for several minutes. He stopped only when she did, and then they both sat in silence and wiped their faces.

"I can't stop crying," Macy said.

"Have you tried this?" Li suggested, demonstrating his rocking motion. "I find it helps. It's an Eastern technique—rather like squeezing the last bit of toothpaste from the tube."

"I'll have to try that," she said, drying her eyes. "The soldier in the biological suit—it was Sato Matsushita, wasn't it?"

"Yes. I didn't know his name until later, when I began my research."

"He killed your wife."

"He dissected her—alive, and without anesthetic."

"In God's name, why?"

"To study the progress of the disease on her internal organs. It was thought that anesthetic might interfere with their observations."

"Was it bubonic plague?"

"Yes—as indicated by the buboes and the skin discoloration. It's a shame I had not yet finished my bacteriology degree. I understood very little at the time. It wouldn't have mattered, I suppose; with my own wounds, I would have been of no help to anyone in the village. No one could have helped, really. One-third of Congshan perished in that attack."

Li lifted his shirt to reveal a pale, twisted line of flesh just beneath his left rib cage. "The Imperial soldiers in China were badly trained," he said. "But then, I suppose it doesn't take a lot of military expertise to deal with unarmed Chinese peasants. The proper technique is to insert the bayonet, then twist as you remove it—that creates a much larger wound. It seems the old boy forgot to twist. Had he done so, I would not be sitting here now."

"How long did it take you to recover?"

"Physically? The better part of a year. Mentally and emotionally, it took a bit longer. I'm hoping to recover anytime now."

"And this is why you've spent your life pursuing Sato Matsushita."

"When I recovered from my wounds, when I regained enough of my sanity to think clearly, I realized that God had given me a mission: I must find Sato Matsushita. I'm just like Simeon in the Gospel of Saint Luke, waiting in the temple for the Promised One—and I know that I will not be allowed to die before I find him."

"And when you do?"

"There's something I want to say to him."

"And that's all?"

Li paused. "No. There's something else."

Macy searched for a tissue. "I wish you weren't such a good storyteller."

"Why? So you wouldn't feel anguish, or anger, or hatred? Those are the very things I wanted you to feel. A story that never makes it past your head remains in your head until it is forgotten. A story that passes into your heart remains in your heart forever."

"I'll never forget it," Macy said.

"That is the greatest compliment you could pay me—and my wife."

"Have you been back to the village since?"

"There's little reason. Jin's body was burned for fear of contagion—so were her clothes and our cottage. The only remaining trace of her, the only proof that she ever existed at all, is this wedding photograph."

"I'm honored that you would show it to me."

"All our friends tried to discourage us from taking it, you know."

"Why?"

"The rural Chinese can be a very superstitious people. On wedding days especially, great care is taken not to incur any bad luck or invite the wrath of malevolent spirits. In those days, photography was looked upon with suspicion—and taking a snapshot on a wedding day was simply tempting fate. To make matters worse, we're posing in front of a well. On the wedding day, the bride is never supposed to look at a well."

"Why not?"

"Wells, and widows, and cats—they're all bad luck, you see. But we loved the well; we considered it the symbol of our relationship. In our early courtship, we used to sneak away and meet there. She would go out to draw water, and for some reason my studies made me very thirsty. Her parents must have thought I had a bladder problem."

Macy smiled. "Do you think they knew?"

Li winked. "Older people know more than you think."

He slid the photograph halfway out of his pocket and peeked at it again. "Her face was supposed to be covered by a veil. She wasn't supposed to remove it until after the ceremony. Thank God she did—can you imagine if my only memory of her was a veil of beads?"

He pulled out the photograph now, studied it carefully, then squeezed his eyes tight. "I look at it every day," he said. "I study it; I memorize her face. If I don't, when I think of my beautiful Jin, an unbearable image comes to mind, something that could take away my sanity. The photograph is a kind of antidote, you see. This is the way I want to remember her."

He put the photograph away again and glanced at his watch. "Look at the time," he said. "I'm afraid I've taken up your whole morning—and here you are with examinations to grade."

"My students will thank you," Macy said. "I'm in a much more compassionate mood now."

"May I use your telephone to call a taxi?"

"I feel bad that you have to take a taxi."

"Not at all—on the way up here, I had a chance to work on my Spanish."

"It won't help on the way home. You'll probably get Arabic."

She showed him to the telephone. Li started to lift the receiver, then stopped and looked at her.

"You know, in the East we have a custom. Whenever a gift is given, it requires that a gift be given in return—a gift of equal value. It's more than a custom, really; it's almost an obligation, and people take it quite seriously. If you give a lavish gift to a poor person, the gift may be viewed as a burden—because now they have to give something in return, something just as precious."

Macy wasn't sure where this was going.

Li smiled. "I've just given you a precious gift," he said. "Perhaps, when you are ready, you'll give me something in return."

Macy nodded but said nothing.

CHAPTER TWENTY-SEVEN

DONOVAN TOOK EAST RIVER Drive north to the Willis Avenue Bridge. The traffic was light, and he was making good time. He took particular delight in watching the southbound lanes, still choked with late-morning traffic creeping its way into the city. He didn't expect to be heading back home just a couple of hours after leaving—but then, he didn't expect his simple request for an address and phone number to set off bells and whistles all the way to Washington.

Pasha Mirovik—that was the name Li had given him. When he searched the Bureau's records, he found nothing at all; when he submitted the name to the Federal Witness Security Program at the U.S. Marshals Service, it was less than an hour before he found himself in Reuben Mayer's office, responding to the angry inquiries of no less than four different government agencies.

More than seventy-five hundred witnesses are sheltered by the Witness Security Program, but not all receive the same level of protection. Those who testify against only minor miscreants may find themselves rewarded with nothing more than a new Social Security card and cab fare to the airport. Those who are willing to defy organized crime bosses or drug cartels receive new identities, relocation for their families, housing, medical care, and even employment. Then there are a very few—maybe the favored ones, maybe the cursed—whom the U.S. government causes to virtually disappear from the face of the earth.

Apparently, Mirovik was one of those. Donovan had made a casual inquiry about a name that should no longer exist, and in the process inadvertently pushed a big red button on somebody's desk. Now a lot of angry people were demanding to know how he knew that name—and much to his embarrassment, he didn't have an answer. "I got it from this old guy" is not an answer that satisfies the State Department or the CIA. So the U.S. Marshals Service made it perfectly clear: Either Donovan would get further information from his source, or they would.

Donovan tried to call Li, but there was no answer at the house. The old man could have been sleeping—after all, he was up half the night. He could have been in the shower; hopefully he wasn't stupid enough to go wandering around the South Bronx alone. Donovan had no choice but to return home and talk to the old man in person.

He pulled up in front of the house, got out, and slammed the door of the Buick a little harder than he needed to. He was beginning to resent the old man's let's-go-fishing approach to information. Li could have warned him about Mirovik. He could have mentioned that this was no ordinary name. He could have told him that this was not a minor request; it was more like asking the Mafia about Jimmy Hoffa's body. He guessed it just didn't fit into the old man's story—not yet anyway.

The front door was locked, but the bolt wasn't fastened. Since Donovan had given him a key to only the doorknob, that meant the old man was out. He poked his head in and called out to make sure—no answer. He walked back down the sidewalk and looked up and down the street—no sign of him. He took out his cell phone and dialed Macy.

"Dr. Monroe."

"Macy, it's Nathan. I'm at home, but Li's not here. By any chance is he with you?"

"He just left. He dropped by unannounced this morning. I thought he might call, but I wasn't expecting a visit."

"Yeah, the old guy is full of surprises. Did he tell you about the photo?"

"He did. He told me a story that you've got to hear."

"I'm sick of stories right now. Can you give me the gist?"

It took less than five minutes for Donovan to get the summary. While he listened, he made his way back into Li's room. "Unbelievable," he said. "They cut her open, and he found her like that? No wonder he wants to get his hands on this guy." He got down on his knees and looked under Li's bed. He pulled out the canvas duffel bag and set it on the mattress. "I'm in his room," he said, "but I don't see the photo."

"He's got it with him. The woman in the picture is his wife—it was taken on their wedding day. They're standing in front of a well where they used to meet. Ask him about it, Nathan—get the details. This is important."

"Why?"

"This is Li's motive. You need to know who you're working with."

"Right. Look, I'll call you back—I want to take care of a few things before he gets back."

He sat down on the bed and opened the duffel. Along one side was the long black case he had seen in Chinatown. He slid it out and set it on the bed beside him. Also in the bag was a medium-sized Bible. Donovan removed it and flipped through the pages; he found a plastic bag containing a small stack of papers. He emptied it on the bed. There were his passport and visa, a document verifying his British citizenship, a list of Chinatown restaurants, and a few financial records. There were no unfamiliar names, addresses, or phone numbers. There were no notes or documents relating to the case at all. He looked through the duffel again. It seemed to contain nothing else but a stack of folded laundry. He reached down into the bag, feeling between each layer of clothing, all the way to the bottom—there was nothing more.

He set the bag aside and picked up the black case. It looked ancient. The edges and corners were nicked and dented. The color was flat black like a barbecue grill, but the surface had an orange-peel texture, and the tiny tip of each raised spot was worn smooth and glossy from sliding across countless surfaces. The hardware was tarnished brass. On the front, on each side of the leather handle, were sliding tabs that released two spring latches. He tried them; the case was locked.

"Please be careful with that. I consider it irreplaceable."

Donovan looked up. Li stood in the doorway, watching, with no expression on his face. "I didn't expect you back so soon," Donovan said.

"Obviously." Li stepped to the dresser, slipped the photograph from his coat pocket, and set it upright. "Is this what you were looking for, or is this a more general search?"

"I talked to Macy. She said you had the photo with you."

"The two of you seem to do a good deal of talking behind my back. Do all of your roommates enjoy this level of privacy? But then, I'm not really a roommate, am I? I'm not even an American citizen; perhaps I'm not entitled to the same legal rights."

"Come off it, Li—you're not just some British tourist vacationing in the U.S. You're cooperating with the federal government on a criminal investigation, and that changes the rules."

Li motioned to his belongings scattered on the bed. "Are these the new rules?" He walked over to Donovan, stopped, and held out his hand. Donovan hesitated, then handed the black case to him.

"Thank you," Li said. He slid the case back into the duffel, then picked up the Bible and plastic bag. "Are all my papers in order, then?"

Donovan ignored the jab. "Macy told me the story about your wife."

"Did she tell it well?"

"I got the basics."

"Then she didn't tell it well at all," Li said with a frown. "Or perhaps you didn't listen well."

"I'm sorry, Li. I can understand how you feel about Matsushita."

"Really? And how do I feel, Nathan?"

"If it had been my wife, I would have killed the man responsible with my bare hands."

"That opportunity was taken away from me. I believe I now understand why."

"I know why you want to find this man. I understand why you've been after him for sixty years. I would do the same thing—just to have a second chance to kill him."

Li looked at him. "Then you're really no different than he is, are you?"

"Look, I'm trying to be your friend here."

"Oh? Is this how you treat your friends?"

Donovan shook his head in exasperation. "What do you want from me?"

"What I would like from you, Nathan, is a little privacy, a little respect, a little *honesty*."

Donovan was losing his patience. "You want honesty? Okay, try this: I think you're hoping the FBI will help you find your wife's murderer so you can dispatch him yourself. You think we'll help you kill Matsushita because he's also a potential threat to the U.S.—but it's never going to happen, Li; *it's never going to happen.* The FBI doesn't want Matsushita dead—we want him *alive.* Counterterrorism isn't just knocking off everybody who might pose a threat to national security—if that's all it took, we'd just shoot everybody who thumbed his nose at us. We want Matsushita alive so we can learn from him. We want to know who he works with, who pays him, and who his suppliers are. We want to know what his methods are. We want to know if he's been able to penetrate our borders, and we want to know about any other vulnerabilities he's discovered. He's worth more to us alive than dead, Li, and that's the problem here. We want you to help us find him, yes—but once we find him, you'd better be satisfied to watch him rot in some federal prison—because once we find him, we won't let you within a mile of him. Do you understand me? We will *not* let you come face-to-face with Sato Matsushita."

There was silence between the men for a few minutes. Donovan reviewed his words; he had spoken in anger, but he regretted nothing. The old man asked for the truth, and that's exactly what he got.

"I appreciate your candor," Li said softly. "Now allow me to be candid with you. My life's mission is to come face-to-face with Sato Matsushita—not to have him found, not to have him killed, and not to simply contribute to his incarceration—to come face-to-face. I will assist your government just as long as it helps me to fulfill my mission. You are interested in Matsushita's entire network; I understand that. My business, however, is with one man. Please allow me to reiterate, Nathan: You will never locate and positively identify this man without my help. If I do not come face-to-face with Sato Matsushita, *neither will you.*"

Donovan glared at him. "You claim this man wants to launch a plague attack against the U.S. Are you saying that if we won't help with your personal vendetta, you're willing to allow hundreds of thousands of people to die?"

Li returned his glare. "Are you saying that your government is willing to risk the lives of hundreds of thousands of people simply to avoid a face-to-face meeting between two old men?"

Donovan took a deep breath and slowly exhaled. "I'm just telling you the way it is, Li. I don't make the rules."

"No—but you do play a significant role in enforcing them. I don't expect you to ignore the rules, Nathan; I'm just hoping for a liberal interpretation."

Donovan pointed to the duffel bag. "What's in the case?"

Li didn't reply.

"Okay," Donovan said. "A little respect, a little privacy."

He looked up at the old man. "I am trying to be your friend, you know. I like you, Li—I want you to know that. You can be an annoying old fart, but I think you mean well."

"Old fart," Li said thoughtfully. "It's not exactly the term of endearment I was hoping for, but it's a start."

"I do understand this mission of yours—and I want to help."

"I'm afraid you understand very little."

"Maybe not. But I want to be sure you understand something: The FBI is using you, Li. They'll accept your help right up until the moment your purposes run contrary to theirs—and then they'll cross you. Do you understand that?"

"Yes. And I want you to understand that I am using the FBI in much the same way."

Donovan nodded and rose from the bed. "I forgot to tell you," he said. "We're seeing your friend Mirovik tomorrow."

"You've found him?"

"He was never lost. The U.S. Marshals Service has been keeping him under wraps. They won't tell us where he is, but they'll take us to him—and only once. Better get some sleep—if you can."

Li followed Donovan to the door and closed it carefully behind him. He locked the door quietly, then pressed his ear against the door until he was satisfied that Donovan had moved away; he returned to the bed and slid the duffel bag out from underneath. He took out the black case and placed it on the bed in front of him.

He lifted a silver chain from around his neck; attached to it was an age-worn, F-shaped key. He fit the key into each of the locks and turned it to the right. The brass latches sprang open with a soft click.

The case opened like two halves of a casting mold. In the top were three cylindrical hollows spaced evenly apart and lined with red silk. In the bottom, three glass laboratory flasks rested in molded indentations. Each flask was topped with a black rubber stopper, and the stopper and neck were further secured by a thick ring of bright red sealing wax impressed with the signet of a Chinese symbol.

Li carefully worked one of the flasks out of the silk-lined case and held it up to the light. The flask was filled with a clear fluid, no more viscous than water, with flecks of some kind of contaminant stirred up by the removal. He turned the bottle carefully and searched for signs of damage or leakage.

There were none. He let out a sigh of relief.

He shook the bottle slightly and watched the sediment drift like tiny bits of ash.

CHAPTER TWENTY-EIGHT

HOW MUCH FARTHER?" LI asked from the backseat.

"We'll get there when we get there," Donovan called over his shoulder. "You're worse than a kid."

"I'm just not used to driving such long distances. It makes me feel very American."

"We're only in New Jersey," Macy said. "You're not an American until you reach the Grand Canyon."

"How much farther is that?"

They had been headed south on the Garden State Parkway for what seemed like an eternity. It took most of an hour just to get out of the city and past the endless concrete jungle of Newark and Elizabeth. South of Perth Amboy, the industrial corridor gradually gave way to endless housing developments, which had slowly replaced the truck farms and orchards that once gave New Jersey its reputation as the Garden State. But they had left the fertile piedmont lowland half an hour ago; now they were in the outer coastal plain and still headed south, into a sparsely populated area known as the Pine Barrens.

Macy leaned over to Donovan. "Do you know where you're going?"

"No idea. I'm just following them."

Directly ahead, an unmarked Crown Victoria from the U.S. Marshals

Service slowed and turned right onto a smaller road. Donovan didn't bother to note the road number. The State Department made it very clear that they would be allowed to meet with Pasha Mirovik once and once only. Without the marshals guiding them, they would never find Mirovik—and they would never find their way back. There were parts of the Pine Barrens that had never been mapped. Donovan hoped the marshals remembered that; he sped up a little and closed the distance between them.

He glanced in the rearview mirror at Li. "I hope this is worth it," he said. "When I asked about Pasha Mirovik, all hell broke loose. The Marshals Service demanded to know what we already knew about him and *exactly* why we wanted to see him—and I didn't have any answers for them. Who is this guy, anyway?"

"I apologize," Li said. "I had no way of knowing how deeply protected Mirovik would be. To answer your question briefly, Pasha Mirovik was once a central figure in Biopreparat. Have you heard of it?"

"The Soviet Union's old bioweapons program," Macy said.

"Yes. When the Soviet Union began to crumble in the early nineties, Mirovik defected to the United States, and he told your authorities everything he knew—about the extent of the Soviet program, about advances in their research, about unheard-of new weapons. To put it mildly, it was a real eye-opener. Your government was scarcely aware the Soviet program even existed."

"No wonder he's in deep cover," Donovan said.

"When Mirovik first defected, his presence became briefly public. That's when I learned of his existence, and I attempted to contact him— but with the help of your authorities, he vanished shortly thereafter. This is one of the reasons I first sought your help; without the consent of your government, I cannot locate Mirovik."

"Why do we need to?" Donovan asked. "He must have already told our intelligence people everything he knows."

"I'm sure Mirovik answered every question he was asked—but there are questions your authorities never thought to ask."

The land was now paper-flat, dotted with scrub oaks and tall cedars.

Between them, stands of spindly pitch pines and junipers crowded together and poked up toward the sun. There were still blackened traces of a fire that swept the area a decade ago, and groups of bright green seedlings sprouted through the cinders. Around the stands of trees the thin crust of ash and pine straw gave way to wide, flowing rivers of white sugar sand.

The Crown Vic turned again—and again, and again, onto ever-smaller roads until they found themselves on an unmarked and unpaved path completely overshadowed by the towering pines. At a clearing a hundred yards ahead, the marshals pulled over and waved to Donovan to pull up alongside. Macy rolled down her window.

"Fifty yards ahead," the marshal said. "You can't miss it."

"Aren't you boys coming in?" Macy asked.

"We'll wait here, ma'am. One of us will stay with the car; one of us will patrol the perimeter on foot. If you need anything, honk your horn."

"Anything else?" Donovan asked.

"Yeah. Don't drink his vodka—he makes it himself."

The path in the clearing curved around to the right. Rounding the bend, they found an open, sandy area. On the right was a plain-looking farmhouse with white beveled siding and a gray corrugated roof. On the left was a small barn with open doors and a long row of chicken coops that ended at a short, tubular silo. A scattering of white, red, and brown chickens wandered across the sand, stopping abruptly to peck at invisible objects.

Donovan pulled up in front of the farmhouse. No sooner had he stopped the engine than the screen door burst open and a stocky, smiling man in a bloodstained apron came charging toward them. He reached Donovan first and eagerly shook his hand with both of his.

"I'm Special Agent Nathan Donovan," he said. "I'm with—"

"I know." He was already around the car, shaking Li's tiny hand in his ham-sized fist.

"Mr. Li."

Macy was just stepping out of the car; Mirovik reached in and took her daintily by the hand and elbow, cradling her arm as if it were a Fabergé egg.

"Lovely lady," he said, grinning from ear to ear. "Dr. Monroe from Columbia University, yes?"

His face had a distinctly Russian architecture, with high cheekbones and a broad, low forehead. His hair was mostly gray, but there were still streaks as red as bog iron. The hair was thick and stiff, and clumps of the stuff seemed to shoot in every direction. His skin was very fair, with a spray of titian freckles across his nose. He was of average height, but his stockiness made him seem somehow shorter. His build was thick and solid—maybe muscle, maybe only fat—but either way, there was little doubt that the man was not an object to be easily moved.

"I am Pasha Mirovik," he said with a thump on his chest. "You will stay for lunch, yes?" And with that, he started off across the open area toward the barn. Along the way, he made a quick dip and snatched a New Hampshire Red by the neck. At the barn, he reached inside the open door and took out a small ax, then started back toward them again.

"We have hen, and potatoes, and cabbage. After, we have blueberry pie. I grow them myself—New Jersey is good for blueberries."

He stopped at a tree stump, where two large nails protruded just an inch apart. He flopped the hen across the stump, positioning its neck between the nails. Then he jerked on the head and stretched the neck out like a feather boa. He stopped and looked up.

"Reds are okay for laying—much better for eating. Not a big bird, but a good breast."

The ax came around in a sudden arc and sank into the stump with a dull thud. There was a quick spurt of blood, and the chicken's body shot away like a punctured balloon. It ran for several seconds before slumping at the ground by Li's feet.

"I grow the potatoes too," Mirovik said. "Some for eating, the rest for— you know." He made a drinking motion, then realized he was still holding the chicken's head. He tossed it away and wiped his hand on the apron.

"We were warned about your vodka," Donovan said.

"Cowards." Mirovik grinned. "Come inside." He turned and headed into the house, letting the screen door bang behind him. A moment later he poked his head out again. "Bring the chicken," he said and disappeared.

The three of them stood staring at the feathered cadaver.

"I don't think he gets a lot of visitors," Macy said.

An hour later they were seated on the back porch around a simple wooden table. In the center was a roasted chicken surrounded by bowls of baked apples, boiled potatoes, and minced cabbage. Mirovik crossed himself, closed his eyes for an instant, then reached for the first bowl. He served himself a generous portion and then dug in, eating as if he were about to run out the door.

"The Bolsheviks came to power in 1917," he said between mouthfuls. "The glorious revolution—then war for four years, Red armies against White, from Siberia to the Crimea. Ten million Russians died, but not from bullets."

Mirovik glanced up. The others were just watching him, with nothing on their plates. He let out a snort. "What is the most dangerous animal in the zoo?" he asked.

Donovan looked at the others; no one had an answer.

"The arctic bear," Mirovik said. "Do you know why? Because the arctic bear never knows when he will eat next—so he kills whenever he has the opportunity, even when he is not hungry. I am from Siberia—we have arctic bear in our blood. I forget that Americans must be *invited* to eat. You would not last long in Siberia." He waved his hand vaguely over the table and returned to his own plate.

"Most died from typhus," he continued. "You are familiar?"

There was a pause from the group; it was Li who responded. "Typhus is a rickettsial disease, usually carried by lice," he said. "Seven to ten days after infection, the victim is stricken by headache and fever. There is a rash that covers the body, accompanied by gangrene on the fingertips, toes, and other extremities. Delirium follows, then death in about 40 percent of cases."

Mirovik nodded at his plate. "Soldiers are not 40 percent accurate with their rifles. Typhus taught us that there are better weapons than bullets. In

1928 the Revolutionary Military Council gave orders to turn typhus into a weapon."

"But the Soviet Union was a signatory to the Geneva Convention," Li said. "The convention banned the use of chemical and biological weapons."

"The *use*," Mirovik said, "not the development." He glanced up at Li and tilted his head. "You look Eastern; you sound Western. What is your country?"

"I am Chinese by birth, but I am a citizen of Great Britain."

"Great Britain signed too." Mirovik shrugged. "Your biological laboratory was at Porton Down. America's was at Fort Detrick in Maryland. Ours was the Leningrad Military Academy. We all agreed not to use these weapons—no one said we could not possess them.

"Our first experiments were all with typhus. We used rats; when the rats neared death, we crushed them in blenders and loaded the mush into small bombs. Crude, yes? But effective. We tested it at Solovetsky, at the gulag there."

"Did you test on human subjects?" Macy asked.

Mirovik looked at her. "You have read Solzhenitsyn? Everyone should read Solzhenitsyn.

"In ten years we had typhus in aerosol form, both powder and liquid. We thought we were geniuses—then came the Great War, and we learned better. In 1945 our soldiers entered Manchuria and captured a Japanese laboratory. Unit 731—you are familiar?"

"We are familiar," Li said quietly.

"We knew about them," Mirovik said. "They tested their weapons on some of our own people, on White Russians living in the North. We heard rumors, but we had no idea. Anthrax, dysentery, cholera, plague—they were years ahead of us. It was an entire industry—as big as the Soviet tank program.

"After the war all their documents were sent to Moscow, even the building blueprints. Stalin put the KGB in charge; within a year, we had our own laboratory at Sverdlovsk, built from Japanese plans."

"What about human testing?" Li asked. "Did that part of their research interest you?"

Mirovik paused. "We used rats, guinea pigs, rabbits—but monkeys are most like humans. A man breathes ten liters of air every minute—a monkey only four. If four particles of a virus kill a monkey, does it take ten to kill a man? That is the mathematical answer—but reality is always different. To know, you must test. But Russia, Britain, America—we are the civilized nations, yes? We were happy to benefit from the research of others, research we would not do ourselves. America was happy too—we all needed to know, you see."

The others had barely started their meals; Mirovik was already finished. He pushed away his plate and lit a cigarette. "In 1953 the structure of DNA was discovered. This changed everything—but not in Russia. We were not allowed to believe in DNA—insane, yes? It was not good Marxism, you see. In the next twenty years the whole world changed, but we did not. We knew nothing about gene splicing, about cloning—we had to smuggle in journals from the West. We could not travel to scientific conferences. We made no advances; we fell behind in everything.

"But our fears brought us to our senses; it was dangerous to fall behind the West in anything. So in 1973 Brezhnev founded Biopreparat. At first we worked in old army factories—at Sverdlovsk, and Kirov, and Zagorsk. Soon we had thirty thousand workers at forty facilities all over the Soviet Union. In Leningrad we made lab equipment and twenty-ton fermenters. At Omutninsk we studied bacteria; at Novosibirsk, viruses. At Chekhov we developed antibiotic-resistant disease strains; at Obolensk our focus was genetic engineering. That is where I worked—at Obolensk.

"Biopreparat took the brightest epidemiologists and biochemists in the country—I was one of them. I went to Obolensk in 1974, fresh from the university. By 1988 I was deputy director for all of Biopreparat. I left in 1992."

"When you defected," Donovan said.

Mirovik winced. "That word suggests betrayal—I betrayed no one. I am here because I wished to be loyal—to mankind and to myself. I was a physician, you see. I took an oath to do no harm—instead, I helped develop weapons of great power. Your people call them weapons of mass destruction; at Biopreparat we called them weapons of mass *casualty*, because they do not destroy buildings or bridges—only people.

"Biopreparat made advances no one thought possible," he said. "Pathogens are very fragile; we learned how to harden them, how to stabilize them. We learned how to protect them from ultraviolet light and changes in temperature. We perfected the aerosol—particles of virus or bacteria in a mist, particles just the right size to enter the lung. We weaponized seventy different pathogens: anthrax, tularemia, Q fever, Ebola, smallpox—"

"Smallpox?" Donovan said. "I thought smallpox was eradicated."

Li took the question. "From the world, yes—but not from laboratories. Smallpox is the most destructive disease in all of human history, Nathan. The last naturally occurring case was in 1977; three years later, the World Health Organization announced that smallpox had been eradicated from the planet. Only two laboratories were allowed to keep samples for future research: your own Centers for Disease Control in Atlanta and the Ivanovsky Institute of Virology in Moscow."

"We used ours for research," Mirovik said. "Weapons research. We kept a stockpile of twenty tons of smallpox weapons at Zagorsk."

"Did we know about this?" Donovan asked.

"America knew very little—until I told them."

Donovan let out a low whistle. "Thanks for coming."

Mirovik paused now and narrowed his eyes at the group. "The things I have told you today—all this I have said before. You did not need to visit me to ask these things. There is something else you wish to know—something I have not been asked before."

Donovan and Macy turned to Li now; they knew they were only spectators here. Li leaned forward and spoke to Mirovik as though they were the only ones there.

"I learned of your defection—your *visit*—to the United States shortly after your arrival, in 1992. Soon after, the American authorities concealed your whereabouts. There is a matter I have been hoping to discuss with you ever since."

"Yes?"

"At the end of World War II, when the Soviet Army captured Unit

731—documents and blueprints were not the only things brought back to Moscow. Scientists were brought back too."

"I have heard this, yes."

"I am searching for one of them—I believe he is still alive. His name is Sato Matsushita."

Mirovik thought for a moment. "I do not know this man."

"Are you certain?"

"You ask me about one man; in Biopreparat there were thirty thousand. Was he military or civilian?"

"He was an officer in the Kwantung Army—but I imagine he would have served the Soviet Union as a civilian."

"Biopreparat was military," Mirovik said. "There were thirty thousand *more* in civilian research."

"Please think carefully; this is very important to me. *Sato Matsushita*—he would have been about fifty years old when you first came to Biopreparat. He was Japanese, about my size and stature. He had two areas of specialty: bubonic plague—and human testing."

Mirovik's eyes widened. *"Dedushka!"*

CHAPTER TWENTY-NINE

I BEG YOUR PARDON?" Li said.

"Dedushka—that is what we called him. It means 'grandfather.' Back then we were all so young, and he was already old—so we called him Dedushka. I did not remember until you mentioned human testing."

"What can you tell me about him?"

Mirovik shrugged. "You must understand, the Soviet Union was very diverse. We had Slavs, Uzbeks, Kazakhs, Tartars, Tajiks—an Eastern man did not stand out as in your country."

"Anything you can remember would be a great help."

Mirovik slumped back and stared up at the ceiling; the back of his chair made a complaining groan beneath his heavy frame. "He was not at Obolensk," he began. "If he was, I would have known. I do not know where he was assigned. I do not know what ministry he belonged to. He was a kind of ghost. I saw him once each year—in April."

"Why April?"

"In April we tested our new weapons—at Rebirth Island, on the Aral Sea. You know this place? We called it *Tmu Tarakan*—it means 'Place of Darkness' or 'Kingdom of Cockroaches.' The sea is drying up, the water is polluted—no fish, no birds, nothing grows there. Desert all around, dust everywhere—a dead place. Just right for us, yes? Rebirth Island is a speck in the sea, shaped like a tear. A hundred of us met there every April—scientists, technicians, soldiers. That is when the ghost appeared."

"The man you called Dedushka?"

"Yes. We tested our weapons on monkeys, you see. But we did not expect to fight a war against monkeys—we needed to know how our weapons would work against Americans. That is the purpose Dedushka served."

"How?"

"He knew about humans. He helped us calculate the Q_{50} for each pathogen."

"The Q_{50}?"

"The amount of pathogen that must be used to infect 50 percent of humans within one square kilometer. It changes for each pathogen, you see. For anthrax, a man must take in ten thousand spores—but only three viral particles will give a man Marburg. You are familiar with Marburg?"

"I am familiar," Li said. "It is a filovirus—a hemorrhagic fever, like Ebola. It liquefies the organs."

"We gave Dedushka our monkey data; he gave us back human data. No one knew how—no one asked."

"He had personal experience in this area," Li said grimly.

"As far as I know, this was his only function at Biopreparat."

"Where was he the rest of the year?"

"I do not know. He was a strange man, a very quiet man. He did not drink; he did not smoke; he did not play cards with the other scientists on the island. He kept to himself. There were rumors; some said he had a small lab at Omutninsk where he did his own research. No one knew. No one cared, as long as he taught us what he knew."

"And what did you teach him?"

"Sorry?"

"He must have learned about the weapons you tested. He must have understood how they were developed, how they were improved from year to year."

"Of course."

"And he probably consulted with other research teams besides your own. It's conceivable that he would have been able to stay abreast of every advancement in Soviet bioweapons technology."

"That is possible, yes." Mirovik looked at Li more carefully now. "Why do you seek this man? What has he done?"

Li looked at Donovan for permission; Donovan nodded. "It isn't what he has done," Li said. "It's what he's planning to do. I believe your Dedushka is planning to launch an attack of bubonic plague against the United States."

Mirovik looked less astonished than any of them expected. Perhaps it was because he had imagined the unimaginable so many times that no new horror had the power to move him; perhaps it was because he had considered this possibility for so many years that the idea was too familiar to cause alarm. Whatever the reason, Mirovik sat in passive silence for a full minute before he spoke again.

"What makes you think this?" he asked.

Li recounted the story of Matsushita, the development of his plague weapon, the aborted Operation Cherry Blossoms at Night—and Hiroshima. Mirovik listened in silence but began to shake his head as the story reached its end.

"The idea is absurd," he said.

"Why is that?"

"This weapon you describe—it is the same one developed by the Japanese? It employs *fleas*?"

"Yes."

"Insect vectors were abandoned decades ago. Too unreliable, too fragile. Plague weapons are all aerosols now, released by cruise missiles—twenty-liter canisters that break apart in the air."

Macy interjected here. "There's reason to believe that Matsushita would keep the flea vector. It has tremendous psychological significance to him. It was his original weapon, the weapon he was never allowed to use. It would have an almost romantic appeal to him—like an old soldier who still wants to fight with his sword."

Mirovik looked annoyed. "Why fight with a sword when you have a rifle?"

"Wouldn't his weapon work?"

"It would have little effect."

"Why?" Donovan asked.

"The bubonic form of plague is not passed from person to person—the flea is the vector. The fleas could not be spread as broadly as an aerosol; the attack would be too localized. And the fleas would soon die—the disease they pass on kills them too. This kind of attack would be clumsy and primitive. After the initial infection, it would be easy to contain."

"Excuse me," Li said from across the table. "I think we must be very careful to separate the vector from the disease itself. First of all, Dr. Mirovik, would the flea vector work? Can fleas be used to spread plague?"

"Of course. Fleas are the natural vector of plague."

"And can fleas be purposely infected with plague for this purpose?"

"We ourselves have used this method—but not for many years."

"Then the weapon would indeed work; your objection is simply that it would not be your weapon of choice. And if the fleas could be distributed broadly, then the infection would not be localized, would it?"

"How would this be done?"

"I have no idea. I'm posing a speculative question."

"If the fleas were spread widely, the initial infection would be larger—but even then the disease would be easy to contain."

"That brings us to the second issue," Li said, "the disease itself. Dr. Mirovik, you said that this Dedushka might have been privy to every advancement in Soviet bioweapons technology. During your tenure at Biopreparat, were there any significant advances in plague research?"

"Wait a minute," Donovan said. "You told us Matsushita would want to use his *original* weapon."

"The handgun you carry," Li said. "Is it the only one you own?"

"No—I still have my Marine service sidearm."

"And when you fire it, do you use old ammunition or new? Your affection is for the weapon, Nathan, not the bullets it fires."

Donovan looked at Macy. "It's possible," she said. "Matsushita might want to retain the form of his original weapon but still enhance its effectiveness—sort of like putting a bigger engine in a classic car."

As they spoke, Mirovik lit another cigarette and rose from his chair. He walked slowly across the small porch and stood by the screen, pressing the ash of his cigarette against the small black gnats on the other side and watching them drop away.

"There were three advancements in plague research," he said quietly.

The group fell silent.

"The first advancement was in the disease itself. All plague is not the same; people do not understand this. Some strains are much more virulent than others. The worst come from the marmots of the Russian steppes. That is the strain we worked with—the one that almost destroyed Europe. It has a peculiar quality—it quickly becomes pneumonic."

Donovan frowned. "I thought all plague was *bubonic* plague."

"There is only one plague organism," Li replied, "*Yersinia pestis*—but plague takes one of three different forms, depending on the system it attacks. Plague is called *bubonic* when it attacks the lymph nodes—the buboes, if you will. Untreated, bubonic plague is fatal in about half of all cases. When plague moves to the bloodstream, it is called *septicemic*; septicemic plague is almost always fatal. When plague attacks the lungs, it is *pneumonic*. It, too, is almost always fatal—and it is the worst form of all."

"Why?"

"Because bubonic and septicemic plagues are rarely passed from person to person. As Dr. Mirovik said, the flea is the vector, and when the flea dies, the disease ceases to spread. But pneumonic plague is highly contagious—it can be passed with as little as a cough or a sneeze. The Black Death of the Middle Ages is something of a paradox: There are countless reports of the symptoms of bubonic plague, but the disease spread much too quickly and much too widely to be bubonic only. Experts believe that the Black Death was both bubonic and pneumonic in nature. It was the pneumonic form that spread the disease to millions—and it would do the same today."

"It was the same strain that Biopreparat used," Mirovik said. "After all, a biological weapon must be contagious to be useful."

No one said anything for a moment.

"Is there a vaccine against plague?" Donovan asked.

"Against pneumonic plague? No."

"Is there a cure?"

"Plague is treated with streptomycin. With rapid diagnosis and treatment, only half will die."

"*Only* half?"

"Yes—but that was before our second advancement. You see, we genetically engineered our plague to resist all major antibiotics."

"*All* of them?"

"All those currently used to treat plague."

"Then what would ever stop it?" Donovan asked.

"The same thing that stopped it in the fourteenth century," Li said.

"What's that?"

"No one knows. Our best guess is that the disease simply burns itself out—as it passes through body after body, it mutates into a less virulent form."

"How long would that take?"

"In weeks and months? No one can say. In human terms? Twenty-five million was the number in Europe, in cities far less densely populated than our own."

Another silence followed, even heavier than before.

Donovan turned to Mirovik again. "You said there were *three* advancements."

Mirovik nodded. "We also learned to splice toxin genes into the plague bacterium. The first was myelin toxin—a chemical that destroys the nerves. We tested it on rabbits; when the first symptoms of plague appeared, their hind legs were also paralyzed."

Donovan shook his head in disbelief. "Tell me something—exactly why is the State Department protecting you? If I had it my way, they'd do the same thing to you that you did to that chicken."

"Nathan," Macy said gently. "Dr. Mirovik is trying to help."

237

"He's trying to help kill a monster he helped create! You heard what he said—Matsushita's original weapon would be localized and ineffective. *He* made it effective—now it could kill millions instead of hundreds or thousands!"

Mirovik glared back at him. "What about your own country, Mr. Donovan? Do you know where Biopreparat obtained Bolivian hemorrhagic fever? We bought it from a U.S. laboratory! And when Iraq began its biological weapons program twenty years ago, where did they get their raw materials? They bought them from America! Thirty-six strains of ten different pathogens, all sent by mail in a nice little box—and Britain sold them growth medium so they could reproduce pathogens by the ton.

"And who developed nuclear technology—who released that demon on the world? Now every little country is trying to produce a bomb of its own. You must understand something: The Soviet Union turned to biological weapons because America had an atomic bomb and we did not. This monster belongs to the whole world, my friend. We all have blood on our hands."

"Gentlemen," Li interrupted. "We have only one chance to meet, and there is a much more important question to consider than who is to blame." He looked at Mirovik. "Sato Matsushita—Dedushka, as you called him—*where is he now?*"

Mirovik took his seat again. "When Biopreparat shut down, our scientists were without work—I know one who sold flowers on the streets of Moscow to feed his family. The terrible economic conditions have caused our people to seek work elsewhere."

"In other countries?"

"Wherever there is work. Our scientists could be very useful to any nation wanting to develop its own bioweapons program. The information they could provide, the experience—it could save them years of research. When the Soviet Union collapsed, many of our top scientists disappeared. Some went to Iran, some to North Korea, some to Europe—twenty-five came to America. Some of them, no one knows."

"And Dedushka?"

"This I know. Dedushka went to Iraq."

"How can you be certain?"

"In April of 1990—one of our last Aprils at Rebirth Island—Dedushka was not there. Everyone noticed—the ghost did not appear, you see. It was just before your war in the Persian Gulf. I was informed by the deputy director of Omutninsk that Dedushka had defected to Iraq."

"Was anything done?"

Mirovik shrugged. "Dedushka was a ghost. When a ghost vanishes, what is to be done?"

"Dr. Mirovik," Li said, "Iraq did not use biological weapons against the Coalition forces in the Persian Gulf."

"No."

"And Dedushka's presence in Iraq was never exposed. Had he remained in Iraq, it seems likely to me that sometime during the last fifteen years he would have been identified by Western intelligence—especially during the most recent conflict there. This suggests to me that he probably moved on to yet another country. Would you agree?"

"I would guess that Dedushka escaped to Syria. It would not surprise me if he took Iraq's entire program with him."

"What?" Donovan said.

Mirovik smiled. "What did you think—that the Iraqis destroyed their entire arsenal just to please the Americans? Tons of liquid anthrax? Nineteen thousand liters of botulinum toxin, plus aflatoxin and ricin? Nothing is easier to hide than a pathogen, my friends. A flask of liquid can fit into a pocket. A vial of freeze-dried powder can be as small as a pack of cigarettes. Dedushka did not need to drive a tanker truck across the Syrian border; all he needed was the *seed stock*—a small sample of each pathogen."

"And once in Syria, all he would need was the equipment to reproduce it," Li said. "Fermentation vessels, filtration equipment—it would all fit into a small laboratory."

"Why Syria?" Donovan asked.

"Syria shares a six-hundred-mile border with Iraq," Li said. "Across the border is Al Hamad—two hundred thousand square miles of Syrian desert. It would be a simple matter to slip across the border undetected and disappear—many parties did so at the beginning of hostilities. And

Syria has long been a haven to terrorists. I know about this—one of the last Nazi war criminals, Alois Brunner, is said to still live in Damascus. Syria denies this, of course, though Brunner would be easy enough to identify—he's missing an eye and several fingers, thanks to Israeli letter bombs. Syria has provided shelter for many terrorist groups—some say even funding and support."

"Try the university there," Mirovik said with a shrug. "They would have the necessary facilities."

After a pause, Macy leaned forward. "I have one last question, Dr. Mirovik. This scenario we've described—an attempt by one man to launch a biological attack against New York—could it really be done?"

Mirovik considered before answering. "One man alone—no. One man with the support of others—perhaps. No nation would be foolish enough to use biological weapons—even Iraq did not when facing destruction. No nation would dare—the world would tear out the throat of that nation like a Siberian tiger. But one man—one man who did not care about the cost or the repercussions . . ."

His voice trailed off, and he said nothing more.

Half an hour later they stood by the car, trading handshakes and final words. No one said, "I'll see you later," or "I'll give you a call." They all knew this was their one and only meeting and that they would never see one another again. Mirovik would finish his days on his tiny New Jersey gulag, raising chickens and picking wild blueberries from the Pine Barrens sand.

He shook Donovan's hand. "I want you to know something," he said, pointing to the tree stump with the ax still angling from its rings. "That is an option I have considered many times. Some of my friends chose that path; I chose instead to come to America, to tell what I know. I did a lot of very bad things. God will forgive me."

He turned to Li now. "Tell me—why do you seek this man?"

"I believe we explained that."

"No—why do *you* seek this man?"

Li paused. "For personal reasons."

Mirovik nodded. "Perhaps only one man can find one man, yes?"

"Perhaps only a ghost can find a ghost."

Mirovik turned to Macy last of all. "Lovely lady," he said again, "thank you for gracing me with your presence. Thank you for allowing me to look at you."

She glanced around the small farm. "Will you be okay here?"

"This is all I ever wanted—just a small chicken farm, like the one I grew up on in Russia. But life sometimes sends you down an unexpected path. Yes?"

She nodded. "Peace to you, Pasha Mirovik."

"Yes—peace."

HALFWAY BACK TO THE city, Donovan's cell phone rang.

"Nathan Donovan."

"Mr. Donovan, this is Elizabeth Mowery with the Art Theft Program. Are you still interested in funerary jars?"

"You bet. What have you got?"

"We've turned up another jar."

"Where?"

"Red Hook Container Terminal in Brooklyn."

"It came by ship?"

"That's right. When the first jar turned out to be a fake, we figured more of them would turn up eventually—so we sent out a heads-up to all the Customs agents and Port Authority officers at the docks and air terminals. We just got lucky; a Customs agent found the jar while he was doing a random search of a shipping container."

"Was the jar empty?"

"No fleas, if that's what you mean."

"What about the jar itself? Is there any way to know where it came from?"

"The ownership of the container is untraceable—but we know where the shipment originated. The ship sailed from the port of Tartus—in Syria."

CHAPTER THIRTY

THE COMPANY FOUND YOUR report very interesting," the man in the navy suit said.

I guess so, Donovan thought. *The CIA isn't in the habit of sending over two of its analysts just to throw an office party.*

"This is very good. Which one of you wrote this?" the younger man asked, looking hopefully across the table at Macy.

"We both did," Donovan said. "I didn't catch your names."

"I'm Dave. I'm a science, technology, and weapons analyst for the agency."

"Hi, *Dave,*" Donovan said with a little too much enthusiasm.

"John Stassen," the other man said. "Clandestine service."

A geek and *a spook,* Donovan thought. *Not bad—we must have caught somebody's attention at Langley.*

"I just thought it was very well written," Dave said, eyeing Macy again.

"Thanks," Macy said, covering a smile. "I'm working on my writing skills."

"Your last report was forwarded to us," Stassen said. "We were asked to evaluate its feasibility and to write an estimate on the threat potential."

"And?"

"Let me see if I understand. This fellow Matsushita—we know his background, we know his motives, and we know his capabilities. The only thing we don't know is whether he really exists."

"That's where you guys come in," Donovan said. "The FBI's charter ends at the border; we need somebody who can do some digging overseas."

"We know that Matsushita was alive as late as January of '91," Macy said. "He was known to be in Iraq, possibly headed for Syria."

"That was a long time ago. He could easily be dead by now."

"Yes—but there's also the matter of the fleas in TriBeCa. They're consistent with Matsushita's modus, and so far nobody's offered any other explanation for their presence."

"Maybe somebody just used his calling card," Stassen said. "That doesn't mean it was Matsushita himself. It could have been a student of his, or a copycat—somebody who just read about his work. It's a pretty big leap to say it's the old man himself."

"It's a very big leap," Macy said, "but it's possible—and it's too important a possibility to overlook."

"We know somebody sent the fleas," Donovan said, "and we know that one of the ceramic jars was shipped from Tartus—in *Syria*. You think that's just a coincidence?"

"Hard to tell," Stassen said. "Syria is sort of a black hole for us—a lot of things disappear there: money, narcotics, terrorists. The current government keeps making overtures to us, but at the same time they look the other way for a lot of bad guys. They may even be funding some of them; we don't know for sure. Your boy just might be there. If he is, he'll be hard to find."

"What assets do you have in Syria?"

Stassen looked at him over the top of his glasses.

"Sorry," Donovan said. "I assume you've got a station there—I know we've got an embassy. Ask your people to do some looking, will you? Ask around—start in Tartus. See if you can find the source of those jars."

"I'll check with Mossad," Stassen said. "If anybody knows what's going on in Syria, Israeli intelligence does. They'll have more sources in place."

Stassen turned to his younger colleague. "Anything from you?"

"Well, the science is all there," Dave said. "The Japanese plague bomb, using fleas as a vector for *Yersinia pestis*, Soviet reengineering of the plague bacterium—it all checks out. It's definitely doable—but frankly, I find it very hard to believe."

"Wait a minute," Macy said. "The *science* says it's doable—*you* say it's hard to believe. Which one did you write in your threat assessment?"

"Well—both," he said sheepishly.

"That was sloppy," Macy said. "Tell me—*as a scientist*—why is this scenario so hard to believe?"

He hesitated. "Well—the technical resources it would take to pull it off."

"We were told this is a fairly primitive weapon—using fleas instead of an aerosol, for example."

"Yes, that's true."

"And I understand that it requires very little equipment to reproduce a biological pathogen—about what you would find in the average microbrewery."

"That's true too."

"Then it really requires very few resources to pull off."

"Well—it requires human resources too. He couldn't do this alone."

"But that's not a scientific objection now, is it?"

He didn't reply.

Macy slid a three-ring binder in front of her and opened it. "Let me explain to you gentlemen why this whole thing is not only doable but believable. This binder contains a document I printed off the Internet. It comes from a Web site hosted by Mr. Li, the Chinese gentleman you read about in our report. This document is an English translation of a book that was originally printed in Russia in 1949. It was part of an eighteen-volume series.

"The series contains the transcripts of the Khabarovsk war crimes trial the Russians held after World War II. This volume contains Sato Matsushita's testimony. If you read it, you'll find that he's barely lucid half the time; his grief almost drove him insane. He talks incessantly about his desire to seek justice for his dead sister. He expresses it in Shinto terminology: In Shinto belief, one of the greatest evils is to take the life of another person without showing gratitude and respect for that person's sacrifice. If you do, that person becomes an *aragami*—a powerful, evil spirit bent on revenge. That evil spirit will hold *urami*—a grudge—until justice is done.

"That's what Matsushita thinks—his sister was murdered without respect and without gratitude, and she will never be at peace until he makes things right. That's a very powerful psychological motive—durable enough to last sixty years and dogged enough to find its way around almost any technical hurdle."

She focused on Dave now. "Have you ever heard of the 'white lab coat syndrome,' Dave? It's what happens when people like you step outside their area of expertise. You're a scientist, so you have authority only when you speak *as* a scientist. But when you speak as a sociologist or a political psychologist, you have no more authority than anyone else.

"Now here's what I'd like you to do, Dave. I want you to go back to that threat assessment you wrote, and I want you to look for every personal-value judgment you made—I want you to look for every recommendation or evaluation you offered outside your area of expertise, and I want you to remove them all. I want you to rewrite that threat assessment, Dave, because you write these estimates for policy makers—for people who have the power to act and to allocate resources. This is an important one, Dave, and I don't want the National Security Council to ignore this because of some casual remark you made as a nonscientist. Okay?"

Dave blinked twice. "Okay."

"Fine. Are we done here? Thank you for your time, gentlemen." Macy closed the binder, rose, and headed for the door.

All three men watched until the door closed behind her. Donovan turned and smiled at Dave.

"Still want to go out with her?"

CHAPTER THIRTY-ONE

KHALID STARED DOWN FROM the long, narrow window of the ship's bridge. Thirty feet below, the deck stretched away from him the length of a soccer field. Three rectangular holes lined the center of the deck, hatchways to three of the ship's four cargo holds—three forward, one aft. Between the hatches, two tall gray king posts rose into the sky, each one capped by a crossbeam, forming the letter *T*. From the crossbeams, black cables draped down everywhere like threads, attached to the booms of the heavy-lift derricks. Aging motors groaned in complaint; cables tightened and went slack again. A long boom arm swung out over the docks, pausing just long enough for longshoremen to fasten straps and hooks to it. Then the cables drew taut again, and a long-ton pallet rose into the air as if weightless. Ten feet above the concrete, the derrick stopped; then a motor clicked and hummed, and the boom arm slowly turned, swinging the pallet up and over the gunnels, dangling the forty-bag pallet over a gaping hatch. Bare-chested men leaned out over the cargo hold to steady the swaying load— then there was a quick shout or whistle, and the pallet was slowly swallowed by the darkness.

The king posts and boom arms were flecked with peeling shards of paint. Motor housings and bollards were covered with rust. The deck's surface was blotched and blemished; rings of various colors marked locations where cable spools and grease drums once rested. The ship's gray hull was striped with long vertical stains of brownish orange, where runoff from the deck above had slowly corroded through the failing paint.

Khalid turned to the ship's master. "How old is this ship?"

The man let out a snort. "Young enough for this job," he said.

"Are you certain of that?" Khalid wondered if the rust was just a discoloration, or more like a cancer. He wondered if the entire hull might crumble apart at sea.

"If you don't like my ship, get off."

Khalid glared at him. "I am in command of this ship."

"You are in *control*—I am in command. You represent my superiors, so I will follow your instructions. But I decide how those orders will be carried out—unless you know more about ships than I think you do."

Khalid looked at his feet; the master nodded. "There can be only one master on a ship," he said. "If I fail to follow your instructions, you can relieve me. If you disobey my orders, I will have you thrown overboard. Do you understand?"

Khalid ignored the question. "How old?" he asked again.

"The *Divine Wind* was built in 1970, at the Austin & Pickersgill shipyards in England."

"An odd name for a British ship."

"She was christened the *Lancaster*. She's traded hands a number of times since then. When a ship gets to a certain age, she is no longer profitable. Her engines get older; she burns too much fuel; she's too expensive to repair and insure. Our friends picked her up fifteen years ago; they gave her the name *Divine Wind*. In case you wonder, most ships are ready for salvage after twenty-five years. The *Divine Wind* is living on borrowed time—but then, she doesn't have to live much longer, does she?"

Khalid shook his head.

"It's just as well," the master said. "I would rather have her end her life this way than have her bones picked clean on some godforsaken beach in Bangladesh."

"How long have you been the master of this ship?"

"As long as our friends have owned it—not that their ownership could ever be proved, of course. I'm sure the ship is registered to some nonexistent corporation."

Khalid looked out again at the patches of bare wood, the unprotected metal, the fungal splotches of orange and green and brown. "They should have bought a newer ship," he grumbled.

"Our friends know what they're doing. Newer vessels cost a fortune; a ship like this can be purchased for barely a million U.S.—an important feature for people who have to pay cash."

"I've heard they own twenty like this."

"We know they own at least two," the master said.

Khalid watched as yet another pallet disappeared into the darkness of the cargo hold. "How much cargo can she carry?"

"Nine thousand tons—plus crew, stores, and bunkers."

"Bunkers?"

"Heavy fuel oil. The *Divine Wind* has a sea speed of twelve knots. She can do fourteen, but she burns twenty-five tons a day to do it. She's got a tank for diesel fuel, too, the kind we're required to burn in port, but we won't need that; we're filling that tank with bunkers too." The master looked at Khalid's blank face. "You know nothing about ships, do you?"

"I'm a soldier."

"Well, you're a sailor now." He pointed out the bridge window. "That's the *bow*," he said. "Behind us is the *stern*. Toward the bow, that's *fore*; toward the stern, that's *aft*. We're standing in the wheelhouse, or bridge. Below us are three cabin decks, then the main deck—that's called the *weather deck*. The *Divine Wind* is a hundred and forty meters long, and she's twenty-one meters wide—that's her *beam*. When she's fully loaded, the weight will sink her eight meters into the water. That's her *draft*—that's what we need to know to keep from running her aground. Understood?"

Khalid nodded.

"The *Divine Wind* is one of two hundred ships that were built just like her; only fifty of them are still afloat. She's a general cargo ship—she loads and unloads herself through deck hatches, just like ships have done for thousands of years. But sixty years ago the entire shipping industry changed. Now everything is shipped in standardized containers. The ships are bigger, faster, and they load through the side of the hull or from dockside cranes. Ships like the *Divine Wind* can no longer compete. They're too slow; they take too long in port; they don't have the cargo capacity. Ships like this used to own the shipping lanes, but now they're just tramp freighters doing odd jobs all over the world. They keep to the smaller ports—ports like Tartus, where there aren't many inspections or regulations. Every year a few more disappear—sold for salvage or broken apart on some reef. No one misses them; as I said, our friends know what they're doing."

"How long to finish loading?" Khalid asked.

"A day or two—the plumbing and wiring will take a little longer."

"And the laboratory?"

"In the aft cargo hold, lower level. There is a bulkhead that separates it from the rest of the cargo hold. The compartment is isolated from the rest of the ship, as was instructed. It is accessible by a stairway from the weather deck."

Khalid studied his face. "You are aware of the purpose of this mission?"

The master smiled. "I would be a fool to begin a voyage without knowing how it would end, now, wouldn't I?"

"And you are willing?"

"I hate the Americans as much as you do," he said. "I serve the cause."

"Then your name will blaze in the heavens for a thousand years."

"I'm just a simple sailor," he said.

"Well, you're a soldier now."

There was a knock at the door. "Come," the master said.

The door opened, and two seamen entered. They were Filipino, very young and very slender. They were shabbily dressed, and their T-shirts were smeared with streaks of grease. They were part of the black gang, the unskilled oilers and wipers from the engine room who helped keep the ship's ancient five-cylinder diesel functioning.

"Your employer wants a word with you," the master said with a nod to Khalid.

They turned to him.

"We have no further need of your services," Khalid said. "When we put to sea in a few days, you will no longer be part of our crew."

They looked at each other. "Why? What have we done?"

"Your service has been exemplary. The decision has simply been made to replace this crew with another."

"Why?"

"That is not your concern."

"Do you have another ship for us?"

"Not at this time."

They were aghast. "You are dismissing us? You can't do that—we have contracts!"

"Forgive me for not expressing myself better," Khalid said. "We are not dismissing you—not at all. We are buying out your contracts." He reached into his pocket and took out a large roll of U.S. currency. He began to count out hundred-dollar bills into two stacks; the amount was three times the remainder of their contracts.

"Have you been ashore in Tartus yet?" he asked. "A port town offers many pleasures—for a man with money."

The two men stared at one another wide-eyed, then darted for the money.

"I want you off the ship within the hour," the master said. "Get your gear together and turn out your bunks. Understood?"

Thirty minutes later the two men bounded down the gangplank of the *Divine Wind*, the wad of dollars already burning a hole in their pockets. Halfway down the gangplank, they stepped aside to let an elderly Japanese man pass, slowly working his way up toward the ship.

"Did you see him?" one of them whispered. "He must have been a hundred!"

"No wonder they're replacing us," his friend replied. "They could pay him half as much."

CHAPTER THIRTY-TWO

Donovan watched as Li took a single french fry and placed it in his mouth. He held it by the very tip and put it all the way in until his fingers touched his lips, then pulled it out again. He repeated the process over and over until he had licked off the last trace of salt.

"This is obscene," Donovan said. "Didn't anyone ever teach you how to eat french fries?"

"Be my guest," Li said, gesturing to the red carton.

Donovan ripped open two ketchup packets and squeezed them out on a napkin. Then he took half a dozen french fries, folded them in half, wiped up a gob of ketchup, and stuffed the handful into his mouth.

Li turned to Macy. "How can he be a barbarian even when he eats french fries?"

"You should see him with soup," Macy said.

Donovan wiped his hands on his trousers. "I'd rather be a barbarian than a sissy," he said. "Who eats fries one at a time?"

"I do," Li said coolly. "I consider them a delicacy—one of the few accomplishments of American cuisine."

They watched while Li slowly savored several more.

"It's called *fast* food," Donovan grumbled.

"Fast food for obsessive people," Li replied. "Dining should be a break from the hurried pace of life. All other cultures seem to understand this; I'm not sure why you Americans are so slow to catch on. Dining should be a time to relax. Dining should be a time for *conversation*."

Neither of them responded.

Li let out a sigh. "You know, you two can be quite dull. Must I always carry the conversation?"

"Okay," Donovan said with a shrug. "The CIA has agreed to check with its assets in Syria. They're going to try to find the source of those earthen jars, and they're going to ask around about Matsushita."

Li turned to Macy with a look of disgust. "That's the best he has to offer. Can you do any better?"

Macy looked at him sheepishly. "What do you want us to say?"

"I am surrounded by cowards. I mention conversation, and the two of you immediately turn to a professional topic—a *safe* topic. It's as though you have no personal lives at all."

"What did you expect?" Donovan said. "We're divorced—it takes time to build a new personal life."

"It takes time *and interest*—but I see no indication of interest. Neither of you is making an attempt to build a new personal life. Why is that? It's as though you're each leaving the space vacant that the other once occupied."

Li looked at each of them, but neither would make eye contact.

"I'm not 'leaving the space vacant,'" Macy said. "I'm just busy."

"You *stay* busy. There's anger between the two of you; that's obvious. What you fail to see is the love that still remains."

Donovan looked up. "What makes you say that?"

"I hear criticism but not contempt. I see conflict, but there is still restraint—as though there is something the two of you are still protecting. Truly hateful people can be quite brutal, you know."

"Maybe we're just being polite."

"To what end? No, there is still love between you. You said it yourself, Nathan."

"Me? When?"

"Just now. When I said, 'Love still remains,' you failed to deny it. Instead, you wanted to know the reason for my observation. That indicates *hope*, my young friend. Either you still love this woman, or you still hope to."

Donovan glared at Li now but still avoided eye contact with Macy. "Is this your idea of stimulating conversation?"

"Honest conversation, yes."

"Well, we could use a little less honesty."

"If you ask me, you both could use a lot more."

"No one asked you," Donovan said.

"I'm trying to be your friend here. Remember the old proverb: 'Faithful are the wounds of a friend.'"

"I was thinking of a different proverb: 'With friends like you, who needs enemies?' Butt out, Li. Macy and I will talk when we're good and ready."

"Will you? I wonder. I see too much pride and stubbornness in both of you."

"Maybe so," he grumbled. "What business is it of yours?"

Li returned his glare now. "I'd like to answer that question. I once loved a young woman very much—more than most people can possibly imagine. I lost her, Nathan, and when I did, my life became a series of endless regrets: things I could have said, things I could have done. It's quite amazing, the clarity of vision that death brings with it. But the mind is like that, isn't it? You never remember the thing you've forgotten until the door clicks shut behind you.

"So here you both are, with things left unsaid and things left undone. But it's not too late for you; the door is still open. So I'm here to plead with you both—talk with one another, say what needs to be said and do what needs to be done before it's too late. Please believe me—no matter how painful it may be, if you leave these things undone, your regrets will be far more painful later."

Li got up from his seat.

"Where are you going?" Donovan asked.

"I'm going home—to your home, that is."

"But I'm your ride."

"I've decided to take a taxi. I need to get my heart rate up after this heavy meal."

"Li—we can't just start talking."

"That's exactly what you can do—start talking. You don't have to finish, but you can at least start."

"It's not that easy," Macy said.

"Did I say it was easy? Forgive me; I meant to say it was *simple*. The two of you need to talk. It may not be easy, but it is that simple."

And with that, he turned and left the restaurant.

Macy and Donovan stared after him until it became painfully clear that he would not return. Then they slowly turned and looked at each other. When their eyes met, it was like crossing two live wires.

They looked away again.

Li WAS WAITING ON the sofa when Donovan opened the door.

"Well? How did it go?"

Donovan threw his keys on a side table and headed for the kitchen. "I don't know whether to thank you or punch you in the nose."

"I'm too old for punching," Li said.

"You're not too old to cause a lot of trouble." Donovan popped the top on his beer and sat down on the sofa beside him.

"What did she say?"

He took a long drink. "She asked me why I wasn't there—when Jeremy was dying."

"And what did you say?"

He paused. "I couldn't tell her."

"Why not?"

"Because I don't know."

"Then what did she say?"

"She said that if I couldn't answer that question, there was nothing else to talk about. We sat there for a few minutes, and then she left."

Li nodded. "This is good."

"This is *good*?"

"In folklore, the hero of the story always arrives at a place of ultimate darkness: a cave, or a pit, or even hell itself. There he must face a test, or answer a riddle, or slay a dragon. When he does, he returns with the golden key—the key to all his troubles."

"Li, this is not a story—this is real life."

"But life imitates stories, and stories imitate life. You've come to your place of darkness, don't you see? Macy knows it, and now you know it too. Why weren't you there when your son died, Nathan? That is the question you must answer; that is the dragon you must slay."

"And what's my prize when I do?"

"Forgiveness."

Donovan looked at him. "Funny thing," he said. "Macy's angry, and I'm angry—but you're the one who's been hunting down an enemy for the last sixty years. You're a strange one to talk about forgiveness."

Li nodded. "Stranger than you know."

CHAPTER THIRTY-THREE

THE *DIVINE WIND* PASSED the Strait of Gibraltar and the Moroccan port of Tangier on the morning of its eighth day at sea. The skeleton crew of fifteen men watched the landmasses of Europe and Africa open behind them like spreading hands. At twelve knots, it would be another three days before they reached the port of Ponta Delgada in the Azores, the last port on the last landmass before the endless expanse of the central Atlantic. They would not put in at the port, but they would pass close by. They needed no fuel or supplies; they needed nothing from Ponta Delgada at all. But Ponta Delgada needed to see the *Divine Wind* pass by.

Halfway to the Azores, the *Divine Wind* departed from the traditional shipping lanes and turned north. After ten miles she crossed the visual horizon, where no part of a funnel or mast would be visible to any passing ship. After twenty miles, she passed out of electronic range and disappeared from all ship and ground radar. At that point, the *Divine Wind* had effectively vanished from the face of the earth.

There the ship stopped.

On deck, crewmen threw ropes over the deck railings and lowered scaffolds loaded with drums of black paint. Atop the bridge, three men rigged blocks and tackles from the rim of the ship's tall stack. On the bow, the faded white letters that spelled out *Divine Wind* were already disappearing beneath strips of glossy black.

Khalid descended a long metal stairway from the main deck to the aft cargo hold. The cargo hold was divided into three separate compartments by floor-to-ceiling bulkheads running parallel to the ship. On an ordinary journey, all three compartments would be stacked from floor to ceiling with cargo or stores—but this was no ordinary journey. For this voyage, the starboard third had been converted into a temporary biosafety lab—Dedushka's lab, outfitted precisely according to his specifications.

Khalid ducked through a hatchway and into the long narrow lab. Ten feet ahead of him, a great sheet of milky polyethylene plastic draped from ceiling to floor, sealed tight around the edges with wide strips of tape. In the center of the sheet was a zippered doorway; beyond this doorway was the decontamination area. On the right Khalid saw a shower, a washbasin, and a cabinet for medical supplies. On the left was a simple wooden bench underscored by several pairs of rubber boots. Above the bench, a row of bulky white nuclear/biological/chemical suits hung from metal hooks like sleeping ghosts.

The decontamination area ended at a second plastic sheet with its own zippered doorway. Through this doorway was the final compartment, the laboratory proper, where Khalid could see the white-clad figure of Sato Matsushita bent over his worktable.

"Dedushka," Khalid called out. There was no response. "Dedushka!" He picked up a Stillson wrench from the floor and banged it against the metal bulkhead. Sato turned and stared at him through the translucent plastic. He raised one hand in greeting, then clumped to the plastic barrier and slowly pulled the zipper. He stepped through the doorway and carefully sealed the opening behind him again. In the decontamination area he stepped under the shower and pulled a long silver chain, rinsing off any clinging particles before removing his gas mask and hood.

The de-suiting process took several minutes; at last the old man pulled the zipper on the outer barrier and stepped out.

"How is the heat?" Khalid asked.

"Very bad," Sato said, mopping his forehead. "I must work in brief shifts to avoid dehydration. Is there nothing we can do?"

"It is a cargo hold," he said. "You are in the lowest part."

Sato nodded. "The fleas are not bothered by the heat—the fleas are all that matter."

"I came to tell you that the other ship has arrived."

"How long will we be stopped?"

"Only until the conversion is complete—perhaps a few more hours." Khalid looked at the old man. The temperatures in the lower cargo hold had caused more than one crewman to stagger to the top deck for air—and yet here he was, working hour after hour in a suffocating NBC suit. Perhaps it would be best if he died this way, slumping over from heat exhaustion in the middle of his work.

"You should get some rest," Khalid said. He turned and started up the stairs again. He could feel the heat lifting and the air lightening with every step.

At the top of the stairway, he turned left down a short corridor, then up three more flights of stairs to the bridge. As he entered, he nodded to the ship's master. Out the window, he could see the fourteen-thousand-ton *Southampton* sitting dead in the water a hundred yards ahead.

The *Southampton* was a virtual twin of the *Divine Wind*. It was the identical class of general cargo carrier, born in the same Sunderland shipyard in almost the same year. The two ships were identical in almost every detail: length, beam, draft, displacement. Their hull configurations were the same; they carried the same complement of heavy-lift derricks and hoists, the same rigging and masts and antenna mounts. Structurally, the two ships were identical; the only thing that distinguished them was their color—and that was about to change.

The *Southampton* flew the British flag and sailed from Cardiff in the Bristol Channel. Her hull was solid black, with her name across her bow in italic letters. Her superstructure was white, and her stack was solid red with a wide black stripe at the top.

The *Divine Wind* had a chalky gray hull, with a white stack topped by rings of gray and royal blue. Her name was in simple block letters, and she sailed under a flag of convenience—the flag of Saint Vincent and the Grenadines.

Crewmen hung from the sides of both ships, dangling from ropes and perching on scaffolds, stretching left and right with rollers and brushes. Within hours, the ships had traded colors. The *Southampton*'s hull was now a slate gray—but she looked too freshly painted to pass for her neglected sister, so buckets of acid were poured down her sides, stripping off some of the paint and exposing the naked steel beneath, followed by buckets of salt water to accelerate the rusting process. Her stack was now a boring white, the paint thinned slightly to lend the appearance of age. In a matter of hours, the pristine *Southampton* had aged twenty years.

Her hard-worn sister, on the other hand, had been rejuvenated. The *Divine Wind*'s hull was now a gleaming black, with a new name emblazoned in script across the bow. The fresh red paint rose up the sides of her stack like a climbing flame, with a crisp black smoke ring at the top. Finishing touches were added to the lettering, and flags were traded; and with those final details, the *Southampton* and *Divine Wind* had miraculously traded bodies—but not voices.

That, too, was about to change.

On the bridge, the ship's master sat in front of a laptop computer with Khalid standing behind him. Beside the computer, a small gray device with its own simple keyboard was mounted to the console.

"This is the Automatic Identification System," the master said. "Since last year, all ships over three hundred tons have been required to carry one. It is a transmitter and a receiver; it constantly sends out information about this ship, and it constantly receives information from others."

"What kind of information?"

"Information about the ship, its cargo, our destination, the number of passengers, our bearing and speed—all these things."

"Where does it get all this information?"

"Some of it we provide. When the unit is first installed, we enter the ship's name, our call sign, and a description of the ship. Length, beam, displacement—these things never change, so they are entered only once. Then there are things that change with each voyage. Our destination, our cargo, our draft—we must enter these each time we leave port. And there are some things that change at every moment. Our speed, our course, our precise position—these things the ship provides. Our speed and position come from the Global Positioning System; our heading comes from the gyrocompass.

"All this is transmitted every twenty seconds; every ship within twenty miles receives our signal. That is why we agreed to meet here, away from the shipping lanes and out of range of other vessels—except that one," he said, pointing to the *Southampton.*

"The information we provide," Khalid said. "What prevents us from changing it?"

"You are not as stupid as you look," the master said. "Watch the screen."

The master picked up the radio and contacted the bridge of the *Southampton.* Khalid saw several lines of text describing every detail of the *Southampton*'s structure, cargo, and destination. Every twenty seconds the image blinked momentarily and then refreshed again. After one blink, the name of the ship vanished; twenty seconds later, the name *Divine Wind* took its place.

"Welcome aboard the *Southampton,*" the master said, typing at the unit's keyboard. "We are now transporting nine thousand tons of steel, machinery, and newsprint from the West Midlands of England to the city of New York. I wish it was always this easy to load cargo."

He nodded out the window at the newly christened *Divine Wind.* "We'll give her a couple of hours' head start," he said. "When she passes Ponta Delgada, the vehicle tracking station there will pick up her signal— she will appear to be the *Divine Wind* out of Tartus, bound for La Guaira in Venezuela. When we pass a few hours later, we will appear to all observers to be the *Southampton.* And when we approach New York Harbor ten days from now, the authorities there will see just what they have been expecting to see—just a friendly little cargo ship flying a British flag."

The transformation was now complete.

CHAPTER THIRTY-FOUR

DONOVAN LEANED BACK IN his chair with his feet propped up on his desk. He'd gotten little done all morning, except to type up a report for Reuben Mayer on his meeting with the CIA analysts the week before. He couldn't seem to focus; when he thought about the meeting, he thought about Macy and the way she handled Dave the Science Guy. You had to admire that kind of ability—if you weren't on the receiving end of it, that is. What a formidable woman. *What made that wonk think he had a chance with a woman like Macy?* Every time he thought about it, he felt angry. But why was he angry? He kept thinking about something Li had said: 'The two of you are still *protecting* something.' Was that it? Was he still protecting Macy from other men? Or was he just protecting himself from imagining Macy with other men?

When he thought about Macy, he thought about Li. He wondered if bringing the old man to his house was a stupid thing to do. Now he had a roommate, and that was the last thing he wanted. Living with Li was like being back in ordnance removal—there was no way to know when he would go off; there was no way to tell what he would say or do next. He had to admit, though, there was something about the old man he liked. Maybe it was the same thing he liked about bombs—the honesty, the uncertainty, the risk.

And when he thought about Li, he wondered how this whole thing would end. The old man had his heart set on finding Sato Matsushita; Donovan wished he could make it happen. He wished he could find Matsushita and tie him to a chair, then leave the room and lock the door while Li did what he needed to do. But Donovan knew that would never happen. He wondered if, deep in his heart, Li knew it too. If he did, he wasn't letting on.

If the CIA found Matsushita in Syria, Donovan had no idea what would happen next. He knew that he himself would be finished with the case—it would be an international matter, under the jurisdiction of the CIA or the State Department. Li would demand to see Matsushita, but he would be refused in no uncertain terms. Matsushita would be extradited, interrogated, and then imprisoned or hidden away on some little chicken farm like Pasha Mirovik. Then what would happen to Li? What happens to an old man when he loses his only reason to live?

The phone rang. Donovan reached for it absentmindedly.

"Nathan Donovan."

"Mr. Donovan, this is John Stassen over at CIA. You got a minute?"

Donovan jerked his legs off the desk and sat up. "What's up, Mr. Stassen?"

"I thought you might like to know what's going on over here. This is purely a professional courtesy, you understand. Since you're the one who brought this to our attention, I thought I'd keep you in the loop."

"I appreciate that."

"We've heard from our people in Syria. We think we've located this Sato Matsushita character."

Donovan was focused now. "You're sure of that?"

"We think so. We took your advice and focused on the two main ports—Latakia and Tartus. Port towns are a great place to pick up information—sailors have a lot of time on their hands while their ships are loading. They tend to hang out in the waterfront bars. They drink a lot, and they talk a lot—about cargoes, and crewmates, and destinations. It's not too hard to listen in."

"What did you hear?"

"It was in Tartus, like you said. Two Filipino crewmen were making a lot of noise in one of the local establishments—flashing a lot of money, buying drinks for the house, that sort of thing. They claimed they got put off their ship. Not fired—bought out. Said the big boss called them in one day and bought out their contracts on the spot. Gave them three times what they had coming—in U.S. currency."

"That's pretty generous."

"No kidding—they pay these guys dirt."

"Sounds like somebody wanted happy campers."

"Somebody wanted them *gone*—off the ship pronto, no questions and no objections. We did some checking around town; we found three more crewmen who were put off the same ship. That makes five in Tartus alone—there may be more who already left town. We think there's a good chance they replaced the whole crew."

"Is that a red flag?"

"That's a big red flag. It takes time to train a crew, and you need veterans to train the new recruits. Nobody turns a crew over all at once—who would do the training?"

"Maybe you've just got a ship with a moron in charge of personnel. What does this have to do with Matsushita?"

"When the two Filipinos left the ship, they said they passed a new guy coming on board. They said he was a very old man—and he was Japanese."

"Did they get a name?"

"No."

"Is there any kind of crew manifest? Some way to get a positive ID?"

"Not that we can find."

"Where is this ship now?"

"In the middle of the Atlantic. It left port two weeks ago. Four days ago it passed the Azores; a VTS station there recorded its transponder signal. It's an old tramp freighter called the *Divine Wind*. The ownership is untraceable—but that's true for a lot of these old wrecks."

"Where's the ship headed?"

"It's headed for La Guaira, in Venezuela."

"Venezuela? Why Venezuela?"

"Beats me. Syria exports a lot of phosphates to South America. Maybe Matsushita is tagging along, looking for a back road into the U.S."

"If it's Matsushita."

"We think it's worth checking out. We know the *Divine Wind*'s exact location; a couple of tankers are passing her transponder signal on to us, and we've picked her up on one of our satellites. Right now there's a Navy missile cruiser on its way to intercept her."

"You're going to board her?"

"If necessary—whatever it takes to positively identify this old man."

"Tell your people to be careful," Donovan said. "If this guy really is Sato Matsushita, and if he's carrying this plague weapon of his, he just might use it. If you back him into a corner, what does he have to lose?"

"We're on top of it," Stassen said. "The cruiser is carrying a SEAL unit and a team from the Centers for Disease Control in Atlanta. They know how to handle these things; they're not going to walk into anything with their pants down."

"What if they won't let you board her? What then?"

"I can't comment on that."

"I understand. Look, do me a favor, will you? Let me know when you ID this old man. I've got somebody here who'd really like to know."

CHAPTERTHIRTY-FIVE

THE SHIP'S MASTER TRAINED his binoculars on the horizon. There was no sign of the American missile cruiser itself, but a fast-run boat from the cruiser had appeared over the horizon and was approaching on the starboard side. He steadied the binoculars on the approaching craft, racing across the water toward him like a skipping stone. He estimated its speed at twenty knots; at that rate, they would arrive in minutes. He counted ten men on board—eight of them were armed, and all wore biological suits.

The missile cruiser identified herself as the USS *Leyte Gulf,* and her orders were simple and clear: Stop your engines and prepare to be boarded and searched. The ship's master complained that such a search was illegal, a violation of their rights on international waters. He demanded the reason for this intrusion. He offered to send them a complete passenger list and cargo manifest—but nothing deterred them. It was clear that the Americans were unwilling to believe anything except what they saw with their own eyes. They were intent on boarding the *Divine Wind*—and that could never be allowed.

He hurried down to the main deck and followed the starboard railing toward the bow. He raised his binoculars again; the boat was so close now that the binoculars were no longer necessary. He could see one of the men standing, holding a bullhorn and issuing demands. The voice was in Arabic. So the Americans knew who they were, and they knew where she was from—but what else did they know?

He turned and looked down into the open hatch of the number three cargo hold. The entire crew was huddled together on the lower deck, kneeling and bowing in as easterly a direction as was possible on a ship adrift at sea.

The master considered his options. He could not run; the cruiser would easily overtake them. His crew had enough weapons to repel this small boarding party, but there would only be another. It was a missile cruiser—it would fire on the ship; it would cripple her and then board her by force. And once on board, the Americans would quickly recognize that this was not the *Divine Wind* at all. It would only be a matter of time before the real *Divine Wind* was discovered—and then all would be lost.

It was a chance he could not take.

He turned to his crew again. "This is a great and glorious day," he called down into the cargo hold. "Today we will offer our perfect sacrifice; today we have been chosen to become *shahids* and to rejoice together in Paradise. Open the seacocks."

They opened two valves, and geysers of water gushed into the lower hull.

The master turned back to the railing again. The inflatable was almost alongside now.

"What is it you wish?" he called out to them.

"Stand down," the bullhorn blared back. "Prepare to be boarded. Instruct all crew members to report to the main deck immediately."

"This is a privately owned vessel, and we are in international waters. You have no right to board this ship."

The two closest men raised their weapons. "Step back from the railing. We are coming aboard."

"Americans," the master said, sneering. "There is no end to your arrogance." From behind his back he pulled a revolver from his belt. Before he could level the weapon, there was a burst of fire from the boat. The ship's master stumbled backward and over the edge of the open hatch; he was dead before his body hit the water in the bottom of the cargo hold.

A crewman stared down at the body, then turned his face to the blue rectangle of sky above him. "*Allahu Akbar*," he said.

Then he lifted the small box and grasped the protruding handle. He twisted it hard to the right.

The ocean erupted in a ball of fire.

CHAPTER THIRTY-SIX

LI WAS SITTING ON the sofa, staring at the television, when Donovan flung open the door and charged into the room. He reached the sofa in three steps and landed beside Li; the sudden counterweight caused Li's end of the sofa to rise three inches higher.

"Are you watching it?" Donovan asked.

"You certainly know how to make an entrance."

"The report on CNN—are you watching it?"

"I'm not certain what I'm supposed to be seeing," Li said. "They are reporting that a U.S. naval vessel intercepted a merchant ship in the middle of the Atlantic Ocean. The merchant ship unexpectedly exploded, killing several Navy personnel and apparently some civilians as well."

"Any other details?"

"Very few. What's this all about, Nathan?"

Donovan leaned forward and switched off the set, then turned and looked at Li. "Sato Matsushita was on that merchant ship," he said.

Li's eyes widened, but he said nothing.

"The ship was from Syria," Donovan explained. "It set sail two weeks ago, headed for Venezuela. Two former crewmen reported seeing an elderly man board the ship—an elderly *Japanese* man."

"Where did you learn this?" Li asked.

"From a contact at the CIA."

"*When* did you learn this?"

"Yesterday."

"Yesterday! Why didn't you tell me?"

Donovan hesitated. Li studied his eyes, then slowly nodded. "I see— you were hoping not to tell me at all."

"I didn't want to get your hopes up. We didn't know for sure it was Matsushita—that's why they sent the missile cruiser, to board the ship and get a positive ID on the old man."

"And did they make this identification?"

"The cruiser sent an inflatable with a SEAL squad and two scientists from the CDC to check out the ship—but when they pulled up alongside, the crew blew up the ship. The blast killed all ten men. The ship sank like a rock—there was nothing left of it."

"Then no one actually saw Sato Matsushita."

"Come on, Li, who else would it be? An elderly Japanese man boards a ship in Syria. We try to board the ship, but before we can, they blow it out of the water. Now, who rigs a ship to self-destruct? Somebody with something to *hide*, that's who. And let me tell you something—it takes a *lot* of explosive to tear a ship apart like that. Somebody wanted that ship to sink without a trace."

Li thought for a moment. "Can the ship be salvaged?"

"In the middle of the Atlantic? It could be three miles down—whatever's left of it."

"Could bodies be recovered?"

"Li—there's nothing left, okay? Nothing at all."

Li paused again. "Then we can't be certain it was Sato Matsushita."

Donovan rolled his eyes.

"You said the ship was bound for Venezuela. Why would Sato Matsushita want to go to Venezuela?"

"We never got a chance to ask him."

"That seems highly unlikely. And besides—"

"Li." Donovan put a hand on the old man's shoulder and spoke as softly as he could. "Sato Matsushita is *dead*. Do you hear what I'm saying?

Your old enemy is *dead.* There's no way around it; you have to face it. I'm sorry you didn't have the chance to kill him yourself—but at least you know he got what was coming to him. I've seen people die in explosions, Li. It's no pretty sight. He was probably torn apart, or—"

"Nathan," the old man said, "you understand so little."

Donovan leaned back. "Maybe so—but at least I understand this: Matsushita is dead, and you just have to get over it."

Li shook his head. "You have no idea what you're saying."

"I know it was your *mission*," Donovan said, "but try to look at it this way: Without your help, we never would have found Matsushita at all. You told us about him; without you, we never would have tracked him to Syria—we never would have known he was on that ship. We only stopped the ship because you warned us about his plague weapon. He didn't die of old age, Li; he died because of *you.* In a way, you did fulfill your mission."

"My mission was not to cause his death," Li said. "My mission was to meet him face-to-face."

"I tried to tell you that would never happen."

"Yes—you did."

They sat in silence for a few moments. "So Sato Matsushita 'got what was coming to him,'" Li said. "But what about me, Nathan? Am I to remain imprisoned for the rest of my life?"

"You've got to let it go," Donovan said.

Li looked at him. "The way you've let Jeremy go?" He got up from the sofa, walked into his bedroom, and shut the door behind him.

That evening, Donovan sat on the front step and pressed the cell phone tight against his ear. The Fourth of July was just three days away, and he could hear the occasional screech of a bottle rocket and the crackle of firecrackers in the distance. Fireworks were illegal in the city of New York, but the NYPD had better things to do than arrest every ten-year-old with a sparkler. After all, it was the Fourth of July, and New York was in a mood to celebrate.

"How did he take it?" Macy asked.

"Pretty hard, I think."

"What did he say?"

"He said his mission wasn't fulfilled—that he was still in prison."

"Where is he now?"

"In his room. He went to bed early."

"Check up on him, Nathan. Don't leave him alone."

"You think he might do something stupid?"

"I think he's a very old man who just lost his reason for living. What do you think?"

"I told him he had to get over it."

"Nathan—"

"I didn't mean right away—I just meant that eventually he has to find something else to live for."

"What did he say to that?"

Donovan paused. "Nothing."

"Stay with him, okay? Let me know how he's doing."

"Maybe we can all get together again. I think he'd like to see you."

"Okay. Call me."

"Hey," Donovan said. "It's nice talking to you again."

There was a click on the other end.

He got up and went into the house. Li's bedroom door was shut tight. Donovan turned the knob as quietly as possible and pushed the door open just enough to peer inside. The old man was lying on his back, staring up at the ceiling. His fingers were interlocked, holding the photograph of Jin against his chest.

"I'm not dead, if that's what you're thinking," Li said without moving his eyes.

Donovan stepped into the room. "Could have fooled me."

"I'm just having trouble sleeping."

"I have that problem too."

"Give it a few decades—you'll get used to it."

Donovan sat down on the end of the bed. "You okay?"

"In what sense? My body is quite well, thank you. My thoughts are extraordinarily clear."

"I mean about the news today."

"I haven't 'gotten over it' yet, if that's what you mean."

"I'm sorry," Donovan said. "I talked with Macy; she told me that was a little blunt."

"The two physicians conferring over their patient," Li said. "Dr. Monroe's specialty is the mind—what's your specialty, Nathan?"

"Survival."

"What a very narrow specialty. Life is more than survival, Nathan—life is about healing. The trick is to continue healing right up until the moment you die. The irony is, I'm more than eighty years old, but I'm healthier than you are."

"All I meant to say is you have to move on. It's all you can do, Li."

"Have you ever taken a holiday, Nathan? It's been my experience that there are two kinds of holidays. In the first kind, the destination is the thing—you cannot wait to get there; you have someplace to *be*. But in the second kind, the trip itself is the holiday. Imagine how dull a holiday would be if one could simply teleport oneself from place to place. Imagine how much you would miss. Life is a journey, Nathan, not a destination. You mustn't be in too much of a hurry to arrive. You really must stop along the way—even at the dark places. They're part of the journey too."

Li's voice trailed off now. He continued to stare at the ceiling, saying nothing, not even blinking. Donovan watched him, wondering how much of a journey the old man had left.

"May I tell you something?" Li said softly. "Something I've never told anyone before." He looked down at Donovan for the first time. "I knew my wife was dead before I approached the village."

"What?"

"Before I saw the first dead rodent. Before I even crossed the final hillside, I already knew."

"How?"

"'The two shall become one flesh'—that's how the Scriptures put it.

When Jin's spirit left this world, I sensed her absence. It was as obvious to me as if we were two children playing on a seesaw, and she stepped off the other end. I knew, Nathan. It wasn't a premonition or a sense of foreboding—I *knew*." He paused. "That's how I know that Sato Matsushita is still alive."

Donovan's shoulders slumped, and he let out a sigh. "Li—"

"I am joined to him, Nathan. If his spirit had left this world, I would know. I've been lying here thinking and praying all evening. God has reassured me that I will not die until I meet Sato Matsushita face-to-face. I will not die in bondage; I will have the chance to release my soul from prison."

"I hate to question God," Donovan said, "but what about the evidence? He was on that ship, Li, and that ship went down. There were no survivors."

"It was the wrong ship."

"What?"

"It was the wrong ship, or Sato was not on it. Perhaps he only boarded temporarily; perhaps he disembarked again before the ship set sail. I have no idea—I'm simply telling you that he is still alive. This is not my imagination, Nathan, or some desperate wish. I'm simply telling you what I *know*."

"And I'm telling you what *I* know," Donovan said. He patted the old man's leg and rose from the bed. "Try to get some sleep," he said, "if you can."

Donovan closed the door behind him and went into his own bedroom. He stripped down to his boxer shorts and stood in front of the air conditioner, trying to shed the evening's heat before he attempted sleep. He parted the drapes and looked out; in the distance, he saw a trail of silver sparks slowly streak across the sky and then explode, dripping down in a shower of white and gold.

In bed, he found himself staring at his own ceiling and thinking about the old man next door. *Some holiday*, he thought. Li was wrong; some vacations were so bad that you'd gladly teleport from place to place—you'd skip the whole thing if you had the chance. But you don't get that chance—maybe that's what Li was saying. Maybe life is the vacation from hell, an endless road trip where you don't know where you're going but you're making really good time. And every town you stop at along the way is dull and disappointing, but you keep telling yourself that the next one will be better. You just keep driving; you never learn.

Li was wrong. Sato Matsushita was dead, and Li would have to get over it—it was a destination, not a journey, and the sooner he could get there, the better off he would be. Li was like some old poem—he sounded so wise, but the words never really made sense. Maybe Macy was wrong too; maybe Li was insane—or maybe he was the sanest man Donovan had ever met.

No—Li was wrong. But something the old man said kept bothering him, kept coming back to him. He couldn't ignore it; he couldn't put it out of his mind.

It was the wrong ship.

Donovan rolled over and reached for the phone.

CHAPTER THIRTY-SEVEN

MACY SAT UP IN bed and switched on the light. It was no use trying to sleep. Sometimes her thoughts were like a freight train, gathering momentum all day long. When she finally turned out the light and commanded her mind to rest, it was like hitting the brake. It took miles to come to a full stop—it took hours.

She dreaded the winding-down process. It was the loneliest part of her day, lying in the darkness and staring wide-eyed at nothing at all. There was nothing to listen to, nothing to touch or taste—no distractions at all. *That's the problem with darkness*, she thought. *It's a theater for the mind.* In the darkness of the bedroom, every thought became louder, every image more distinct. She tried sleeping on the sofa, with all the lights on and the television playing in the background, hoping to somehow pass directly from consciousness into perfect oblivion. It didn't work—nothing did.

"It's nice talking to you again," Nathan had said. It was a thoughtful sentiment, they were gracious words, but they made her furious. What did he think—that Jeremy was a topic they could just ignore, that they could just forget the whole thing and be pals again? Nathan was absent from his own son's death. Jeremy died alone, wondering why his father had abandoned him. That was over—that was history. But Nathan couldn't just show up again now, without apology and without excuse, and pretend that it never happened. It *did* happen, and it hurt worse than anything in Macy's whole life.

The more she thought about it, the angrier she became—angry at Nathan and angry at herself for letting her mind go there again. She could feel the adrenaline creeping into her system. *Terrific*, she thought, *there goes another hour. Maybe I can look through Jeremy's baby pictures again—that'll keep me up all night.* She turned to the nightstand and picked up the small book Li had given her at the restaurant. Might as well put the time to use. She slipped on a pair of reading glasses.

Just inside the cover was a note in Li's own immaculate handwriting. It read:

> *My dear Macy,*
>
> *The book you are holding is known as The Decameron. It was penned by Giovanni Boccaccio in 1353, while the Black Death was still ravaging Europe. It is the tale of ten young friends who fled to the countryside to escape the plague in the city of Florence. Each day, the group took turns entertaining one another with stories. The book is a collection of their stories. Some contain eyewitness accounts of the plague and its effects. I have earmarked one particular section for you; I think you will find it most interesting.*
>
> *With all respect and affection,*
> *Li*

Macy flipped through the pages. Near the center was a small sheet of rice paper marking the first page of a chapter. She set the paper aside and began to read.

> *I say, then, that the years of the beatific incarnation of the Son of God had reached the tale of one thousand three hundred and forty-eight when in the illustrious city of Florence, the fairest of all the cities of Italy, there made its appearance that deadly pestilence . . .*

In Florence, despite all that human wisdom and fore-thought could devise to avert it... towards the beginning of the spring of the said year the doleful effects of the pestilence began to be horribly apparent by symptoms that shewed as if miraculous...

In men and women alike it first betrayed itself by the emergence of certain tumours in the groin or the armpits, some of which grew as large as a common apple, others as an egg, some more, some less, which the common folk called gav-occioli. From the two said parts of the body this deadly gav-occiolo soon began to propagate and spread itself in all directions indifferently; after which the form of the malady began to change, black spots or livid making their appearance in many cases on the arm or the thigh or elsewhere, now few and large, now minute and numerous... Almost all within three days from the appearance of the said symptoms, sooner or later, died...

They stayed in their quarters, in their houses, where they sickened by thousands a day, and, being without service or help of any kind, were, so to speak, irredeemably devoted to the death which overtook them. Many died daily or nightly in the public streets; of many others, who died at home, the departure was hardly observed by their neighbours, until the stench of their putrefying bodies carried the tidings; and what with their corpses and the corpses of others who died on every hand the whole place was a sepulchre...

It was the common practice of most of the neighbours, moved no less by fear of contamination by the putrefying bod-ies than by charity towards the deceased, to drag the corpses out of the houses with their own hands... and to lay them in front of the doors, where any one who made the round might have seen, especially in the morning, more of them than he could count... It was come to this, that a dead man *was then of no more account than a dead goat would be today . . .*

They dug, for each graveyard, as soon as it was full, a huge trench, in which they laid the corpses as they arrived by hundreds at a time, piling them up as merchandise is stowed in the hold of a ship, tier upon tier, each covered with a little earth, until the trench would hold no more . . .

How many brave men, how many fair ladies, how many gallant youths, whom any physician . . . would have pronounced in the soundest of health, broke fast with their kinsfolk, comrades and friends in the morning, and when evening came, supped with their forefathers in the other world.

Macy shuddered. She picked up the piece of paper to mark the place again, and only then realized that the paper bore Li's handwriting too. It contained two short excerpts from a book titled *In the Wake of the Plague*.

The level of mortality in the Black Death was so high and so sudden that—until germ warfare on a large scale occurs—to find a modern parallel we must look more toward a nuclear war than a pandemic . . .

Nothing like this has happened before or since in the recorded history of mankind.

Suddenly, she heard pounding at her front door. Someone was hammering it with his fist, shouting something through the door. Macy threw off the covers and scrambled into her robe. She stopped at her closet just long enough to grab the first shoe she could find—then she thought about her chances of fending off an attacker with a black Mary Jane, and she threw it back into the closet.

"Who is it?" she shouted through the door.

"It's Nathan and Li! Open up!"

Macy peered through the peephole and saw the fish-eyed images of the two men. She unlocked the dead bolt and knob. The door was only halfway open when Donovan pushed past her.

"Where have you been?" he demanded. "I've been trying to call."

"I took the phone off the hook—I was trying to sleep."

"That was a stupid thing to do. We wasted half an hour getting up here."

"What's the hurry? What's happened?"

"You've got five minutes to get dressed. They want us down at 26 Fed—*now*."

CHAPTER THIRTY-EIGHT

THE CONFERENCE ROOM AT 26 Federal Plaza was crowded with people, high-ranking representatives of the thirty-odd organizations composing the Joint Terrorism Task Force. The conference table was littered with papers, maps, and open laptops with cellular uplinks to government offices, military bases, and the FBI's own Strategic Information and Operations Center in Washington. There were uniforms from three different services, though there were more civilians in number; there were men and women in formal business attire, and there were open collars with shirttails out. People hustled everywhere, making quick verbal exchanges and handing off papers to administrative assistants who darted in and out of the doors. On the far wall, a rear-projection screen displayed a satellite photograph of New York Harbor.

No one noticed Donovan, Macy, and Li when they entered. Donovan spotted Poldie and Reuben Mayer across the room; he motioned to Macy and headed for them. The room was in chaos—there was no podium, no microphone, no indication of who was in charge.

Donovan leaned over to Poldie. "Who's running this show?"

"It's opening night," Poldie said. "I think we got a few bugs to work out."

Donovan looked around the room, waiting for someone to take charge—but no one did. He put two fingers to his lips and produced a whistle that would stop any cab in New York.

The room fell silent. Donovan stood up.

"My name is Nathan Donovan," he said. "I'm with the FBI. I was in charge of this case; I'm not sure who's in charge of it now, but we need to figure that out fast. Let's start by finding out who's here. He's NYPD," he said, gesturing to Poldie. Then he nodded at Macy: "And she's Columbia University."

He began to point to people around the table. No personal names were given, only the names of represented agencies. There were intelligence experts, analysts, and state and local law enforcement. There was the CIA, the Department of Homeland Security, Customs and Border Protection, and the Transportation Security Administration. A Coast Guard Port Security Unit was present; so was a top official from the Centers for Disease Control in Atlanta. The Navy would ordinarily be represented by the Naval Criminal Investigative Service—but on this occasion a SEAL commander had replaced him, from the Naval Special Warfare Development Group out of Dam Neck, Virginia.

"Okay," Donovan said. "Time is short, so let's get right to it. CIA, we need a situation briefing—the short version, if you don't mind."

A man on the opposite side of the table rose from his chair. "By now you all know the basics," he said. "About twenty-six hours ago the USS *Leyte Gulf* intercepted a Syrian cargo ship called the *Divine Wind*. We now have reason to believe that the ship was not the *Divine Wind* after all.

"The vessel tracking station in the Azores picked up the *Divine Wind*'s transponder signal about four days ago. We worked backward from that date, tracing her course using satellite photographs. We found this," he said, pointing to the projection screen. He hit a button on his laptop, and the screen changed to show a satellite image of two ships so close together that they looked as if they were about to collide.

"About six days ago the real *Divine Wind* headed north, out of commercial shipping lanes. She stopped here, at this point; the other vessel you see in the photograph joined her a few hours later. We've traced that ship back to her point of origin—she's the *Southampton* out of Cardiff. She's exactly the same kind of cargo ship as the *Divine Wind*—and I mean exactly.

"Now watch," he said, changing the image again. "This was taken a few hours later. The top ship in the photo is departing first—that's the *Southampton*. But when she passed the Azores, her transponder signal identified her as the *Divine Wind*. We believe the two ships traded identities—flags, colors, transponder data, the works. We think it was a ruse to conceal the whereabouts of the real *Divine Wind*."

"Where's the real one now?" the Coast Guard asked.

"About ten hours out of New York Harbor."

There was a second of complete silence—then the room erupted in noise.

"Let's hold it down!" Donovan shouted over the din. "Okay—that's the situation. You've all read the briefings on Sato Matsushita; you know about his possible plague weapon. We're proceeding under the assumption that Matsushita is on board this vessel and that he is carrying the weapon with him. Our job is to stop him. Options?"

Questions and comments began to be shouted from all around the table. Donovan held up both hands.

"How many of you represent the 'response and recovery' side of things? FEMA, first responders—all the disaster management agencies?"

Half of the hands in the room went up.

"Okay—for the next thirty minutes I want you people to keep your mouths shut. The rest of us represent the assets we have available to prevent this thing from happening. Now—how do we go about it?"

"The first priority is to stop the ship," the Navy said. "Deny her access to U.S. territorial waters—keep her out of range of the coast."

"How?" Donovan asked.

"We send out a CPB—a coastal patrol boat. It's small, it's fast, and it can carry a large weapons package and a full SEAL team. There are nine stationed at Little Creek, Virginia."

"Too far away," the Coast Guard said. "We can send one of ours directly out of New York."

"Hold it a minute," the CDC said. "This plague bacillus—what form is it in?"

"We don't know," Donovan replied.

"Well, is it weaponized? Is it a missile? Is it ready to be launched? What's its range?"

"Again, we don't know."

"Those are crucial questions," the CDC said. "We can't go sailing up to this ship in broad daylight—you saw what they did to their decoy. If they see a naval vessel approaching, they're likely to launch that weapon— if it's launchable, that is. What would they have to lose?"

"It's very unlikely it would have that kind of range," the Navy said.

"*Unlikely?* You've all seen the briefings; this strain of *Yersinia pestis* is reported to have been genetically altered. That means there's no vaccine and there's no cure. There are millions of people in New York. We can't afford to take a chance—we have to assume that the bacillus is weaponized and within range of the coast."

"Then our only option is to sink her," the Navy said. "A coordinated strike from a series of Tomahawk cruise missiles. They can travel just above the water at three-quarters the speed of sound—the terrorists would never see them coming."

"We'd better be sure about this," the State Department said. "We're talking about a military attack on a merchant vessel in international waters without any prior notice or warning. This is a political nightmare—are we sure about our intelligence here? We can't afford another 'We thought they had weapons of mass destruction' debacle."

"The intelligence is solid," the CIA said. "We can prove that the ship switched identities."

"That's circumstantial evidence. Can we prove that they definitely have this plague on board?"

"Sir—we don't *know* what she has on board. We're talking about a pre-emptive strike against a potential threat."

"We'd better decide how important this *proof* is," the Navy said. "If we hit her with a couple of Tomahawks, there won't be anything left."

There was a pause. "Well, I don't see any choice," the State Department said. "The potential threat to the U.S. is too great. We'll just have to take the heat later. I agree—we need to sink the ship."

Heads began to nod all around the room.

"Wait a minute," the CDC said, slowly rising from his chair. "There's something we're not considering here—something absolutely crucial. This strain of plague—it's unknown to us. If it's on this ship, then it's probably in a laboratory somewhere else too. That means even if we sink this ship, there could be another attempt to use this weapon against us later on. We need a sample of this plague. The CDC needs time to develop a vaccine. We can't afford to wait until the next attack—it'll be too late then."

"What are you suggesting?" the State Department asked.

"I'm saying we can't just sink this ship. We need to put somebody on board who can retrieve a specimen for us."

There were groans from all around the table.

"That's possible," the Navy said, "but not without some element of risk."

"Why?"

"Because it's almost dawn—the ship will be arriving in broad daylight. No matter how we try to approach, there's always a chance of being spotted."

"Can't you use divers?"

"That's our best option: Put a swimmer delivery-vehicle team on a passing merchant ship and drop them off a few miles away—approach from underwater. But they'll still have to scale the side of the ship—and then there's open deck to cross. There's always a chance they'll be spotted—we need to be clear about that up front."

"Any chance is too great a chance," the Coast Guard said. "These people aren't going to sail into New York Harbor with their hands in their pockets—they're going to be ready to act. And they're going to have lookouts all around the perimeter of the ship—if they've gotten this far, they're not idiots."

"We're losing sight of the priority here," the CIA said. "Maybe this plague is in some other laboratory; maybe it's not. Maybe there will be some future attack; maybe there won't. We can't prevent all possible future scenarios—we have to prevent *this* one. The priority is to sink this ship—*now*."

"That's incredibly shortsighted," the CDC said. "Suppose they fire this weapon—suppose ten million people die from it. We all agree that would be unthinkable. Now suppose we sink the ship so there is no attack, but they still find a way to use the weapon next month, or next year, and we still have no protection against it—then ten million *still* die. Ten million now or ten million later—what's the difference?"

"There's a *big* difference," the CIA replied. "It's a real ten million now versus a theoretical ten million later."

"But maybe it's twenty million later—maybe a *hundred*. The minute we get our hands on this strain, we can get to work on a vaccine—and the minute we have a vaccine, this weapon is rendered useless at all times and in all places. If there's *any* chance to get a sample of this plague, it's worth taking."

"Is it worth ten million lives?"

"No, of course not—we have to reduce that risk."

"There's no guarantee that we can put a man on that ship unseen—it can't be done."

"We have to find a way."

"This is lunacy!"

Objections and opinions came from all around the table. The pace quickened, voices rose, and tempers flared. Donovan looked around the table. This was the problem with the JTTF: thirty organizations with very different perspectives and priorities and no clear lines of authority. The *Divine Wind* could sail up the Hudson to Albany while these guys were still arguing.

"Harbor pilots," said a voice across the table.

Donovan looked. The voice came from a very ordinary-looking man in civilian clothing. He sat quietly with his hands folded on the table in front of him. He had no computer, no cell phone, no administrative assistant. Up until now he had been just part of the wallpaper.

"Hold it down!" Donovan shouted over the group. He turned to the man. "I'm sorry—what did you say?"

The man looked a little embarrassed. "It just occurred to me that there's a way to put a man on that ship without anybody noticing. Come to think of it—make that three."

CHAPTER THIRTY-NINE

THE MAN HAD EVERYONE'S attention now.

"Stand up!" someone shouted. He slid back his chair and awkwardly rose to his feet.

"Who are you with?" Donovan asked.

"Sandy Hook Harbor Pilots."

"Okay, Sandy Hook, you've got the floor. We're all ears."

"See, it's this way," he said. "Any foreign ship entering U.S. coastal waters has to have a U.S. harbor pilot on board to guide her into port. It's the law."

"Why?"

"The ship's master knows his vessel, and he knows the open sea—somebody else has to know the harbor: the tides, the currents, the sandbars and shoals. A master can't be familiar with every port he calls on—and even if he could, conditions change. Some of these ships are the largest moving objects in the world. We can't have some fool running a thousand-foot bulk carrier aground and blocking the shipping channel just because he doesn't know the terrain. That's our job—we go out to meet the ships as they approach, and we pilot them in."

The man pointed to the projection screen. "Somebody had a shot of the harbor up there—can we get that back again?" A few seconds later the image reappeared. "Can you back it out a little? I need a wider view." The image refocused at a lower resolution, showing a broad overview of New York Harbor. At the top of the screen, the tip of Manhattan was just visible. Below it was a huge, hourglass-shaped body of water.

"Up top is Manhattan," he said, stepping up to the screen. "You can see Liberty Island and Ellis Island there and there—that's the Upper Bay. The bay narrows down here, where it passes between Brooklyn and Staten Island. See this little line? That's the Verrazano-Narrows Bridge—that's where our offices are, just above the bridge. Below the bridge, all this water down here, that's the Lower Bay—and you can see that the Lower Bay empties into the Atlantic over here.

"Now, you see this?" He pointed to a spot at the bottom of the screen where a narrow strip of land curled up and into the Lower Bay like a crab's claw. "That's Sandy Hook—there's a Coast Guard station there. And this," he said, tracing a line with his finger due east into the Atlantic, "is Ambrose Channel. It's the main shipping channel in and out of New York Harbor. This is the channel your cargo ship will follow to enter the harbor."

He put his finger on the eastern end of the channel. "Right about here is Ambrose Tower," he said, "a floating lighthouse that marks the entrance to the channel. Ambrose Tower is about twenty-five miles east of the Verrazano Bridge. Whenever a ship passes that tower, one of our pilots is there to meet it."

"How do they get out there?" Donovan asked.

"We keep a pilot boat floating in this area here—it's out there 24/7, twelve months a year, in good weather and bad. There are always pilots on board; we're like doctors—we're always on call. When a ship is about three hours out, she radios us to confirm her arrival. When she does, we put a pilot on a smaller, faster boat—we call it a launch. The launch ferries the pilot out to the ship."

"How does the pilot get on board?"

"The launch pulls up alongside, they throw a rope ladder down, and the pilot climbs up."

"You're kidding."

He shook his head. "I've climbed a couple and found nothing holding the ladder on but a couple of crewmen."

"And once the pilot's on board?"

"He's taken straight to the bridge, where he takes over for the ship's master."

"You do this for *every* ship?"

"Every domestic ship over sixty tons. And *every* foreign ship—no exceptions, no questions asked. See, that's the beauty of it: They're *expecting* a pilot to come on board—in fact, they'll get suspicious if he doesn't. And another thing—since 9/11, it's been common practice for a couple of Coast Guard guys to come along with the pilot, just to do a random inspection from time to time. They're called sea marshals—sort of like the air marshals on planes. Every ship's master knows about it; they all know they have to put up with it. The Coast Guard guys are always in uniform—and they're always armed.

"So I was thinking: When this ship passes Ambrose Tower, we send out a launch just like we always do—only this time, our pilot brings along two of your Special Forces guys dressed like sea marshals. They go straight to the bridge, where they take over the ship; then the pilot steers while the other two search the ship."

The group fell silent, and the man slowly returned to his chair.

"It's good," Donovan said, nodding, "but we don't need one of your pilots—we don't need to steer the ship; all we need to do is stop it. We don't want to put one of your men at risk—and if we're only putting three men on board, they all need to be professionals."

Donovan looked at the Navy SEAL commander. "Can you pick me two good men?"

"No problem. Who's the third?"

"Me. Somebody from the JTTF needs to be there—and this is still my case, if there are no objections."

He glanced quickly around the room. From the corner of his eye, he could see Macy slowly shaking her head.

"Done," Donovan said. He turned to the CIA. "How far is the *Divine Wind* from Ambrose Tower right now?"

He looked at his laptop. "Best estimate: less than six hours."

Conversations erupted all around the table again as all the details of logistics were considered. Suddenly, there was a sharp rapping sound from the far end of the table. Heads slowly turned. It was Li, rapping his knuckles on the hard wooden surface until the room grew quiet and every eye was on him.

"I have a question," he said. "How many old Japanese men are aboard this vessel?"

No one responded.

"It seems like a reasonable question," Li said. "After all, our goal isn't simply to board this ship—our goal is to locate and identify one individual *on* this ship."

"Li," Donovan said, "I think we can find one old Japanese man on the ship."

"That's very reassuring, considering the fact that until a few hours ago, you couldn't find the ship itself. It seems to me that these people went to extraordinary lengths to disguise this vessel—mightn't they attempt the same thing with the most important individual *on* the ship?"

"Sir, once we seize the ship, we have everyone on it," the Navy said.

"And while you're talking to the wrong Sato Matsushita, the real one launches a missile into the sky. Or perhaps he destroys the weapon rather than allow it to fall into your hands—and the plague along with it." He looked at the CDC. "It would be very simple to do, and then you would have no specimen."

"He's right," the CDC said. "We have to find this Matsushita as quickly as possible—that should be the number one priority."

"Is there a photo of this guy?" the Navy asked. "Is there some way to positively identify him?"

"Indeed there is," Li said. "I can identify him. I am the only one on earth who can."

"Sir," the Navy said, "with all due respect, there is no way—"

Li held up both hands. "I'm not suggesting that I replace one of your Special Forces men. That would be very foolish—though I must admit I find the idea exhilarating. I'm simply suggesting that I be close by in order to serve as a reference." He turned to the harbor pilot. "This 'launch' of yours—how big is it?"

"About fifty feet in length," he said.

"Sounds quite roomy. I assume this launch requires a pilot; in addition, it must carry Mr. Donovan and his two sea marshals. That makes four. By any chance, would there be room for me as well?"

"No problem."

Li smiled and looked at the group. "There you have it," he said. "I can tag along on the launch, safe and out of harm's way. When Mr. Donovan and his team secure the vessel, I will be available nearby to confirm the identification of Sato Matsushita. My services may never be required; perhaps Dr. Matsushita will be wearing one of those friendly name badges that says, 'Hello—my name is Sato.'" He glanced around the room. "Perhaps not."

Donovan looked at him; Li returned his gaze. The old man's dark eyes were perfectly still, unflinching. There was no apology in them, no evasion, and no shame. Donovan remembered Li's words: *I don't expect you to ignore the rules, Nathan; I'm just hoping for a liberal interpretation.* The old man knew it might come down to this. Donovan was in charge now, and if he stuck to the rules, he would end the old man's dream right now.

Li seemed to read his thoughts. *It is my mission,* his eyes said.

Donovan paused—then he nodded almost imperceptibly, and the old man blinked gratefully in reply.

"It's not a bad idea," Donovan said to the group. "We're only going to get one shot at this; we might as well have all the resources available that we can."

"Then you'll want me too."

It was Macy's voice. Donovan turned, but before he could say a word, Macy rose to her feet and began to address the table.

"I'm Dr. Macy Monroe. I'm a professor of political science and international relations at Columbia. I've been consulting for the FBI on this case, working in conjunction with Mr. Donovan and Mr. Li. I'm a specialist in terrorist psychology and hostage negotiation—I have regional expertise in both the Middle East and Japan. I speak both Arabic and Japanese." She looked around the table. "I know many of you personally. I've trained some of your people in hostage negotiation."

Donovan rolled his eyes. She was laying out her credentials one by one as if she were dealing cards.

"Mr. Li and Mr. Donovan are correct," she said. "We should have all the resources available that we can. Suppose Mr. Donovan and the sea marshals secure the ship, then immediately search for Sato Matsushita. It's possible they'll encounter no resistance, that they'll find Matsushita and take him completely by surprise. It's possible—but it's not likely. There could very well be some resistance, some exchange of hostilities, something to warn Matsushita that things have gone wrong. Suppose Mr. Li's scenario occurs; suppose Matsushita has enough time to consider using his weapon—or destroying it. Suppose he locks himself in his cabin or barricades himself in some corner of the ship. Who's going to talk him out?" She looked at Donovan. "How's your Japanese?"

Before he could respond, she continued. "I propose that I accompany Mr. Li and the others on the launch. I think we'd be foolish not to prepare for this contingency. If my services are needed, I'll be available. If not, like Mr. Li, I'll be out of harm's way. Are there any objections?"

She glanced around the table, turning to Donovan last of all. Her eyes were different from Li's—they were angry, defiant, challenging. Donovan paused, hoping that someone else would offer an objection. But no one did, and he knew he couldn't either. He had plenty of objections—but they all came from his heart and not his head.

As Macy took her seat again, Donovan slowly rose. "I think that completes our team," he said. "Let's cap it off here before this launch turns into a cruise ship."

Donovan, Macy, and Li were hustled down a corridor to an elevator, headed for the rooftop where a Coast Guard Dolphin recovery helicopter waited to ferry them directly to the Coast Guard station at Sandy Hook. On the elevator, Donovan turned to Macy.

"What are you doing?" he whispered.

"What are *you* doing?"

Li leaned forward and looked at both of them. "At least we all know what *I'm* doing."

On the rooftop, under the deafening *thup-thup-thup* of the beating blades, the Navy SEAL commander pulled Donovan aside.

"I don't buy the CDC's argument," he shouted over the roar. "Trying to grab this plague is insanity—it's just too big a risk."

"It's done, Commander," Donovan shouted back. "Anything else?"

The Navy nodded. "We need a contingency plan—a way to shut this thing down if it all goes bad. You understand what I'm saying?"

"What do you have in mind?"

"I'm going to instruct my two men to send out a radio signal from the bridge the minute the situation is under control—that will let us know that everything's going according to plan. I want to set a ten-minute time limit, Mr. Donovan—from the time you climb aboard until the time that signal is sent out."

"No good," Donovan said. "Equipment fails and signals get crossed—even for the SEALs. I'm not risking the lives of my people because a battery goes dead. Besides, the issue here isn't time; it's distance. The closer this ship gets to the harbor, the greater the danger."

"Okay, what do you suggest?"

"A distance limit, not a time limit. When we take control of the ship, we'll shut the engines down—we'll stop her dead in the water. We'll do our best to send that radio signal—but if you don't hear from us, keep an eye on the ship. If the ship stops, you'll know everything's okay."

"We need to agree on a limit," the Navy said.

Donovan considered. "The harbor pilot said it was twenty-five miles to the Verrazano Bridge. Give me ten miles—that should be enough to stop her, and that still puts us fifteen miles from shore."

"Fair enough, Mr. Donovan; we'll listen for the radio signal, *and* we'll keep an eye on the ship. But I'm requesting that a missile cruiser out of Naval Station Norfolk be kept on full alert; if we don't hear from you, and if the ship doesn't come to a full stop within ten miles, the cruiser will launch four missiles targeting the rudder, the engine room, the bridge, and the main deck. Are we clear?"

"Ten miles," Donovan said. "Let's hope it's enough."

"If I were you, I wouldn't do any sightseeing on the way to the bridge."

"Thanks for the advice." Donovan turned and ducked under the whirling blades.

They loaded into the helicopter and belted in. As it slowly lifted from the rooftop, Donovan looked down at the SEAL commander below, who held up the fingers of both hands.

"What's that all about?" Li asked.

"Ten minutes to Sandy Hook," Donovan said.

CHAPTER FORTY

T HE HARBOR PILOT BOAT *New Jersey* bobbed like a cork in the rolling swells.

"Sorry about the weather," the boat pilot said. "Wish we could have arranged a better day for you."

"Is it always this rough?" Donovan asked.

The pilot shook his head. "This is what we call a 'summer southerly.' Just came out of nowhere this morning—looks like it might get worse. Too bad—this time of year the weather's usually good."

"Lucky me."

The *New Jersey* was no rowboat; at 145 feet in length, she had room to sleep twenty-four, complete with galley, lounge, and TV room. But to the waters of the Atlantic, the *New Jersey* was just another speck of floating debris. Donovan estimated the swells at ten feet, but in the wheelhouse high above the deck, the effect of the waves was amplified—it felt like twenty. The tall wheelhouse swayed from side to side like the top of a tree in a storm.

There were handrails on every wall and handgrips all across the ceiling, so harbor pilots never had to take a step without some way to steady themselves—but harbor pilots didn't need to steady themselves. Their trained legs were like shock absorbers, bending and flexing with the rolling water while their torsos remained stock-still. Donovan had lost his sea legs a long time ago; try as he might, he still found himself lurching with each unexpected wave.

Suddenly, Macy squeezed between them, swinging white-knuckled from handgrip to handgrip like a little girl on monkey bars. She had a look of panic on her face; she stared directly ahead, out the window at the horizon line. She inhaled and exhaled through her mouth, sucking and blowing as if she were in the final stages of labor.

"How much longer?" she asked, looking at neither of them.

"No way to tell," the pilot said. "A ship is supposed to radio us when she's three hours away, but sometimes they don't; sometimes they just show up. We call those 'ringers.' We don't like it, but there's not much we can do about it. All we can do is wait."

"Three *hours*?" she said.

"Maybe less."

Macy nodded fiercely, as if she had just been told, "We have to remove the leg." Then she turned and lurched away across the cabin.

The pilot looked over his shoulder at her. "Is she okay?"

"She gets seasick," Donovan said. "And I'm not talking about the garden-variety, green-around-the-gills type either—I'm talking about puke-your-guts-out comet vomit. I hope she hangs on; she was okay on the dispatch boat on the way out here."

"That's 'cause the dispatch boat is fast—it's when you slow down that the waves get to you. It's the rolling, you know?"

Donovan nodded. "We went on a cruise for our honeymoon—can you believe it? She lasted one day, then we had to airlift her back to Miami."

"What's she doing out here?"

"She volunteered."

"Did she know what she was getting into?"

"You mean the mission or the marriage?"

Donovan turned and looked at Macy. She was panting her way along the aft wall of the cabin now, following a long chrome handrail hand over hand from starboard to port.

"I'd better go talk to her," he said. "She's going to suck all the air out of the room."

He intercepted her in the corner of the cabin. "How're you feeling?" he asked.

"How do I look like I'm feeling?"

"You look like the Hulk—not the figure, just the color. Want to sit down?"

"No."

"Want to—"

"No!" She pushed past him and stared out the forward window. "Got to keep moving," she said. "If I look at you, I'll throw up."

"Well, that's normal anyway."

"Don't make jokes," she growled.

Donovan shook his head. "Macy, what are you doing out here? Why did you volunteer for this?"

"Don't you know?"

"I'm a guy, okay? I don't know anything I'm supposed to know."

"We've got unfinished business," she said.

"You think we'll get time to talk about it out here?"

"No," she said with a quick sideways glance. "I think you might die out here."

"I'm just doing my job, Macy."

"So am I."

Donovan looked at her. "I want you to promise me something," he said. "I want you to promise me that you'll keep your head down out here."

"Will you?"

"As much as I can."

"Me too."

"That's not good enough," he said. "I want you to promise me."

She glanced at him again. "Why should I?"

"You know why."

She shook her head. "I don't know anything unless you tell me,

Nathan. That's been our problem all along." She lurched forward again, continuing toward the front of the cabin. Donovan turned away.

In the center of the wheelhouse was a row of padded seats. In the far seat, Li sat peacefully with his hands folded in his lap, swaying like a pendulum with the motion of the waves. Like Macy, he was dressed in his civilian clothes. At his feet was a large backpack that was given to him by the Coast Guard at Sandy Hook. Each member of the team received one; each contained a white NBC suit and an integrated gas mask and hood.

But Donovan noticed an addition to Li's backpack: Protruding from under the flap was the corner of a small black case.

Donovan worked his way over and took a seat beside the old man. "I want you to listen to me," he said. "You've gotten this far only because of me. You were allowed to attend that meeting only because I got you clearance. All I had to do was say the word, and you'd be in a taxi right now headed for LaGuardia."

"I believe I'm being scolded," Li said. "Have I done something to offend you?"

Donovan pointed to the backpack. "You never told me what you've got in the case."

Li paused. "I've thought about telling you more than once—but all things considered, I think it's best that you don't know."

"C'mon, Li—I need to know."

"By this point in our relationship, I was hoping you might trust me."

Donovan glared at him. "Look, I stuck my neck out a long way just to get you here."

"Forgive me," Li said. "In all the excitement, perhaps I've failed to express my appreciation. To feel gratitude and fail to express it is like buying a lovely gift but never giving it away. Gratitude should be expressed liberally—*tangibly* whenever possible, don't you agree?"

"My point is that there's only so far I can go to help you."

"And *my* point is that gratitude should go both ways. You did not seek me out, Nathan—I sought you. As you said before, without my help you never would have found Sato Matsushita—you never would have known

297

he existed. If it weren't for me, a disaster of unprecedented proportions might have taken your nation completely by surprise."

"Believe me, I appreciate that."

"How very kind—but as I said, gratitude should be expressed *tangibly* whenever possible. You'll forgive me, but at the present time your words mean very little; what I need right now is your assistance."

"I'll help you if I can," Donovan said, "but I need you to remember something: *I have a mission too.* If you force me to choose between your mission and mine—I'll choose mine."

"As you must," Li replied. "But I believe there is a way for both of our missions to be accomplished successfully."

"How?"

"I haven't the slightest." Li shrugged. "If I knew that, we wouldn't be having this—"

"There she is!" the pilot shouted back.

Donovan leaped from his seat and stumbled forward to the wheelhouse window.

"Where?"

"About ten o'clock, just coming over the horizon. See her? We're picking up her transponder signal now—the *Southampton* out of Cardiff. She's a ringer, all right—sailing right up to the front door without so much as a hello. She's still about three or four miles out; we'll meet her at two. Better get your team on the launch."

Donovan turned and looked once more at Li; he was working the black case deeper into his backpack.

Then he glanced at Macy. She stood perfectly still in the center of the cabin, staring at the approaching ship with no expression on her face.

"She looks a lot better," the pilot said.

"Yeah," Donovan replied. "Fear can do that."

CHAPTER FORTY-ONE

THE ALUMINUM HULL OF the launch plunged into the swells like a pelican diving for its dinner. The swells were almost twelve feet high now. The fifty-foot boat seemed to leap from peak to peak, and its engine raced audibly when the propeller broke free of the water.

Donovan and the two "sea marshals" stood beside the pilot in the wheelhouse. Li stood slightly behind them, bracing himself with a ceiling grip. The old man was surprisingly steady; his smaller mass was somehow less affected by the sudden shifts in speed and direction.

Just behind Li the wheelhouse ended, and three short steps descended to a main cabin where Macy sat quietly in a pilot's chair. Her condition was 100 percent improved, though the launch plunged in and out of swells at twenty-four knots. The pilot was right: Faster was better—anything was better than the rolling.

"How long?" Donovan asked the pilot.

"Seven, eight minutes tops. The ship will make a lee—that means she'll bear west a little, and we'll come up along her starboard side. The ship will block the wind, so the sea should be calmer on that side—but don't count on it."

Donovan turned to the two Special Forces operatives, who looked convincingly like a pair of Coast Guard petty officers, from their navy blue trousers, windbreakers, and shoulder-mount radios to their ball caps with gold brocade. There was one significant difference that only a professional would notice—the custom-made .45-caliber U.S. Special Operations Forces offensive handguns that hung from their belts. Donovan tapped his left ankle against the helm and felt the reassuring bulk of his own handgun tucked into its ankle holster.

He looked down at his clothing; he had been given a dark wool business suit with a flaming red tie. "Are you sure this is right?" he asked the pilot. "I look like George Bush."

"All our harbor pilots work in business suits," the pilot said. "It's tradition. Until just a few years ago, we wore fedoras too—sorry to see those go. Oh—one more thing," he said, handing Donovan a copy of the *New York Times*. "When you get to the bridge, the first thing you do is hand the ship's master a copy of today's newspaper. That's a tradition too—he'll be expecting it. You're supposed to be a harbor pilot; you should know that."

"What else do I need to know?"

"You expect me to teach you how to pilot a fourteen-thousand-ton freighter in seven minutes?"

"I don't need to know what I'm doing—I just need to talk a good game."

"Okay. What do you want to know?"

"For starters, tell me where we are."

"We're just outside the entrance to Ambrose Channel," the pilot said, "the main shipping channel into New York Harbor. The channel is two thousand feet wide and forty-five feet deep all the way to the piers."

"Forty-five feet? I figured the water would be a mile deep here."

"Uh-uh—they dredge it just deep enough for the biggest ships. A big container vessel might have a draft of forty feet; that means there's only five feet between her keel and the bottom."

"What if she steers a little wide?"

"Then she runs aground—an old wreck like that one might even break apart."

"So what does the pilot do, just steer down the center of the channel?"

"It's not that simple. It's about three or four hours from here to the piers, and there are thirty-five or forty course corrections you have to make along the way. One wrong turn and you're the *Exxon Valdez*."

"How do you know where to turn?"

"The channel is marked by buoys, and the ship's GPS system tells you exactly where you are. You have to know where to turn—that's what they pay you for."

"All kinds of ships must come in here," Donovan said. "How can you know how to steer them all?"

"We don't have to," the pilot said. "Every bridge has a helmsman; all we do is tell him where to turn. Come left ten degrees; reduce to half speed; dead ahead slow. We give the orders; they do the steering."

"They all speak English?"

"By law, every ship in American waters is required to have someone on the bridge who speaks English."

"Do they?"

"Most of the time—no. We just use a kind of pidgin English. They figure it out." The pilot looked at him. "Anything else you want to know?"

"Like you said—not in seven minutes."

"More like four," the pilot said.

Donovan turned to the sea marshals. "Let's go over it one last time."

"I think we've got it, sir," the first man said. "We board the ship using the pilots' ladder—the two of us will go first, and you'll bring up the rear. At the top, we'll be escorted to the bridge. There we should encounter three crew members: the ship's master, a helmsman, and a mate. We will immediately neutralize the crew."

"Excuse me," Li said from behind them. "Does that mean you will kill them?"

"That will be up to them, sir," the man said, glancing over his shoulder. "As soon as we secure the bridge, we will immediately cut the engines and contact our people by radio."

"That's important," Donovan said. "Let's not forget that part."

"We will then work our way down through the crew cabins, repeating the process as necessary. When all topside crew members are secured, we will move below deck to the engine room, followed by the cargo holds."

"Good," Donovan said. "And the target?"

"Dr. Sato Matsushita. Japanese, about eighty years of age, small stature." He nodded at Li. "Are we sure that's not him?"

"We're quite sure," Li said in annoyance.

"Sir," the second man said to Donovan. "If you don't mind my asking, how long has it been since you've pulled this kind of duty?"

Donovan looked at the two men. "Is either of you a Marine?"

"We're Navy, sir."

He nodded. "Try to keep up with me, then."

Donovan looked out the window again. The *Divine Wind* was approaching fast now, bearing almost directly toward them. The launch began to make a wide arc to the left, preparing to circle around behind her and come up along the starboard side. To Donovan the ship looked enormous, maybe ten times longer than the launch, but it didn't fare much better than they had in the rising swells. The mammoth ship rocked and swayed like a sea buoy.

As they swung wide to the left, Donovan could see the pilots' ladder dangling over the railing and down the starboard side. It drifted in the wind like a ribbon, swinging out over the water one minute and crashing back against the metal hull the next. *This has got to be a joke*, Donovan thought. Scaling that ladder would be like holding on to a loose fire hose.

"Please tell me that's not the ladder," Donovan said.

"Relax," the pilot said. "Here's how it works: When we come up alongside, the ship will reduce her speed to a slow bell—maybe seven knots. The ship will be *pitching*—that means rocking from bow to stern. It will also be *rolling*—swaying from side to side. And it'll be rising and sinking with the swells too. That means the ship will be moving in three directions at once—up and down, back and forth, and side to side. Now, our boat will be doing the same thing—only worse, and not at the same time. If our boat goes down when the ship goes up, you may find yourself looking up at the bottom of the ladder. If they pitch forward when we pitch back, the ladder will swing past you like a grapevine. Got the idea?"

"Tell me the truth," Donovan said. "How hard is this?"

"It's kind of an art."

"It takes time to learn an art."

"Yeah," he said, "it does."

"Have you ever tried this in swells this big?"

"I've done it in swells twice this size."

"Does anybody ever get killed this way?"

The pilot glanced at him. "You don't want to hear about that now, do you?"

"It's not so bad," one of the SEALs said with a grin. "But then, you're not Navy, are you?"

The pilot pointed out the window at the deck of the launch. "When we come up alongside, your team will move out to the foredeck."

Donovan looked. The foredeck was rising and dropping like the end of a diving board, and he wondered if it would have the same effect. "We go out *there?*"

"There are railings all along the way, see? You always have something to hold on to. You work your way out to that break in the railing—that's where I'll line up with the ladder. Then all you do is wait for the right moment and jump."

"And if I pick the wrong moment?"

"Then watch the propellers."

Donovan turned to Macy; she had been staring at the back of his head. He started toward her and motioned for Li to join them. They sat down together in the row of pilots' chairs.

"I want you both to stay back here, out of view," Donovan said. "We're going to secure the bridge and locate Matsushita—if we need either one of you, we'll send for you. Otherwise, you are *not* to approach the ship. Is that clear?"

They both nodded.

Donovan started to get up, but Macy grabbed his arm. "There's something I want to tell you," she said. "You're a stubborn, pigheaded fool."

"Thanks," Donovan said. "I'll treasure that always."

"I wasn't finished—I was about to say, 'but you're a good man.' I still believe that, Nathan. This is a good thing you're doing, and you're a good man."

Donovan wrapped his arms around her and pulled her in tight. He felt grateful; it was almost worth all this just to have the chance to hold her one more time.

"I want to finish that business," he whispered into her ear.

She nodded against his chest. "You know where to find me."

Donovan released her and stood up; so did Li.

"Nothing for an old fart?" the old man said.

Donovan hesitated, then extended his hand. Li looked at it, smiled, and took it.

"When I find Matsushita," Donovan said, "I will *not* bring him back to this boat. Do you understand? This is as close as you'll get, Li. Are you okay with that?"

"Of course not. I still believe that God will allow us to meet face-to-face. But if, as you say, this is as close as I get—then thank you, Nathan. I do not wish to be thought ungrateful. Thank you for helping an old man with his dream."

Donovan nodded, then turned and climbed the three short steps to the wheelhouse. They were coming up close on the starboard side now; through the window, the ship's black hull loomed over them like a wall of coal.

"This is it!" the pilot called back.

Donovan glanced over his shoulder one last time. Li smiled and nodded, but Macy looked away.

CHAPTER FORTY-TWO

THE LEAP FROM THE launch to the ship's ladder looked impossible. Both vessels pitched, and rolled, and rose and fell with the swells—but the huge ship rocked slowly, like the pendulum of an old grandfather clock, while the little launch bobbed like a bar of soap in a tub. One minute the ship's hull loomed so close that Donovan could almost stretch out and touch it; the next minute it tipped so far away that he couldn't reach the ladder with a running start.

Neither of the SEALs looked concerned. Why should they? They did this kind of thing every day. They were trained to throw grappling hooks up and over stern railings and climb ropes hand over hand. *Sure, they can do it*, Donovan thought. *They can do it because they're ten years younger and thirty pounds lighter*. Donovan felt old, and he felt angry—and he felt grateful that he had two men to watch before it was his turn to try.

The first SEAL crouched down on the edge of the foredeck, steadying himself with the railings on both sides. His eyes were glued to the ladder. It swung left and right before him, first tantalizingly close, then impossibly out of reach. Donovan watched, too, second-guessing him. Seconds went by; then the great ship dipped low in the water while the launch rose, and the ship tipped toward them while their own boat remained level.

"Now!" Donovan shouted—but the SEAL didn't flinch. An instant later, the ship pitched forward and the ladder swung away toward the bow.

The SEAL turned and glared at Donovan.

"Sorry," Donovan said. "Your call."

A few seconds later the SEAL sprang from the deck like a panther, catching the ladder perfectly by both ropes. Then the two vessels rocked away from each other and the SEAL seemed to rocket into the sky. For a moment he hung on only by his hands; then he fitted his feet against the wooden rungs and began to climb.

Now the second SEAL stepped up to the edge of the deck. His wait was a little longer; he was a little less decisive. But Donovan knew he would make it—after all, he had a larger margin of error than Donovan did. It helps to have legs like a thoroughbred and a body made of nothing but sinew and bone. Donovan wondered what would happen when his own 220 pounds left the deck. He wondered how far he could still jump; he wondered if the aging ladder would support his weight.

The second SEAL caught the ladder and began his ascent. Now Donovan gripped the railing and eased his way up to the edge.

He tensed and waited, studying the movement of the ships—but there was no repetition, no cadence to count or pattern to predict. Now he realized that the decision was a lot easier to make when someone else was doing the jumping, the same way strikes and balls are easier to call when someone else is standing at the plate. He could see now that it had to be a split-second judgment—and there was no room for error.

Suddenly, the launch swerved left just as the ship rolled right, and the two vessels crashed together. The thick black bumper that surrounded the launch made a dull, rubbery sound as it bounced against the ship. The hull and ladder slammed into Donovan, knocking his hands from the railing. As he fell to the deck, he grabbed the rope ladder with his left hand.

An instant later the two vessels veered apart again, and Donovan was catapulted off the deck and into the air. He still held the rope in his left hand; as he rotated clockwise in the air, he could see the launch lunging along below him. Then it suddenly swerved to starboard, and there was nothing under him but churning water.

Now the ladder swung back hard toward the ship, and Donovan's back and shoulder slammed against the hull. The impact rippled through his body like a bomb blast, and he felt his grip loosen. It was sheer luck that he was looking down when he hit—if his head had struck the iron hull, he would be sinking unconscious into the sea. He swung wildly to his left and grasped for the ladder with his right hand. He found it. He repositioned his hands and tried to strengthen his hold, but his legs still swung free. His hands slipped down a little on the ropes, and he felt a pop in his right shoulder.

The launch slowly eased under him again, offering whatever assistance it could. When the ship rolled right again, Donovan found himself dangling directly over the boat's foredeck. For an instant he thought about releasing his grip and dropping to the deck below, but he no longer trusted his timing or his judgment. He knew that by the time he reached the deck, the boat could be gone again. The only thing to do was hold on.

When the ship rolled left again, the ladder started its long swing back toward the hull, and Donovan braced for impact. His body snapped against the hull like a whip—first his hands and arms, then his torso, then his legs and feet. He felt the Glock in his ankle holster slip out and drop away.

The impact knocked his wind out; he knew he couldn't survive another one like it. He had to climb; he had to shorten the radius of the ropes. He drew his aching legs up under him and felt for the rungs. He found one, and he started up toward the railing. He climbed slowly, checking each rung for reliability and testing each new handgrip before releasing the last.

A minute later he felt two powerful pairs of hands grab him by the shoulders and drag him onto the deck. He took a second to catch his breath, then rolled to his feet and began to stand.

"Thanks," he said, "I really—"

The bodies of the two SEALs lay on the deck before him, each shot through the forehead as he stepped over the side of the ship. Three crewmen stood in front of Donovan; two of them shouldered Russian-made AK-47s, both trained on his own forehead. The third man pulled a handgun from a leather holster and stepped forward. He spoke in broken English. "You are the pilot?"

CHAPTER FORTY-THREE

DONOVAN WATCHED AS THE crewmen stripped the bodies of their shoulder radios. He felt numb. He looked down at the two Navy SEALs, still alive only minutes ago. He thought of their youthfulness, their training, their physical prowess—all gone in a flash of muzzle fire, vanished before they even had a chance to draw their weapons. This was more than murder; it was disgrace—disgrace that men so utterly inferior should be able to take their lives.

"You—this way." The man with the handgun motioned for Donovan to follow.

Donovan looked down at the bodies one last time as he stepped across them. He remembered a part of the SEALs' cherished creed, never to leave a fallen comrade behind, and he felt as if he were betraying them. But he also recalled another part of the SEALs' creed: *I will always place the mission first; I will never accept defeat; I will never quit.* He stared at each of the crewmen as he passed, and he made a silent promise.

They entered the superstructure on the starboard side—Donovan first and the gunman behind. They passed down a short corridor, then turned right and started up three flights of metal stairs. Donovan walked slowly, his mind racing. *How much do they know?* Did they somehow know about the plan? Did they know the men were Special Forces? No, they couldn't—

if they did, they would have known that he was FBI and they would have killed him too. No, they believed the men were Coast Guard sea marshals—they killed them just to avoid inspection. That meant they still believed Donovan was a harbor pilot—and as long as they believed that, he still had a chance.

But what would happen if they stopped believing?

He kicked himself when he remembered his words on the launch: "I don't need to know what I'm doing," he'd told the pilot. "I just need to talk a good game." Well, he needed more than talk now. These people expected him to steer this ship all the way into the harbor. Forty course corrections along the way, and the first one he missed would give him away. "You have to know where to turn," the pilot said. "That's what they pay you for." Why didn't he listen more closely? Why didn't he ask more questions? He tried to remember every word the pilot had spoken to him, piecing the memories together like the fragments of an old manuscript.

They reached the top of the stairs now, and there was a wooden door directly ahead.

"Inside!" the man behind him barked.

Donovan opened the door and stepped onto the ship's bridge—the first bridge of any commercial ship Donovan had ever seen in his life. The room was not deep, but it was very wide. Along the far wall was a long instrument console filled with glass-covered gauges, illuminated indicators, and chrome-handled levers. There was an open laptop computer in the center, and a gray metal box beside it with a small keyboard of its own.

Above the console was a row of rectangular windows that stretched from wall to wall, looking out on the ship's long deck and forward cargo holds. Donovan was astonished at the sense of height and the expanse of the forward deck. It seemed impossible that an object so large could be controlled from such a tiny room, and by only one man—especially if that man was him.

There was a voice inside his head that told him to blurt out, "Wow! Look at this!" It was a voice he recognized, a voice soldiers hear when their lives are on the line. "Stand up and wave your arms," it says, or "Lie down here and fall asleep." Donovan remembered the voice from his days in ordnance removal. "Cut all the wires at once," it told him. "Just grab a handful and rip them out." It was a child's voice, the voice that told you to scream before your hiding place was discovered. Every soldier knows it; it's a siren's voice, and if you listen, it will get you killed.

The man behind him closed the door and stepped around to Donovan's right, still leveling the gun at his chest. Donovan took his first good look at the man. He was Arab—thirty-five, maybe forty years of age. He was dressed like a soldier, though he wore no insignia or rank. He had a thick salt-and-pepper mustache and black hair. And when the man turned to face the console, Donovan saw that his left ear was just a stump.

The man said something in Arabic. At the console, a helmsman stood facing the window and made no reply. Instead, a captain's chair to the left of the helmsman swiveled around, revealing a taller man, leaner and with darker skin. He was dressed in civilian clothes, but he wore a weathered captain's hat. This was undoubtedly the ship's master. He nodded to the gunman and spoke a single word in reply—then he turned to face Donovan.

"Good morning," he said in perfect English.

Donovan winced—so much for the language barrier. He had hoped that the pilot was right—that no one on the bridge would speak English. Then no one could ask him questions, and his ignorance might be concealed.

"What's the meaning of this?" Donovan demanded. "You've murdered two Coast Guard sea marshals. Why?"

"I'm not at liberty to explain," the ship's master said. "Let me simply point out that they are dead, while you are still alive. You will remain alive as long as you are needed to pilot this ship."

"And if I refuse?"

The ship's master smiled. "Personally, I consider you nothing but a convenience. We had to allow your people aboard, or your port authorities would have been contacted immediately. But I have called on the port of New York before, and I believe I am capable of navigating the harbor myself."

"You think so?" Donovan said. "Take a look at the weather out there—those are twelve-foot swells. We've had some sandbars shifting lately—do you know where they are?"

The man paused. "All right," he said. "Perhaps you are more than a convenience—for now."

"What's this all about?" Donovan asked. "What's this ship carrying, anyway?"

"Again, I'm not at liberty to say."

"You've already killed two men. Even if I take you into the harbor, you'll kill me anyway."

"Perhaps—perhaps not. One thing is certain: If you refuse to pilot this ship, you will be of no value whatsoever—you will die immediately. You have two choices, my friend: certain death or possible survival. The choice seems clear to me."

Donovan's mind was spinning. His only way to stay alive was by piloting the ship. But if he did pilot the ship, if he somehow managed to guide it successfully more than ten miles ahead, he would die anyway—they all would, in one colossal ball of fire caused by four Tomahawk missiles. He had no idea what to do—but he remembered something he'd learned years ago when a mission went bad: Sometimes the only thing to do is to do the next thing.

"Okay," he said. "You've got a pilot—for now."

"Then let's get started," the ship's master said. "We do have a schedule to keep."

Donovan slipped off his backpack and opened it carefully so that no one caught a glimpse of the NBC suit inside. He pulled out the copy of the *New York Times* and handed it to the ship's master. "I wish it was next week's," he said. "It would have your obituary."

"Perhaps beside your own," the man replied. "Where is your computer?"

Strike one, Donovan thought. "In this weather? Are you kidding? We'll use yours."

"But mine has no charts of the channel."

Donovan rolled his eyes. "I know where to turn—that's what they pay me for." Now he paused, carefully considering the wording of his first instruction. He made a split-second inventory of every nautical term he knew. "Take her into the channel," he said—that seemed vague enough.

The ship's master repeated the instruction to the helmsman in Arabic; then he turned back to Donovan. "At what speed?"

What speed? How fast does a ship like this go? He thought about the launch: *It did twenty-four knots, the pilot said—but it was a tenth the size of this behemoth. He did the math. That couldn't be right—a ship couldn't cross an entire ocean at two or three knots—it would take forever. It must go faster—maybe half as fast?*

"Twelve knots," he said with authority.

"Twelve knots? We proceed into the channel at sea speed?"

Strike two. "We're only in the entrance to the channel," he said. "We'll slow her down in a minute." *Terrific*, he thought. *I just gave the order to proceed at full speed. How long will it take us to cover ten miles at this rate?*

Donovan stepped up to the helm now and glanced over at the helmsman. "Where you from?"

"He speaks no English," the ship's master said.

"Yours is good," Donovan replied. "Where did you learn it?"

"I was educated here. America educates most of her enemies—I find that delightfully ironic."

Donovan nodded to the gunman. "How about your boy there? Looks like somebody talked his ear off."

The ship's master smiled. "His name is Khalid, and he is not my 'boy.' He is my employer—that means he is your employer too. Fortunately for you, Khalid speaks only a few words of English. If I repeated your comment to him in Arabic, he would kill you."

Three men on the bridge—only one speaks English; only one is armed. If only I had my gun, Donovan thought. *If only it hadn't fallen into the water. Three men and only one armed—that's workable. All I'd need is a distraction, something to give me time to draw the Glock from my ankle holster.* He shook his head. *Might as well wish for a bazooka while I'm at it.*

He stared ahead out the window now. There was no sign of land on the horizon yet—but there would be soon enough.

CHAPTER FORTY-FOUR

THE LAUNCH HUNG BACK slightly, giving the pilot a view of the ship's entire starboard side. He kept a beam's width away, trying to avoid another unexpected collision. He leaned forward over the helm, staring up at the ship's railing.

"She's increased her speed to twelve knots," he called back to Macy and Li.

"Is something wrong?" Macy asked.

"I'm not sure. We should have heard from them by now—they were supposed to stop the ship the minute they got the bridge under control. But they've increased their speed like they're going ahead into the channel."

"What should we do?"

"My instructions are to get out of here as fast as I can if the ship doesn't stop."

"That's excellent advice," Li said quickly, "and we should obey those instructions—*if* the ship doesn't stop. But all we know is that the ship hasn't stopped so far. She may stop at any moment now."

The pilot shook his head. "I'm not sure how long to hang around here."

"Dr. Monroe and I are vital elements of this operation," Li said. "It's crucial that we remain here as long as possible. If Mr. Donovan sends for us and we are unavailable, this entire operation could be put in jeopardy."

"Okay," the pilot said. "We'll wait and see what happens."

CHAPTER FORTY-FIVE

I N THE AFT CARGO hold, Sato Matsushita selected another rat from its cage. The hairless rats were perfect for the procedure. *If only we'd had them at Ping Fan*, he thought, *how much more efficient we would have been.* Hairless rats offered two distinct advantages: They had no thymus, which crippled their immune system, making them especially susceptible to the plague; and they had no hair, which rendered their entire bodies accessible to the ravenous fleas.

Sato worked in his NBC suit. The late-morning heat was already unbearable; he blinked constantly to keep the sweat from dripping into his eyes. He stared into the cages—there were hundreds of rats, pink and silky smooth. The rats wandered about slowly, lethargically. Some stumbled haltingly around the cage; others lay on their sides, prematurely stricken by the bacteria ravaging their internal organs. Below the cages, the shriveled bodies of hundreds of dead rats rested in hermetically sealed containers.

Sato lifted the Plexiglas cover from a tray and gently placed the rat inside. He had to be careful; if the rat turned on him and managed to penetrate his glove with its teeth, then he would be infected. That would happen soon enough, but it must not happen prematurely—not before he had the chance to see the blackness with his own eyes.

The sides of the tray were made of simple wood. The bottom was covered with coarse screen wire, with openings more than large enough to allow a flea's narrow body to pass through. There were a dozen rats in the shallow tray, all approaching the final agonies of death—but all still full of blood, warm blood, blood now dominated by a strain of *Yersinia pestis* for which there was no known cure.

Sato carried the tray to the opposite wall, where dozens of other trays rested on an elaborate shelf. But these trays were different—they were slightly larger and made of white porcelain. He lifted the lid from one of them and looked inside. The bottom of the tray was covered by an inch of water—and the water was covered by a speckled gray crust consisting of thousands and thousands of Oriental rat fleas.

The fleas remained motionless; the water prevented them from jumping. Sato took the tray of rats and lowered it into the porcelain tray until it rested just a few inches above the water. Then he opened a valve, and the water slowly drained away.

As the last of the water disappeared, the fleas began to ricochet off the porcelain like microscopic bullets. A handful of tiny dots began to appear on the rats' naked skin—then more, and more, until no pink at all remained. Each rat looked as if it wore a tiny wool suit, with only its glistening eyes, its tail, and the nonvascular tips of its toes still visible.

Now Sato opened another valve, and a thin layer of water returned to the bottom of the tray. He must wait now. The fleas would feed until they were engorged, and then they would drop off onto the water one by one, where they could be skimmed off and loaded into the shells.

The ceramic shells rested on a table along the aft bulkhead, nested in a layer of thick, high-density foam. Each shell was about four feet long and eight inches wide. The bottom two-thirds of each contained the cherry tree firework effect, the product of hundreds of thousands of dollars and years of research. The top third of each shell held five kilograms of infected fleas, an oxygen supply, and a canister of dried blood for sustenance. When the shell detonated at precisely eight hundred meters, the explosion would send the top third hurtling even higher, safely above the heat of the firework display. Then, as the cherry tree vanished from the sky, the fleas would gently rain down all around in search of their next meal.

Sato looked at the shells proudly. They were works of art—not like the primitive, hand-thrown pottery shells they used at Ping Fan. They were bullet-shaped, like large artillery shells, but they were as smooth as glass and gleaming white in color. And each shell was embellished with a brilliant hand-painted image of a cherry tree in the classic style of the Edo period.

Four of the shells were already loaded and rested on the tabletop. Four more waited on the floor under the table, ready to receive their tiny passengers.

Sato started back for another tray of rats—but as he turned, his bulky sleeve caught a flask of acid and sent it crashing to the floor. He looked down at the puddle spreading slowly across the floor toward the plastic barrier. He had to clean it up—he couldn't take a chance on the acid dissolving the seal and allowing the dressing area to become contaminated.

He looked around the laboratory; there was nothing suitable. He needed a mop and a bucket—surely he could find those things somewhere in the cargo hold. He unzipped the doorway into the dressing area, then sealed it carefully again behind him. He stepped under the disinfectant shower and pulled the chain; then he pulled off his hood and mask, grateful for the chance to release the pent-up heat.

He considered removing his NBC suit entirely, but he decided against it. Why bother? The process took several minutes, and he would need to return to his work as soon as possible. He looked around the dressing area—no mops, no sponges, no rags. He unzipped the second doorway and stepped into the outer compartment. Again he found nothing.

He looked at the hatchway and thought of making the long climb to the main deck—but he was already exhausted from the heat; he didn't need additional exertion. He looked around the outer compartment again and spotted a sealed hatch in the metal bulkhead that separated his laboratory from the rest of the aft cargo hold.

He had been sternly warned never to open this hatch. Khalid reminded him that they were guests on an ordinary merchant vessel, and they must not interfere with the vessel's cargo or schedule in any way. In return, Sato's own facilities would be strictly off-limits to the crew. To open the hatch was to risk revealing everything, and that was the last thing Sato wanted to do.

But this was an emergency—surely this was an exception.

He turned the handle on the metal hatch. Two bolts withdrew from the top and bottom frame, and the door swung outward. Sato poked his head through and looked. There was no sign of anyone—but there was a utility sink, and beside it was a mop and a metal pail.

He stepped through and pulled the hatch shut behind him. He quickly picked up the mop and bucket and turned back toward the lab. But as he did, he glanced around the cargo hold—and he was astonished at what he saw.

The cargo hold was stacked from floor to ceiling with wooden pallets, each bearing forty bags of unmarked paper sacks. Each stack of sacks was wrapped in layer upon layer of transparent plastic, forming a kind of huge cocoon. Near the top of each pallet, a small plastic pipe punctured the cocoon, and the hole was tightly sealed off with gray duct tape.

And protruding from each hole was an electrical wire.

Sato let out a gasp. He dropped the mop and bucket and hurried back to his laboratory. He unzipped the first doorway, not even bothering to seal it behind him again. In the dressing area he opened the medical cabinet and removed a scalpel and a rubber glove.

Back in the cargo hold he cut through one of the plastic cocoons and into the side of a paper sack. White granulated powder poured out. He scooped up some of it and poured it into the rubber glove; then he took the glove to the utility sink and added water. He twisted off the open end of the glove and shook the mixture. He pulled off one of his own thick gloves and felt the rubber with his bare hand.

It was cold.

Sato charged through the hatchway and up the stairs toward the bridge.

CHAPTER FORTY-SIX

ONOVAN HAD NO IDEA how long they'd been traveling at twelve knots—five minutes? Ten? It seemed like an hour. The ship was plunging straight down the center of the channel. How long could it be before one of those forty course corrections would be required? One thing was for sure: He was in no hurry to cover the next ten miles. He needed time to think. He had to slow it down.

"Reduce speed to five knots," he said confidently.

The ship's master stepped closer. "That's a bit cautious."

A series of responses ran through Donovan's mind, but none of them sounded convincing. He turned to the ship's master with a look of disdain.

"This is the way I learned it," he said. "If you know better, be my guest."

The ship's master turned to the helmsman and repeated the order. "You wouldn't be trying to slow us down, would you?" he said to Donovan.

"The sooner we get this over with, the better," Donovan replied.

"How long have you been a harbor pilot?"

"Seven years," he said without missing a beat. He started to add, "Before that, I was an apprentice for three," but he stopped short. *Play it safe*, he reminded himself. *Don't volunteer information—that's an amateur's mistake.*

"I assume you were once a ship's master yourself."

"Sure." Donovan had to stop this line of questions. The only way to do it was by asking his own. "What's the draft on this vessel?"

"You don't know?"

He paused. "I thought I did—but this ship isn't exactly what she seems to be, now, is she?"

"Her draft is twenty-nine feet."

"Is she fully loaded?"

"She is."

"With what?"

He smiled. "I'd rather talk about your ship. When you were a ship's master, what type of vessel did you command?"

He was thinking fast now. "She was called the *South Bronx*. How old is this ship, anyway?"

"Thirty-five years. You sailed from New York Harbor, then?"

"Yeah. You said you've called here before—how many times?"

"What class of vessel was she? What was her displacement?"

Strike three, Donovan thought. *I'm out.*

Just then the door opened with a crash. The ship's master spun around, and so did the helmsman—it gave Donovan an excuse to turn and look too. In the doorway was a small man, dressed in a bulky white biological suit, but with no hood. He was an old man, and he looked very angry— and he was Japanese.

Donovan took his first look at Sato Matsushita.

The old man charged up to the gunman and thrust out his right hand. He was holding something—it looked like an inflated rubber glove. The bloated fingers dangled down like a cow's teats. The old man shouted something in Arabic; the gunman's shoulders rounded, and he shuffled backward a step or two. *Khalid may be the employer*, Donovan thought, *but Sato looks like the boss.*

The conversation that followed was all in Arabic. Donovan didn't understand a word of it—but he watched carefully, picking up anything he could.

"Feel it!" Sato shouted, holding out the glove.

Khalid hesitated. Sato took another step forward and thrust the glove in Khalid's face. "I said *feel it.*"

Khalid slowly reached out and touched the glove. "So?"

"I know what this is, Khalid! I am not a fool! Ammonium nitrate is endothermic—it becomes cold when water is added!" He threw the glove to the floor; it landed with a squashing sound, sending water flecked with white granules everywhere.

"Where did you get that?" Khalid demanded.

"Where do you think? The cargo hold is stacked from floor to ceiling with it!"

"You were instructed never to go in there!"

"And now I know why! This ship is designed to be a bomb, isn't it?"

A pause. "Yes."

"Why did you not tell me?"

"I was instructed not to. The plan was—changed."

"Changed! Don't these people understand? Did you not tell them that I will allow no further interference, no variation from my plan? These people are fools, Khalid! They almost destroyed my strategy once—are they trying to do so again? What is this change you speak of? All I required was transportation and a simple laboratory—was that so difficult?"

"I told you," Khalid mumbled. "It is their money."

"Idiots!" Sato shouted. "My plan is perfect—it requires no additions and no alterations! There is no need for a secondary attack! There is no—"

Sato fell silent. His mouth dropped open, and he stood staring at Khalid, blinking hard. Khalid looked away.

"This change you speak of—what is it?"

Khalid stared at the floor.

"Please, Khalid—tell me."

Khalid looked over at the ship's master.

"Tell him," the ship's master said with a shrug. "I would want to know. What harm can it do now?"

Khalid stared back at the floor and began to speak. "The ship is a bomb," he said quietly. "It carries nine thousand tons of nitrate fertilizer. Each pallet is wrapped like a sack; the sacks are joined by pipes to the main fuel tank, and each one is wired with a detonator. When the command is given, the oil from the fuel tanks will be pumped into the sacks."

"An understandable precaution," Sato said hopefully. "But if there is no interference, if my strategy goes according to plan, then there will be no need for this alternative. Is that correct?"

He didn't reply.

"It is only a precaution, is it not? Khalid?"

Khalid closed his eyes. "When the ship enters the Upper Bay, the command will be given and the fuel oil will mix with the fertilizer. When the ship reaches a point halfway between Liberty Island and Manhattan, the bomb will be detonated—about two hours from now."

Sato gripped his head in his hands and let out a cry like a little child.

"Think of it," Khalid implored. "It will have the force of a small nuclear bomb. It will destroy far more than a simple pair of towers—it will collapse buildings all along the shores, it will destroy ships and piers, and it will ignite fires everywhere. And think of this, Dedushka: It will destroy the statue too."

Sato looked at him in horror. "Are you so simpleminded, Khalid? Is that the extent of your vision—to knock down a *statue*? I thought you were different from the rest of them. Your people are ignorant and primitive, barely out of the Stone Age. They're like children with firecrackers, running around the streets, making big sounds but accomplishing nothing at all. I offered them something more—something great, something inspired, something to be spoken of for generations to come. But your people know nothing of these things, do they? Arabs and their bombs," he said in disgust. "All they want is to make a little noise, a little puff of smoke, and then they are satisfied."

Khalid still made no reply.

Now the old man looked at him with sorrow in his eyes. "I should have expected this from these people," he said. "But not from you, Khalid, not from you. You have betrayed me."

Khalid slowly looked up from the floor and glared at the old man. "I have *not* betrayed you," he said. "I do not serve you; I serve the cause. You are wrong, Dedushka; *you* are the one who acts like a child—a spoiled child, a child who receives many gifts but still pouts because he doesn't get the very one he wanted."

"This is my *mission*," he said. "Can you not understand that?"

"Your mission is to strike at the Americans."

"Not in some clumsy, brutish way! Not without poetry, or beauty, or grace!"

"I could have left you behind to rot in Damascus," Khalid said, "dreaming of your precious *mission* that would never take place. Instead, you have been given the honor of participating in this great cause."

"By perishing in some mindless explosion? By being acted upon rather than acting? This is not an honor, Khalid; this is a death sentence! Your people feared what I would do if they rejected my plan. *That* is why I am here!"

"They were wise to fear you," Khalid said. "Perhaps I should fear you too." He raised the gun and pointed it at the old man's chest. Sato looked down at it, then back at Khalid.

"Is this to be my end?" he said quietly.

"That is your choice, Dedushka."

Sato paused. "If I have but two hours to live, I wish to prepare myself. Will you allow me?"

"Go."

Sato turned and exited the bridge. Khalid stared after him.

The ship's master spoke up. "The old man could still make trouble," he said. "I'd follow him if I were you."

Khalid handed the gun to the ship's master and followed.

Donovan listened to every word but understood nothing. Something was seriously wrong—but he had no idea what.

CHAPTER FORTY-SEVEN

KHALID TOOK THE THREE flights of stairs down to the main deck. He turned left at the bottom, down the narrow corridor toward the starboard side of the ship. Dedushka had a few seconds' head start on him, and he had no idea where he went. Where does an old man go to spend the last two hours of his life? *Where would I go?* Khalid asked himself. *To a stinking laboratory in the bowels of a ship? No—I would go out into the fresh air, out to feel the sun on my face one last time.*

He opened the hatch and stepped out onto the deck. The wind was strong, and the swells were still high. The rolling of the ship felt even more pronounced in sight of the heaving waves. He glanced to his right; to his surprise, the pilot boat still followed astern, just off the starboard side. But why would the boat still be following them? Perhaps they were waiting for some kind of signal, something that told them all was well and they could return to port. But what if the signal was never received? What if, by killing the sea marshals and seizing the pilot, they had prevented the signal from being sent? The pilot boat had a radio; it could contact the authorities—and if they did, there was still time for the authorities to intercept the ship.

Khalid raced back up the stairs to the bridge. He burst through the door, breathing hard.

"The pilot boat is still following!" Khalid shouted to the ship's master. "Ask the pilot why—ask him what we need to do to send it away!"

The ship's master repeated the question for Donovan. He listened, then calmly replied.

"He says it is the sea marshals," the ship's master explained. "The boat is still waiting for a signal from them. He says if they fail to receive the signal, they will contact the authorities. He asks permission to contact the boat by radio."

"No radio," Khalid said. "I will take care of it myself."

Back on deck, Khalid approached the bodies of the two SEALs. He grabbed one of the dead men by the shoulder and dragged him over onto his back. He removed the belt, then began to unbutton the shirt. A few minutes later he was dressed in the sea marshal's navy blue uniform. He removed the safety from his handgun and slid it into the empty holster. He donned the cap last of all, pulling the bill down low over his face.

He backed over the railing of the ship and began to descend the ladder. He let go of the rope with his right hand; keeping his face to the hull, he waved to the pilot boat to come up alongside.

"ONE OF THE SEALs is coming back," the pilot called to Macy and Li.

"Why would he do that?" Macy asked.

"No idea—but it's a good sign. If something was wrong, they sure wouldn't let him come back."

"Why didn't he just radio?"

"Perhaps they require our services," Li said. "Perhaps the young man is returning to assist us in boarding the ship."

"Could be," the pilot said. "We'll know in a minute."

The pilot pushed forward on the throttle, and the launch accelerated. He turned the wheel slowly, bringing the boat closer to the hull of the ship. The SEAL descended the ladder a few more rungs; he was level with the boat's bridge now, but still several feet above the foredeck. He waved again for the boat to draw up alongside.

The ladder was even with the foredeck now, and the pilot waited for the SEAL to descend the last few rungs and drop onto the deck—but he didn't. Instead, he waved for the pilot to pull up even farther.

"What's he doing?" Macy asked.

"I don't know. Maybe he just wants to give us a message—maybe their radios aren't working."

The pilot steered away from the ship slightly; if the SEAL wasn't coming aboard, there was no sense risking contact with the ship's hull. He nudged the throttle and eased the boat forward until the SEAL was even with the port bridge window. The man still clung to the ladder, facing the side of the ship.

As the pilot turned his head to the port window, Khalid released the ladder with his right hand and drew his gun. He spun around wildly, firing a spray of bullets into the bridge. The window's safety glass shattered into a thousand tiny pieces. The first three bullets struck the helm; a fourth caught the pilot in the left shoulder, and the final shot found the side of his head. He died instantly, slumping forward on the controls. Khalid turned back to the ladder, holstered his weapon, and looked up toward the ship's deck.

Inside the boat, Macy and Li sat frozen. Against the sound of the engines and the crashing waves, the gunshots sounded tiny and faraway—not like gunshots at all, but like the cracking of a stick. Even when the window shattered, it was unclear what had occurred. Maybe something had struck the window; maybe something had come loose. But when Macy saw splinters of wood and plastic fly off the helm, she thought something must be wrong—and when she saw the pilot slump forward, she knew.

She lunged forward and grabbed the pilot with both hands, thinking to pull him out of the line of fire. But as the body slid off the helm and onto the floor, it pulled the wheel sharply to the left, and the boat veered hard to port—directly toward the side of the ship.

Just as the launch began to turn, the ship pitched down into a deep trough. Now Khalid was no longer above the boat's deck—he was even with it. The boat's black bumper crashed against the iron hull with a shuddering thump, catching Khalid across the back of the legs, pinning him against the hull. He screamed in agony. Now the ship slowly started to rise again. Flesh ripped open, tendons tore, and bones splintered like dry wood. His legs hung limp and lifeless; his grip loosened, and he slid down the ladder a full rung.

The impact of the collision sent the launch rebounding away, but its rudder was still turned to port. The boat veered back again, this time crushing Khalid's pelvis with an audible crack. The next collision caught the center of his back—then his shoulders—then his skull. His arms fell limply to his sides, but he didn't fall. He just jerked slowly downward like a sheet of paper disappearing into a shredder, ground to dust between a giant's fingers, until he silently dropped away into the rolling water.

CHAPTER FORTY-EIGHT

The ship's master stared anxiously at the bridge door.

"Problem?" Donovan asked.

"Pilot the ship!" the master shouted, waving the gun wildly in the air.

Donovan watched the way he handled the sidearm. He was obviously not a soldier, like the rest of them. He looked awkward and self-conscious with the handgun; he carried it like a lit stick of dynamite. Donovan had no doubt that the ship's master would use the weapon. But his aim might be off, and he just might hesitate for an extra second or two—and that could be all Donovan needed.

The ship's master charged toward the bridge door—but he stopped abruptly and looked back at Donovan, seeming to reconsider his decision. He walked slowly back toward the helm again.

"If you interfere with the progress of this ship in any way, I will kill you," he said.

Donovan did his best to look disinterested. "If you want to go check on your employer, go ahead. I'll be here when you get back."

The ship's master stood motionless, considering.

Go, Donovan thought. *Get out of here. Leave me alone with this helmsman. I can break this guy in half; I can kill the engines and use the ship's own radio to send the signal. I can contact the launch—I can tell the pilot to get*

Macy and Li out of here; then I can bar the door and buy myself some time.
He knew this was his chance; he searched for something additional to say,
something that might sway the man, but he said nothing more. This was
no time to overplay his hand. Donovan just stared ahead out the bridge
window, willing the man to leave.

The ship's master barked something at the helmsman, who nodded
and glanced quickly over at Donovan. Then the master slowly turned
away and walked to the bridge door.

But just as he reached for the doorknob, the door opened. It was
Matsushita again, still dressed in his NBC suit—but this time he was
wearing his hood. He stepped forward, directly toward the ship's master,
until they were only a few feet apart.

The old man raised his left arm and motioned for the ship's master to
come closer. The man hesitated, then took a step forward and leaned
down. As he did, Matsushita brought his right arm up; in his hand he held
what looked like a small spray bottle. There was a quick hiss and a mist of
clear liquid—and the ship's master crumpled to the floor like a puppet
dropping on a stage.

It all happened in a single second. There was no gasping for breath, no
clutching at the throat, not even a look of shocked realization. It was a
sudden and instantaneous death. *It must be VX,* Donovan thought, *or
maybe some other nerve agent the old man cooked up himself.* He'd heard
about these chemicals in Bureau briefings—toxins that were absorbed
through the skin, nerve agents so potent that a single drop caused instant
death. Donovan never would have believed anything could kill that fast—
but it was hard to argue with results.

Now Matsushita started toward the helm, holding the spray bottle in
front of him as he walked. The helmsman stumbled backward into
Donovan, who shoved him aside. Matsushita shouted an order in Arabic;
the terrified helmsman nodded, then crept back to his position at the controls and pulled back on a series of levers. Donovan felt his weight shift
forward as the ship slowed to a stop.

The old man barked a second command, waving the bottle menacingly in the air. The helmsman scrambled away from the console again, staying well out of Matsushita's reach. Donovan had no idea what was said, so he stood motionless and waited. Matsushita looked at him and paused; then he said in English, "Please step away from the controls."

Donovan moved to the back wall. He watched as the old man turned back to the helm and began to spray every lever, every switch, and every knob with the clear fluid. He sprayed the keys of the laptop computer; he sprayed the radio; and he sprayed the throttles most of all. One thing was for sure—the old man didn't want this ship to budge.

As soon as Matsushita turned his back, the helmsman used the opportunity to scramble through the doorway and off the bridge. But Donovan waited, considering his options. He could run too—but where was he supposed to go? This was Sato Matsushita; this was the man he had come for. He measured the distance to the hooded figure. There was no way; he could never reach him before the old man had a chance to turn and raise that spray bottle of his. And this was not like the ship's master; this was not some gunman spraying 9mm chunks of lead. The old man didn't have to aim for the heart or the head, and Donovan wouldn't be able to take a hurried shot in the shoulder or leg and keep charging forward. All it took was a single drop, and it would be lights-out.

The ship's master. Donovan turned and looked; the body lay facedown with the right arm bent underneath—on top of the gun. Would he have time to reach the body, turn it over, and grab the gun before the old man could get to him? And even if he did reach the gun first—was anything on it?

One drop was all it took.

Before Donovan could move, before he even had a chance to speak, the old man wheeled around and charged out of the room, leaving Donovan on the bridge all alone with no idea what to do next.

CHAPTER FORTY-NINE

FBI Headquarters, 26 Federal Plaza

THE SHIP IS DEAD in the water," a young technical assistant announced, watching the radar image on his laptop screen. There were expressions of relief and enthusiasm all around the table.

Over the last few hours, the Joint Terrorism Task Force had changed. It had evolved into something larger, something far more powerful. The National Security Council had been briefed on the situation in an emergency session, which included the secretary of defense and the chairman of the Joint Chiefs of Staff. The decision was quickly made to keep the Incident Command Center where it had originated, at FBI headquarters, rather than take the time to transfer all the task force members to a new location—but the members themselves had each been slowly replaced. One of the four deputy directors of the CIA was now in attendance; so was a more senior State Department official. The military representatives had all been superseded by officers of higher rank, including the Navy SEAL commander, who had been replaced by a vice admiral—a man with the authority to push much larger buttons.

Additional technicians and support personnel had also crowded into the room, providing access to every possible asset and source of information. There were open lines to government offices all over Capitol Hill; even the president and vice president were updated at regular intervals. It was a truly national task force now, like a giant neuron with axons stretching all over the eastern seaboard. But at this moment in time, the nerve center was still at 26 Federal Plaza in New York.

"Let's hold it down," the CIA director shouted over the din. "Have we received the radio signal yet?"

"Not yet, sir."

"That's more than an oversight—the radio signal should have been the first priority. Something's gone wrong."

"What's the exact position of the ship?" the Navy said to a technician.

"Just under nineteen miles out, sir."

"That's cutting it awfully close. They were given ten miles to bring the ship to a stop—they did it in just over six."

"If everything was on task, we would have received the radio signal by now," the CIA said. "We're blind here—we have to assume the worst."

"But they did manage to stop the ship."

"Somebody did—but we don't know why, and we don't know for how long. For all we know, they could be setting up this plague weapon right now. I think we should launch the missiles; it's our only safe bet."

"I've got two men on that ship," the Navy said.

"We've got eight million here," said a woman from the mayor's office.

The CDC representative was still the same individual, though his status in the group had decreased significantly. The sudden loss of seniority had made him a little more supplicating and a lot less demanding. "Maybe there's another option," the man said. "These cruise missiles of yours—how accurate are they?"

"Within one meter," the Navy replied.

"Well—do we have to destroy the ship? How deep is the channel here? Does anybody know?"

Half a dozen support personnel clicked away at their keyboards. Just a few seconds passed before someone said, "Less than fifty feet."

"Okay then," the CDC said. "Suppose we just sink her—quickly, I mean, so that no one on board has a chance to respond. Can that be done?"

"We can strike just above the waterline," the Navy replied. "We can target the fore and aft cargo holds. We can use tactical warheads designed to open the hull but not tear the ship apart. What's your point?"

"We need that plague specimen," the CDC said. "The safest way to get it is to board the ship and carry it off. But if that option has failed, then there might be another way: We can sink the ship and send in divers to retrieve it. The bacillus has to be contained in some way—it should be protected from the seawater. And at that depth there's not much pressure—even a glass container might survive."

"If it survives the blast."

"That's a chance we have to take. Speaking on behalf of the Centers for Disease Control, we need that plague specimen. But the mayor's office is right: We've got eight million people to think about—maybe more."

The Navy considered. "We can do a tactical strike with two missiles," he said, "then launch two more with conventional warheads a minute later. If anything goes wrong with the tactical strike, we can guide the second two in and destroy the ship completely—but if everything goes the way we want, we can abort the second two missiles and drop them in the water."

Heads began to nod all around the room.

"Excuse me," a low voice said from across the room. Reuben Mayer slowly rose from his chair and smoothed his tie. Mayer was no longer the senior FBI agent present; the assistant director in charge was in attendance as well. But Reuben Mayer was the only man in the room who knew Nathan Donovan.

"I have a man on this ship too," Mayer said. "Some of you met him earlier—his name is Nathan Donovan. He's a CT agent for the Bureau, and he's an ex-Marine. I've been with the Bureau longer than some of you have been alive, and in all that time there's one thing I've learned: You always back your people. The CIA director said something that I think is important here: *We're blind.* We don't know what's going on. We tell our men to send out a radio signal—no signal. We give them ten miles to stop the ship—the ship stops. So why are we assuming the worst? Sounds to me like the job is half-finished—and for that we send in missiles and take them all out? I don't think so. That's not how you do business. That's not how you back your people. We put three good men on board this ship, and we gave them a job to do—I say give them a chance to do it."

There were objections and comments everywhere, but Mayer just raised his voice. "All I'm saying is, we set that ten-mile limit for a reason. This ship is no greater a threat to us now than it was six miles back. As long as it stays where it is, we can afford to give our people time. We told them ten miles; I say we give them ten miles."

"The men might survive the tactical strike."

"What if they're below deck? What if they're searching a cargo hold? Your 'tactical strike' will send the ship to the bottom with everyone on it."

"And what do we do if the ship starts forward again?"

Mayer paused. "If we have no radio signal *and* the ship starts forward again, then I agree—we have no choice. *Then* we launch. But let's wait until then." He looked slowly around the table, then sat down again.

"This man of yours," the State Department asked. "How good is he?"

Mayer shrugged. "He's FBI. What else do you need to know?"

There was silence around the table.

"Maybe he's right," the Navy said. "These men are our only assets in place; our best chance of taking that plague specimen intact is to give them a shot at it. The ship's not going anywhere—we don't have to pull the trigger just yet."

No one said anything for a minute.

"I'm willing to give the men more time," the CIA director said, "but I want to add a stipulation: If that ship moves a single foot closer to our coastline, I say we consider the mission scrubbed and we launch the missiles—no conditions; no questions asked. I see no reason to wait until she crosses the ten-mile mark; the missiles will take a few minutes to get there anyway."

The Navy looked around the table. "If there are no further objections, let's get on the phones and get the necessary approvals—and fast. We'll convene again in ten minutes."

As the group scattered, the CIA director worked his way across the room to Reuben Mayer. "I have a question for you," he said. "If this man of yours is so good, why do you think we haven't heard from him? What's your theory?"

"How many men are on this vessel?" Mayer asked.

"We have no way to know. They falsified all their documents."

"You suppose they're armed?"

"I would think so, yes."

Mayer nodded. "He could be a little busy."

CHAPTER FIFTY

THE LAUNCH CONTINUED TO pound against the side of the ship's hull. Macy grabbed the wheel and jerked it to the right, steering the boat away. At the same time she grabbed the throttle lever and pulled it back hard, and the boat lurched to a stop. She looked out the bridge window, expecting to see the ship pull away from her and continue on down the channel—but it didn't. For some reason, the ship had also come to a stop. Now the two vessels floated side by side like a great black swan and her tiny cygnet, slowly drifting closer again with each rolling swell.

"He's dead," Macy said.

"Yes," Li replied, struggling to drag the pilot's body away from the helm and into the main cabin. "May God rest his soul."

"No—Nathan's dead."

Li looked up at her. She stood motionless at the helm, her hands still gripping the steering wheel, staring straight ahead out the window. Li put his arm around her shoulders and gently turned her away, leading her down the three short steps to the row of pilots' seats. They sat down together, and Li took her hands in his.

"We don't know that," he said gently.

"That man was wearing one of the SEALs' uniforms—how do you think he got it? Something went wrong, Li. The SEALs are dead—and so is Nathan."

"We must not jump to conclusions. Apparently, the SEALs were unable to take control of the ship—that's all we know for certain."

"He was wearing his *clothes*."

"One does not have to be dead to surrender his clothing. Perhaps the men were only taken captive."

"They murdered the pilot of this boat. Do you think they treated Nathan any better? He's dead—I can feel it."

"Nonsense," Li said sharply. "We must not give up hope—and we must remain focused. We are now in command of this vessel, and we must decide what to do next."

Macy tried to clear her thoughts. "We should radio for help," she said. "Let the others know what's going on."

"We don't know what's going on. What would we tell them?"

"That the mission has failed."

"Has it? Are we certain of that? We must be very careful here. If we announce to your superiors that this mission has failed, what do you suppose their next alternative will be?"

Macy considered. "They'll destroy the ship."

"Of course they will. Why do you suppose the pilot said that if anything went wrong, we were to 'get out of here fast'? If we declare this mission a failure, we will ensure the deaths of everyone on that ship—*everyone*. Are you willing to take that risk, Macy? Are you *that* certain that Nathan is dead?"

They felt the boat shudder, and they heard a sound like a tire swing rubbing against a tree. The waves had carried the two vessels together again. They looked out the port window and saw nothing but black.

"And another thing," Li said. "If we use the radio, the crew of the ship might overhear our message—and they may be unaware of our presence here. Even if that gunman caught a glimpse of us when he fired at the pilot, he's dead now—as far as the crew of the ship knows, there's no one left on this launch. That's a very great advantage, Macy—it means no one will be looking when we board the ship."

Macy's jaw dropped open. "What?"

"That's why we came here, isn't it?"

"Li—you saw what happened to that gunman."

"Yes—that was rather unpleasant, wasn't it?"

"You could be crushed—or you could fall into the water and drown."

"What a shame," Li said. "I was hoping to die in perfect health."

"You saw what happened when Nathan tried it."

"That wasn't particularly graceful, was it? I think we can do better."

"But—I can't drive this boat. Can you?"

They felt the hulls bump together again. "I don't think we'll have to—if we act quickly, that is."

"Li—this is crazy."

The old man smiled. "I didn't come along just for the ride, Macy—and neither did you. It's been my intention all along to board this vessel. And if I'm not mistaken, you came along to assist your husband."

"My ex-husband."

"Really," Li said. "Do you also repair past houses and work at past jobs? No, my dear, no one goes to this much trouble for an *ex*-husband."

"That's a different matter."

"That's the *heart* of the matter," he said. "Everything else is peripheral. You need to forgive him, you know."

"I'm not sure I can."

"I know—but you want to, and that's what's important. That's why you're here."

"You think I came all the way out here to forgive Nathan?"

"May I tell you something? Something that Nathan does not yet understand. Your mission and my mission—they are the same. Do you understand what I'm saying?"

"No."

"You think we came out here because of a plague—and we did, in a sense, but the plague is not on that ship. *We* have the plague, Macy, you and I. We both came out here in pursuit of a cure."

"It's too late now," she said.

"No, it isn't. Nathan is still alive."

"How do you know?"

"Because *I* feel it—and I have more experience with these things than you do. Of course, we'll never know for certain until we board that ship."

Another dull thump from the two colliding hulls. Macy looked out the broken window at the rope ladder still dangling over the ship's starboard side. The ladder dipped low and then hesitated for a moment, as if inviting her to climb aboard—then it suddenly jerked up and away until the last rung of the ladder was above her head. It was like dangling a string in front of a cat's face, waiting until its paw reached out before snatching the string away.

"We'll never make it," Macy said.

Li patted her hand. "God has brought me this far; I don't believe He will abandon me now. Who knows? Perhaps He'll assist you with your mission too."

Li pulled on his backpack and stepped out onto the deck. He worked his way down the railing and stepped into the opening. He stood perfectly erect, like a plastic figurine on the dashboard of a car. He stared directly ahead at some fixed point. He raised both hands until he looked like a bear that was about to attack—and then he waited. Seconds passed—then a minute.

Macy held her breath. She wondered if he was frozen, if fear had paralyzed him. She started to call out to him—then the ladder dipped low and close again. When it did, Li simply extended his arms, gripped the ropes, and stepped onto one of the rungs. A moment later he was whisked away into the sky.

Macy shook her head in amazement. The old man knew what he was doing. The younger men threw themselves at the ladder, but Li let the ladder come to him. *Maybe that's what you have to do when you grow old*, she thought. *Or maybe that's what you learn to do when you grow wise.*

Macy worked her way out on the deck now. She looked up; Li was already at the top of the ladder, pulling himself over the side of the ship. She hoped he was right—she hoped no one knew they were coming. She stood in the opening now, waiting just as Li did for her golden opportunity.

Then the ships began to drift apart.

At first she thought it was just a momentary separation, and she waited

338

for the waves to bring her in closer again. Then she realized to her horror that the hulls were slowly separating. This was as close as she would get—and she was getting farther away all the time.

She began to panic. She measured the distance to the ladder. She thought about jumping out and trying to land on the ladder on all fours. But it was too far away for that now; she would miss the ladder entirely and disappear into the waves. And then a terrifying thought occurred to her, worse than anything she had contemplated yet: Maybe it was too late. Maybe she had missed her chance—maybe she had no choice now but to stand on the deck and watch helplessly as Nathan drifted away.

I'm sick of separations, she thought, *and I hate being helpless.*

She crouched down low, swung both arms out, and dived for the ladder.

CHAPTER FIFTY-ONE

S HE SEEMED TO HANG in the air for an eternity. When her feet first left the edge of the boat, her fingertips were pointed at the middle of the ladder—but in midair the ship began to rise again, and she watched in dismay as the rungs flashed past her one by one. She couldn't bear to look down. She kept her eyes straight ahead, fixed on each rung until it disappeared from her sight, praying that there was at least one more to follow.

Her hands caught the final rung, and for a split second she looked like an arrow shot into the side of the ship—then her body swung down hard. She managed to bend her legs slightly and turn her side into the impact. It was still a gut-wrenching blow, but she kept her grip. Now she hung there, staring up at the ladder, knowing she didn't have the strength to pull herself up hand over hand.

And she wondered if the boat was drifting closer behind her.

Then the ship rolled to starboard again, and Macy found herself dipping into the ocean like a tea bag. She was up to her neck now, and the ladder kept going down. She released her hands and used the water's buoyancy to lift her, taking a new grip several rungs higher—and this time placing her feet on one of the rungs below. When the ship rolled back again, she was out of the water and on the ladder—and she was starting to climb.

A minute later she pulled herself over the gunnels. She saw Li, standing motionless and staring down at the bodies of the two SEALs. One of them was dressed only in his underclothes; both had gaping bullet wounds in their foreheads.

"Oh, no," she said with a moan.

"Come on," Li said. "We can't stay here—we have to get out of sight."

He took her by the arm and led her to the hatchway in the starboard side of the superstructure. He peered around the corner—there was no one in the corridor. They both stepped inside. At the first door they came to, Li quietly knocked. There was no answer; they entered and shut the door behind them. It was an empty cabin.

Li immediately sat down on the edge of a bunk and opened his backpack. He pulled out the NBC suit and began to unfold it.

"What are you doing?" Macy asked.

"I'm going to find Sato Matsushita, of course. Help me with this, will you?"

The suit was a single unit from head to foot. A long zipper ran from the crotch to just below the hood. He pushed his legs down into the lower half and worked his feet into the boots; then he stood up, and Macy held the suit while he slid his arms into the sleeves. He pulled the hood over last of all, positioning the gas mask over his mouth and nose and the lens in front of his eyes. Then he slowly drew the long zipper, closing the seal.

"How do I look?"

"Li—how are you going to find Matsushita?"

"I'm going to ask someone. Unlike most men, I'm not ashamed to ask for directions."

"Be serious."

"I'm quite serious." He looked in his backpack again. It was empty now, except for a small black case with tarnished brass hardware. He fastened the flap on the backpack and pulled it over his shoulders.

"I need a box of some sort," he said, "something heavy. Look around, will you?"

Under the bunk they found a corrugated box containing medical supplies. Li lifted it, testing its weight.

"This will do nicely," he said and started for the door.

"What are you going to do?"

"Wait for me here. When I find Matsushita, I will come back for you."

She stepped in front of him. "Li, you can't just walk around the ship. You don't exactly look like an Arab."

Li looked up at her through the lens of his hood. "No—but I just might pass for Japanese."

CHAPTER FIFTY-TWO

LI STEPPED OUT ONTO the main deck and looked to both sides—there was no one in sight. He turned to his right and headed toward the rear of the ship. Over the railing, to his left, he could still see the launch floating in the water below.

At the corner he turned right and started across the back of the superstructure toward the opposite side of the ship. On the port side of the deck, he spotted a crewman coiling a steel cable around a capstan. Li lumbered toward him, waiting for the crewman to glance up; then he set the box down heavily, straightened, and slowly rolled his shoulders in his best imitation of exhaustion. The crewman shouted something across the deck in Arabic; Li responded in Chinese.

The crewman approached. Li pointed down at the box, jabbed his finger impatiently at the crewman, then planted his hands on his hips and glared at him.

The crewman shook his head, muttered a colorful Arab expression, and hoisted the box. He started back across the deck in the direction from which Li had come. Li turned and followed.

Li trailed the crewman through a hatchway and down a long flight of metal stairs. At the bottom of the stairway, there was a second hatch. When Li stepped through, he found himself standing before a huge sheet of white translucent plastic draped from ceiling to floor. Li tapped the crewman on the shoulder and pointed to the floor. The crewman deposited the box without comment and disappeared through the hatchway again.

Li peered through the first sheet of plastic; beyond it was some kind of locker area, and then a second plastic barrier with a sealed doorway of its own. Beyond that barrier he could just make out the dreamlike image of a biological laboratory. He recognized the screen-wire fronts of the animal cages; he saw shelves full of porcelain basins draped with surgical tubing—and on the far wall, he saw something that looked like a series of tall white cylinders. No, wait—they tapered at the ends, like bullets.

He carefully unzipped each flap and stepped through.

Li found the laboratory horrifyingly familiar. He examined the cages; there were hundreds and hundreds of rats, like the ones the rat-catchers combed the alleys of Singapore for sixty years ago—like the ones the Indian and Malay boys were forced to pick fleas from with pincers. But these rats were different—they were hairless; no one would have to shave their bellies as they did at Ping Fan.

He stared into the porcelain basins and saw the speckled crust of fleas, exactly like the ones they had raised in oil cans at Ping Fan. He saw the hardwood trays with their mesh bottoms, and he shook his head in astonishment. Every piece of equipment in the lab was of the latest design, precision-engineered to the highest modern standards—but it was exactly the same as the process developed by Unit 731 scientists more than six decades ago.

Li stopped for a moment and drew a few deep breaths. The heat and humidity in the lower cargo hold were oppressive, and in the heavy NBC suit, there was no relief at all.

He turned to the aft wall now and examined the items on the long worktable. In the center, standing in a transit case lined with thick protective foam, were the four bullet-shaped cylinders. He pried one of the cylinders from the foam; it was extremely heavy. It took all of his strength just to ease it onto the worktable and slide it forward to the edge. He worked slowly, pacing himself; this would be a most unfortunate time to faint from heat exhaustion.

He turned the cylinder and ran his glove over the surface. It was certainly a thing of beauty, a flawless ceramic piece fire-glazed to a glassy finish. He studied the intricate painting now. It was a tree, the unmistakable image of a Nanking Cherry—but there was one significant difference. In the place of each puffy pinkish-white blossom was something that looked like a spiny thistle. The spines of some pointed straight out, while others draped down slightly like the ribs of an umbrella. What were they? What did they symbolize? Li stepped back from the cylinder to take a wider view—and then, suddenly, everything came into focus.

They weren't thistles—they were showers of sparks.

They weren't cylinders—they were mortar shells.

They were fireworks, and today was the third of July.

Li looked for a place to sit down.

CHAPTER FIFTY-THREE

MACY PEERED DOWN THE corridor from behind the cracked door, watching for Li to return. She had been able to see him until he stepped through the hatchway and onto the deck—but once he turned to his right, he vanished, and she had seen no sign of him since. She looked down at her watch. How long was she supposed to wait here? How long would it take Li to find Matsushita and return for her? And what if he never came back—what if he was discovered first; what if he suffered the same fate as the two Navy SEALs?

And if he did, how would she ever know?

It was too much to think about now. Macy knew from experience that imaginary roads are the darkest to travel, and the mental side trip only makes you more afraid to face the genuine item when it comes along. She shook it off and tried to focus on what she would say to Matsushita when they met—if they ever did.

Suddenly, she heard footsteps in the corridor. Someone was approaching from the opposite direction, moving fast. She pressed the door tighter until only a slit remained, and she waited with her heart pounding in her throat. She thought that at any moment the door would burst open, crashing into her and sending her flying across the cabin—but the figure hurried past, racing toward the same hatchway that Li had used just a few minutes before. The form that passed by was only a silhouette in the darkness of the corridor; all she could tell was that he was a big man, broad-shouldered, wearing something across his back. But in the light flooding through the hatchway, she could see him in every detail.

Nathan!

She threw open the door and shouted his name. It was a stupid thing to do, announcing their presence to everyone within earshot—but she didn't care. She imagined Nathan stepping out onto the deck and vanishing just as Li did, and the thought was more than she could bear. There was a basic human instinct that Macy was compelled to obey, foolish or not—it was the voice inside her that said, *I don't want to die alone.*

Donovan spun around and looked at her. For an instant he stood paralyzed, incredulous—then he charged toward her and into the cabin, swinging the door shut behind him. He wrapped her in his arms and held her—then he took her by the shoulders and pushed her away.

"What are you doing here? I told you to stay away from the ship!"

"The launch pilot is dead," Macy said.

"What?"

"Somebody from the ship put on one of the SEALs' uniforms. He climbed down the ladder—we thought it was one of the SEALs coming back for us. When we pulled up alongside, he shot the pilot in the head."

"Why didn't you get out of here?"

"And just leave you here?"

"I can take care of myself."

"Just like the SEALs?"

"Macy—now I have to look out for you too."

"I don't need a babysitter," she said. "I came here to help."

"Did you try the radio? Did you tell them what was going on here?"

"I didn't *know* what was going on—I still don't!"

"Still no radio contact," Donovan said. "We could have a problem here."

"What's wrong?"

"The Navy gave me an ultimatum. They said if they didn't hear from me, I needed to stop the ship within ten miles—or else."

"But the ship did stop."

"Yeah—but I have no idea how close we are to the line, or which way the tide is carrying us. I don't know how long we've got."

"Then we can't afford to wait. We have to go after Li."

"Li! Isn't he still on the launch?"

"No—he's here, Nathan; he went to look for Matsushita."

"You let him go after Matsushita—by *himself*?" Donovan sank down on the end of the bunk and put his head in his hands.

"What else could I do? I can't go walking around the ship. Li put on his NBC suit—he can pass for Matsushita; he can look around without being recognized. He's coming back for me as soon as he finds him."

"He's not coming back for you, Macy."

"Why not?"

"Did he take anything with him?"

"He was wearing his backpack—that's all."

Donovan groaned.

"What's wrong?"

"I don't have time to explain—and we don't have time to waste. How much of a head start does he have on us?"

"Maybe ten minutes."

"Then we have to hurry. Wait here a minute—I'll be right back."

Donovan ducked out the doorway and down the corridor to the hatch. He poked his head out and looked left toward the bow; the bodies of the two SEALs were still lying faceup on the deck. Donovan searched up and down the deck—there was no one in sight. He crept quickly down the deck to the still-clothed body and drew the sidearm from its holster. Then he hurried back to the cabin, hopefully unobserved.

"We've got to find Matsushita before Li does," Donovan said, tucking the weapon into his belt.

"How do we find him?"

"We'll just have to search the ship. I checked the other cabins on the way down from the bridge. There's nobody up here—they must all be below deck."

"There don't seem to be many people on this ship."

"I thought the same thing. When I boarded the ship, there were two with automatic weapons; there was a third with just a handgun. On the bridge there were two more—but one of them is dead."

"How?"

"I'll explain later. Have you seen anybody else?"

"Just the crewman who shot the pilot. But he's dead too—he got caught between the ships."

"That leaves only three—that we've seen, anyway." He looked at her. "He got caught between the ships?"

"It was terrible."

"Sorry I missed that," he said. "How did you get up here, anyway?"

"I climbed the ladder, just like you did."

"*Just* like I did?"

"Well—I like to think I looked a little better."

"So do I. Come on, let's get out of here."

"Where are we going?"

"Which way did Li go? If we can't find Matsushita, we can at least find Li."

"He turned right, toward the rear of the ship. That's all I could see."

"Then that's where we'll start—with the aft cargo hold."

He waited by the door as she pulled on her backpack with her NBC suit inside.

"Nathan—why do we have to find Matsushita before Li does?"

"Because Li is going to kill him," Donovan said, "and I don't think it's going to be pretty when he does."

CHAPTER FIFTY-FOUR

IDIOTS, Sato thought, *INCOMPETENT morons and fools! I offer them the chance to stand on the shoulders of giants, but no—they prefer to grovel like rodents in their little desert burrows, gnawing at the soles of the Americans when they could be striking a death blow to the head!*

He charged down the stairway and through the hatch, blind with his own rage.

I give them the benefit of sixty years of my own research—and before that, the work of hundreds more at Ping Fan! I grant them access to the astonishing discoveries of all of Biopreparat—I offer them the collective genius of the greatest scientific minds of the last century, and when it comes time to strike, what weapon do they prefer? A bomb—a clumsy, barbaric device that a Chinese peasant could devise!

He stepped through the first plastic barrier and into the dressing area. He returned the plastic spray bottle to the medical cabinet, then pulled down the long zipper on his NBC suit and ducked his head out from under the hood.

A boat filled with explosives! A floating tin of gunpowder! And the only detonator their feeble minds can devise is a handful of their own people—one to push the button, no doubt, and the others to bolster his courage. Truly a ship of fools! If only we could load all of these people onto a single ship—then perhaps we would have a bomb worth detonating!

He wrestled the suit down off his shoulders and pulled his arms from the sleeves. He squatted down on the wooden bench and bunched the leggings down around his shins, then worked his feet up and out of the boots. He hung the suit up on the wall, then turned to the second plastic barrier and opened the zipper.

And what glorious purpose will this brilliant weapon fulfill? It will destroy a statue*! What idiocy is this? Why strike at the giant's shadow and hope for the giant to fall? This bomb will destroy a single row of waterfront buildings, and the first row will shield the second row from harm. What genius! Why strike at useless buildings instead of at the lives they contain? It is not the buildings that will strike back—it is the enemy within, the enemy left alive because of their ignorance and shortsightedness!*

He stepped into the laboratory now and sealed the flap behind him. He turned immediately to the cages on his left. He absentmindedly ran his fingernail down the screen wire of one, half observing the dull response of the dying rats.

I will not allow this to happen. I will not allow my weapon and my mission to be destroyed in a clumsy puff of smoke. This ship will not proceed until I say so. Khalid will reconsider—Khalid will recognize his foolishness, and he will come to me, and we will talk. I will make him understand that here, on the other side of the ocean, we are under no obligation to obey the foolish commands of his so-called superiors. We are the ones who must decide, we are—

He stopped and drew a sharp breath.

In the center of the worktable he saw his foam-lined transit case—but one of his beautiful shells was missing. He jerked his head to the right—there it was, standing upright on the far corner of the table. Standing beside it was an elderly Chinese man, smiling and resting one hand on the tip of the shell. Beside the old man, on the floor, was an NBC suit and an empty backpack.

And on the table beside the shell, a small black case lay open, with three glass vials inside.

CHAPTER FIFTY-FIVE

DONOVAN STEPPED THROUGH THE cargo hatch with Macy right behind him. He held the .45 at eye level, with the butt of the gun resting in his cupped left hand. He swept the room as he entered. He kept his right finger outside the trigger guard, knowing that the Special Forces handgun would have a very light pull. He only had a single clip, and he didn't want to waste a bullet on the first sudden noise that made him flinch.

"I still don't see anybody," Macy said.

"Me neither."

"How many people does it take to run a ship?"

"Beats me—I sure figured more than this."

"Where do you think they all are?"

"Maybe in the engine room—but I don't think Matsushita would be with the rest of the crew. I think he'd have his own space; I'm betting they set him up in one of the cargo holds."

"Is this a cargo hold?"

"I think so. Let me find the lights."

A moment later there was the click of a circuit breaker, and rows of yellow incandescents went on high above. Macy let out a gasp. The room around them was cavernous. It was at least forty feet wide, and it was impossible to tell how deep. It was stacked floor to ceiling with palletized sacks, forming a wall so high that it seemed to curl over them like a breaking wave.

There were less than two feet of clearance between the bulkhead and the first row of pallets, creating a narrow aisle just wide enough to squeeze through sideways. They peered down the aisle in both directions. To the right, the aisle ended at the outer hull of the ship; to the left, it ended at a second metal hatch.

"That way," Donovan said. "That must lead to the next cargo hold."

"Wait," Macy said, breathing hard. "I need a second." She bent over and rested her hands on her knees.

"You okay?"

"It's this heat," she said. "It must be a hundred and twenty down here. I felt bad enough already—this isn't helping."

"Let's take it slower," he said, "but we've got to keep moving."

They sidestepped down the aisle with their backs against the bulkhead. As they passed column after column of stacked pallets, Donovan stared down the long narrow spaces between them. As his eyes adjusted to the dim light, he began to make out strange shapes in the shadows between the columns. There seemed to be something attached to the top of each plastic-wrapped pallet, something long and straight like a board. And there was something around it or beside it, something that wound and curled like surgical tubing.

He stopped to take a better look, but the spaces between the pallets were too deep in shadow to reveal any more details.

"Back up," he said to Macy.

They worked their way back to a space where the incandescents hung directly above, casting their yellow light deep into the narrow gap—and then Donovan saw it.

They weren't boards; they were pipes—and it wasn't surgical tubing; it was electrical wire.

He studied the layout of the pipes; the side of the column of pallets looked like a family tree. Pipes from the lowest pallets joined with larger pipes above, merging as they rose into ever-larger diameters until they all joined together near the ceiling into a single six-inch conduit that traveled back through a hole cut through the bulkhead.

The wires from each level of pallets gathered with others at a metal junction box. A single wire emerged from the top of the junction box, joining with others above it and traveling in undulating bundles through the same hole as the pipe.

Donovan looked at the pallet directly in front of his face. Through the thick plastic wrapping, he saw layer upon layer of hundred-pound sacks bearing no apparent label or identification. He grabbed at the plastic and tried to tear it open, but it was too thick. He pressed the distorting plastic tighter against the brown paper and searched more closely for some distinguishing mark that might identify its contents. On the end of one sack, in tiny dot-matrix letters, he found the phrase *ENGRAIS CHIMIQUE*.

"What does this say?" Donovan asked Macy.

She squinted at the tiny line. "Chemical fertilizer."

Donovan leaned back against the bulkhead and slid down to the floor.

"What's wrong?"

Donovan just stared straight ahead.

Macy sat down on the floor beside him. "Nathan, what is it?"

"The ship is a bomb," he said. "The sacks—they're filled with ammonium nitrate. This whole ship is rigged to explode."

"What?"

"Sixty years ago, in Texas City, they were loading a ship like this one with ammonium nitrate. They had about two thousand tons of it on board when the ship caught fire. A couple of hours later the ship blew up—and it destroyed half the city. Pieces of the ship came down a mile away. The blast knocked two planes out of the sky—they say you could hear it a hundred and fifty miles away." He pointed around the room. "Look at the pallets," he said. "Each one is wrapped in plastic, like a bag, and each bag has a pipe attached to it—see there? Those pipes carry fuel oil from the ship's tanks."

"Why?"

"Because ammonium nitrate is a low-grade explosive—until it's mixed with a hydrocarbon like oil. Then it's known as ANFO: ammonium nitrate/fuel oil. Remember the Oklahoma City bombing? That's what they used there—ammonium nitrate mixed with nitromethane, a kind of racing fuel. In Oklahoma City they only used about two tons—a thousand times less than in Texas—but it still took off half the Federal Building. The difference was the fuel oil, plus a sophisticated triggering sequence." He pointed up at the ceiling. "See the wires? I'll bet the triggering sequence is computerized."

Macy looked around again at the cargo hold. There were pallets everywhere, as far as the eye could see.

"How much do you think is here?"

"I have no idea. This is just one cargo hold—if they plan to blow up the ship, they probably loaded them all. There could be five times more ammonium nitrate here than there was on the ship in Texas City—but it's rigged for maximum effect, like the bomb in Oklahoma City. If this thing goes off anywhere near the harbor . . ." His voice trailed away. "Well—at least we know why there's nobody on the ship. Talk about a skeleton crew."

"I don't get it," Macy said. "They already have Matsushita and his plague weapon. Why the bomb?"

"I have no idea. But there's some kind of conflict going on here. They're fighting among themselves—maybe not everybody is on the same page. I was on the bridge when Matsushita came in."

"You saw him?"

"Yeah—and he was *ticked*. He was in an NBC suit, and he had a spray bottle with him—some kind of nerve agent. He killed the ship's master, and he ordered the helmsman to stop the ship—then he sprayed all the controls so no one could touch them. Apparently Matsushita doesn't want this ship to move."

"Why not?"

"We'll have to ask him," he said, climbing to his feet. "Come on—we've got to hurry."

"Nathan, wait. This ammonium nitrate—is there any other way to set it off?"

"Like what?"

"Say, for example—a missile?"

CHAPTER FIFTY-SIX

"WHO ARE YOU?" MATSUSHITA demanded.

"My name is not important," Li replied.

"How did you get on this ship?"

"Again, a trivial detail. We have very little time together, Dr. Matsushita, and we must focus on more important matters."

Matsushita's eyes began to dart around the laboratory.

"Nothing is missing, if that's what you're thinking. Nothing has been tampered with, and nothing has been taken—except this," he said, patting the white shell beside him.

Matsushita started toward him.

"I would not do that," Li said, tipping the shell precariously over the edge of the table.

Matsushita froze. He raised both hands in an entreating gesture and backed slowly away.

Li rocked the shell back again. "It would be rather embarrassing for two eighty-year-old men to end up in a wrestling match," he said. "I think discussion is more appropriate to men of our station in life, don't you?"

"What do you want?"

"I want to tell you a story. I know you'll enjoy this story, because it involves you—and I imagine that by this point your twisted soul is interested in nothing else."

356

"I do not have time for this."

"You took sixty years of my time," Li said. "The least you could do is give a few minutes in return. Now then—where shall I begin? There are so many possible starting points, and the beginning of a story is the most important part. How about this: Once upon a time there was an ambitious young man who wished nothing more than to become an excellent doctor. But it was not to be. Instead, he was conscripted into the Imperial Japanese Army, where he was assigned to a biological warfare facility in Manchuria known as Unit 731."

"How do you know this?" Matsushita demanded.

"Please—you're interrupting my story. At first, the young man found the practices of Unit 731 abhorrent. But then, like many men in times of war, his heart grew hard and unfeeling. But war does not make men demons—it simply releases the demons within them. And within his own heart there were demons, though he was too young to know them yet—things like arrogant nationalism, and intellectual snobbery, and racial bigotry. Soon these demons had taken over his heart, and he became an eager and willing accomplice of Unit 731. The dissections, the bloodletting, the human testing—they were all just daily activities to him. And the Chinese peasants who begged for mercy while he cut them open to study their living remains—they were just like laboratory animals squealing in their cages."

Li paused. "Are you enjoying my story?"

"No."

"Then perhaps I should begin somewhere else," he said. "I know: Once upon a time there was a young Chinese man. He, too, wanted only to be a doctor one day—but along the way he discovered that he wanted something else: He wanted to be a *husband*. He was quite surprised to discover this; he had never thought of being a husband before. But one day he met a young Chinese woman, a simple peasant girl—but she was as beautiful as the Yangtze at sunset and as gentle as a woodland fawn. The young man was captured by this vision; he was enraptured with love for her—and to his great and undeserving delight, she loved him in return.

And from that day forward, in all the world there was only one thing he really longed to be: her husband. But it was not to be.

"One day, an airplane flew over her village and ejected something from its tail that looked like smoke. The people of the village thought little of it, but a few days later they were stricken with a strange disease. My wife was among them. She was in agony, Dr. Matsushita. She was told that medical help was available if only she would report to the village temple. She did so—and when she got there, do you know what happened? She was tied to a chair and vivisected."

Li's voice was trembling now. "Is this story familiar to you, Dr. Matsushita?"

"No."

"The village was called Congshan. Does that help?"

"I cannot remember."

"When you finished with my wife's internal organs and discarded them on the floor, you returned to your truck. Do you remember? A young man approached you from behind. He put a hand on your shoulder and turned you around. He looked at your face; he stared into your eyes. He memorized every contour and pore. He charted the blood vessels in your eyes. Do you recall this? You looked back at him, Dr. Matsushita. Do you remember his face? Would you recognize him if you saw him again?"

Li took a step closer but stayed within arm's length of the shell. "One of the soldiers—he pushed you aside. The soldier stepped forward and plunged his bayonet into the young man's belly." Li slowly lifted his shirt, revealing the jagged scar below his ribs.

"Do you remember me, Dr. Matsushita?"

The old man shook his head.

"But why should you?" Li said. "It was only a bayonet wound, barely two inches in length. Now, a vivisection—that's something different; that's something to *remember*."

Li's voice began to break; he paused for a moment to compose himself.

"I really don't mind if you don't remember me," he said. "But I must know if you remember my wife. Her name was Jin Li. Did you hear me? *Jin Li.* Please, Dr. Matsushita—tell me that you hated her, or tell me that her memory has haunted you every day since. Tell me that you're glad you butchered her, that her death has been a source of constant satisfaction to you. Tell me that you selected her for a reason—tell me there was something different about her, something that to this very day makes her stand out in your mind. But please, in the name of all that is holy, don't tell me that you can't *remember.*"

"I cannot be expected to recall a single person," he said.

"You mean you cannot remember one murder among thousands? How very odd the human heart is. If I commit a single murder, it weighs on my soul like a mountain of fire. If I commit a second murder, my burden is increased—but not doubled. And when I commit a thousand murders, my burden is somehow relieved. How fortunate for your conscience that you were a mass murderer and not some petty assassin."

"It was a time of war," he said.

"Yes—that's what the Americans said when they dropped the bomb on Hiroshima and incinerated your precious sister. Did that justification satisfy *you*, Dr. Matsushita? That it was a time of war, and ordinary morality had to be set aside for the sake of ultimate victory? Is that what you tell yourself even now?"

Matsushita's face flushed. "How dare you speak of my sister!"

"I do dare—I dare to speak her name: *Emiko Matsushita.* I speak her name that she might be remembered. Have you ever spoken my wife's name, Dr. Matsushita? Of course not—you never knew her name, did you? I'm curious: How was my wife distinguished from all your other human experiments? Was she assigned a case number? Was she simply described as 'Congshan female'? Or was she not interesting enough for that—perhaps her organs were too ordinary to merit any notation at all."

"It was *war*," he said again. "All nations had to sacrifice."

"Nations don't make sacrifices—people do. Strange, isn't it? Nations win victories, but individuals make sacrifices. Take me, for example: My nation was among the victors, and yet I lost everything I held dear in the world. I am a victor, yet I suffer among the vanquished. Do you know why? Because there is no victory great enough to compensate me for the loss of my beloved Jin."

"What is it you seek from me—an apology?"

"In your current spiritual condition, that would be far too much to expect."

"I will not apologize! When my helpless sister was scorched to death in atomic fire, who offered an apology to me? And now her soul is in agony!"

"I assure you, it is not Emiko's soul that is in agony."

"Tell me what it is you want!"

"I want you to listen. I want you to try to allow some tiny shaft of light into that blackened soul of yours. You think that the taking of a million lives will somehow compensate you for the loss of your sister—but it never will. You *loved* your sister, and when you truly love something, you assign it a value above everything else in the world. Nothing can repay the loss of your sister—*nothing*. Not a single life; not a million. You think the destruction of the Americans will somehow satisfy you, but their deaths will mean nothing to you. You felt nothing after the thousandth death—why should you be satisfied with more? But if you do this wicked thing in the name of Emiko Matsushita—if this is how you allow her to be remembered—then I assure you, your poor sister's soul *will* be in agony."

"You have no right to say these things to me!"

"I have *every* right. Do you know why? Because you are the victim of the Americans, but I am the victim of *you*. You have pursued the Americans for sixty years, and I have pursued you. The hatred you harbor for them is the hatred I have harbored for you. The debt that is owed you is the debt you owe me. Look closer, Dr. Matsushita—do you still not recognize me? Do you still not know who I am? I am your cell mate—I am your fellow prisoner."

"You wish to prevent my mission!"

"No—I wish to fulfill mine."

Li turned to the black case. His hands were shaking so badly that he could barely remove one of the vials. He twisted the top, and the old wax seal cracked and crumbled into pieces.

"I brought something for you," Li said. "Something I brought with me from China; something I have saved for a very long time."

Matsushita took a step back. "What is it you want from me?"

"Right now, I want you to stand still."

Just then, there was a heavy metallic sound from beyond the two plastic barriers. Li turned. He saw the shadowy figures of a man and a woman stepping through the hatch.

CHAPTER FIFTY-SEVEN

DONOVAN SAW THE HUGE sheet of plastic with the zippered doorway in the center. Beyond it was another; they hung like flat curtains from the ceiling, dividing the cargo hold into three airtight compartments. He stared through the plastic and saw the blurred images of two men at the opposite end of the room. They were about equal in stature and build—and neither of them wore biological suits.

"Li!" he shouted. "Is that you in there?"

"Hello, Nathan. Your timing is always extraordinary."

"We're coming in!" He pulled the first zipper.

"You must not come in yet," Li said. "The doctor and I have unfinished business to attend to."

"Who are these people?" Matsushita demanded.

"Friends of mine," Li said. "I believe they have business with you too."

Donovan and Macy were through the first barrier now. With just a single sheet of plastic remaining between them, Donovan could make out more details. Li and Matsushita were standing face-to-face at opposite ends of a table. Li's right arm was extended—his hand was resting on something that looked like a white artillery shell. His left hand was holding something, too, something smaller—something made of glass.

Then he saw the open black case.

"Li—we're coming in there!"

"As usual, Nathan, you're not listening. I said you must not come in just yet."

"Stay back!" Matsushita shouted through the plastic. "You must not enter my laboratory!"

"You see?" Li said. "The doctor and I are in agreement."

When Donovan reached for the second zipper, Matsushita lunged forward and grabbed the shell from Li's hands. He pulled hard on the ceramic tip, rocking it off the table and onto the floor. It landed nose-first, shattering into a dozen gleaming white shards, and a mound of pepper-gray powder poured out from inside.

Donovan and Macy stood frozen outside the plastic, staring at the floor.

"Li," Donovan gasped. "What is that thing?"

"Well, now," Li said, staring at the pile around their feet, "I really didn't anticipate this."

"Are those the fleas?"

"I'm afraid so. These bullet-shaped capsules you see are fireworks—some type of skyrocket or aerial display, no doubt intended for New York's Fourth of July celebration tomorrow. The good doctor here has loaded his plague-infected fleas into the tops of these shells. Just imagine all the people lining the waterfront on the Fourth of July—I must say, you have to appreciate his ingenuity, twisted though it is."

"Li!" Macy said. "You've got to get out of there!"

"I'm afraid it's a little late for me—for both of us, in fact. The doctor and I can no longer leave this ship; the risk to others would be too great. Oh well, I suppose it seems appropriate that our missions would end here, together—a poetic justice, one might say. And now if you two will excuse me, I have one more matter to attend to."

"Li—don't do it! I still need to talk to him!"

"Now, Nathan," Li said, "by now you must know that I'm really quite intent on this—and now I have all the more reason. Perhaps you'll have time to speak with him when I am finished."

"Li, I have a job to do!"

"And I have a mission to fulfill. Which comes first, the mission or the job? You were assigned yours just a few weeks ago. I was assigned mine six decades ago—and by a much higher authority."

Nathan pulled the gun from his belt and leveled it at Li.

"Nathan!" Macy shouted. "What are you doing?"

"My job," he said.

"You and Dr. Matsushita are kindred spirits," Li said. "He once did his job too."

"I mean it, Li. Step away from Matsushita."

The old man looked back at him sadly. "Could you kill me, Nathan? Please don't imagine you could merely wound me—to stop me you would have to kill me. Could you do that?"

"Don't make me find out."

"I must do what I came to do," Li said, "and you must do what you must." He took two steps toward Matsushita.

Donovan clicked the safety off and slid his finger inside the guard.

"Nathan, don't!" Macy shouted.

Li turned and looked at him. "I'm confident you will do the right thing," he said, "but perhaps I should take this opportunity to point out that if you shoot me, you will also poke a hole through this plastic barrier—and the two of you are hardly dressed for the occasion."

Donovan lowered the gun and looked at the plastic. It was all that stood between them and a disease for which there was no cure.

"You old fool!" he shouted, "Come on," he said to Macy, "we've got to suit up—fast!" They both wrestled off their backpacks and dropped to the floor.

Li turned back to Matsushita, who continued to stare down at the remains of his broken shell, watching the mound of fleas slowly dissipate as tiny specks collected on his trouser legs and shoes.

"Now where was I?" Li said. "Oh, yes—my story. I've attempted two different starting points, Dr. Matsushita, and you've failed to appreciate either of them. Perhaps I should try one more."

Donovan and Macy were dressing as fast as they could. Donovan shoved his left foot into the boot so fast that he almost ripped through the butyl coated nylon. Macy had both legs inserted into her suit, and she lay back on the floor for a moment, panting. The heat was draining the last bit of energy from her body, and her head was starting to swim.

"There once was a young man who loved someone very much—more than anything else in the world. But that person was taken from him most cruelly, and then he was terribly alone. At first he thought he would go insane with grief—in fact, he wished for it, preferring madness to the inescapable horrors of his rational mind. Some say he did go insane; others simply say that he was never quite the same again."

Donovan and Macy were on their feet now, helping one another pull the bulky suits up over their shoulders. Donovan's business suit rode up his back, bunching up in a ball between his shoulders. He took an extra few seconds to rip it off and throw it aside.

"Over time his grief became anger; then his anger turned to bitterness; then his bitterness cooled and hardened like magma until his heart was as hard as stone. His soul collapsed like a dying star, folding in on itself in hatred and loathing and rage.

"Some said the man was a tragic victim, imprisoned by the injustice of others. It was something he desperately wanted to believe, something he told himself over and over again, because it justified all the darkness in his heart. But it was a lie. He was a victim, yes—but he lived in a prison of his own making, a prison without locks or bars or even walls. He sentenced himself to a life in solitary confinement, where he could wallow in sorrow and self-pity—where he could nurture his longing for revenge."

Li stared at Matsushita. "Do you recognize the man in this story?"

Matsushita said nothing.

He shook his head sadly. "Of course you don't—how could I expect you to? You see, the man in the story is *me*. Sixty years ago, you took my beautiful wife away from me—and I have lived in a prison of anger and hatred ever since. But you and I are different, Dr. Matsushita. Unlike you, I am not willing to die in prison. For sixty years I have been on a journey to free my soul—and today my journey ends here, face-to-face with you."

Donovan and Macy were almost suited up now. Macy's skin was dry and clammy; when she pulled the hood and mask down over her face, she felt as if all the air had left the room and the walls were beginning to close in on her. She only had the zipper halfway up when Donovan grabbed her by the arm.

"Come on!" he shouted, opening the plastic barrier.

Li stood directly in front of Matsushita now. He raised the glass vial to eye level and spoke slowly and solemnly. "Sato Matsushita," he said. "Freely I have received; freely I give. In the name of the Father, and the Son, and the Holy Ghost—*I forgive you.*"

He brought the vial down quickly in a diagonal, slashing motion, and the clear fluid splashed across Matsushita's face and chest. The old man staggered back, sputtering.

Macy and Donovan stood frozen, waiting—but nothing happened.

"It didn't work!" Donovan said.

"What ever do you mean?" Li said indignantly. "It worked perfectly."

"Maybe it lost its potency."

"How does water lose its potency?"

"It was *water*?"

"I suppose holy water does have a certain potency, but I'm unaware of any expiration date."

"*Holy* water?"

"Yes—from a certain well near the village of Congshan."

Just then, Macy's eyes drooped shut, and she slowly sank to her knees at Matsushita's feet. The old man looked down at her and saw the half-open zipper. He leaped forward and grabbed her by the hood, ripping it back and off her head, exposing her face and neck.

"No!" Donovan shouted. He lunged in front of her, butting Matsushita out of the way with his shoulder. He grabbed Macy by both arms and jerked her kneeling body up from the floor like a limp doll. Then he charged forward with her, directly into the first plastic barrier, ripping it from the walls and ceiling. The thick plastic wrapped around them like a clinging shroud, but Donovan kept plowing forward, through the second barrier and toward the hatch at the opposite end of the room.

The cargo hold was in chaos. The collapsing barriers dragged everything along with them: benches, cabinets, biological suits—even a row of rat cages crashed to the floor and sprang open, and half-dead hairless rodents wandered out onto the floor.

Donovan kicked and tore the plastic away from him, shoving Macy through the hatch and onto the metal stairs. "Can you walk?" he shouted in her face.

She stared at him through half-open eyes.

He shook her by the shoulders. "Macy! Can you walk?"

"I think so."

"Then get away from here! Get up to the top deck and get out of this suit!" He spun her around and shoved her up the first few stairs; she stumbled, but she kept moving upward.

Donovan turned back to the room—it was a ruin. The floor was covered with mounds of crumpled plastic, and various objects hung suspended in the folds like flecks of debris in foam. On the far side of the room, he saw Li still standing by the table.

But Matsushita was nowhere in sight.

CHAPTER FIFTY-EIGHT

Donovan waded back through the sea of crumpled plastic toward Li. He saw the old man wrestle a second of the four loaded shells onto the table and then send it crashing to the floor beside the first.

"What are you doing?"

"I think it's best to destroy them all," Li said, prying a third shell from its padded case. "That old devil is really quite shrewd, you know. He thought that by sacrificing one of his shells, he would make us all flee—leaving him with seven shells still intact."

"But he killed himself in the process."

"I suspect Dr. Matsushita only planned to live a few days longer any-way—just long enough to witness his revenge. With this attempt he lost only a single day of life and potentially saved his mission in the process. An excellent wager, all in all."

"Where is he? Where did he go?"

"There are only two exits to this room," Li said. "You and Macy occu-pied one of them; I imagine he left through the other. I didn't really see—things were rather busy. I must say, you really have a flair for entrances and exits."

"Li, do you think Macy was infected?"

The old man stared sadly at the floor. "I pray not," he said. "She was exposed for only an instant—but she was on her knees, so close to the floor. You snatched her away so quickly. But her face, her bare neck . . . I pray not," he said again.

Donovan looked the old man over. "How do you feel?"

"Free," he said. "It's a wonderful feeling—you should try it."

"I mean physically."

"Oh, that. I feel like a dog in need of a flea bath. These things are really quite irritating." He pulled the third shell onto the floor—it shattered beside the others.

"I've got an idea," Donovan said. "If these suits can keep bacteria out, then they can keep bacteria in. We'll suit you up—then we can find a way to get you off the ship."

"For what purpose? There is no cure for this disease, Nathan. I am covered with these annoying creatures, and I am undoubtedly infected. Removing me from this ship will not add a single day to my life. And besides, I can't just walk out of here like a sackful of pestilence—the risk to others would be too great."

"I can't just leave you here."

"I'm afraid you have no choice."

Donovan stared at him. "I can't leave you."

The old man smiled and patted his sleeve. "You called me an 'old fool,'" he said. "That's much better than 'old fart.' Is this what you call a growing relationship?"

"He's killed you, Li. He murdered your wife, and now he's killed you too."

"He's only sped up the process. One thing an old man learns is not to be too greedy. Life mustn't be measured only in days, you know—you're looking at a man who lived to fulfill his mission."

"Your *mission*," Donovan said. "You told me you wanted to kill him!"

"I never said any such thing."

"You led me to believe that!"

"I led you only where you wished to go."

"Why, you old fox."

369

"That's even better than 'old fool.' We're moving right along."

"Li—why didn't you tell me?"

"Now, Nathan. Suppose I told you from the beginning, 'Please let me come along—I wish to forgive him.' What would you have said?"

"I would have said, 'Stay *home* and forgive him. You don't need to come along for that.'"

"Precisely. The only reason you allowed me to come along is because you thought I wished to kill him—because you thought I needed to get my hands physically around his throat."

"But, Li—why *did* you need to come along? If all you wanted to do was forgive him, why didn't you just let it go? Why all this trouble? Why all the risk?"

"Forgiveness is serious business, Nathan—forgiveness is the business of life. There is enormous power in forgiveness—but for that power to be experienced, forgiveness must be *expressed*. Forgiveness is a transfer of title; it's a canceling of debt—it's infinitely more than a simple change of heart."

"He didn't deserve to be forgiven."

"It was never about him, Nathan; don't you see that? I was the one imprisoned; I was the one who wished to be released. So I sought out my tormentor, and I handed him the title to my hatred and my bitterness—and then I was free."

"But your forgiveness meant nothing to him."

"That's an entirely different matter. There is enormous power in forgiveness—but for Dr. Matsushita to experience it, he must choose to *receive* it. I choose to believe that somewhere deep inside he wants to be forgiven—because that is what every human heart longs for, to be released from a debt it can never repay."

Donovan shook his head. "You waited sixty years and traveled halfway around the world just to forgive this guy? You must be a saint."

"You mustn't think that," Li said. "We label others 'saints' to avoid our own responsibilities—yours, for example."

"I know my responsibility," Donovan said. "I'm going after Matsushita."

"You'll do nothing of the kind."

"I still need to talk to him, Li. I need to find out who his backers were, where his lab was, if anybody else has this plague of his."

"Be reasonable, Nathan—you're talking about a bitter old man whose dreams have been shattered, who now has only days to live. What will you do, *interrogate* him? He'll tell you nothing, and you'll waste precious time finding whatever rock he's slithered under."

"I should find him just to kill him."

"Do you think I forgave this man just so you could destroy him? Don't be a fool—and don't make a mockery of my life. You're still thinking about your job, Nathan. Your job is finished—now you have a mission."

"What mission?"

"Nathan—*the business of life is forgiveness.* Up on deck is a woman who has pursued *you* halfway around the world—halfway across the city, anyway, because she desperately wants to forgive you."

"You'd never know it."

"You've hardly made it easy for her, now, have you? You must not expect Macy to be like me, Nathan; you must not expect her to do all the work of forgiveness herself. And *you* must not be like Sato Matsushita— you must not harden your heart against her; you must not let your anger and pride keep you apart. I hate to have to say this, Nathan, but Macy and I may leave this world together. You have no more time for stubbornness; you have no more time for delay. You never did—but you were too foolish to know."

"What do I say to her?"

"Tell her why you ran away when your son was dying of cancer."

"I *didn't* run away—"

"You did run away, because you were afraid."

"I've never been afraid of anything in my—"

"*Please,*" Li said. "We have very little time here, and I don't intend to waste it listening to your empty clichés. Of course you've been afraid, Nathan. All men are afraid—only a fool fears nothing. You and I have something in common, you know: We were both forced to watch someone we love suffer while we stood helplessly by. Did you ever wish that you could switch places with your son? Did you ever wish that you could suffer *for* him?"

"Every day."

"And you would have done it, gladly, if only you were given the chance. But you weren't given that chance, Nathan; there was nothing you could *do*. Let me tell you something: The worst form of suffering is not to suffer yourself, but to watch someone you love suffer and not be able to stop it. That's what it means to be *powerless*—and that's something all men loathe and fear.

"And so you ran away. And ever since, you have been walking through fire and throwing yourself in front of bullets to prove to yourself that you are not a coward. You are not a coward, Nathan—you simply could not stand to see your child in pain. I was luckier than you; I saw the results of my wife's suffering, but I didn't have to bear it day after day. I'm not sure I would have had the courage either."

"Macy did."

"Yes, she did."

"What do I say to her, Li—'I'm sorry for being weak'?"

"I think that covers it nicely."

"She could never forgive me."

"Give her a chance, Nathan. Perhaps all she needs is something to forgive."

Donovan looked into the old man's eyes. "Li," he said, "I want you to know something. It's been an honor—it's been my privilege—"

"I know," Li said with a smile. "I've become quite fond of you too."

Donovan wrapped his arms around him and pulled him in tight. Li was right—if he could somehow draw the plague from the old man's bloodstream and put it in his own, he would do it gladly.

"Enough now," Li said, pushing himself away and swatting the gray specks from Donovan's NBC suit. "You have a mission to fulfill, and I'm not one to interfere with a man on a mission. Go now."

"Wait," Donovan said. "I've got to get a specimen of that plague. It's what we came here for."

"I've taken care of that," Li said. He handed him his own black case, sealed tight again. "What you want is in here," he said. "This is what you came here for."

Donovan tucked the case under his arm. "What are you going to do now?"

"I'm going to look for Sato Matsushita."

"Why?"

"I think he could use some company."

"You never give up, do you?"

"No—and I hope you don't either."

"Li, you need to know something. The Navy, they told me—"

"I know." He nodded. "That's why we both must hurry. Good-bye, Nathan. Thank you for helping an old man fulfill his dream."

Donovan turned and hurried toward the hatch. Halfway across the room, he turned back. He tried to speak, but nothing came out.

Li smiled. "Give your wife my love, won't you?"

CHAPTER FIFTY-NINE

ON THE BRIDGE, THE helmsman crept slowly up to the controls. He held his arms upright, like a doctor preparing for surgery. On his hands he wore an oversized pair of yellow rubber gloves.

He hesitated over the controls. He touched the throttle with a single finger and backed away again, waiting. Nothing happened.

He stepped forward now and grabbed the throttle in his fist. Still nothing.

He pushed slowly forward on the throttle, and the ship began to move.

"SIR!" THE TECHNICIAN SHOUTED across the table. "The ship is moving again, and it's headed for the harbor!"

Quick glances were exchanged all around the table. The State Department said, "If anybody has any second thoughts, he'd better speak now."

There were none.

"Okay," the Navy said. "I'm giving the order to fire."

ON AN AEGIS-CLASS MISSILE cruiser somewhere in the North Atlantic, two hatch doors opened, and a pair of cruise missiles lifted off on plumes of white smoke.

CHAPTERSIXTY

MACY LEANED OVER THE railing, still trying to regain her strength. She shed the remains of her NBC suit as soon as she got to the deck, and she felt instant relief—even the glaring midday sun was an improvement over the sweltering cargo hold. The sea had calmed considerably; the giant swells were only rolling hills now. Her legs were still rubbery, and her head ached terribly, but overall she felt considerably better.

She wondered how long she would feel that way.

Suddenly, she noticed something: The launch was no longer beside the ship. It was a hundred yards behind them now and slowly drifting away.

Behind her, Nathan burst through the hatchway and onto the deck. He stopped for an instant and looked at her, then ripped his own NBC suit off and threw it aside. He started toward her.

"Stay away!" Macy said, backing away from him.

"We're getting off this ship," he said.

"Not me—I can't, Nathan; I've been exposed. I'm just like Li—I can't leave this ship; the risk would be too great."

Donovan kept walking toward her.

"Stay back! Don't touch me!"

But he threw his arms around her and pulled her close to him. She struggled in his arms, twisting like a wild animal—but he wouldn't release his grip.

"Get away from me! There could be fleas in my hair!"

"You need to bathe more," he said. "You've really let yourself go." He began to stroke her long brown hair again and again. "You were only exposed for a second, you know."

"That could be all it takes."

"Then I guess I've got it too—I've been stroking your hair longer than that."

He released her now, and she pushed away and looked at him.

"Why did you do that? You could have left."

"I didn't want to leave—not without you."

"Nathan, there's no cure for this strain of plague. Now we *both* have to stay."

"No, we don't," he said. "We'll swim to the launch—we'll quarantine ourselves there and wait. We'll just—" He looked over the railing; there was nothing but empty sea. "Hey! Where's the boat?"

She pointed. "Back there."

Nathan looked—the boat was now two hundred yards away and diminishing fast. Then he spotted the churning wake behind the ship.

"The ship's moving again," he said. "Come on—we're out of time!"

"Nathan—I don't think I can swim that far."

"You'll make it," he said. "I'll help you."

She looked down at the water below. "It's too far to jump."

"Macy, we don't have time to argue. Either you climb over that railing and jump, or I'll throw you in myself."

She glared at him. "I hate bullies!"

"And I hate whiners!"

She sat on the railing and swung her legs over. "I have *never* whined," she said, "without good reason." She pushed off from the railing and hurtled silently toward the waiting water.

Donovan put one hand on the railing, swung his legs up and over, and plunged into the ocean beside her.

It seemed to take forever to reach the launch. They were able to swim only as fast as Macy's exhausted body could manage. Donovan hooked his arm around her chest and tried carrying her like a drowning victim, but the pace was even slower. All he could do was swim along beside her, encouraging, cajoling, and threatening. There was a moment when she almost panicked—when she was still a hundred yards from the launch, and she glanced back at the ship and saw it receding away—but Donovan took her by the arm and pulled her along, half gliding and half swimming toward the boat.

They reached it at last and dragged themselves onto the deck. They made their way onto the bridge; the pilot's lifeless body still lay facedown in the cabin behind it. Donovan tried the engine and prayed—it started the first time. He shoved forward on the throttle, and the boat tipped back and accelerated.

"Where are we going?" Macy asked.

"Away from the ship—that's all that matters right now. Get on the radio—tell them everything. See if we can call off those missiles."

"What if they've already fired them?"

"They can still call them off—but we don't have much time."

Macy reached down for the microphone. She picked up the cord—but there was nothing on the end but a shattered chunk of plastic and a few tangled wires. She held it up and showed it to Donovan. "A bullet must have hit it," she said.

"Then we've got a problem—there's no way to call off the attack."

"What happens if those missiles hit all that ammonium nitrate?"

He quickly did the math. "At twenty-four knots, we couldn't get far enough away in an hour—and I don't think we have an hour."

Donovan scanned the horizon; to his left, he saw an enormous container ship approaching in the channel, heading out to sea. It would be even with the *Divine Wind* in just a few minutes, passing on her starboard side about a thousand yards across the channel. Donovan estimated the distance to the container ship—then he turned the wheel and steered directly for it.

"What are you doing?"

"If we're in open water when those missiles hit, we won't have a prayer. Our only chance is to duck behind something—and out here, there's just not much to duck behind."

"Can we make it in time?"

"You want the honest answer or the hopeful answer?"

"The hopeful answer."

Donovan looked at her. "I doubt it."

CHAPTER SIXTY-ONE

DONOVAN SHOVED HARDER ON the throttle, but the launch could go no faster. At first it felt as if they were flying across the water, but now, in the open expanse of the channel, they seemed to be almost standing still. The gap between them and the *Divine Wind* widened with agonizing slowness because they were fleeing at a diagonal, in the same direction the ship itself was moving. But that was the path they had to take—that was the shortest route to the oncoming container ship.

From a distance, the container ship looked no larger than the *Divine Wind*—but as it grew closer, its enormity became apparent. It was more than twice the size of the old cargo ship, at least a thousand feet in length. Its weather deck was forty feet above the water, and the deck was stacked another forty feet higher with row upon row of multicolored shipping containers. It was the perfect shelter, a virtual floating fortress—that is, if they could reach it in time.

Donovan glanced over at Macy. She stood beside him on the bridge, with one hand gripping the edge of the helm and the other clinging to an overhead grip. He thought about telling her to go back to the main cabin, to lie facedown and find something to cover her head—but what was the point? It wouldn't make any difference—and besides, he was glad for her company.

She looked over at him, and their eyes met.

"I want you to know I'm sorry," Donovan said.

"I don't want to hear it," she said, turning back to the window. "We'll have plenty of time to talk later."

"Well, just in case we don't—"

"Later."

"Isn't that what you call 'denial'?"

"No, that's what you call 'focus.' I know you, Nathan—whenever you start talking, you take your foot off the gas. Just drive."

"Yes ma'am."

They heard the first deep bellow of the huge container ship's horn. Someone on her bridge had apparently spotted them and must have recognized their collision course. Not that the big ship had anything to worry about; the launch's aluminum hull would smash against the great ship's iron side without even leaving a dent. But then there would be wreckage to recover and survivors to fish out, and that would involve a costly break in schedule—and so the bellow of the horn came in repeating blasts, warning the smaller boat away.

Donovan aimed for a point just ahead of the ship's bow. There were only a hundred yards left between them, and the two vessels were closing fast. He suddenly realized that he had misjudged the ship's speed—the container ship was approaching faster than he'd estimated. If he failed to reach the ship before it crossed his path, he'd have to veer left and travel four hundred yards down her starboard side, and that was a chance he didn't want to take. If the *Divine Wind* did go off, it would be bad enough to be caught in open sea—but trapped against the container ship's iron hull, they would be smashed like a bug on a windshield. He steered farther to the right, trying to increase the clearance—and now they really were on a collision course.

And now the ship's horn was a constant thundering roar.

"We're not going to make it!" Macy shouted.

"We'll make it."

"Turn left!"

"Too late."

The ship was on top of them now. Her massive prow sliced down on them like the blade of a guillotine. The bow of the launch just managed to squeeze past.

The rest of the boat did not.

CHAPTER SIXTY-TWO

L I FOUND MATSUSHITA IN the far corner of the cargo hold, squatting in the darkness by the ship's hull, staring up forlornly at the tall stacks of pallets. A stream of white granules slowly trickled from the side of the pallet directly in front of him, forming a cone-shaped mound on the floor. There was a vertical gash through the plastic wrapping, and the side of each brown sack had been ripped apart. At the old man's feet was something that looked like a crowbar.

"There you are," Li said. "I've been looking for you."

Matsushita made no reply.

Li turned and squatted beside him. He stared up at the endless towering stacks, then down at the single vandalized pallet. "You have a ways to go," he said.

Matsushita stared directly ahead. "What do you want?"

"Have you ever read the book of Job? It's one of the oldest books in the world. Job was in anguish over the loss of everything he held dear, and three of his friends came to comfort him. They sat down on the ground with him for seven days and seven nights, and no one spoke a word to him, for they saw that his pain was very great. Later, they started offering advice and got into all sorts of trouble—but I think their original intention was quite admirable."

"What do you want?" he asked again.

"I offered you my forgiveness," Li said. "I suppose I wanted to know if that meant anything to you at all."

"Go away," he said. "I owe you no apology."

"You know, when you tipped that shell over and released those fleas of yours, you sentenced me to a rather gruesome death."

"I will die too."

"Is that supposed to be a consolation?"

"You interfered with my mission."

"And I suppose this is the price I pay for fulfilling mine. Fair enough, then—my life for your mission. But what about my wife? What about Jin?"

Matsushita sneered. "She was Chinese."

"I find it hard to believe that a man of your intelligence could so quickly descend to ethnic bigotry. But I suppose I shouldn't be surprised; even a demon can be well educated."

"She was one woman," Matsushita said. "Thousands died for a greater cause."

"Your sister died for someone's greater cause. Is that satisfying to you? I know you find this hard to accept, but your purebred sister and my mongrel wife were sisters of a sort: Either they both deserved to die, or they both deserved to live. You can't have it both ways."

"Go away!" he said. "Leave me to die in peace."

"That's exactly what I'm hoping to do," Li said. "You know, I've had only two dreams in my life: One was to become a doctor, and the other was to become a missionary to my people. I wanted to help heal bodies and save souls—nothing more. You took the first dream away from me— I never became a doctor. I thought you ended my second dream as well— but it's just now occurred to me that I did become a missionary of sorts. I am a missionary to a single man—*you*. I now understand that the Lord has sent me halfway around the world in pursuit of your soul—so great is His love even for you."

Li reached around behind his back and pulled Donovan's handgun from his belt. "I must say, I feel rather dashing carrying this. My friend left it behind, you see, and I've appropriated it." He turned the gun in his hands, examining it. "Now let's see. I've never been very good with these things." He pulled back on the slide a little and found a bullet ready in the chamber. He turned the gun over; he pushed a small lever on the bottom of the handle, and the clip ejected. He rose and stepped up to the pallets; he tossed the clip into a space between two of them, and it disappeared into the darkness. Then he turned and extended the gun to Matsushita.

"This is for you," he said. "Please, take it."

Matsushita slowly stood up, glaring at him. "What is this?"

"This is your salvation—or your damnation. The choice is up to you." He placed the gun in Matsushita's hand.

"You stand before me an angry, bitter, resentful man," Li said. "Your mission is unfulfilled, and your sister is unavenged. You will not get your chance to repay the Americans. Your soul is still in agony, still searching for someone to lash out at for all your misery and pain. Well—here I am. I am not personally responsible for the failure of your mission, Dr. Matsushita— I wish I could claim that honor, but I cannot. I believe the powers of heaven itself have opposed you, but I represent those powers—I as much as anyone.

"And now the Lord asks you a question, the same hard question He put to me many years ago: Who is to blame for your suffering? Who is responsible for all the torture and misery of your life? I offer you one last chance to understand. Think, my friend. *Think*."

Matsushita stared down at the gun in his hand. He began to tremble from head to foot. When he finally raised his eyes, they were still as hard as flint, seething with hatred and rage. He slowly raised the gun and leveled it at Li.

Li looked back at him with sadness. "I am so sorry for you," he said. "Sato Matsushita, may the God of all grace have mercy on your soul."

CHAPTER SIXTY-THREE

THE CONTAINER SHIP STRUCK the launch astern, splintering the deck and caving in the port-side hull like an old beer can. The big ship never flinched; it swatted the tiny boat aside like an annoying insect and continued on its way. The launch rocked hard to port and the stern pitched down; the impact of the collision threw Donovan and Macy against the wall and then to the floor. For a moment it seemed as if the ship might plow the boat right under—then the stern bobbed up again, and the boat was pushed clear of the ship's prow.

Donovan scrambled to his feet and tried the throttle. It was useless—the engines were dead. But at least they made it past the great ship's bow; at least they were behind her now.

At that instant two Tomahawk cruise missiles hissed past just ahead of the container ship, skimming six feet above the water's surface. At five hundred miles per hour, it took the missiles less than four seconds to travel the final thousand yards across the channel. They carried limited warheads, designed only to penetrate the ship's hull—but just behind that hull lay nine thousand tons of ammonium nitrate fertilizer.

They struck just above the waterline, one fore and one aft.

And then came the blast.

There was a blinding flash of light from behind the container ship. A pulverizing shock wave instantly filled the air around them, and Donovan collapsed to the floor again. It reminded him of the flash-and-bang stun grenades they used in the Marines, the kind that could turn your legs to rubber—only amplified a million times. He felt as if his bones would turn to powder and his muscles liquefy, reducing his body to a blob of quivering jelly. He thought for sure the boat would shake apart into all its component pieces and drop into the water like a bucket full of rocks.

And lying on his back on the floor, staring up through the shattered windows, he saw the container ship come crashing down.

The ship rocked so abruptly and so far to port that its hull looked like a giant black flyswatter arcing down. The hull slammed down on the boat's roof and crushed it in, jamming the boat to the side and shoving it down into the ocean until water poured over the deck and halfway up the bridge door. And Donovan wondered if the ship would continue to roll, pressing them under the water and holding them there, maybe even taking them with her to the bottom of the sea.

But an instant later the crushing stopped. There was a moment of stillness, and then the ship began to lift up and right itself again. Donovan struggled to his knees and peered through the remains of the bridge window—and right before his eyes a twenty-foot-long metal shipping container dropped out of the sky.

It caught the starboard edge of the boat, smashing down the railings and tearing the black bumper from the side. The impact pitched the bow forward, and the boat rocked like a seesaw, launching Donovan off the floor and smashing his head into the crushed-in roof. Now a second container landed in the water beside them, sending up a geyser of water like the blast of a depth charge. A hundred yards ahead, a massive chunk of the ship's white superstructure tore away and dropped into the water like a bomb, sending a five-foot wave surging in all directions. Another shipping container landed to the right—then another, and another, and then a hailstorm of metal began to rain down and dot the water for a mile all around.

Donovan spun and threw himself to the floor, crawling up and over Macy's unconscious form, uselessly shielding her body with his own.

CHAPTER SIXTY-FOUR

T HE DISPATCH FLOATED SILENTLY on the now-glassy ocean. Her crumpled hull and cabin rested in exactly the same spot where her engines had ceased to function almost three days before, moving only with the drifting tides. There was nothing around her but open sea—but on the horizon, a virtual armada of naval vessels surrounded her, cutting her off from all contact with the outside world. No ship of any size or nature was allowed within that protective perimeter. Any unfortunate vessel wandering into the quarantined area would be warned once and then summarily destroyed—no questions asked; no apologies accepted.

The *Divine Wind* vanished without a trace, scattering pieces of her hull like shrapnel over a ten-mile area. In homes and businesses facing the ocean, plate-glass windows shattered over a thirty-mile stretch of the Long Island and Jersey shore. The blast was registered by university and Department of Defense seismographs all over the eastern seaboard. The greatest monetary damage was caused by the resulting wall of water that destroyed boats and piers and flooded low-lying areas up and down the coast.

Apart from the handful of passengers on the *Divine Wind*, the only loss of life was on the bridge of the ill-timed container ship, which was towed away for salvage the following day.

The genetically altered strain of bubonic plague was incinerated by the blast. The only remaining specimen lay in a small black case on the tiny broken launch—and possibly in the bloodstreams of its two passengers.

Half an hour after the blast, the first Coast Guard patrol boat approached—but Donovan waved them off. He fastened a yellow life raft to a gaff and hoisted it aloft, the age-old signal for a quarantined vessel. The authorities heeded the warning, clearing the area and forming a floating wall of iron around her. A few hours later, the patrol boat broke from the perimeter and approached again. A hundred yards away she stopped and fired a line across the launch's bow. Donovan reeled it in; attached to the opposite end was an inflatable raft loaded with provisions, supplies, and a portable radio. They made themselves as comfortable as possible. Their instructions were simple: Sit and wait.

Macy's symptoms began on the morning of the second day.

It began with a cold sweat that left her feeling feverish and weak. Her skin grew pale and tender, and she couldn't bear the slightest touch. Then came the nausea and the hours of gut-twisting vomiting and dry-retching that left her in utter exhaustion, longing only for death.

"Give me your gun," she groaned to Donovan. "I'm begging you."

"Sorry—I left it on the ship. Besides, in your current state of mind, you'd probably shoot me first."

"You've never been seasick—you don't know what it's like."

"Let me guess: not a lot of fun, right?" Donovan started to peel the plastic off an egg-salad sandwich.

She struggled to a sitting position. "If you open that in front of me, I swear I'll tear your arms off."

He handed her a bottle of water. "Better keep your fluids up," he said. "They want us to do one last blood draw in an hour."

"I thought they said we were all clear."

"They're doctors. They probably want to bill us for another appointment."

Macy looked over at the small black case resting on the floor in the corner. "I wish they'd get that thing out of here. I don't like having it around."

"They say they don't want to risk sending it over on the raft—too much chance of something going wrong. They want to wait until we're in the clear, then get the CDC to take it off the boat themselves."

He set the case on the floor in front of him and started to open it.

"What are you doing?"

"Just taking a peek."

"Nathan, leave it alone! What if you break it?"

"I jumped off the ship with it," Donovan said. "If it hasn't broken by now, it isn't going to."

Macy shook her head. "Men."

He swung open the lid and rested it on the floor. Inside the case were two glass vials filled with a clear fluid; beside them was a third, empty indentation.

"Wait a minute," he said. "These are the same two bottles that were in here before. Look—they're still sealed with wax. He lied to me—there's no sample of plague in here."

"You're sure he said there was?"

"Of course I'm sure. I said, 'I need to get a specimen of that plague,' and he said—"

He stopped.

"What?"

"He said, 'This is what you came here for.'"

Donovan stared down at the bottles for a long time. When he finally looked up at Macy again, he said quietly, "I was afraid."

"What?"

"That's why I wasn't there when Jeremy died—I was afraid."

She waited for him to continue.

"I wanted to be there," he said. "I know you don't believe me, but it's true."

"Then why weren't you?"

"I just couldn't bear it. I couldn't stand to watch him suffer and not be able to help."

"I couldn't bear it either," she said, "but I didn't have much choice."

"I know—and I'm sorry—and I'll be ashamed of that for the rest of my life."

"Where were you, Nathan? Where did you go?"

"I was working double shifts. I was responding to every late-night call; I was volunteering for every high-risk activity I could find. I was crazy—I was out of my mind. I was picking fights, I was taking stupid risks. I think I was trying to experience all the pain I could—I was trying to absorb it, to draw it all away from *him*. Does that sound nuts?"

"Yes—but very human."

He shook his head. "I've never been afraid of anything in my life—but that's because there was always something I could *do*. This time, there was nothing—and I was afraid that I just wouldn't have the strength to stand there and watch him die."

He pried each of the bottles from the foam packing and slid the case aside.

"Li said this is what I came here for—he said this is what I needed. He was right, Macy. Is it possible—do you think—could you ever find a way to forgive me?"

She took the two jars from his hands. "What exactly is this?"

"Holy water—from the well in China where Li used to meet with his wife. I thought it was some kind of biological agent—something that would rot the flesh right off you."

"We could use some powerful stuff," she said. She handed one of the jars back to Donovan.

"What's this for?"

"That one's for you," she said. "I think you need to use it on yourself."

"What about the other one?"

"I'm going to hang on to it. I need a little time to think."

He nodded. "Well, like you said—we've got plenty of time."

"Yes, Nathan—we've got plenty of time."

THE MAKING OF PLAGUEMAKER

UNIT 731 WAS AN ACTUAL BIOLOGICAL warfare research laboratory constructed by the Japanese at Ping Fan in Manchuria in 1939. At least twelve different organisms were studied there for their weapons potential, including plague, glanders, anthrax, and typhus. The facility covered six square kilometers and was as large as the concentration camp Auschwitz-Burkenau. Extensive human testing took place at Unit 731, as horrible as anything conducted by the Nazis in Germany. Anda Proving Ground actually existed, and outdoor tests on prisoners tied to stakes were conducted exactly as described.

The perpetrators of Unit 731 were never prosecuted. They were granted immunity in exchange for the results of their research. The Allies wanted to prevent this information from falling into Soviet hands at the start of the Cold War.

A flea-infested plague bomb was developed at Unit 731 in June of 1941. It was actually scheduled for use against the city of San Diego in September of 1945, but the war ended just six weeks earlier.

The village of Congshan is a real village, and a test of a bubonic plague weapon was conducted there in August of 1942 exactly as described. As a result, 392 of the 1200 residents perished from plague over the next two months. At its peak, the plague killed twenty villagers each day.

THE MAKING OF PLAGUEMAKER

Vivisections were a common part of the human experiments, because researchers wanted to study the effects of different pathogens before the body began to decompose.

The opening chapter of the book is based on a real story. In March of 1999, a man named Chua Kaw Bing needed to transport a sample of the deadly Nipah virus from Malaysia to the CDC in Fort Collins, Colorado. No courier would agree to transport the substance, so Chua packed it up and carried it himself on a commercial airline.

Because bubonic plague resides in rodent populations, it can never be eradicated. There have been three great plague pandemics throughout history, claiming the lives of an estimated 200 million people. There are 10–15 cases of bubonic plague in the United States each year. There is currently no vaccine against plague. Plague is listed by the CDC as one of its "Critical Biological Agents."

Over a twenty year period beginning in 1972, the Soviet Union conducted extensive research on biological weapons in general and plague in particular. In the city of Kirov, twenty tons of plague were maintained in their arsenals every year. Soviet scientists discovered ways to splice toxins into the plague bacterium, making it far more deadly than it is in its natural state.

When the Soviet Union collapsed in 1991, many Soviet bioweapons scientists were forced to look for work in other fields. Many left the country. Some disappeared.

The character of Pasha Mirovik is loosely based on a real figure, Kanatjan Alibekov. Alibekov was Chief Deputy Director of Biopreparat, the Soviet Union's bioweapons program, until 1992 when he defected to the United States and gave U.S. authorities their first comprehensive picture of the Soviets' weapons program. Alibekov holds two PhDs, one for research and development of plague and tularemia as biological weapons.

ACKNOWLEDGMENTS

I WOULD LIKE TO THANK the following individuals for their assistance in my research for this book: Special Agents Chris Anglin and Sally Jellison of the FBI; Captain Bill Sherwood of the Sandy Hook Harbor Pilots; LCDR Michael Hunt of the U.S. Coast Guard; Ken Kohl, Assistant U.S. Attorney; Gary Souza of Souza's PyroSpectaculars; Dr. Wes Watson, Associate Professor of Entomology at North Carolina State University; Dr. Ken Sorensen, Extension Entomologist at NCSU; Scott Bergeron of the Liberian International Ship and Corporate Registry; Warner Montgomery of Wilmington Shipping Company; Tom Joyce; Norma Ailes; and all the others who took the time to respond to my e-mails, letters, and calls.

And thanks to all the others who helped make the publication of this novel possible: my literary agent, Lee Hough of Alive Communications; story editor Pat Lobrutto for his experience and insight; copy editor Deborah Wiseman for her command of the English language; and Allen Arnold, Jenny Baumgartner, and the rest of the staff of WestBow Press for their kindness, vision, and hard work.

AN EXCERPT FROM HEAD GAME

CHAPTER 2

Kuwaiti Airspace, February 1991

Cale Caldwell sat strapped to a web seat in the forward cargo hold of the massive MC-130. The aircraft flexed and groaned with every pocket of turbulence—and there were plenty of them in the rising plumes of heat above the Arabian Peninsula.

Cale's eyes wandered over the cavernous interior. It was like being in the belly of a whale. Just like Jonah, he thought, swallowed by a monster and dangling from a strand of seaweed. The floor was like the monster's belly, with alternating rows of gleaming silver rollers and nonskid patches of sandy gray. The walls were a rib cage of arching aluminum struts joined together by pale green strips of vinyl-covered flesh. Cale stared into the shadows at the rear of the plane; that was the monster's maw, and he wondered when it might gape open again to swallow up another victim—or maybe to vomit him out along with the wooden crates and tarpaulin-draped equipment that lined the monster's gut.

An hour ago Cale was standing on the tarmac at King Fahd Airport, and now here he was riding in the belly of a beast through an ocean of air. Less than twelve months ago he was still a student at the University of North Carolina at Chapel Hill—just a Tar Heel from the Piedmont town of High Point, the "furniture capital of the world," paying his way through college with an Army ROTC scholarship. Tuition, books, and a monthly stipend that just about covered room and board—it sure made sense at the time. Vietnam was a distant memory, the cold war was ending, and there were no military conflicts anywhere on the horizon. "Iraq" was just a thing that held your .30/.30 in the back window of your pickup, and ROTC was just a free ride through Chapel Hill followed by an easy six-year payback in the Army Reserves.

Who could have known?

Last spring Cale was still an advertising student at the Kenan-Flagler Business School at UNC; by summer he had landed a to-die-for position as a creative director at Leo Burnett, a Top Ten ad agency in Chicago; but by autumn the buildup in the Persian Gulf had begun, and Second Lieutenant Cale Caldwell found himself summarily summoned to active duty and attached to the Fourth Psychological Operations Group, commonly referred to as 4POG. The group was stationed at Fort Bragg in Fayetteville, just a stone's throw from High Point—but a world away from that nice little office in Chicago. And now he was another world away, thousands of feet above the rocky plateaus of Saudi Arabia's eastern province, preparing to rain down propaganda leaflets on frontline Iraqis defending the stolen oil fields of Kuwait.

Cale shook his head. Does life get any stranger than this?

Across the aisle from Cale sat a second passenger, clutching the vertical supports with blanching knuckles like a child on his first swing set. The man was almost exactly the same age as Cale; he also wore "butter bars" on his lapels; and he, too, hailed from the Piedmont Triad of North Carolina. All this was more than coincidence—the man was Cale's onetime college roommate and his oldest friend in the world.

"Hey, Kirby, you having fun yet?" Cale said with a grin. "You're supposed to be enjoying this."

"Says who?"

"It's a chance to get out of the office. You know: Join the Army, see the world."

"I joined the Army, not the Air Force."

"Who are you kidding? You didn't join anything."

"You got that right," Kirby grumbled.

One short year ago Kirby was also a student at UNC, courtesy of a scholarship from the Reserve Officer Training Corps—but he was not in the business school like his roommate. Kirby had no interest in business, or psychology, or any other field of study at UNC. Kirby was an artist, and ever since he was a boy in High Point he'd been interested in only one thing: comic books. Kirby's life goal was to one day move to Manhattan and work for Marvel or DC Comics, spending his days penciling massively muscled superheroes and curvaceous superheroines in spandex suits. That was Kirby's dream—and it was his reality, too, until he was also called up to active duty and assigned to 4POG at Fort Bragg.

Kirby was born Alderson Dumfries, a name that for many years hung around his neck like an albatross. And so, upon entering college, he simply announced to Cale one day that he was changing his name—to King Kirby, after the legendary Marvel artist Jack "King" Kirby, in hopes that he would soon become known across campus as "King." But royalty eluded Kirby; it took only one glance to recognize that Kirby was a Kirby and not a King. But even "Kirby" was preferable to "Dumfries," and so the man who would be King was forced to settle for a parallel move instead of the promotion he had hoped for.

Cale found the floor surprisingly stable. The enormous aircraft seemed to give with the turbulence, softening the motion. "Let's get the leaflets ready," he said. He looked over at Kirby, who was staring at the metal rollers that lined the floor. "What's wrong?"

"Those rollers go right up to the door. It's like a big slide."

"Just step over them."

"Didn't you ever see Jaws? Remember that scene where the old guy went sliding down the deck, right into the mouth of the shark?"

"Not many sharks around here."

"That's what the old guy said."

Cale nodded at Kirby's shirt. "This looks like a job for Superman."

Kirby fingered the buttons on his desert BDU.

Ever since childhood Kirby had worn a red-yellow-and-blue Superman tee under every button-down shirt or jacket. He wore it to school, and to church, and under his pajamas at night—he even wore it under his high school prom tuxedo. Kirby would no more forget his Superman undershirt than Clark Kent would, because it served the same purpose. It was his secret identity, his means of leaving Alderson Dumfries on the floor of the phone booth and emerging as someone else—someone bigger, someone braver, someone stronger.

Cale remembered playing dodgeball with Kirby in their grade school gym class back in High Point. Whenever their team was being mercilessly pounded, mild-mannered Alderson Dumfries would strip down to his Superman T-shirt and save the day—or at least think he did. Once, delivering a speech in front of his high school English class, Kirby was overcome by stage fright. He grabbed his oxford button-down with both hands and ripped it open, revealing a scarlet S emblazoned across his bony chest. Buttons ricocheted in every direction and the class erupted in laughter, but Kirby felt no fear or shame. How could he? Superman is invulnerable. Whenever a little more courage was needed, whenever a little more strength was required, all Kirby had to do was unzip his jacket and reveal the man beneath—the man he really was.

Kirby opened just the top two buttons of his BDU. At the first glimpse of that royal blue field, he felt the power flowing through him.

"Let's get those leaflets," he said.

Cale and Kirby were not alone in the cargo hold; a flight engineer and two loadmasters made notations on clipboards and tested the restraining tethers that held crates and equipment in check. Cale turned just in time to see another figure enter the cargo hold through a narrow door in the forward bulkhead. The man was a captain in rank, two decades older than Cale or Kirby. He appeared to be much shorter, though mathematically it was only a difference of two or three inches. The difference was not one of height but proportion; squeezing through the narrow doorway the man looked as wide as he was tall. He had a neck like a water buffalo and the trunk of a century oak. His arms were like pipes, thick but without definition, and his catcher's-mitt hands ended in five blunt stubs. Like the udder of a cow, Cale thought.

The most interesting thing about the man was his face—interesting, Kirby once said, the way a camel's face is interesting. His nose was broad and flat and his eyes were set wide but not deep, giving him a look of constant alertness or surprise. His forehead seemed flat, too, like all of his facial features. Kirby said that most faces are like mountain ranges, but his was more like a plateau: just a few boring landmarks and not much change in elevation.

Overall, the man looked like a boxer whose features had been permanently fixed by one massive blow to the center of his face, which probably accounted for his nickname: Pug. The name tape on his right shirt pocket said MOSELEY in large block letters, and "Captain Moseley" was the required form of address by all subordinates—but to everyone else he was simply Pug. Nobody knew his Christian name; nobody cared. Pug was a career PsyOps officer whose tour of duty extended back to Vietnam. In the Army, Pug said, you call it like you see it: An infantryman is a "grunt," an Iraqi civilian is a "Haji," and a Muslim woman in traditional garb is a "BMO"—a Black Moving Object. In 1965, somewhere outside Da Nang, some wise guy in a moment of boredom or divine inspiration referred to young private what's-his-face as "Pug," and the moniker stuck—for good.

Pug spotted Cale and Kirby and headed toward them. As he approached, Cale noticed that Pug seemed completely unaffected by the rolling and lurching of the plane; his stride was just as solid and deliberate as always. Cale once quipped that in the event of an earthquake Pug would be the only stationary object around; you could duck and cover or you could just grab on to Pug.

"How you two doin'?" Pug called out.

"Just getting our sea legs," Cale said.

Pug glanced down at Kirby's open battle dress uniform and the nonregulation undershirt beneath. "Excuse me, Lieutenant, but your underwear is showing." Pug enjoyed addressing Kirby by his inferior rank, and he had a knack for making the word "lieutenant" sound like a derogatory term.

"That's my uniform," Kirby replied.

"That is your uniform," Pug countered, jabbing Kirby's BDU with one of those cigar-shaped fingers. "That thing is your underwear—and it's supposed to be white."

Kirby reluctantly refastened the top two buttons.

"Look, Superboy, if this Combat Talon takes a nosedive, stripping down to your skivvies won't save your hide."

"Superman," Kirby corrected.

"Coulda fooled me."

"Pug's got a point," Cale said to Kirby. "Suppose the plane does go down, and suppose the Iraqi army finds your body in the wreckage. Think of what the headlines would say in Baghdad: SUPERMAN DIES IN PLANE CRASH. What would people think back home?"

"Yeah, but what if I survived?" Kirby said. "Suppose the Iraqi army approaches the wreckage and the only thing left intact is me, standing like this." He widened his stance and placed his fists on both hips. "Man, this war would be over."

Pug shook his head in disgust. Kirby's nonregulation undershirt was a point of contention between them, but it was just one of many. Virtually everything about Kirby was nonregulation. Pug found it difficult to imagine anyone less suited to military life than this skinny, hyperactive artist with delusional fantasies. As a Vietnam volunteer with no education beyond a GED, Pug had a general disdain for what he called "ROTC pretty boys"—but Kirby was almost more than he could bear.

Yet at the beginning of the conflict in the Gulf, the Army in its infinite wisdom assigned Pug, Cale, and Kirby to the same three-man PsyOps team at 4POG's Propaganda Development Center in Riyadh. Their mission: to create propaganda leaflets designed to strip the enemy of his capacity and will to resist—or as Pug so eloquently expressed it, "to put an idea in his head instead of a bullet."

Cale served as the PsyOps officer of the team, the one responsible for developing the original propaganda "theme." Cale was highly qualified for this role, though his Army training consisted of nothing more than a four-week Basic PsyOps course at Fort Bragg. In fact, Cale was simply doing for the Army what he did back at Leo Burnett: He was selling a product—a different kind of product, granted, but the Army was betting that a man who could talk a welfare kid into shelling out a hundred bucks for a pair of Nikes could also talk an Iraqi soldier into laying down his rifle and raising his hands in the air.

It was a good bet, because Cale possessed an exceptional natural ability: a horse trader's uncanny insight into human motivation and behavior. Cale listened to the human heart the way a concert musician listens to his instrument, and he knew how to tighten one string and loosen another until the instrument produced precisely the sound he wanted to hear. Cale's study of advertising didn't produce this ability—just the opposite: It was his inborn talent that made advertising such a hand-in-glove fit. Cale's natural gift was what allowed him to land a coveted internship with Leo Burnett before his senior year of college, and the same gift helped him create a campaign for Nintendo that brought home a Clio in his very first year at the agency. And now Cale found himself working for a different kind of agency—the Hell, Fire & Brimstone Agency, Kirby liked to call it. Their motto: "Repent—or the end is near." The product was different this time; Cale was no longer selling shoes, or light beer, or popping-fresh dough. The client was different too: Now it was the U.S. Army instead of McDonald's or GM or Hallmark cards. But the process was still the same—only this time the Arab culture was the market segment, and the Iraqi soldier was the consumer.

The product the Army was selling was simply life: survival; continued existence; the chance to see your loved ones again; the chance to get your first decent meal in weeks; the chance to abandon your outdated Soviet equipment and walk away before the Second Marine Division ground you into desert dust. But at first the product wasn't selling—not the way the Army hoped it would anyway, and Cale knew why: We were selling down to them. The product wasn't tailored to fit the consumer's needs. To a devout Muslim—to a man guaranteed a place in Paradise simply for dying in battle—the offer of life was just not enough. The offer needed to be life with honor; survival with dignity; and continued existence with the respect of family and friends.

Cale understood this intuitively. He told Pug, and Pug knew he was right. "Just like the end of World War II," Pug said. "On islands in the South Pacific they were trying to round up all the Japs still holed up in the hills. The PsyOps boys tried dropping a leaflet on 'em. The title said, 'I Surrender'—but nobody did."

"How come?"

"'Cause in the Japanese culture 'surrender' is a dirty word—better to die than to surrender. So we changed the title to read, 'I Cease Resistance,' and the Japs came down in droves. Go figure."

To Cale, it did figure. The Army had subtly but shrewdly changed its sales pitch—from simple surrender to surrender with honor. The distinction might be lost on some, but to an ad man it was no different than a fast-food restaurant changing its pitch from "Great-tasting food" to "You deserve a break today."

So that's what Cale began to do—change the pitch. The propaganda themes that he began to create were specifically designed to capture that missing sense of honor. He began to address the enemy with dignity, as a powerful and worthy opponent instead of a second-rate force doomed to annihilation. His themes appealed to Arab brotherhood; they made surrender sound like an investment in the future of the Arab world instead of capitulation to an arrogant foreign power. With Cale's savvy and cultural insight, a different kind of PsyOps theme began to emerge.

But someone had to take Cale's concepts and visualize them—that was Kirby's job. Words can be ambiguous, and translations from English to Arabic are notoriously problematic. One leaflet produced by another PsyOps team bore the message, "Brother Iraqi soldiers, our great tragedy is we do not want you to come back to Iraq dead or crippled." But due to a subtle error in translation the message actually read, "Brother Iraqi soldiers, our great tragedy is to want you to come back to Iraq dead or crippled."

That's why images were so important, and that's why reservists like Kirby with artistic abilities were so eagerly snatched up by 4POG. Images are a universal form of communication—though images are not without difficulties of their own. One leaflet portrayed the face of an Iraqi soldier; in a "thought bubble" above his head was the image of his wife and children back home. Unfortunately, the Arab culture has no equivalent for the "thought bubble." An Iraqi POW, asked for his opinion of the leaflet, asked, "Why are those people floating in the sky?"

But images say things that words alone cannot: images of exploding bombs, and dismembered bodies, and grieving loved ones—and no one captured those images better than Kirby. When Kirby first arrived in Riyadh he reviewed all of the current propaganda leaflets, summarizing the level of artwork as "Crap, crap, and more crap." And he was right—though his candor didn't win him many friends.

"In the Army you call it like you see it," Kirby said, reminding Pug of his own words.

"That's right," Pug replied, "but after you call it, remember to duck."

Kirby brought a whole new level of artistry to 4POG. His images were simple, clear, and powerful; his representations of Iraqi soldiers were respectful and dignified—even heroic at times. Kirby's leaflets had become collector's items among the Coalition forces, gathered and traded with the same enthusiasm as any past issue of the X-Men or Fantastic Four. Kirby drew constantly; there was almost always a pencil in his hand, as though it were an extension of his arm. He doodled on every flat surface—every notebook, every desktop, every restaurant napkin. His knowledge of anatomy was flawless and his caricatures were unerring. At the headquarters of 4POG in Riyadh, Kirby was almost a legend. Lonely GIs brought him tiny, faded snapshots of sorely missed wives and girlfriends, and Kirby returned to them enlarged and generously enhanced caricatures that were featured on many a wall and locker.

Pug served as the Intelligence Officer on this three-man team. His assignment—one he had done without peer since Vietnam—was to gather intelligence on specific enemy units, to identify targets of opportunity, and to evaluate the results of previous propaganda efforts. Pug was the old warhorse of this team; his was the voice of practical knowledge and experience. Cale understood human motivation and Kirby knew art—but Pug knew PsyOps inside and out, and the mere offer of a beer was enough to get Pug started on some bizarre story from the history of psychological warfare.

In the Hell, Fire & Brimstone Agency, Pug served as market researcher, identifying new markets and suggesting products to fit. One of his favorite duties was interviewing prisoners of war, employing them like focus groups to fine-tune upcoming campaigns. One leaflet in development had displayed a bowl of apples and oranges, suggesting a bounty of food for hungry soldiers who surrendered.

"Add some bananas," one prisoner suggested. "To the Arabs, bananas are a delicacy." Pug made a note, and bananas were added to the menu.

Another leaflet portrayed a friendly, clean-shaven American soldier extending his hand in friendship to an Arab soldier—but to the Arabs a beard is a sign of maturity, brotherhood, and trust. Under Kirby's hand, images began to show American soldiers sporting Arab-style chin beards.

Just as General Motors spent millions every year to remind the buying public of basic themes like safety, reliability, and trade-in value, so the Army worked to keep four basic messages in front of their "consumers": "Your Defeat Is Inevitable," "Abandon Your Weapons and Flee," "It's All Saddam's Fault," and "Surrender or Die." That last message was the Army's particular favorite, and that's why MC-130s like this one were currently dumping more than eleven million leaflets bearing that simple and powerful message—with Cale's special spin.

"Your drop zone is coming up," one of the loadmasters called out over the drone of the engines. "Get your boxes on deck."

Cale, Kirby, and Pug began to carry a series of simple corrugated boxes to the rear of the plane, arranging them side by side on the rollers of the cargo ramp. Each box was about eighteen inches on a side, packed with thousands of five-by-eight-inch leaflets. The top of each box bore a fifteen-foot tether secured to a tie-down on the floor of the plane. The bottom of each box had been crisscrossed with a razor knife to weaken the cardboard. When they reached the drop zone—a specific location calculated by their altitude, prevailing wind speed, and distance from the target—the cargo ramp would lower and the boxes would roll out. When the tethers jerked tight the bottoms of the boxes would rip apart, scattering their contents into the wind—and hopefully into the hands of impressionable Iraqi soldiers.

Kirby didn't loiter on the cargo ramp; the instant each box touched the floor he released it and leaped aside in a kind of grand jeté that Superman was rarely known to make.

Pug rolled his eyes. "Whatsamatter, your underwear give out on you? Superman's not afraid to fly."

Kirby muttered something that the engines drowned out.

"Aren't you boys enjoying our little field trip?" Pug asked. "That's gratitude for you. I went to a lot of trouble to set this up."

It was true. Ordinarily, PsyOps teams are deskbound and rarely ride along on leaflet drops. But a sergeant in the Dissemination Battalion at King Fahd Airport owed Pug a favor, so today they had a rare opportunity to witness the fruit of their labor firsthand.

"Thirty seconds," the loadmaster announced. "Clear the ramp."

Kirby didn't have to be asked twice.

A few seconds later the ramp actuators activated. The cargo ramp began to lower as a hatch above it began to rise, and the two sections of the fuselage slowly separated like the jaws of an opening pliers. Pug and Cale stood in the center of the deck, watching, but Kirby kept one hand on the cargo behind him, fearing a sudden vacuum that might suck him out—but there was none. In fact, it was surprisingly still; the opening ramp flooded the cargo hold with sound and light but remarkably little wind.

Now the boxes began to move, and one by one they slowly rolled forward and disappeared over the edge of the ramp. The tethers snapped taut, and then—nothing. The three men stood staring at empty sky and a dozen nylon tethers dangling into space.

"What a rush," Kirby called out. "Let's do it again."

Cale looked over the ramp at the ground below. He had expected to see nothing but a vague, khaki-colored landscape, but found to his surprise that he was able to make out specific details.

"We're a lot lower than I thought we'd be," he shouted to Pug.

"You can thank the flyboys for that," Pug shouted back. "They've knocked out all the ground-to-air defenses—all it took is a couple thousand air sorties. It's a big help for us; better to fly low when you're dropping leaflets. More accuracy—less wind drift."

Now tiny bits of paper began to appear behind the plane, spinning in the air like a blanket of confetti. The leaflets were designed to spin—to "autorotate," that was the word that 4POG used—to disperse the leaflets as they slowly descended toward the ground.

"Don't they have any antiaircraft?" Cale asked.

"They don't have much of anything. That's one of the reasons our leaflets work. They've got nothing and they know it—we're just reminding 'em. Hey, there's a leaflet idea for you—an Arab guy singing, 'I Got Plenty of Nothing.'"

Pug turned and grinned at Kirby. "Hey, doughhead, whaddya think about—"

Suddenly, there was a sound like a hammer rapping on the side of the plane. A series of small holes appeared in the padding on the starboard fuselage, as though someone had plunged an invisible ice pick through from the other side.

Kirby let out a cry and collapsed.

Pug grabbed Cale by the shoulder and dragged him to the floor. "Stay down!" he shouted. "The floor's got plenty of metal—those shots came through the wall." He twisted toward Kirby and started crawling. Cale was right behind him.

At the same instant the loadmaster lunged to the port side of the plane. He slammed his fist against a large switch and the jaws of the monster began to hiss and slowly grind shut again. Through a wall-mounted intercom he shouted instructions to the pilots. A moment later the cargo plane rolled left and began to rapidly climb, baring its armored underbelly to the direction of fire.

Kirby was in agony. He pressed his hands against wounds on both sides of his left thigh, and blood trickled freely between his fingers. Pug grabbed Kirby's right hand and pried it away.

"What are you doing?" Kirby shouted.

"Gotta see if they hit an artery," Pug said. "They didn't—lucky you."

"I thought they didn't have antiaircraft," Cale said.

"That was just small arms fire. If it had been an AA round he might not have a leg left. I'll take a bullet over shrapnel any day."

By now the loadmaster was at Kirby's side with a portable medical kit. He quickly jabbed an antibiotic syringe into the muscle and began to unwrap sterile gauze pads and a compression bandage.

"Bullet went clean through," the loadmaster said, noting the exit wound. "Must have missed the bone completely. Lucky guy."

"Everybody says I'm lucky," Kirby moaned. "I don't feel so lucky."

"Relax, doughhead. You'll need a couple units of blood, that's all. Might be a while before you can leap tall buildings with a single bound, but you'll be fine."

Within minutes the bleeding was under control and Kirby was lifted to a stretcher rigged in place of the web seats, his left leg so thickly bandaged that it resembled a Thanksgiving drumstick. Cale did his best to remain by his friend's side, but the plane's steep angle made standing difficult. When the loadmaster had first shouted his warning to the pilot, the plane's engines roared so loudly that Cale thought they were going to explode. Then the plane began to climb and he felt as if his body weight had suddenly doubled; he wondered if he would have collapsed to the flight deck if he hadn't been there already. He felt glued in place until their angle of ascent grew so steep that he gripped the floor for fear of rolling back onto the cargo ramp.

Cale pulled himself to his feet next to Pug, half standing and half hanging beside his wounded friend.

"How you doing, buddy?" he asked, patting Kirby on the shoulder.

"I'll feel better when I get off this plane."

"Guess the Superman long johns didn't work," Pug said. "I'd take 'em back if I were you."

Kirby looked up at him. "You think this is my ticket home?"

"Forget it. You sit on your butt all day. So what if you got a hole in your leg?"

Kirby groaned.

"Hey, I just thought of something," Cale said. "You get a medal for this."

"A medal?"

"Yeah—the Purple Heart. And guess who gets to pin it on you? Your commanding officer." He grinned at Pug.

Now it was Pug's turn to groan. "There is no way I'm pinning a medal on this two-digit midget."

"It's regulations, Pug."

"Then I'll pin it with a nail gun. That'll be your ticket home."

Kirby winced. Humor was a distraction, but it wasn't an anesthetic.

Cale turned to the loadmaster. "How much longer back to Riyadh?"

"Sorry, Lieutenant, we've got another drop to make first."

"We've got a wounded man here."

"The lieutenant's in stable condition. We can't scrub a mission unless it's a critical injury. Besides, we can't land the plane with this thing still on board." As he spoke, he dragged a canvas tarpaulin off an object the size of a Volkswagen in the center of the cargo bay.

Cale looked. The object was metallic, cylindrical in shape, tapering to a point at the fore end and slightly rounded at the tail. It looked like the stub of a pencil magnified a thousand times. It was at least four feet in diameter and ten feet long—maybe fifteen end to end. At the tapered end a slender rod protruded forward another three feet. The entire object was fastened with thick straps to some kind of movable sled.

"What is that thing?" Cale said. "It looks like a grain silo turned on its side."

Pug stepped forward and ran his hand along its side. "It's a BLU-82—used to be called a Daisy Cutter."

"Largest conventional bomb in the world," the loadmaster said. "Fifteen thousand pounds of GSX slurry—ammonium nitrate, aluminum powder, and polystyrene."

"You're going to drop it?"

"That's the general idea, Lieutenant."

"We started using 'em in Vietnam," Pug said. "It was tough to find clearings in the jungle big enough to land a Huey, so we started using these babies. It's got a blast radius of six hundred yards. You drop one of these, you got a landing site." He walked around to the tapered front and pointed to the protruding rod. "See this thing? That's called a fuse extender. The bomb drops nose-first, lowered by a parachute. The minute that rod touches down the bomb goes off. That keeps the blast aboveground—keeps it from cratering."

The loadmaster nodded. "At ground zero a BLU-82 causes an overpressure of a thousand pounds per square inch—that's about the same pressure you'd find two thousand feet underwater. Turns everything around it into mush."

"Is that why we're still climbing?" Cale asked.

"You better believe it—you don't want to be anywhere around when this thing goes off. Coupla weeks back we dropped one of these; there was a British commando unit a few miles away. They thought it was a nuke."

"But this is a cargo plane," Cale said. "Why isn't it on a bomber?"

"Won't fit," Pug said. "There isn't a bomber in the world that can carry it."

"I thought we were just dropping leaflets."

"We have to consolidate missions, Lieutenant," the loadmaster said. "It's not exactly cost effective to take this big boy up just to drop off a few cardboard boxes."

"So what's the target? There are already plenty of places to land a helicopter around here."

"This isn't Vietnam," Pug said. "The BLU-82 has a different operational objective here."

On his stretcher, Kirby rolled his head to the side and looked. "I've seen that thing somewhere before. Where was it?"

"Probably on a leaflet," Pug said.

"That's right. I drew that thing for a leaflet—it was a series of three."